Fragile Wings

By the Author

Truths

Ghosts of Winter

The Locket and the Flintlock

A Queer Kind of Justice: Prison Tales Across Time

Fragile Wings

Fragile Wings

by

Rebecca S. Buck

2016

FRAGILE WINGS

ISBN 13: 978-1-62639-546-6

This Trade Paperback Original Is Published By
Bold Strokes Books, Inc.
P.O. Box 249
Valley Falls, NY 12185

First Edition: January 2016

Credits
Editor: Ruth Sternglantz
Production Design: Stacia Seaman
Cover Design by Sheri (graphicartist2020@hotmail.com)

Acknowledgments

The first draft of this book was written about a decade ago. It has been read by friends and family, rewritten and reread on many occasions. It's impossible to thank everyone who has helped and influenced me through that period. You all know who you are, and I hope you know I am grateful.

A few people do deserve to be mentioned by name. The earliest beta readers of this book were Michelle Lisbona and Amanda Tindale. The novel is immeasurably changed from the first draft, but your influence remains. In its present form, I thank Cindy Pfannenstiel (and Michelle Lisbona once again) for careful reading and thoughtful comments. Mum (Jayne Timmins) and Dad (Jeff Buck), you both read this book and offered encouragement when being a published writer was just a distant dream. Thank you.

That this final version is a huge improvement on the first draft is partly due to my amazing editor, Ruth Sternglantz, not just for your well-judged editing of this novel but for the way you've helped me improve and grow as a writer in the five years I've now known you. It's still an honour to have you help me craft my words and to consider you a friend.

I thank the whole Bold Strokes Books team, those involved in creating this beautiful book and the wider team, who are all fabulous. A family I feel grateful to be part of.

The changes in what was a draft manuscript called *Butterfly* to the finished novel *Fragile Wings* are many and varied, Evelyn's changing fortunes, loves, and emotions reflecting my own over the years. The journey this manuscript has been on has been, in many ways, a personal journey too. Allowing it to fly free into the hands of its readers is at once liberating and frightening. Thank you to each of you who picks it up and reads my words.

For all those who did not directly influence my writing, but who have been part of my journey, I extend a huge thank you. Again, you know who you are. That there are now too many to name where once there were very few is a measure of how far that journey has taken me. You've all played a part.

A final acknowledgement must go to my literary influences. I don't believe I'd have been able to create the world of 1920s London and that desperate, decadent post-war era without reading the words of Aldous Huxley, Evelyn Waugh, Michael Arlen, D. H. Lawrence, and Virginia Woolf.

And to Chris Morris. For everything you are and for loving me. When I write romance now, I know what it means.

To my great-grandparents who lived through the Great War. Particularly to William J. Buck (c.1892–1928), my paternal great-grandfather, who survived the conflict only to succumb, ten years after the end of the war, at the height of the Roaring Twenties, to the long-term effects of being gassed, leaving his wife and two young sons.

We are not very far removed from the generation who witnessed it and lived beyond it, remembering.

PROLOGUE

London, 1916

The skies above Greenwich were dark, cloudy, and starless that night. But still the shadow was visible as it loomed into view. The unworldly visitor from a foreign place, bringing only destruction. A vast black oval against the night sky, a darkness against the dark. Then the fire was unleashed.

Searchlights roamed through the night, their vivid beams illuminating the giant Zeppelin, but being able to see it only made it more terrifying. Floating above the houses and factories of London, it dropped its bombs with no apparent effort.

The night was quiet no longer. The explosions, so loud they made the ears ring, caused walls and floors to shake, filled the air with the rumble of collapsing masonry. Fires crackled, springing to life where hearths and gas mains had been. The acrid stench of smoke, the dry dust of crumbled brickwork, made it difficult to breathe.

This was the horror of this Great War. Wars, for centuries, were something fought on a faraway field. But the massive Zeppelins brought the war to London. As if it wasn't enough that the people had sent sons, husbands, and fathers to die in the trenches, now the Germans aimed their bombs at the families waiting at home.

Joselyn Singleton crouched under the heavy kitchen table of her family home, her hands over her ears. All she could think of were her twin brother and her parents. She had not seen them since she had returned home and had no way to know where they were in the house, or even if they were home. She had only been inside for a few minutes when the raid had begun. The first bomb had shattered the windows and she had taken shelter under the table.

Joselyn, halfway through her eighteenth year, had been working as a conductor on the buses all day. It suited her rather more than being a volunteer nurse, the option many of her friends had taken. She was rather squeamish about the sight of blood and, besides, she did not think she could bear to see suffering on so great a scale. Before the war, she'd been cultivating a career on the stage, but that had felt very frivolous in such a time of desperation. So now she clipped tickets on buses in her smart uniform, rather enjoyed the freedom to roam around London, and tried not to remember that she did so because there was a war raging across the sea.

Of course, she could not forget. Her own brother was part of the war. Vernon was not away fighting, but rather serving a clerical duty at a desk in London, as a result of a string of childhood diseases that had left him with reduced lung capacity and made him unfit for active duty. She supposed she should be ashamed that she was glad, but he was the other half of her, her twin, and she could not bear the idea of hearing of his death via telegram one bleak day. His administrative role was just as fundamental to British victory, and both of them were rather scornful about the supposed glory in battle and prayed for an end to the madness.

Now, Joselyn cowered under the table and desperately wondered where Vernon was. He sometimes worked late into the night, but he could equally be somewhere in the house, or visiting their neighbours. Bombs were exploding across Greenwich and with every explosion she winced. Her parents had been to visit her mother's sister in Chelsea but she had no way of knowing if they were still there.

Another bomb fell, closer this time, so close that she heard objects in the house falling. The dark room was now illuminated with an orange glow from the fires burning outside. She could hear men's voices, shouting urgently.

Then there was a crash above her, a flash. And then, nothing.

Devon, 1918

"Promise me, Evelyn!"

Evelyn sobbed and struck her brother on the shoulder, with no intention to harm him, simply to express her anguish. He stood solid, his eyes imploring her.

"How can I promise that, Eddie? How can you ask me to even think about it?" Evelyn's voice was hoarse with crying. She'd barely stopped since Edward had received his papers, demanding he go to fight for his country.

"How can you not promise it, Evie?" There were tears in Edward's eyes too, a strain in his voice.

"Because I don't want to even consider that you won't come back, Eddie! I can't think about it. If I promise you, it's like tempting fate. I couldn't live with myself." She looked up into his familiar face. Other young men from West Coombe had gone to fight, and had died. But it couldn't happen to her brother. He was too kind to kill, too vital to die. She reached up a hand and stroked his cheek.

"Evie"—Edward cradled Evelyn's face in his hands—"I don't want to think about it either. I don't want to die. I don't want to see anyone else die." Evelyn could hear the fear in his voice and anxiety gripped her heart tighter. "But I don't have a choice. You wouldn't want me to refuse to go, would you?"

"I wish I could…" She knew there was no alternative. Edward was no conscientious objector—his patriotism, though latent, had been stirred by the struggle against Germany. Although it had not turned out to be the quick and glorious war they had hoped for, that day in '14, he still thought there was something worth fighting for. They had always known he would reach the age where he would have to go to the front if the war did not end. There was still no sign of it ending.

"I know, Evie. And if it wasn't for duty and all that, I wouldn't go. But since I have to, please, promise. If I don't make it back, live your life for both of us. Do something extraordinary. Don't just live and die here in West Coombe. Strive to be happy—don't settle for contentment."

Edward's eyes had grown wide and desperate. Evelyn could sense his pain. It wasn't an idle expectation he had of her. On many nights she'd sat up with him in the sitting room, talking about how she found life rather too small, how she wanted something more but wasn't sure what that was. He always told her he felt the same, that one day they'd leave together if they had to. Now he demanded she commit to that, even without him.

"But you won't die." Her protest was quiet.

"I might, Evie. I might. And if I don't, then we'll go on as before. But if I do, in the moment when my life is slipping away, if I can think of you doing everything we've talked about, and more, then I will be satisfied and at peace."

Evelyn held his gaze for a long moment. The pain in her throat was so intense she could no longer speak above a whisper. "I promise, Eddie. I promise. But please, don't die."

Edward smiled sadly. "I'll try. I promise you that. And thank you." He bent to place a light kiss on her forehead. Tears rolled down her cheeks, but she did not try to stop them.

"I love you, Eddie." Edward did not answer. He simply held her close. Her memories of their childhood together, of that innocent happiness, tormented her. He was just over a year older than her. It was a gap of three years down to their younger sister, Annie, and another two years again to Peter, who was just twelve. Edward and Evelyn had always felt themselves different to their siblings, older, wiser, and more worldly. Edward, as the eldest son, had received the best education, but everything he'd learned at the High School, he'd shared with Evelyn. His help had dulled the pain, three years ago, when she'd been required to leave school and help her mother and father in the town grocery shop. A girl's education did not matter so greatly, providing she knew enough not to be ignorant as a wife and mother.

Her mind went back further, to playing on the beach in the bay with Eddie, digging deep holes in the sand. Eddie would tease her and say she'd dig all the way through to Australia. The picture in her mind changed again. Eddie at her dolls' tea parties, pretending happily to drink from the miniature china tea set. Eddie at his birthday just last year, delighted with the cake Evelyn had made for him. It had always been Eddie and Evie. Although she felt a sisterly love for Annie and Peter, she did not share the level of friendship and the meeting of minds that she did with her older brother.

And now he would be snatched away from her and taken to a foreign land, where men who did not know him at all would try to take his life. She felt the sobs rising again and held him tighter.

CHAPTER ONE

November 1927

Evelyn Hopkins slipped out of the back door of her home about half an hour before the time her father would usually rise. She'd not slept at all, lying awake for a while in the empty room. She reflected on the stories of women she had read in the newspapers. These were modern times—the war had changed everything. There were women who were lawyers now, civil servants, doctors. Women who lived alone and knew their hopes of marriage had died in the mud of Flanders. These surplus women, as she'd seen them referred to, had no choice but to be independent. Even before the war, the suffragettes had made their voices heard, and not always quietly. These people made her world seem small, her expectations so limited. Now it was her time to be brave and see what came of it.

She thought of her brother, too, and wanted to go back to him. Had he slept last night? What impact would her decision have on a body and mind already so damaged, a man who had lived through such trauma?

She whispered into the early morning silence. "This is that moment, isn't it, Eddie? That we always talked about, like birds and butterflies. The moment where you take to the air and find out if you can fly, or if you'll just plummet to the ground. But even if you plummet, at least you had the chance of flying."

If Eddie could go to war, live through a war, she could do this. Edward had climbed onto a train, then a ship, and had been transported to a foreign land where men were trying to kill him. So many other men had done the same. So many had not returned. This unexpected trip to London with a half-planned scheme to stay awhile and see a little of the world was really nothing more than a tourist jaunt in comparison. It was certainly nothing like as dramatic as it felt.

As she walked the three miles to the station, she thought about Edward. He had returned from the war, although, for a while, they'd believed him dead. After the Battle of Valenciennes, they'd received a telegram to say he was missing. So many of the missing turned out to be dead that her family's grief was instant and deep.

Other families in town had lost sons, fathers, uncles. The community tried to support each other, as they all tried to fathom the loss. But Evelyn had not wanted their comfort. Eddie was gone and she was certain no one felt it as deeply as she did. Of her promise to Eddie, she'd thought very little. Loss and emptiness pervaded everything.

But a few months after the end of the war, they'd received a letter from a military hospital near Brighton. A solider who had been transported there from France at the end of hostilities. His face had been badly wounded and heavily bandaged, as had both of his hands. His uniform had gone and somehow there was no trace of his identification papers. He had not spoken since he had first arrived at the hospital. Eventually he had written his name and place of birth on a piece of paper. Tracking down the Hopkins family in a town as small as West Coombe had not been difficult.

Evelyn remembered her parents' delight. Edward was not dead and he was coming home! She was delighted too, the heavy weight of grief finally lifted. But the thought of Eddie so injured he could not speak made it impossible to dispel the darkness entirely.

They'd gone to meet him from the train, walking the same roads and lanes as she did this morning. Evelyn's memory of the day was vivid still, seven years later. The steam from the train, the black coal smoke, hung heavy on the platform. Passengers alighted into a haze and looked around confusedly for those who had come to greet them. Evelyn and her family peered through the fog for the figure so familiar to them. They could not see him anywhere, and her mother had begun to wonder out loud if there was some kind of mistake.

Evelyn's attention had been drawn by a tall, exceptionally thin figure moving slowly towards them. He was on crutches, his gait awkward. A dark suit was all she could make out of his clothing. His head was bowed, his attention apparently focused on the ground. She almost looked away. Then recognition dawned.

"Mother, Dad, it's him! There!" She'd run towards him even as she finished the exclamation. "Eddie, we're here! You're back home now." As she reached him, she instinctively took his face in her hands and looked into his eyes. What she saw, to her shame, made her cry out in awful surprise.

Edward's face was scarred. His left cheek bore evidence of lacerations that had healed badly and his forehead and the area around his right eye looked shiny and contorted, as though he'd been burned. The scarring bothered Evelyn less than the dull, hard expression on the face, the clouded eyes that had once been so bright. It was as though Edward saw and recognised the world around him but was somehow removed from it.

Evelyn had willed herself not to look away. She lowered her hands to his shoulders, noticing how much weight he'd lost since she'd last held him. "Oh, Eddie, what happened?"

The question would never be answered.

It had taken Evelyn some minutes to realise that Edward's awkward stance, dependence on the crutches, was a result of his left leg missing from below the knee. The horror of war was suddenly embodied by her Eddie, and Evelyn did not know whether tears or anger was the correct emotional response.

In the seven years since that day, Evelyn had read what she could about shell shock. But no matter what she read, Evelyn did not find anything to help Edward. The doctors and psychologists were at a loss, arguing amongst themselves. In the end, Evelyn tired of reading their educated commentaries. They were irrelevant to her experience of living day-to-day with Eddie.

He made progress, of sorts. The moments of eye contact grew longer, with more meaning. He would reach out and touch members of the family, usually in thanks or apparent affection. As though he was remembering the bare essentials of communication, his manners were the first part of his speech to return; he began, quite abruptly one day, to say please and thank you at the appropriate moments. The names of his family also crept in. In the last two years he'd occasionally passed comment on the weather, or the quality of the roast meat put in front of him.

Still, he remained mostly silent. And he did not leave the house. So now, Edward was left to his own devices. He spent his days in the parlour, mostly gazing out of the window. They kept him supplied with tea and left a pen and paper next to him. One day Evelyn found that he'd written his name over and over again on the paper. Another day was a sketch of a face, crudely drawn. She received no response when she asked him who it was. Only those brief touches of the hand, the moments of eye contact, told her that he was still here.

And now, at his urging, she was leaving him behind. In the drive he had shown to make her leave, to escape claustrophobic West Coombe, she had seen more of his former self than she had since he went to war. Rationalising this morning's actions was easy in that context.

She had written letters to explain and had entrusted them to Edward before they had retired for the night. Although she knew there would be worry and pain, she felt sure that the notion that Edward had plotted this with her, that somehow Edward approved, would distract her parents from her own actions. Pragmatic as they were, her parents would undoubtedly be shocked, but not in a way that would greatly affect their day-to-day existence.

She felt more guilt about Michael. A few hours ago, desperate to move forward in her life, seeking something she did not understand, she had accepted his proposal of marriage and let him kiss her. He'd been so happy when she'd left him, just the evening before. Their time at the dance, and the fireworks, seemed a world away now, not just a few hours. That seemed ludicrous now.

Michael would be disappointed. Worse than that, he would be hurt. He'd pursued Evelyn for years, patient, waiting. She knew he loved her. Michael was popular though, he had friends enough to occupy him, women enough who would readily be courted. She was, surely, doing the right thing by him. Condemning him to a marriage in which she would never be a satisfied partner could not be the fair action for either of them. She hoped her letter would make that plain, and that he would forgive her.

She could not explain her motivations in encouraging him and then rejecting him. He would not understand that West Coombe was so small, so suffocating, that she needed to leave. Nor would he understand that, at twenty-five, she still did not feel ready to marry. That her affection for him did not translate into enough of a regard to be ready to promise to spend the rest of her life with him, to obey him, to do everything a man and woman did together. Michael was a good man but she could not marry, as her sister Annie had done, a good man who would give her respectably, content life. She needed more. Michael would never understand. She hoped, very much, that he would recover quickly and move on.

Saying goodbye to Edward was the hardest. She'd crept into his room before she went down the stairs for the last time. She found him sitting up in bed. He smiled when he saw her and, for an awful moment, she thought he'd forgotten their conversation of the evening before and was just pleased to see her. If Edward did not want her to leave, she could not. She saw his eyes move to the small suitcase she carried with her, calm and happy still. He remembered.

She had returned home from the Bonfire Party she'd attended with Michael, to find Edward still awake, sitting in the shadows of the parlour. He'd been sitting in his usual chair, but on the edge, as if agitated. The fireworks of Guy Fawkes Night had left him weeping, shivering slightly. She stroked his face and he was quieter, seemed soothed by her presence. He'd looked like a child again, and she wanted nothing more than to embrace him and tell him everything would be all right. However, she could not ignore the sheets of crumpled and torn paper around him, covered in his uneven handwriting. They were on his lap, on the floor, on the arms of the chair, on the side table. There were ink blots all over his fingers, even a smudge of ink just above his top lip.

"What's all this, Eddie?" she'd asked gently. Edward looked at her, watching. She bent to pick a scrap up from near Edward's foot. All that was written was her name. "That's my name, Eddie. Is this for me?" Edward did not respond, simply stared at the fragment of paper in her hand. She bent and picked up another. "Is it a letter, Eddie, to me?"

Edward nodded furiously. "A letter. To Evie."

Evelyn stared. This was the closest to a conversation she'd had with her brother since before he went to war. He barely ever responded directly to questions. "What were you writing to me about? What does this mean, Eddie?" she asked him, turning the paper, with its indecipherable scribblings, to show him. His eyes dropped to look at what he had written, but he said nothing. His right hand began to tremble and Evelyn grasped it between her own, abandoning the scraps of paper for a moment to soothe him. She saw the tears rising in his eyes. Her mind flew back to the last time she'd truly seen him cry, the night before he'd left for the war. The night he'd made her promise.

The realisation dawned suddenly. "My promise."

"Yes, yes, yes, promise. Evie, promise." Edward nodded furiously again.

She'd rarely seen him so agitated, she knew she should try to calm him. But she needed to know what he was thinking. She'd barely given the promise a second thought herself. So much had happened since that night. She was so far from keeping that promise. What she had said tonight, to Michael, was the final step. She'd never keep the promise if she married him.

"Is that it, Eddie? That you think I've not kept my promise?" Edward stopped nodding and stared at her, but the stare was accusatory. "I still think West Coombe's too small, just like we always did. But I don't know how to leave. Do you know what I did tonight? I said yes when Michael asked me to marry him. I said yes. I'm going to be Mrs. Michael Godfrey and there's nothing I can do to stop it. I can't keep that damn promise, Eddie, even though I want to and you have no business being angry with me about it unless you have some sort of magic and can get me away from here!"

And he had then produced a kind of magic, Evelyn mused. Crumpled from his pocket, a letter in an unfamiliar hand, on yellowed paper. The final letter written by a fallen comrade, a captain of Edward's regiment, entrusted to Edward to be delivered to his sister in Mayfair, should he not survive. Edward, for reasons he could not explain, had kept the letter for eight years. She'd read the letter with tears in her eyes. Frank Grainger and his sister Lilian were unknown to her, but to read this brief, intimate insight into their life affected her deeply.

Edward had taken a deep breath. "Go!" He paused for a moment, waiting for her response. "Promised!"

"But you can't go to London, Eddie!" Evelyn was surprised he'd even considered it. "I know you promised this Frank that you'd try, but you can't." Edward was suddenly shaking his head again. "It's all right, Eddie. Maybe we can put the letter in the post, or enquire if Lilian still lives there." She reached out a hand and tried to soothe him.

"No!" His voice was loud and Evelyn thought about her parents sleeping in the room above. "You go."

Evelyn stared at him, realisation finally beginning to dawn. "Me?" Now Edward was nodding, more gently. He knew she understood. "You want me to go to London and take this letter to Lilian Grainger on your behalf." Evelyn felt her hands shaking. "And you think it would fulfil what I promised, don't you, Eddie? It will get me out of West Coombe. Away from Michael." She reached the finally conclusion quietly, almost to herself.

Edward had stopped nodding and was simply regarding Evelyn quietly, calmer now.

"I couldn't do it, Eddie! Mother and Father wouldn't allow it and I've said what I said to Michael. And I don't have any money. You can't just go to London, especially not a woman on her own. What do you expect me to do, just turn up at Lilian Grainger's door and ask to stay?"

In silent response, Edward had reached into the pocket of his pyjamas. Into her hands he scooped a raggedy heap of folder pieces of paper. "Saving," he said, then returned to his silence.

It took Evelyn a moment to realise that they were bank notes. Most of them only pound notes, but she saw at least one worth twenty pounds. Her heart started to thud heavily in her chest, as the possibilities offered by the money opened to her.

Evelyn stared at him. For a moment he had almost been Edward from before the war. It had been so brief, but it was enough to confirm he was still there, somewhere.

"There must be over a hundred pounds here, Eddie." More than enough for the train and a respectable hotel, even in London. The voice in her head told her she could do it. She gritted her teeth and tried to ignore it. "But that still doesn't mean I can go! It's unheard of!" Not entirely unheard of, perhaps. The Rawson family from Back Street had moved to Kent a few months ago. A girl she'd been at school with, Cathy Clarke, had visited an aunt and uncle in London every summer. London was not a foreign country. It was one simple train ride away. And now, when she was so desperate to escape, he held this in front of her. Her chance to fulfil promises for both herself and Edward, her chance to see something of the outside world.

Yet she knew there would be no going back. If she went, her engagement to Michael was in tatters. There would be no one else. Her parents would not understand her need to see the world outside of West

Coombe. Besides, Edward had clearly hidden both the letter and money for years, not wanting their parents to know. Whatever his reasoning, it would be a betrayal to tell them. In the end, her loyalty was to Edward.

She thought of that hot July day, a year or two before the war. Side by side on a clifftop bench, watching the seagulls, the little brown butterflies in the meadow, they'd wondered aloud how such creatures realise they can fly. And suddenly it had seemed to represent everything in their limited, grounded lives. One day, they'd sworn to each other, they would fly.

Now Evelyn could try, for them both. There would be no further chances. Feeling drunk suddenly, as the adrenaline pulsed through her body, she knew she had to make the attempt. And if she failed, what had she really lost?

"I'll do it, Eddie." It was a whisper at first. "I'll do it."

Edward had smiled then, one of the broadest smiles she'd seen him manage since his return. She smiled back, a surge of youthful excitement filling her. She reached her hands out to Edward, clasping his face in her hands. "The only thing I'll miss from here is you, Eddie. I love you. And I'll write, and tell you everything. Can you believe it? I'm going to try to fly, Eddie!" She bent and kissed his forehead, then threw her arms around him and embraced him wholeheartedly.

And this morning she'd had to part from him. "I came to say goodbye, Eddie. It's only for now of course. Who knows, I might be back in a few days, when the money runs out. I mean, I'm hoping there'll be something useful I can do. But if not, I'll be back really soon. I don't know what I'll do then, of course…" Edward was still smiling. Whatever happened, this was worth it to see that smile. "Anyway, it might be for a little while, with any luck. You make sure you give those letters to Mother and Michael, won't you?" Edward's eyes flickered with understanding, though he said nothing. "And I'll write to you too, Eddie. I'll be thinking about you the whole time. I love you."

Evelyn had embraced her brother and felt him put his arms around her shoulders. A barely perceptible whisper: "I love you, Evie." She squeezed him harder, then straightened up again before the tears could fall.

This was her time to fly.

Chapter Two

Lost in her thoughts, Evelyn was alert enough to be relieved to find an empty road ahead of her. There was little cause for anyone from West Coombe to head for the station, which the village shared with the nearby inland town of Markham, in time for the early train. The first train into the station was a different matter, for it brought mail, fresh fruits and vegetables, stock for her father's shop, and all manner of items ordered by residents of the town. But the first train out of the station had overnighted here and would set off half an hour before that arrival.

There were several men in smart suits on the platform of the small station. A family waited patiently with three children in uniform, clearly returning to school. A couple stood close to each other at one end of the platform. Evelyn did not recognise any of them, to her relief. She'd caught very few trains and the man in the ticket booth had never seen her before either. His eyes registered mild surprise when she asked for a single ticket to London.

"On your own, miss?"

Evelyn found she rather resented the implication that she could not manage a train journey on her own. "Yes. I'm going to visit relatives, they'll meet me at Paddington."

"Right you are. Staying awhile are you then?" He was only bored and trying to liven up an early morning, but Evelyn really wished he would stop questioning her.

"Yes, probably until Christmas at least," she said, marvelling at how easily the lie came to her.

"Ah, well, don't fancy it myself. Air full of smoke, that's what London is. Went there once, tail end of the century it was. Smoke and fog and nasty smells."

"Oh, well, my family are in a suburb. It's not so bad," Evelyn assured him.

"If you say so. Have a good trip, miss." He handed Evelyn her ticket.

"Thank you. And you have a good day." She smiled and turned gratefully away from the window. On the platform, she glanced at the big station clock. There were just twenty minutes before the train. Her family would be awake by now, her father preparing the shop for the day, her mother making a start on breakfast. They would not have noticed her absence yet, for she was usually still asleep or reading in her room, especially on days she wasn't expected to help in the shop. She felt another pang of guilt. Without herself or her recently married sister Annie to help, her father would have to work longer hours in the shop. Perhaps Peter could step in. As the youngest, he'd never been expected to before, so it was really only fair.

The waiting was unpleasant since it held with it the possibility of being noticed, or of turning back before she was missed. A heavy nervousness settled in the pit of her stomach. The brightening daylight made it worse. What had seemed reasonable in the rather fraught hours of the night, with Edward next to her, suddenly felt dangerous, impossible even. She stood with feet glued to the platform, not daring to move lest she turn and run back home. She saw herself reflected in the glass of the waiting-room window. Curly chestnut hair framed a rather pale face, a slightly too-slender body. The reflection was not clear enough to show the apprehension in her hazel eyes. She made herself move and watched her reflection take the step to the side with her. It connected her to the reality of the moment, somehow. She was really here at the station, and really going to London.

Eventually, with a hiss of steam and a plume of black smoke, the train was ready to depart. Evelyn found herself in an empty compartment, glad of the quiet. She was really very tired, her nerves overwrought, and did not relish the idea of sharing the closed space with a stranger who might expect manners or conversation.

As the train pulled out of the station, Evelyn closed her eyes, unwilling to watch the familiar place disappearing. Even through closed eyes though, it was impossible not to think of the landscape she left behind. Her mind took her to her favourite clifftop vantage point, a place she had often gone to read or just to be alone, away from the judgement of her family, the gossip of the town. She did love to be high on the cliffs, the salt in her hair. Below her she could see down into the valley. West Coombe, the most southerly town in Devon, lay on an estuary, the whole town squeezed into the V-shaped valley, teetering on the edge of the blue water. Considering the open countryside above, it was unfortunate the town had crammed itself onto the slopes and the water's edge. The buildings were too close, the streets too narrow. Evelyn was immune to the charm that the tourists from the cities saw in the summer months. For her, it was claustrophobic. She remembered that claustrophobia now, trying not to dwell on her departure from the sea and cliffs and beaches she loved.

Soon, she thought of Edward again, and of his friend Frank, whose letter was safe in her pocket. This was not just a selfish bid for freedom from a life that was too restrictive. This was a duty she had to fulfil, for both of them.

The countryside slid by the window quickly. At Newton Abbot and Exeter, more passengers joined the train. A man and a woman came into Evelyn's compartment but seemed to require no more interaction than the polite nod she gave them. She continued to gaze out of the window. Exeter was the furthest she had ever travelled on the train. Leaving that particular station felt truly like the point of no return.

The train flew through fields, past beaches and sea views, more fields. Evelyn did not really appreciate the scenery, being preoccupied instead with what her family would be doing at that precise moment. Breakfast, dressing, opening the shop, setting a fire in the parlour hearth…

Evelyn felt drowsy as the train passed through Dorset, as though her body was suggesting sleep as an alternative to anxiety and overwrought emotions. She was asleep before the train left the county. When she opened her eyes, she was just moving out of Reading Station. Her compartment was empty again, though she had not noticed the couple leave. Disorientated, she rubbed her eyes and looked at her wristwatch, unable to believe she'd slept for so long. But sure enough, it was midmorning and she was now very close to London indeed. Excitement rushed through her and almost eradicated the loss of home

Evelyn shook it, still smiling. "It's been a pleasure, Miss Hopkins. I hope you enjoy your stay in London. If you're near Paddington again, keep an eye out for me."

"Thank you, Mr. Williams. And I will do." Evelyn gave him a final smile and headed towards the waiting cab, almost sorry to have to leave him behind. She turned and realised he was watching her go, so she waved a hand. He waved in return, then strolled back towards the station building. Evelyn wondered if he worked on the railways.

"Afternoon, miss. Hays Mews, yes?"

"Yes, please." Evelyn climbed awkwardly into the back of the cab. The driver started the engine, the vibration travelling through Evelyn's body. It was an odd sensation, being in a motor car. The car started moving and Evelyn watched the pavement slide by outside the window. Before long she saw railings with a green expanse behind them. It had to be Hyde Park! The simple fact she was divided only by a thin piece of glass from such a famous location made her stare, as though she'd never seen a park before.

All too soon, the cab turned from the broad road at the perimeter of the park into a narrower road, with tall buildings on both sides. Cream stone gave way to red brick; there were steps and doorways and every style of construction from the last century. Evelyn thought there were probably more buildings on this one small street than in the whole of West Coombe.

The further the cab took her, the grander the buildings seemed. At a recently built Georgian-style mansion they turned, only to be surrounded by taller, red-brick, authentically Georgian buildings. They drove past doorway after doorway. At first, Evelyn tried to imagine what was behind each door, who lived in such a place. But after a minute or two, she found it dizzying to watch the street and turned her attention to the way ahead, peering past the driver and out of the windscreen.

Eventually, the driver slowed the cab as they turned into a narrower street. The buildings were still several storeys high but appeared narrower, not quite as spectacular. They were still graceful, with a type of elegance Evelyn had never before seen. But this looked like a street where people could actually live, rather than the stage-set grandeur of the previous thoroughfares.

A moment later, the cab stopped and the driver turned. "Here you are then, miss. Hays Mews. Number 15a wasn't it? That's the yellow brick one there, with the steps up to the front door."

"Thank you." Evelyn peered in the direction he pointed, nervous again now she was actually here.

"Welcome, miss."

Evelyn paid the driver with some of Edward's money she'd kept out of the suitcase in case of need. She watched the cab drive away and found herself alone again. A few steps along the road and she was outside the door of 15a. She paused, looking at the polished brass numbers on the gloss-black painted door. Then she tilted her head to look up at the building. Neat sash windows formed two rows over four storeys. There was an upper floor with smaller windows, just below the roof. The building was beige-yellow bricks except for cream-coloured columns on the facade at street level and a Greek-style portico over the front door. Three steps led to the door, and next to the door, a button for the bell.

Evelyn contemplated the bell for a moment. The idea of ringing it, of bringing out a complete stranger from this rather grand house and trying to explain her purpose, all seemed very daunting. How did she even know that Lilian Grainger still lived here? If the woman had moved, what would she do then? Be on the next train back to West Coombe, most likely. She could hardly stay in London alone. It began to dawn on her just how little she wanted to return to West Coombe. Despite everything, London seemed exciting, a place she wanted to get to know better. The first step towards that, towards fulfilling her promise to Edward, was to ring the doorbell.

As she pushed the brass button, Evelyn listened for the sound of the bell inside the house. She did not hear it but the door looked heavy and as though it would block sound from within. She tried to smile and waited expectantly. After a few minutes, she began to grow tense once again. If no one was home, how long did she stand on the doorstep before giving up? Or it was possible that someone was home but did not want to be disturbed. She was reluctant to keep ringing the bell and discover she'd simply irritated whoever was in the house. Still, the letter she had to deliver was important. Important enough to risk ringing the bell again.

Evelyn listened for the sound of the bell again, and again heard nothing. After waiting a final minute, she tried the brass knocker on the door, hearing that sound echoing in the hallway within. She knocked three times and waited, almost holding her breath. Moments later, she was sure she heard movement. She bit her lip and tried to set her expression to friendly, but not too friendly.

The door opened and Evelyn found herself looking into a round pink dimpled face with bright green eyes, surrounded by cropped red hair which curled around the jawline and sat in a straight line just above the eyebrows. A woman, who looked a little older than herself. The woman wore a blue silk housecoat with an Egyptian pattern embroidered onto the fabric. Her feet were bare. Evelyn drew breath and found herself lost for words.

"Oh, hello there!" The woman spoke loudly and cheerfully. She did not have an accent like the people Evelyn had heard in London so far. Rather her voice was clipped and proper. Clearly this was an educated and wealthy woman. Still, her smile was open and warm. "Did you ring the bell? Oh no, you haven't been waiting there for ages, have you? I've told James we have to get someone to fix it, but somehow neither of us ever gets around to it! Simply ridiculous of us really. Sorry."

"I wasn't here very long before I knocked," Evelyn responded, rather taken aback at the robust manner of this woman and her flow of words, all delivered at quite a pace.

"Oh good, good, that's all right, then. Now, how can I help?"

Evelyn had rehearsed her explanation several times on the train, but now she was here her planned words evaporated from her mind. "Well, I'm looking for a Miss Lilian Grainger. I was given this address for her."

"You've found her then," the woman said, now beginning to look curious. "I'm Lilian. Who are you?"

"My name's Evelyn Hopkins."

"Pleased to meet you, Evelyn. I can call you Evelyn, can't I? You can call me Lilian. I can't stand all of the formalities, we're just two people after all."

"Yes, of course." Evelyn felt herself being blown further and further off course by Lilian's breezy personality and seeming inability to stop talking.

"So why are you looking for me, Evelyn? Is it to do with my singing?"

"No, it's nothing to do with singing. It's, well, it's about your brother."

"So it's really James you're looking for?"

"No, I'm looking for you. It's not James. It's your other brother."

Lilian's smile faded. "I've not had another brother for a long time now," she replied. Some of her friendly demeanour had diminished. "He was killed in the war."

"I know," Evelyn said. She could see the pain in Lilian's eyes and feared making the other woman angry.

"What do you mean? What do you know about Frank?" Lilian demanded.

"My brother, Edward. He served with him, you see. And Eddie came back from the war with a letter. For you, from Frank."

"A letter?" Lilian was staring at Evelyn now, as though she was trying to comprehend the words.

"Yes."

"But the war ended eight years ago. Why would you only bring it now?" Lilian's tone was suspicious suddenly. "And why you and not this brother of yours?"

Resentment rose in Evelyn's heart at the implication that Edward had done something wrong in not sending the letter before now, the hint of mistrust in Lilian's voice. She wanted to defend her brother, defend her own sense of loss. "Eddie came back, but he was shell-shocked—you must know what that can mean. He's barely spoken since he came home. He struggles to let us know what he wants, what he thinks, or to do anything at all, really. It took him a huge effort to make me understand what he wanted, when he asked me to do this. I can't say why he waited until now…I'm sorry."

Lilian's face softened again. She reached out a hand and touched Evelyn's. "No, I'm sorry. That must have been hard for you." There were tears in Lilian's eyes. "The war was so ghastly, wasn't it?"

"Yes," Evelyn replied. For a moment they were lost in mutual remembrance. "Do you want to see the letter?"

"You better come in." Lilian stepped back from the door, and Evelyn passed into the hallway.

Chapter Three

"Sometimes I think of emigrating," Jos Singleton declared, taking a sip of her scotch and running a hand through her untidy short black hair. She looked across the table at her friend Courtney Craig. "America is a place of opportunity isn't it?"

Courtney smiled indulgently, red-painted lips parting to reveal white teeth. "Depends on the opportunity you're looking for, Jos, darling. I prefer London to New York when it comes down to it." The accent of her home city, across the Atlantic, made this a surprising conclusion in many ways. Courtney's beaded dress shimmered in the electric lights of the cafe bar. She would be at home in any big, bright city, Jos suspected.

"Ah, but that's because *I'm* here," interjected the third woman at the table. Courtney's long-term partner in love and life, Clara Bridgford, reached out and wrapped a shirtsleeved arm around her lover's shoulders, smiling broadly. Courtney rubbed a delicate hand over Clara's brown-trousered thigh. Jos watched their easy affection with something like envy.

"There is that, of course. But Jos here is asking my advice about emigration, dear, and I don't think she's in love with you too." Courtney smiled sweetly.

"I don't see how she could resist. You couldn't," Clara said, with a wink at Courtney.

"It's a chore, Clara, I'm sure, but I manage." Jos smiled, shaking her head slightly. It would undoubtedly be hard to leave her friends, if she really were to leave the country. She did not really relish the idea of starting anew in an unfamiliar place. Her friends were, in many ways, the anchors which stopped her drifting aimlessly.

"What's responsible for this sudden wanderlust, then?" Clara asked. "You didn't mention this when we dined together last week."

"Oh, I don't know. I hadn't really thought of it last week." Jos sipped more scotch, almost wishing she'd not started the conversation. She'd been feeling lonely and a little low-spirited, and afternoon drinks with two of her most beloved friends had seemed like a good idea, but now she wished she'd stayed in her flat and enjoyed her scotch with no need for conversation or musing on her future.

"We're not having that, and you know it." This was Courtney. "You're always the same, Jos, darling—you start to tell us how you feel and then back out of it. Well this is important. We don't want to lose you."

"I don't suppose I'm really going anywhere. I'm in London for the whole of pantomime season at least. And it's not really wanderlust, more a sense of having rather exhausted all there is for me here."

"But you'd hate to leave us," Courtney said, "and you'd miss Vernon too."

Jos nodded her acknowledgement of this. "Yes, I would. Although my dear brother is making rather a good fist of being a small-business owner, I have to say. I never knew he had it in him."

"But he was born to be the perfect host," Clara said.

"I know, it's more that I didn't expect he could keep his own accounts or manage his staff. He surprises me daily. I don't feel like I need to look after him any more, really." Jos missed the feeling of being responsible for her brother. She was pleased to see his increasing success, but it was odd to see him building a life while hers just ticked along, day by day.

"Now, now, Vernon will always need a chaperone. To save him from himself, of course." Clara rolled her eyes. "He's making some questionable choices these days."

"I don't interfere in his affairs and he stays away from mine." Jos shrugged. She did not necessarily approve of the string of women Vernon had seduced, but she could hardly claim a more decent track record. "And I'm happy he's keeping himself entertained. You know it was hard for both of us for a while." She thought of the dark days after their parents' death, when the war had seemed likely never to end. Of the scars on her leg, which still ached on cold days. Vernon had coped remarkably well on the surface of things, but she remembered his sleepless nights and slide into self-destructive hedonism when given a chance. In many ways, it had been her feelings of responsibility for him that had arrested her own spiralling into drink and despair. She had been the one to talk him into starting a business of his own, of pursuing his love of socialising and music to start a jazz club. There was no point, she told him, in taking the sensible and safe option. Life had to be lived, its pleasures pursued. And now he was leaving her behind. Not that he was aware of how she felt. She didn't like to share feelings that would be a burden on him. Not on anyone.

"Well, you don't live just for Vernon, do you now? What do you really want, Jos? For yourself?" Clara was looking at her in earnest.

Jos tried to shy away from the question. "Could you even answer that question yourself, Clara? Either of you? If I asked you what you really, truly want?"

Clara looked thoughtful. "I suppose not entirely. But I have an idea. I want Courtney by my side, a circle of friends who know me deeply, enough money to live the life I've chosen, and to never be bored."

"And I want to be with Clara, to visit my parents only sporadically, to never put on any weight, and to have reason to smile for at least half of every day."

Jos looked evenly at Clara and Courtney. However many jokes they made, being with each other was the essence of what each wanted. She didn't have that. But could she claim it was a woman she wanted? Not really. Perhaps. "It's easy for you two. You have each other. I honestly don't really know what I want. To be happy, I suppose. I just don't know how to find it. I never intended to stay in London, you know."

"You didn't?"

"No, it's one of the reasons I've stayed in the theatre. Opportunity to travel the country, or even the world. I didn't want to feel tied down to one place."

"And yet you're still here."

"Perhaps because sometimes it feels as though the world comes to London so I don't need to go anywhere."

"Well that's awfully lazy, darling."

Jos felt a stirring of resentment at Courtney's words. She wasn't lazy, she was scared, and she knew it all too well. Scared to live life. Scared to leave London in case something terrible happened while she was off pursuing that elusive happiness. Sometimes it felt as though the fear was so consuming that it paralysed her. Scotch was one of the solutions, but she knew it was not a wise or helpful one, in the long run.

"I'm not lazy. I just haven't really found my direction yet, I suppose. It was so clear, once upon a time, when I knew I wanted to be on the stage, to act, whatever my parents thought of that ambition. But, lately, it's been rather blurred. I just thought moving elsewhere might, well, sharpen things a little."

Clara reached across and rested a hand on her arm. "You know, Jos, you don't need to actively search it out. I know that's what everyone in London's doing now, tearing about on a madcap treasure hunt for happiness and passion and something so bright it eclipses everything that went before it. But that's not you, my dear. Be yourself and happiness might just find you."

"I've been trying though, Clara, these seven years at least," Jos protested. "A fresh start somewhere is starting to seem appealing."

"Well, you're stuck here while the pantomime's on. I know you won't leave a job half-done—you're too reliable for that," Courtney said. "So my words of wisdom are that you should stop worrying about it until then. In the new year, see how the land lies. If you think leaving London is the right thing to do, we'll surely support you. But be open to other options. Don't try too hard. See what comes along."

"Nothing good ever comes along," Jos said sullenly, aware that she was beginning to sound sulky.

"And don't you dare start feeling sorry for yourself like that," Clara said with a firm tone. "We simply won't allow it. In fact, we're heading to the Orchid tonight. Come with us. You can see Vernon, hear some fine jazz, and drown your sorrows in a far brighter place than this. Plus, all the prettiest girls flock there…"

Jos rolled her eyes but acquiesced silently. An evening with Clara and Courtney in her brother's club was better than a night alone. She was, however, determined to ignore all the women, pretty or not, since that was a complication she really did not want or need right now.

Evelyn smiled, not surprised that Lilian's uncle would have a house near West Coombe. It would be one of the large villas with the views of the estuary, very different from the houses of the ordinary citizens of the town, but still a welcome source of income for the businesses in the area. More and more wealthy visitors were coming to enjoy the mild climate, turquoise seas, and rocky cliffs. Once they discovered the beauty, they bought land and built their extravagant villas, all balustrades and terraces and formal gardens. "Yes, that'll be West Coombe," was all she said. Now she was on the other side of the divide. Lilian was of the other world; she was related to those wealthy outsiders. And yet she was friendly and welcoming, apparently not forming any judgements about Evelyn. People were, she reflected, only people after all.

"Then you've come a very long way indeed! You must be exhausted, darling." Lilian looked genuinely surprised. Evelyn guessed she did not leave London any more frequently than she left West Coombe.

"I am rather tired."

"Well, I have to say thank you for coming all this way." Lilian sipped her tea, a hesitant expression on her face. Clearly she wanted to ask for her brother's letter, but Evelyn supposed she was not sure she was prepared for it. She took another sip of her own tea, feeling awkward to be part of such a private grief.

"Would you like to read the letter now?" she said finally.

Lilian put her cup down unsteadily. "Yes, yes, I would, please." Evelyn opened the top of her case and retrieved the letter, handing it to Lilian. She took the envelope and stared at the handwriting on the envelope. Without looking up, she spoke to Evelyn. "Please do have some cake. I think you'll excuse me while I read this."

"Of course." Evelyn reached for one of the slices of cake, purposely not watching Lilian, who sat back in her chair, still looking intently at the envelope. In some ways, Evelyn wished she could leave the room and give Lilian her privacy. Yet, at the same time, she suspected her presence, her own suffering, could help Lilian.

She focused her attention on the delicious, sticky ginger cake, each bite renewing her energy and strength. She heard the sound of paper moving as Lilian opened the letter and began to read. Her cake finished, Evelyn sipped her tea and watched the low flames in the fireplace. Her gaze rose to the mantelpiece where there was a framed photograph of three children. One girl, recognisably Lilian, and a boy who looked about the same age. Another boy, younger, with fairer hair, sat between them. Evelyn knew she was looking at Lilian and her two brothers, that the one who looked so much like Lilian was Frank. How strange it was, the way the war had made so many men disappear, leaving photographs, letters, and memories as the only evidence they'd ever lived. So many of them did not even have decent graves at which their families could mourn. She was lucky to have Edward, however damaged. At least he was not entirely lost, vanished as if he had never lived.

The sound of a sob brought Evelyn out of her contemplation. She looked across to Lilian, who had the letter clasped between her hands and tears running down her cheeks. In that moment, it did not matter that Lilian was a stranger who inhabited another world so different from Evelyn's. It only mattered that she needed comfort and friendship. "I'm so sorry, Lilian." Evelyn rose to her feet and went to crouch at the side of Lilian's chair. She laid a hand on the other woman's arm and squeezed gently.

"It's so strange to read his words." Lilian's tone was strained, the pain very clear. "I can hear his voice, you know, saying them. I can see him walking in here now. It doesn't matter how many years go by, I still can't quite believe it. This almost makes it more real…Now he's said goodbye." Lilian's face crumpled in grief once more.

Evelyn took her hand and pressed it between her own. "I think it must've helped him, knowing he'd said goodbye," she ventured. There really were not any satisfactory words of comfort.

"He said he was friends with your brother. Does your brother know how he died?"

Evelyn felt tears welling in her own eyes at the thought of Eddie, of what he and Frank had suffered through together. "He might know, Lilian, he might have seen it with his own eyes, but he can't tell us. He just can't."

Lilian, apparently sensing her pain, returned the pressure on Evelyn's hand. "I'm sorry, I shouldn't have asked. It's just that we've never known, you see. His name's on a wall at a cemetery called St. Roch, in France, and they buried a lot of unknown men there. But we've never been really certain what happened. It's hard…You want to imagine it, but you don't, at the same time."

"I wish I could tell you more. We know Eddie was shelled, they say that's what caused him to be the way he is. So maybe the same thing happened to Frank."

"He'd survived nearly the whole war, you know. It makes me so furious to know that he'd have only had to make it another ten days."

"I've thought the same about Eddie. I mean, I know we didn't lose him entirely, but—"

"Don't worry, darling, I'm not in the business of comparing who suffered the most and who lost the most. At least Frank's at peace. Your Eddie got to come home but he has to remember it. I don't know which is the best, really."

Evelyn was moved by Lilian's understanding of her sense of loss. She crouched quietly, still holding Lilian's hand and trying not to let the urge to cry overwhelm her.

Eventually, Lilian broke the silence. "I'll be all right. Do drink the rest of your tea, won't you." Lilian smiled at Evelyn and gestured to the chair she'd been sitting in previously. Evelyn returned to her chair and drained the remainder of her tea, nodding as Lilian offered to pour her another cup. "I don't think any of us will ever really get over the war, will we?" Lilian sat back in her chair and looked at Evelyn thoughtfully. Her face was pale and her eyes rimmed with red.

"I don't think so. How can we? Everything changed," Evelyn said.

"It's been such a long time now. I mean, I certainly don't think about it every day. And I've got used to the fact that Frank isn't here. But I've never really grieved and moved on, like they say you're supposed to. I can't help the anger, the sadness, that it even happened in the first place. And those idiots who go on about the glory of it. It didn't do anything except kill a lot of our men. And their men too. No one won, if you ask me."

"I know what you mean." Evelyn was startled by Lilian, even while she found herself in agreement. People in West Coombe did not tend to be so blunt about their feelings. The war had been accepted as in the country's best interests against a sinister foe. If people questioned it, as the death toll had mounted, they did it quietly, at home. They certainly didn't share their views with complete strangers. And yet Evelyn found it liberating to be able to talk as freely as Lilian. "I've always been angry too. It doesn't seem like they were fighting for anything, really. And I'm not sure anything's worth all that death and destruction."

"Nothing can be worth it." Lilian sighed. "And how do we know it won't happen again? I find I'm frightened of losing everything, whenever I stop for a moment, if I sit and think about life. If I can lose Frank, if so many people can lose someone they loved, how do we know it won't all be taken away in a moment?"

"I know exactly what you mean." Evelyn agreed enthusiastically, relieved to finally find someone who shared her sense of fear. "And it makes you think that you shouldn't waste a day, but somehow you don't know exactly how you should use those days either. You feel you should make the most, but it's so hard to actually do it."

"Yes, that's it." Lilian smiled at Evelyn. "I see I don't need to explain it to you."

"No. But I'm so happy you understand. No one in West Coombe seemed to."

"Really? I'd have thought the war would've touched you more there, in a small town."

"Oh, it's not that the war didn't touch us. It's just that people carry on with life in the same way as they did before. Nothing really changes. It's like they soak up the loss quietly and just move on, doing the same thing day in, day out. It's so frustrating."

"And here in London we seem so very desperate to get over it. To do anything other than what our parents did before. To be young and honour the men who didn't get to be. Hard to say which approach is best, really, don't you think?"

Evelyn pondered Lilian's words. "At least you acknowledge that there was a war," she said, finally.

"Well, we do try to forget, of course. Quite successfully." Lilian managed a smile, though there was a tired look in her eyes. Silence descended again, as both women sipped their tea. "So, tell me, what are you doing in London?"

"What do you mean?" Evelyn asked, surprised. "I'm not doing anything, other than bringing you the letter." Evelyn felt as though it was a lie, even though, on the surface, she told the truth.

"You came all this way? Couldn't you have posted it?" Lilian's questions betrayed curiosity, not suspicion now.

"I could've done. But you know, you could've moved and it could've meant the letter was lost. I wanted to be sure that didn't happen. And, well, I wanted to see London too, of course."

"So not an entirely unselfish act then? Oh, don't look so worried, I'm glad. I'd feel awfully uncomfortable if you were an entirely selfless angel, descended into my terribly selfish world! So what do you think of London so far?"

Lilian seemed to have forgotten most of her sadness, and Evelyn was glad, encouraged by her good natured questions. "I've not seen much of it. Just Paddington Station and what I saw from the cab. But it seems very exciting and interesting. And big, even bigger than I expected."

"Oh, London's just the tops, I can tell you. I spent a good part of my life at a school out in the sticks in Kent and I'm happy to be in the city. You can always find someone to spend an evening with in London."

"I can imagine..." Evelyn realised that such a thing had never really been a consideration in her life.

"No, darling, you can't imagine." Lilian's smile was broad, her twinkling eyes hinting at a world far beyond Evelyn's imagination. "No one can, until they've really seen it. So, where are you staying?"

Evelyn felt her face flush. "I was hoping to ask your advice on that. I do have some money and I obviously can't return home today."

"Money? Ha, you'll stay here then, if you have no other plans, with me of course! I can't have you coming all this way with a letter for me and send you off to a hotel, can I now? Besides, you're interesting to me."

Evelyn stirred uncomfortably, not sure she liked feeling like an interesting specimen, at the same time as Lilian's words brought a flood of relief to her nerves. "I'm really not that interesting," she protested, "but that's ever so kind of you. Are you sure?"

"Of course, I don't say what I don't mean. And James won't mind. He's my brother, you know, my baby brother. He and I share this house."

"Oh, but I don't want to intrude."

"You won't be, darling. Besides, I think you probably half expected me to offer, didn't you?"

"I didn't like to presume..."

"Oh, don't take me so seriously, Evie. I can call you Evie, can't I? Topping! So you'll stay?"

"Yes, thank you." Evelyn barely had time to consider her good fortune before Lilian continued.

"In that case, I'll show you to your room. You can have a wash if you like. And tonight, you can hear me sing at the Yellow Orchid."

"You sing?" Evelyn found this fascinating.

"Yes, jazz. At the Orchid. It's a fabulous place. You'll learn a whole lot more about London than I can tell you, from one visit there." Lilian's smile again hinted at dark and glamorous mysteries. Evelyn was not sure whether she should feel excited or frightened. A sense of anticipation reduced her feeling of fatigue. So far, she had been right to trust Edward.

Chapter Five

Their tea finished, Lilian showed Evelyn to a room on the first floor of the house. The window looked out onto the street and was framed with maroon curtains. There was a thick carpet on the floor, soft underfoot. A matching wardrobe, dressing table with mirror, and bedside table gave the room a harmonious appearance, for all that it felt rather more sparse than the downstairs sitting room. The bed was far larger than Evelyn's own. Currently the bedding was folded on the bare mattress.

"I'll make sure Grace makes up the bed for you before she leaves for the day. I won't have my domestic help living in, you see—she deserves to have a home of her own, don't you think?"

"Oh yes, of course." Evelyn agreed without giving her response much thought. She placed her suitcase next to the one other piece of furniture in the room, a narrow, straight-backed armchair, upholstered in the same colour as the curtains.

"Will this be all right for you, darling?" Lilian looked around at the room without much concern.

"Yes, it's lovely," Evelyn replied.

"Don't worry about flattery, my love. It's not that lovely. We're well-off enough but there just seem to be more important things to spend money on, you know, than prettying up the guest rooms and suchlike. Mater persists in being shocked by it, mind you. You should see what it's like in The Cedars. That's where Mater and Pater live, by the way, with our sister Katy. James wanted to be in the city for his work—he's an architect—and I wanted to be here for, well, for everything you can have here that you can't have out in the Hertfordshire countryside."

Evelyn blinked, trying to take in everything Lilian had told her about herself in that one short monologue. Everything triggered additional questions in Evelyn's mind but, for now, she hesitated to ask them. She could not presume friendship with Lilian yet, especially when she had yet to meet James Grainger, who might not be quite so accommodating.

"Well, if you're coming out with us this evening, and I really think you should, you've got until about seven o'clock to be ready. So you might want to have a rest, but make a start soon."

"Oh yes." Evelyn looked at her watch. It was now just after four o'clock. She could not imagine how it would take her three hours to be ready for anything.

"I have to go myself, but I'm just on the floor above. If you need me, come to the bottom of the stairs and shout."

"I will, thank you." Evelyn smiled at Lilian, who returned the gesture and went towards the door.

"I'll send Grace up with the things for the bed as soon as she has a moment. Do you need her to bring anything else?"

"No, I don't think so. Thank you."

Lilian smiled again and disappeared through the doorway, pulling the door closed behind her. Evelyn was suddenly alone, in silence.

Lilian's presence had so filled every moment since she had answered the door to Evelyn that the absence of it affected her strongly. The air was still; even distant sounds were muffled. The light was fading outside. Standing in the centre of the room, rubbing her hands together, Evelyn felt more of a stranger here, in London and in Lilian's house, than she had expected to. There was nothing in her experience to prepare her for this. How was she supposed to respond to Lilian's warm, robust hospitality? Could she allow herself to be drawn into Lilian's exuberance when, at home, she'd caused heartache, pain, and shame? The excitement of being in London waged a war with her anxiety and guilt and, neither winning, she found herself numbed, unsure what to feel.

Dazed, she perched on the side of the unmade bed. The mattress springs creaked softly. She was facing the window and her eyes were drawn to the buildings across the street. More windows, more rooftops. Who sat behind those panes of glass? Were they happier than she was? More sure of themselves? Or feeling just as lost? She thought of Edward, and tears sprang to her eyes. What was he doing now? However much of him they had lost, her separation from him now hurt more than she had guessed it would. She wished there was a way he could see her and know she was all right, that she was here, in London. She wished there was a way to reach out to West Coombe and relieve some of the guilt. She could not go home but she had no wish to leave a wake of pain behind her.

A brisk knock on the door startled her out of her reverie. "Yes?" she called.

The door opened to admit a young woman, younger than Evelyn, in a neat grey dress. Her dark hair was short and waved and she was remarkably slender. In her arms she carried bed linen.

"Is it all right if I come in? To make the bed up? I'm Grace."

Evelyn jumped to her feet, feeling awkward. "Oh yes. That's fine. I mean, if you want to just leave the sheets, I'm perfectly capable of making my own bed."

Grace smiled. "You're a guest here and I'm being paid to work, so I'll do it."

"Oh, thank you. I'm Evelyn, by the way."

"Pleased to meet you. Will you be staying long?" Grace moved towards the bed, removed the pillows and blankets, and started to fold the flat sheet over the mattress. Evelyn stood awkwardly to one side.

"I don't know, if I'm honest." Evelyn could be no more specific. She'd not thought to bring up the topic with Lilian and found herself entirely uncertain how long her invitation to stay was valid for.

"Well, it doesn't matter, only that I'll need to know to make the fire up in here if you're not to freeze. And what do you eat for breakfast?"

"I don't mind at all." To contemplate such ordinary considerations was a little remarkable on such an extraordinary day.

"Well, there's always bread—or toast—and butter or marmalade. And I make a pot of porridge most days in winter. Tea or coffee, whichever you want, it's no trouble. You'll have to let me know if you want eggs or bacon or anything fancy."

"Thank you. Toast is just fine."

"No trouble." Grace had finished with the sheet and also put the two pillows into their cases. She began work on the top sheet and woollen blankets. Evelyn watched, wondering what it was like to grow up with someone to do such simple tasks on your behalf. She did not really enjoy the experience of being made to watch rather than do the job herself. She was relieved when Grace had finished and headed towards the door.

"Did she show you where the bathroom is?" Grace's tone was indulgent.

Evelyn wasn't sure if she was trying to be kind, or patronising her. "No. Would you mind?"

"This way." Grace led Evelyn out of the bedroom to a closed door at the end of a narrow landing. "It's this one." Grace opened the door and Evelyn peered inside, astonished at how comfortable and opulent the bathroom seemed. The walls were all tiled in dark green. There was a large enamelled bathtub, a basin, and a toilet. Although her West Coombe home did have inside running water, the very small bathroom, with its metal tub, was a purely functional space which was also the area in which they washed clothes, and their lavatory was in an outbuilding.

"This is just for this floor of course, there's one upstairs as well. Just as well, since Lilian can be some time, once she decides she's getting ready for an evening out."

"So this is just for me?"

"Well, James has his room over there"—Grace pointed to the furthest door from Evelyn's room—"so he uses this one as well. But he's out most of the day, working, so it's mostly yours."

"Well, thank you." Evelyn did not feel inclined to express her impressions of the bathroom to Grace, who already seemed to have judged her naive and perhaps a little stupid.

"If you need me, ring the bell or come and find me. I'm going to put some supper on so there's something to come back to later."

"Of course, thank you."

Grace left Evelyn standing on the landing as she went back down the stairs. Evelyn retreated quickly into the room, now looking more welcoming with the bed fully made up. She closed the door and looked around. The room smelled of lavender, and Evelyn wondered if there were sachets in the drawers.

In an attempt to feel more at one with her surroundings, Evelyn reached for her suitcase, laid it on the bed, and opened the lid. She lifted out the first garment, a dark green woollen cardigan, and held it to her face. The smell of home surrounded her. She wanted nothing more than to sit with Edward, hold his hand, then retire to her own bed, her place of safety, and sleep. Emotion welling, she sank onto the bed, her face still buried in the cardigan. For the first time since she had begun this adventure, she cried, from loneliness and fear and with the realisation that, whatever happened, she could not go back.

❖

A loud banging jolted Evelyn out of the restless sleep she had fallen into. Her eyes stung with the tears she had still been crying when sleep had overtaken her. Her face felt flushed and her mouth dry. Another bang. On the door.

Hurriedly, Evelyn climbed from the bed, quickly running her hands over her hair in an attempt to look decent. There was no time to check her eyes for signs of her tears.

"Evie?" Lilian's voice, slightly impatient, called from outside.

"Yes? I'm coming." Evelyn opened the door. Lilian entered immediately, brushing past Evelyn and into the centre of the room.

"I was hoping you'd help me with the fastenings of this." Lilian gestured at her dress. She hardly needed to draw Evelyn's attention to it, for Evelyn was already staring. Lilian's dress was a vivid salmon pink, the tone of which had also seemed to inspire the fish-scale pattern which covered the bodice in silver thread and sparkling stones. The waist sat low on Lilian's rather broad hips and the skirts fell in stripes of the same pink and a lighter-toned fabric. The stripes were defined with more silver thread and embroidered patterns. The sheer fabric reached only just about to Lilian's knees, showing the whole of her stockinged calves. She was currently without shoes or slippers.

Lilian had clearly noticed Evelyn staring. "Do you like it? It's new for Christmas, this one."

"Yes, it's beautiful." Evelyn was not sure if she meant the compliment or not. Certainly the detailing of the dress was exquisite, but Lilian's appearance was also rather startling.

"It's not as though I'd wear so much sparkle every day, of course, darling. But I will be onstage, you know."

"Of course." Lilian's outfit was certainly more of a stage costume than anything Evelyn would have expected a woman to wear out for the evening.

"But I do love it. Of course, I can't do anything to shave the inches from my hips, but this hides them well enough, don't you think?"

"Well, yes, I suppose…" Evelyn flushed at being asked to make such an assessment.

"But, darling, why aren't you dressed yet?" Lilian had apparently just noticed that Evelyn had not changed since her arrival.

"I had to rest a little. But I've just started to look through my clothes for something suitable," Evelyn assured Lilian. She hoped her face did not look as tear-stained as it felt.

"Excellent, that means I can help you, then. At least until James gets here."

"Oh. Thank you." Lilian's help was not something Evelyn felt she needed. In her mind she catalogued every outfit in her suitcase and knew instinctively that Lilian would approve of none of them.

"So show me what you have!" Lilian was clearly excited.

Evelyn removed the plain white blouse and navy skirt, which sat on top of her case, and reached under the grey, functional dress beneath them to pull out the dress she'd worn for Annie's wedding. It was, after all, the best dress she owned. Plain, dull, and with no embroidery at all, it was nothing compared to the astonishing sight Lilian presented, but she had liked it well enough until now. "This is my best," she told Lilian, letting the dress unfold and holding it up for inspection.

Lilian stood back, head tilted to one side in consideration. "That's really all you have?"

"I have my blue dress, that's smart too. But really, there wasn't much call for evening wear in West Coombe."

"The colour is good, that's something. It's just not very on fashion, is it?"

"We didn't really have fashion in West Coombe." Evelyn's tone was flat. Lilian's approval felt more important than she wanted it to. It was almost as though Lilian embodied London and Lilian's approval was, therefore, London's approval.

Lilian sighed, as if confronted by an intractable problem. "I'd lend you something but you're so much taller and narrower than me, it'd be an indecent tent. So it will have to do."

"Oh, good, thank you." Evelyn let the dress drop.

"If I give you some pearls, that will liven things up a little."

"You don't have to do that."

"Yes, I do. Darling, the Yellow Orchid is the height of fashion. You can't just wear anything to a place like that."

If the place was as Lilian described, Evelyn failed to see how a string of pearls would help her. However, it seemed to pay to humour Lilian, so she smiled her acquiescence and thanked her.

"You put the dress on and we'll see what we can do, darling."

Lilian turned to leave the room. Evelyn did as she was told, stripping her travelling dress and stepping into the lighter, smarter garment. Looking at the pale green fabric, with the darker pattern of leaves, her mind flew back to Annie's wedding. The yearning for home twisted with the fear of suffocation, of ending up in a marriage like Annie's, reminding her of one of the reasons she'd come to London. The despair that had led to her tears had gone, and a sort of determination replaced it. She had to make this work.

Lilian returned bearing not just the pearls, but a dark green scarf with silver embroidery and a hair decoration of pearls and sparkling white stones. "These will help create the right impression, darling."

"If you say so." Despite herself, Evelyn was drawn to the beautiful creamy pearls, the glistening of the stones and embroidery. As Lilian passed her the scarf, it shimmered, the silk trickling into her hands. For a moment she wondered how much such an item would cost, then cast the thought from her mind. She did not have to worry about that, not now. For now she could simply enjoy the luxury. She smiled as Lilian passed her the hair ornament and the heavy string of pearls. "They're beautiful."

"Well, put them on." Lilian looked pleased by Evelyn's reaction.

Evelyn draped the scarf over the end of the bed and carefully rested the hair ornament beside it, leaving her free to place the pearls around her neck. The string was long enough not to need a fastening. Against the skin on the back of her neck, the pearls were cold, heavy, strange. They hung between her breasts, pressing the fabric of her dress closer to her body, accentuating the curves of what was beneath. Even as they warmed with her body temperature, Evelyn was not sure she was comfortable with the pearls. Yet she had to admit, as she looked in the mirror, they were beautiful. Just because they were unfamiliar didn't mean she couldn't grow accustomed to the sensation.

"Excellent. That's a big improvement. I was going to suggest you tie the scarf around your hair, but I actually think you should wear it as a sash. It'll hide the fact that your dress isn't really as low-waisted as it should be." Before Evelyn could protest, Lilian was reaching around her body to position the scarf. Evelyn could do nothing but submit. Lilian tied it expertly so that it draped elegantly over her hips. Evelyn's dress was not altogether old-fashioned; the waistline did sit low on her hips. But with Lilian's handiwork, it was now hidden and the illusion created that her dress had a similar shape to Lilian's. The hem was lower, the fabric plainer, but even Evelyn had to confess that she found it to be an improvement, especially if she was expected to brave the world of a fashionable evening in London.

"I like it," she said to Lilian, who was watching her reaction.

"Me too. I'm going to lend you my green cloak to keep you warm, and if you keep your hair up, I think you're nearly there. Do you have rouge or kohl?"

"No."

"Of course you don't. Well, I'll see if I have time to do those for you too. It really does enhance the way you look, you know—" Lilian was interrupted by the sound of a male voice, shouting her name from downstairs. "That's James! Excellent. I have to show him Frank's letter. And introduce you, of course. If you don't mind, I'll talk to him first—it's bound to be a surprise, you see. You just keep on getting ready, there isn't that much time. Come downstairs in about thirty minutes, that should do it."

"I will do. Thank you, Lilian."

"Welcome. See you in a bit." Lilian left the room, the crystals and silver thread of her dress glistening and shimmering. Such a gaudy outfit seemed entirely inappropriate for the sombre memories she went to share with her brother, but Evelyn guessed that James was used to his sister.

Left alone, Evelyn did as she was told, reaching for the hair ornament Lilian had given her. It was a beautiful filigree pattern of silver metal, decorated all over with pearls and sparkling white stones, at once delicate and ostentatious. Evelyn held the decoration against her hair as she looked in the mirror. It sat very well, her chestnut hair the perfect background for the silver and white. She could not help a smile. Reaching for the pins holding her hair on her crown, she removed them one by one. Her naturally curly hair tumbled down onto her shoulders. Thick and lustrous, her hair was one of the attributes she'd been complimented on since she was a child. To see it tumbling down, loosed from its restraining pins, was remarkably freeing. She shook her head slightly. She lifted a lock of her hair and twisted it, before sliding the silver and pearl ornament in, feeling the cool metal slide along her scalp. She let it rest there and examined her appearance again. She looked like a different woman or, at least, a woman she'd only ever seen in the privacy of her own room. Her hair cascaded below her shoulders, showing all of its autumn tones of brown, chestnut, and auburn. It curled luxuriantly, as if enjoying the freedom. And, to one side, the ornament glistened and gleamed, perfectly positioned to lift her hair from her face. Her eyes seemed darker and larger somehow, the way her hair framed her face accentuating its shadows and planes. Yes, Lilian had told her to keep her hair up, but Evelyn had decided. This was the face she wanted to present to fashionable London, if present a face to it she must.

To give her confidence a physical representation she went to her suitcase. In a pocket sewn into the lining nestled her grandmother's butterfly brooch. She watched the diamonds and rubies sparkle for a moment, then carefully pinned the brooch to her dress, over her heart. *See me fly*.

Smiling to herself now, Evelyn found her shoes and slipped into them. They were a neutral cream, perfectly suitable for her outfit, although Evelyn was sure they weren't decorative enough to meet Lilian's approval. She even thought they looked a little dull herself, in the light of Lilian's loans.

Dressed and ready, Evelyn checked her wristwatch. It had not been thirty minutes yet. She opened the door of her room gently and listened. She could hear Lilian and a male voice, but she could not make out any words. What would James Grainger be like, she wondered. Would he welcome her in his house the way Lilian had done? Her situation was still really rather precarious. How ridiculous it was to be dressed for the evening, in borrowed pearls, in a house half-owned by a man she'd never met. Though she should have been distressed by it, now Evelyn laughed at herself. She laughed at what Edward would say, how surprised anyone in West Coombe would be to see her now. Life would go on there without her. Things would be the same one day to the next. But here she was, in London, with complete strangers, with a silk scarf around her waist, pearls hanging heavy between her breasts, and her hair caressing her shoulders. The laughter came again, so Evelyn closed the door and perched on the side of the bed to gather herself. She suspected this was only the beginning of a night of surprises. She rather hoped that would be the case.

Chapter Six

Evelyn allowed thirty-five minutes to go past before she ventured, a knot of apprehension in her stomach, down the stairs to meet James Grainger. Lilian heard her coming and opened the sitting room door to admit her.

"Excellent, Evie! What a splendid idea with your hair, even I didn't think of it. Now, let me introduce you to James." She took hold of Evelyn's wrist and pulled her into the centre of the room. "Evelyn Hopkins, this is my brother, James. James, this is Evie."

Evelyn smiled awkwardly at James, unsure how to respond to an introduction which was both formal and startlingly casual.

"And now, my darlings, I have to finish beautifying, so I will leave you to it." With that, Lilian left the room. Evelyn wanted to call her back, but found she did not really have a choice.

James was almost a foot taller than his sister, though Evelyn knew him to be younger. He was broad-shouldered and possibly a little too plump for a man still in his prime. His neatly cropped and Brylcreemed hair was auburn, but not as fiery as Lilian's. He had similar green eyes, already showing signs of age at the corners. He wore a short moustache which did not extend beyond the corners of his mouth. The slightly pink tone of his skin was exaggerated by the electric light in the room and the fact that the suit jacket he wore was a tone of light beige. Beneath were a crisp white shirt with rather too much starch in the collar and a sky-blue bow tie. James looked a little like a prematurely aged schoolboy, to Evelyn's mind. He was handsome and yet also pink and a little pudgy.

James was regarding her in a way that suggested he was also

taking in her appearance. From his smile, she assumed he did not disapprove of her lack of modern fashion in quite the way his sister did. "It's my pleasure to meet you, Miss Hopkins."

"And mine to meet you. You can call me Evelyn—Lilian already does."

"Thank you. Then I'm James. Although I'm not sure we should be basing our interactions on Lilian's rather loose grip of social etiquette." James rolled his eyes and Evelyn smiled. She had half supposed James would be awkward; his appearance suggested it. But, instead, he seemed at ease, more formal than Lilian but just as comfortable. "Before we all get carried away with the joys—and spirits—of the evening, I wanted to thank you. For bringing Frank's letter. I know it was for Lilian, not for me, but he did mention me by name, and it was good to hear some of his final thoughts. He was my big brother, you see, and I'd always rather looked up to him when we were children. Then he was gone." James did not speak with emotion in his voice, simply a matter-of-fact acceptance of the tragedy. Evelyn guessed there was more beneath the surface, but good manners and bravado would not allow him to express it.

"You're very welcome. I'm glad I had the chance to bring it to you. I suppose Lilian told you why it was so delayed."

"She mentioned your brother and how he was shell-shocked."

Evelyn would have liked a little less bravado and a little more compassion in James's tone. She guessed this was just his way of dealing with awkward situations. "Yes. He is. Well, that's what they call it, anyway. He's not ever been the same since he came back. I don't really know why he suddenly found himself able to communicate now." It was a lie, of course. Edward had been triggered by Evelyn's intentions with Michael. Michael. The image of him flooded into Evelyn's mind, but it seemed so incongruous in this well-to-do if slightly shabby London sitting room. She could not imagine Michael standing in this room. She could not imagine introducing him to James, as her fiancé or as any kind of acquaintance. It had been such a short time since she had seen him, he still did not know just how badly she had treated him, and yet he seemed distant, a phantom of a remote past.

"Are you quite all right?" James was looking expectantly at her.

"Oh yes, I'm sorry. I was just thinking about home, and my brother, you know."

"Devon, isn't it?"

"Yes." Evelyn managed to smile at James's interest. "Apparently I have quite an accent."

"Well, maybe you do, but Lilian told me."

"West Coombe. I think your family knows it."

"Oh yes! Well, I never. I've spent some excellent days sailing there."

"A lot of people do." Evelyn found it harder to smile now, at this further reminder that James and Lilian were very different from her and her family. Even when they'd been in the same town, they'd been divided, moved in different circles.

"Beautiful place."

"Yes, it is. But I wanted to say thank you for letting me stay with you."

"Oh, it's no bother at all. Lilian's always asking all kinds of waifs and strays to stay here. Not that I consider you a waif. Or a stray." He added the last hurriedly, blushing slightly.

"I suppose I am. I don't have anywhere else in London."

"You don't? Gosh, then we really are lucky that you took a risk to bring us the letter. Didn't you have anyone you could bring to London with you?"

"Well, not really, you see Edward couldn't travel himself, and my sister was recently married. So—"

The door burst open and Lilian appeared. Her face was now powdered and rouged and there was black kohl around her eyes. In the dull yellow electric light of the sitting room, she looked rather like a clown. Evelyn supposed it would be more effective when they were in different lighting and Lilian was onstage. She had a cloak of red velvet draped over her shoulders, her face now framed by a trim of fox fur, almost the same colour as her own hair. That red hair was now encircled by a band of the same colour as her dress, which held a decorative concoction of feathers and jewels at the right side of her head. In her hands was a dark green fabric, trimmed with cream fur, which she thrust towards Evelyn. "Top hole, you're becoming friends, excellent. Evie, here's the cloak I promised you." Evelyn took the heavy velvet garment and made her best effort to swing it elegantly around her shoulders. "And what a pretty little brooch you have! Now we need to go or I shall be late for my first song. And you know how tiresome Vernon gets when I'm late." She rolled her eyes but she was smiling coyly at the same time, a detail which intrigued Evelyn.

"Vernon is always tiresome, Lilian. I really think we should find somewhere new to pass the dark evenings."

"Vernon lets me sing, even pays me to sing. Not every club would let me do that. Besides, it's where all of our friends are."

"They're your friends really, my dear."

"Only because you don't have any." Lilian's retort was gentle and followed by a little blown kiss. "Are we all ready now?"

"Let me help, Evelyn." James helped Evelyn finally settle the cloak about her shoulders, fastening with two ribbons at the front. It swung around her body, heavy and rich, very different from her very functional brown winter coat. The soft fur brushed her neck and made her feel very sophisticated indeed. She did not miss James's approving glance. Then they both went after Lilian, who was already heading for the front door.

❖

The walk through the Mayfair streets to the Yellow Orchid was not very far. They left Hays Mews and walked towards Hyde Park. A few turns to the left and right and they passed through a very short alleyway, opening from the facade of a red-brick Georgian town house. Moments later they emerged onto a wider street. Evelyn looked around her for a landmark and noticed the name of the street. Clarges Street.

"Don't worry, Evie, it's not far now at all, just down this street." Lilian, who was setting the pace and walking slightly ahead of Evelyn and James, sounded excited.

"I wasn't worried," Evelyn replied. "I'm just taking it all in."

"Of course. I simply can't imagine having never seen these dear streets before!"

"Well, there's a lot of streets in London for Evelyn to see," James chimed in. "Perhaps we'll have to take her out. We can't have her not knowing anywhere but the Mews, Clarges Street, and Hyde Park, can we now?"

"I arrived at Paddington," Evelyn told him, keen that he should know she'd managed to make her own way to the house from the station.

"Even that's not far though. What about seeing the sights? Westminster, Buckingham Palace? The Tower?"

"I would like that," Evelyn replied. She realised she'd been so caught up in travelling to London and Edward's mission to get the letter to Lilian that she'd almost forgotten she was in the same city she'd always hoped to visit as a tourist. "If you wouldn't mind showing me one day."

"I'm sure we can make time." James looked pleased. Evelyn was glad of his kindness, which was rather less demanding than Lilian's.

"Yes, we can," Lilian interjected, "as long as we can round out the day with tea at Claridge's."

"Of course. That's one of the sights of London too, after all."

Lilian smiled, satisfied. A few more paces along the road, and she paused. "And now, here it is! One of my favourite places in the whole city."

Evelyn looked at the building they had halted outside. A town house, like the others on the street, it had all the appearance of being nothing but a rather large house. The exterior was brown bricks and there were white-framed Georgian windows, like most of the houses in this part of London. The only sign that it was something other than a house was that the area immediately outside the door was tiled in white and black tiles and surrounded by a wrought-iron railing. Above the black painted door was a very small sign, with a picture of a yellow orchid. Very small black writing beneath it read *Cafe. Jazz etc.* And that was all. Evelyn was surprised that Lilian could be so enthralled by somewhere so unassuming and lacking in obvious display or glamour. It made her all the keener to venture inside, to understand Lilian and her world a little more.

Lilian was watching her with a big smile. "It doesn't look much at all, does it? But you wait, my darling. In here, this is where life feels like it's worth something."

"I think that's rather an exaggeration, Lilian." James sounded tired, yet still indulgent.

"For you, perhaps. But not for me."

"Well, perhaps we should go in and allow Evelyn to decide for herself, what do you say?"

Lilian grinned and reached for the brass door handle.

❖

Although the exterior of the building looked like a grand residence, this belied the interior which was like nothing Evelyn had ever seen. The whole of the ground floor was one large room, which narrowed towards the rear, where there seemed to be a bar, behind which Evelyn glimpsed rows of bottles on neat shelves. The bar was built from a wood so dark it was almost black, which was matched by the lower half of the walls, the wood panelling reaching as far as a decorative dado rail. The upper part of the walls were a light shade of yellow, dotted with the sconces which provided the electric light. These lights were muted with grey and white stained glass shades with a geometric sunburst pattern. On all of the walls were large mirrors, the shape of which mirrored that straight-edged sunburst style, with black and white enamel accents. The whole impression was something extraordinary to Evelyn, so modern it seemed a vision of the future, not the present, and yet without a trace of vulgarity. She thought it graceful and exciting. All over the black and white mosaic floor were positioned tables and chairs, and these had clusters of people gathered, a riot of bright colours, sparkling gems, feathers and velvet cloaks, black ties and dinner suits and all manner of patterns. It appeared Lilian's outfit was not so extraordinary after all. The air was heavy with tobacco smoke, mostly from the cigarettes being smoked at every table, but with the sweet fragrance of cigar and pipe to make it a headier, more cloying odour. The smoke and relatively dim lighting made the place seem almost mysterious, only adding to the subversive glamour Evelyn was already half in love with.

A rising swell of conversation and piano notes met Evelyn's ears as she followed Lilian through the door and deeper into the room. This burst into a series of delighted exclamations, as those gathered inside looked up and recognised Lilian.

"Lilian! Good to see you!"

"Are you singing for us this evening, Lilian? I was so hoping you would be!"

"Lilian Grainger, it's been far too long since I saw you!"

"Lilian, how are you this evening. Oh, and your brother's with you too. How nice…"

Evelyn was suddenly surrounded by the attention of a whole flock of smiling faces. She noted that James was not welcomed in the same way as his sister, and she also noted that Lilian did not respond to every well wisher individually. Rather, head held high, she glided towards the rear of the room, smiling and nodding, reaching out to shake an occasional hand. It rather put Evelyn in mind of a royal visitation. Lilian clearly enjoyed the attention and the feeling of being special to those who knew her, but not so much that she felt it necessary to return the same warmth of greeting.

"You'd think we were in the presence of Queen Mary, wouldn't you?" James asked from close behind Evelyn.

She turned, with a smile. "Lilian certainly is popular."

"I'm just happy they pay more attention to her than they do me," James replied. "Aha, looks like we've found our table."

Evelyn looked back to Lilian, who had made her way to a small table against one of the walls, towards the back of the room, and not too far from the bar. At the table was a woman, her dark hair cropped dramatically into a bob shorter than Lilian's, the line of her fringe across her forehead surely only achieved with the help of a ruler. The points of dark hair ended just below her cheekbones, drawing attention to a pale face and eyes as heavily kohled as Lilian's. Dressed in a midnight-blue and mint-green gown, but with bare shoulders and arms as far as elbow-length blue gloves, the woman was less exuberantly outfitted than Lilian, but made just as startling an impression. Crystals sparkled all over her dress, as she stood to welcome the newcomers.

"Lilian, dear, I was beginning to think you weren't going to make it. James, darling, good to see you." She glanced at Evelyn with inquisitive dark brown eyes.

"We've had quite an evening," Lilian began, oblivious that she had not explained Evelyn's presence, "if you don't mind—"

"You too, Dorothy." James clearly set more store in the etiquette of introductions than his sister. "And may we present Miss Evelyn Hopkins. Our house guest."

"Oh yes, of course." Lilian grinned at Evelyn. "Evelyn's from Devon, and she's staying with us for a while. She's never been to London before."

Evelyn glanced helplessly at James, wondering how to actually take a part in this introduction.

"Evelyn, this is Dorothy Bettany, one of our good friends."

"Pleased to meet you." Evelyn held out a hand.

Dorothy took it. "Delighted, my dear." Dorothy contrived to say the words without sounding at all delighted, or even interested. Evelyn noticed what a still person Dorothy was. Her expression had barely moved or changed; she extended her hand with the minimum of movement and did not shake Evelyn's hand, merely squeezed it with her fingers. Gracefully, she returned to her seat, gesturing laconically for Lilian, Evelyn, and James to join her in the remaining seats at the table. Evelyn sat between James and Lilian, opposite Dorothy, and tried not to stare at her latest new acquaintance. Dorothy was puzzling, but Evelyn found herself intrigued by this odd woman and keen to spend more time in her company.

Dorothy reached into the embroidered bag which sat in front of her on the table, drawing out a cigarette, which she placed in a long ebony holder, before offering the packet around the table. Lilian and James both took cigarettes, then Dorothy held them towards Evelyn.

"No thank you. I don't smoke." Evelyn found herself wishing she did, just so she could be the same as the others at the table.

"Why ever not?" Dorothy asked with a slightly raised eyebrow.

"I never have, so I suppose I never thought about it." In fact Evelyn disliked the smell of cigarette smoke and could not imagine inhaling it. However she did not really feel like explaining this to Dorothy.

"Very well. But I think you should try. It's awfully relaxing."

"I can't imagine not having a ciggie, especially when we're here." Lilian accepted a light from James, who then reached across to perform the same service for Dorothy.

"I suppose Evelyn could teach us all that there's a different way to live." James was smiling at her, but Evelyn felt slightly patronised by his tone. James seemed to at once be part of this high-fashion world of wealth and glamour and at the same time constantly making an effort to seem as though he was not. Evelyn wondered if his apparent cynicism was purely for her benefit.

"Yes, it is good to get some outside blood into the place!" Lilian grinned and then looked up as a waiter arrived at their table. "What'll you have, Evie?"

Evelyn flushed, startled as the waiter turned his gaze on her. "I can't say that I know," she said hurriedly to Lilian.

"You do drink, don't you?" Lilian replied.

"Well, not often, but I don't mind…" Evelyn had drunk sherry at Christmas and brandy in her tea in winter and been given a warmed glass of stout when she had been recovering from a particularly nasty cold. But she rarely consumed alcohol and hardly ever for its own sake.

"In that case, I'll order for you." Lilian looked as though she would enjoy the duty. "I'll have a gin rickey for Evie here, and a Between the Sheets for me, please, Clive." Lilian smiled a wide, lascivious smile at the suggestive name of her own order. The waiter, who was clearly also a friend, smiled and winked in response.

"Anything for you, Miss Grainger."

"Oh, Clive, you're too kind." Lilian fluttered her eyelashes.

"And I'll have a mint julep, please," James interjected, apparently not enjoying his sister's flirting. The waiter looked to Dorothy.

"What was that delicious honey-flavoured drink I tried last week?" she asked.

"The Bee's Knees. Vernon got the recipe from one of the singers, straight from New York."

"Really. That prohibition malarkey's really working over there, then?"

"All the Yanks who come here drink like fish. Thing is, though, they're all making the gin in their bathtubs over there and we've got the proper stuff. Does mean they've got some good ideas for what to do with it—they do it to disguise the taste, of course."

"Well, providing you've not made any of it in a bathtub, I'll take a Bee's Knees, please." Dorothy smiled slightly at the rhyming end to her sentence.

"Right away, ladies." Clive nodded, his eyes lingering for a moment on Lilian, then departed in the direction of the bar.

"Is a gin rickey awfully strong?" Evelyn asked. She'd never tried gin and really was not sure what to expect.

"It's gin, lime, and soda. Just imagine lemonade, but with a delightful twist," Lilian responded. "Only don't gulp it as you would lemonade or we might be picking you up from the floor."

Evelyn smiled, anticipating her first drink in fashionable London with pleasure. Nagging doubts were quickly vanishing, the thought of

West Coombe more easily pushed to the back of her mind. She felt surprisingly comfortable with these people, in these surroundings. And this world was so full of colour, sparkle, and curiosity, it was impossible not to want to drink in more and more of it.

Lilian had the best view of the bar area from their table and Evelyn noticed that she glanced in that direction every few seconds. She followed Lilian's eyeline and could not see anything to warrant such attention. A few men in black suits were clustered close to the bar, holding their cocktails in their hands and debating something robustly, but otherwise there was nothing remarkable. Yet Lilian kept looking. Evelyn wondered just how much she wanted the drink she'd ordered. Or perhaps she and Clive were courting. It was possible, although a humble waiter seemed a little down-to-earth for Lilian.

Evelyn looked away from the bar to find Dorothy regarding her with those large brown eyes. "So, what brings you to London, Evelyn?"

"I visited on behalf of my brother. He served with Frank Grainger in the war and had a letter to give to Lilian. Only he was shell-shocked and I didn't know anything about it until this week. And since I've always wanted to see London, and it seemed important, I came right away." Evelyn reflected that her story was more or less the truth and it sounded quite plausible when expressed that way. Dorothy, however, quickly saw the holes in Evelyn's story.

"You just came to London? On your own?"

"Yes. It seemed so very important, you see, to deliver the letter."

"Do you have family in London?"

"No, I don't. My whole family are in Devon, most of them in West Coombe itself."

Dorothy's eyes narrowed, as though she was seeing the truth but could not quite make it out. Evelyn felt uncomfortable under such scrutiny. "Did you know you could stay with the Graingers?"

Evelyn considered her answer. She did not want to make it sound as though she had taken advantage of the letter to gain Lilian and James's hospitality. And yet that was almost exactly what she had done. "No, I didn't. I brought enough money to stay in a hotel, if necessary."

"That was awfully brave of you, my dear. Was there perhaps a reason you wanted to get away from home?" Dorothy smiled but it did nothing to dispel Evelyn's unease. Dorothy's tone suggested nothing but curiosity, yet Evelyn would sooner not explain her motivations, especially since James and Lilian were now paying attention to their conversation.

"No, no reason. I've always wanted to see London."

"Of course." Dorothy nodded. There was a pause, but she was not out of questions yet. "So, are you—*were* you—attached to anyone in West Coombe? Is there a fellow waiting for your return?"

Evelyn flushed as the image of Michael rose in her mind. She shook her head and said, rather too firmly, "No, no there's not. Nothing like that."

Lilian smiled broadly at this. "Well, London is the perfect place for you to find one, Evie! By the time you go home, we might even have you engaged!" Dorothy and Lilian both giggled. James rolled his eyes and Evelyn tried to smile. She was relieved when Lilian's attention was drawn back towards the bar and a man approaching their table with a tray of drinks. Evelyn followed Lilian's gaze.

"I suppose we'll have to endure Vernon's company for a while, I see." James spoke the words quietly, to Evelyn, though she was fairly sure Lilian would have heard. So this was Vernon, the owner of the establishment, whom Lilian seemed fond of and James apparently had no respect for at all. He was a handsome man, with black hair, slicked back smoothly from his forehead. He was dark complexioned, tanned despite the winter weather. Tall and slim, with angular shoulders, he wore dark tweed Oxford bags and a shirt with pale gold and blue stripes. He wore no jacket or vest and his collar was open. A dark blue bow tie hung loose and untied beneath his collar. He looked, compared to some of the other men in the cafe, as though he had not quite finished dressing before he entered the room. Evelyn found this made him more compelling than some of the more formally dressed people around her. He walked over to their table gracefully and bent to place the tray of drinks in front of them. His manner was confident, comfortable in his domain. Evelyn could not help drawing a comparison with James, who looked even more uncomfortable now Vernon was at the table.

"Lily, darling, wonderful to see you again. And on time, for once. Very good of you." Vernon smiled at Lilian, who blushed slightly and smiled back at him.

"Vernon, my love, polite as ever. You'd wouldn't have half of tonight's customers if it wasn't for me, and you know it."

Vernon reached for Lilian's hand and kissed it with a show of mock gallantry. "Of course, Lily, dear, how can I ever make it up to you?" Vernon's voice was rich and deep, a quality he seemed to make an effort to draw out. Each word was spoken slowly, as if for dramatic effect. Before Lilian could respond, Vernon turned his attention to Dorothy. "Dorothy graces us with her presence too. This is a delightful evening, I must say."

Dorothy pointedly did not offer her hand to Vernon for a kiss. "Good evening, Vernon. Have you been on the champers already?"

"But of course, sweetheart. One can't reach this point in the day without a glass or two of champers, you know that."

Dorothy smiled slightly. "Quite."

Unperturbed and clearly used to Dorothy's manner, Vernon turned to James. "Good evening, James. You look ever so disapproving tonight."

"No more so than usual, Singleton."

"Oh, how can I impress you, convince you I'm a good man?"

"I think it's unlikely." James did reach out and shake Vernon's hand. Evelyn wondered just how strong James's disapproval was. Surely he wouldn't even visit the cafe if he really disliked Vernon. Before she had chance to contemplate this further, Evelyn found herself looking directly into Vernon's eyes. They were a vivid, piercing blue, quite at odds with his dark hair and complexion. He was smiling at her, so she smiled back, dumbly, hoping someone would introduce them.

"And who is this delightful creature?" Vernon glanced at Lilian, then looked back to Evelyn.

James took on the duty of introductions, after what seemed like a long time. "Singleton, may I present Miss Evelyn Hopkins, our house guest. Evelyn, this is Mr. Vernon Singleton, the proprietor of this fine establishment."

Vernon's eyes swept over Evelyn's face and she felt as though he took in every detail of her appearance, even as he reached out a hand. She allowed him to take hers lightly in his fingers. "Miss Hopkins, I am very pleased indeed to meet you." Keeping his eyes on hers, Vernon raised Evelyn's hand to his lips and kissed it, close to her knuckles.

Evelyn was surprised at just how the gentle kiss made her nerve endings tingle. "I'm happy to meet you too," she replied, wondering why Vernon was still holding her hand. She drew it back abruptly.

"Are you just passing through, or will we have the pleasure of your company again?"

Evelyn hesitated. "Well, I haven't got fixed plans—"

"You'll see her again, Vernon. We haven't talked about how long she's staying with us, for now, but we're in here so often, I'm sure this won't be the only time Evelyn's here." Lilian's interruption rather ended the need for conversation between Vernon and Evelyn. Vernon simply smiled once more and responded,

"That's excellent news, thank you Lily. In that case, Miss Hopkins, welcome to our exquisite demi-monde." With a last lingering look, he turned away. A few steps later, he paused, to turn back to Lilian. "On stage in ten minutes, yes, darling?"

"Whatever you say, Vernon." Lilian touched her fingers to her painted lips and blew a kiss in Vernon's direction. He winked in return and then returned to the back of the room, near the bar. Evelyn watched him go, thinking he was rather fascinating but also quite an unnerving presence in their group. She was actually rather glad he had not stayed, however much she was intrigued by him.

"Vernon never changes, does he?" James asked, a hint of annoyance in his voice.

"Can't see why he should," Lilian retorted.

"I think the word is incorrigible, James, darling," Dorothy added. Evelyn was not sure whether she referred to Vernon or Lilian.

"What did he mean by *demi-monde*?" Evelyn asked, thinking of Vernon's last words.

"It's nonsense," James replied dismissively. "It means half-world in French."

"So typical of Vernon," Lilian said, apparently enjoying James's exasperation.

Dorothy smiled a seductive, knowing smile. "James is right, it does mean half-world, if you translate it literally. But it means a good deal more than that. It means a world that is not quite part of the respectable world you know. It means a world that admits our parents were wrong and there's something more to strive for. It means that drink and fashion and making love are all important in the pursuit of draining what life has to offer, of living in all the ways that can be lived. It means looking for that something more that you know is there but can't quite reach." Dorothy concluded, still smiling, then licked her lips and winked at Evelyn.

Evelyn stared, transfixed, into Dorothy's dark eyes, part entranced by the alluring words and part confused by their implications. These seemed like decent people, yet Dorothy's words suggested something altogether deeper and more subversive was at play. Dorothy did not drop the eye contact and Evelyn wished she could question her further, try to understand what Dorothy was telling her.

"Oh, Dorothy, don't tease!" Lilian exclaimed. Evelyn relaxed, and Dorothy turned her attention to the drinks, still on the tray where Vernon had deposited them. She handed the glasses around. Evelyn contemplated her own drink with consternation. Dorothy had placed a tall goblet in front of her, filled to the rim with sparkling clear liquid and ice. It was decorated with a slice of lime, a sprig of mint, and a bright red cherry. She caught a perfumed, dangerous aroma from the glass.

"Aren't you going to try it, Evie?" Lilian asked, taking a sip of her own cocktail. Lilian's drink was a startling yellow colour, in a conical glass with a long stem. Dorothy's looked a lot like Lilian's, and James's a lot like her own, despite her having heard them order distinctly different cocktails. She wondered if she should've trusted Lilian to order for her. A glass of water would have been safer.

"Oh, of course I am," she replied to Lilian, trying not to appear nervous. She picked up the cold glass and took a very small sip of the drink. The cold hit her first, followed by the bitter sting of lime, balanced quickly by the perfume of the gin. It was cool and refreshing as it slipped over her tongue and down her throat. Slowly, savouring the taste, she smiled.

"I think you ordered well, darling," Dorothy told Lilian.

"I can always guess what someone will like," Lilian replied. "It's a gift I have."

"Well, thank you," Evelyn said, before taking a rather larger gulp of her drink.

"Don't you think you should be heading for the stage now?" Dorothy said to Lilian. "You can't always keep Vernon waiting. Besides, it looks like the band are about to be ready."

"Yes, yes. You're such a nag, Dorothy, dear. But you're right, of course. It's a hard life, being the star of the show. I'll see you all later."

"Break a leg," James replied, as Lilian got to her feet with a swirl of beads and embroidery, making her way toward the low stage area in the centre of the cafe.

"We tease her, but she really is rather good," Dorothy confided in Evelyn. "Just don't ever let on that I said so."

Evelyn turned to the stage, eagerly anticipating Lilian's performance. As she waited, the perfume of the gin teased her taste buds and she reached for another cool sip.

"Steady on with the gin, Evelyn!" came from James, at her side. For some reason, his tone rather annoyed her. If she wanted to swallow the whole of the cocktail in one go, surely that was her prerogative. She took another small sip, to make the point, then returned the glass to the table without looking at James. Just as she began to feel that she had perhaps been a little rude, Vernon was centre stage, Lilian at his side.

Vernon approached a device Evelyn had never seen. He bent his head slightly to speak into the metallic box on a stick and, miraculously, his voice echoed around the room, so much louder than its natural level. "Ladies and gentlemen, I hope you're all having the most wonderful evening. It's time for me to present one of the most rarefied beauties the Yellow Orchid can offer to you, my honoured patrons. Ready here in her glad rags to delight you with her top-notch warbling, I give you Miss Lilian Grainger."

"How is he so loud?" Evelyn asked James, as Lilian stepped forward, nodding her gratitude for the ripple of applause.

"Vernon's had the place equipped with all the latest developments, you might be sure of it. The microphone's what makes it so loud—all the American singers are using them now. And thank goodness, since it means my dear sister doesn't have to burst her lungs trying to project to the back of the room!"

Before Evelyn could reply, the band began to play. A broad-backed man in a black tuxedo ran his hands over the keys of the piano, playing an upbeat melody, supported by a tall man with a clarinet. Another man played a small set of drums. Quite suddenly, another tune merged seamlessly with the established flow of the music, as a young man with brown hair lifted the tone with his trumpet. The syncopated rhythm filled the cafe, sweeping Evelyn along. She could not help but tap a foot. The music was like nothing she had heard before, more jovial, more liberated than she'd ever heard a band play. Lilian's red-lipped smile was broad as she stepped up to the microphone and waited for her moment to sing.

"If only I could fall in love…" The first line echoed into the room, jaunty and teasing. The song, it seemed, was not really about wanting to fall in love but a light humoured parody of those who did.

Lilian's voice had a richness Evelyn had not expected. She swayed in time with the music, a constant swirl of sparkling, swinging beads and crystals. Her face came to life when she sang; now she was casting a flirty look at a man close to the stage, then she was winking conspiratorially with a woman to her right. She smiled into the microphone, sharing the exuberance of her performance with everyone in the room. Evelyn could not help but be captivated. Lilian, who seemed so breezy and shallow, connected with every word and emotion in the songs she sang, be they comic or sentimental.

After her opening number, Lilian sang two slower songs, both about lost loves and lingering memories. As she sang the last note of the second, she looked down at the floor, then raised her big green eyes to gaze into the distance as the tune trailed off quietly, and Evelyn could imagine she was dreaming of a true love, far away. Lost perhaps. It was not surprising really. Their generation was accustomed to loss. Caught in the emotion, Evelyn began to understand the sentiment Dorothy had expressed. Life had to be lived in the aftermath of so much loss. Only they, the young people, could understand that. Even if it did mean doing things their parents would not have dreamed of.

As if to prove the point, the next song was perhaps the most upbeat and full of life of any Lilian had performed so far. Apparently carried away with the music, as she sang, Lilian danced on the spot, stepping forwards and backwards, kicking her legs from the knees, moving her hands. She was perfectly in time with the music, though it looked odd to Evelyn to see a woman dancing in such a risqué way, and on her own. To see a woman so filled with confidence in herself, dominating a room, was something she was unused to. It filled her with hope. She'd heard there was a spirit of anything goes in London, and now she started to believe it was true. What options would be open to her here?

Dorothy leaned over to speak to her. "How do you like our very own Ruth Etting then, darling?"

"Oh, I think she's marvellous!" Evelyn replied.

Lilian was still dancing, the band playing an interlude in her song.

"Did they Charleston back home?" Dorothy asked.

"Charleston?"

Dorothy nodded her head towards Lilian. "That rather hotsy-totsy little jig she's doing. Do you not dance in Devon?"

Evelyn flushed a little. Dorothy's tone was teasing but Evelyn did not like to be reminded that she was an outsider in this world she was rapidly growing to wish she was a part of. "Of course we dance. Only the military two-step isn't quite like what Lilian's doing."

Dorothy laughed. "I think it's marvellous she can do that and sing at the same time. A talented girl. Of course, when she's edged, she'll be bound to demonstrate even if she's not onstage!"

Lilian's song ended, and Vernon appeared onstage to offer her another cocktail, which he presented with showy gallantry, making a bow as he gave it to her. One or two of Lilian's audience called out jokes. Lilian grinned mischievously at those who did, took a large swallow of her drink, and handed the glass back to Vernon, dismissing him with a brief wave of her hand, to even greater merriment on the part of those watching. Lilian clearly adored the attention and she knew how to keep it.

Now she spoke into the microphone, her voice unnaturally loud in the room. "You're a simply top-hole audience. I need to thank Vernon Singleton for asking me to sing here again. He clearly recognises a good thing when he sees it, eh, Vernon?" There was a small cheer from the crowd, who seemed to respond to Lilian's energy, loving her even when her vanity came to the fore. "For my last song, I'm going to sing a song that I think is the cat's pyjamas. And I think it's time you pushed some of those chairs out of the way and danced! When I finish, the band will keep playing. So sip your giggle water, take the hand of whoever's near you, and dance!"

With her final word, the band struck up again, playing a song clearly written to be danced to. Bouncy and jovial, the words Lilian sang were secondary to the rhythm. And that rhythm spread around the room infectiously, with many couple sliding their chairs to the side and dancing. All of them danced the swivelling, twisting movements Lilian had been performing herself. Evelyn watched, fascinated.

"Don't feel like a dance yourself?" Dorothy asked her.

"I wouldn't know how." Evelyn found she regretted the fact.

"It's not hard to learn. Ask Lilian to show you. It really is super good fun."

"I'm sure." Evelyn wondered if she could make her joints move in the way the dancers were managing. She hoped so.

Dorothy had not finished. "You know, Evie, it's funny, you being here really makes me see what a performance this all is. Our lives. There's nothing we do that you can't learn. How awfully shallow we all are! Isn't it just shocking?"

"I suppose so." Evelyn was not really sure how to respond to Dorothy, who seemed intent on offering philosophical interpretations of their day-to-day existence with rather alarming consistency. Evelyn had never known anyone to think so much about the way they lived their life as Dorothy seemed to.

Lilian's song finished just as Evelyn drank the last of her cocktail, reluctant to drain the glass. It was difficult to say if the gin was affecting her, since she didn't usually drink gin and she wasn't really sure just how it was supposed to affect her. She was looking down at her empty glass and assessing if she felt anything different when Lilian returned to the table breathless, her face flushed pink, her skin damp with perspiration, and her eyes shining.

"Brava, my dear," Dorothy said, without any great enthusiasm.

"Marvellous as ever, Lilian. Sometimes it surprises me you're my sister." This was James, whose praise did not sound wholly approving.

"Thank you, both." Lilian beamed at them and turned to Evelyn. "Well, Evie, what did you think?"

"I found it extraordinary," Evelyn said, before realising that Lilian might misunderstand. "I mean, you were wonderful, but I've never heard anything like it either, so it was also, well, enlightening, I suppose. I'd love to hear more."

"Oh, you'll have plenty of chances for that, don't worry," James said, good-naturedly. "She sings at every opportunity."

"I don't blame her. It must feel just wonderful to be up there, to have everyone in here watching you and dancing with you."

"Oh and how! You just don't know until you've tried it, Evie!" Lilian spoke loudly, clearly still filled with the energy of her performance.

"I don't think I'll ever try anything of the sort. I can't perform."

"Oh, fiddlesticks! Everyone can perform in some way. I bet you can sing."

Evelyn was surprised Lilian didn't view singing as a unique talent of her own. "Not really. I mean, I used to sing with a choir at my school, but that was years ago now, I was just a girl."

"Well then, perhaps I'll give you singing lessons, darling. I love to teach." Lilian seemed quite taken with her idea.

"Don't believe her, Evelyn," James warned. "I once watched her trying to teach our young cousins to speak French. She reduced two perfectly decent children to tantrums in less than half an hour."

"Hush, brother dear. I'm not offering to teach her French and she's not ten years old. This is entirely different."

"That remains to be seen."

Evelyn smiled, understanding that James was teasing his sister. Something about their relationship made her think of Edward, and a shock of loss and pain made her catch her breath.

"Anyway, you're scaring Evie," Lilian declared, glancing at Evelyn with something like concern in her expression. "How about we get more drinks?" She suited the action to the word, standing up and waving across the cafe. "Yoo-hoo, Vernon, dearest? Same again over here, please!"

Evelyn followed Lilian's gaze and saw Vernon roll his eyes and give a wearied nod of acquiescence. She watched him disappear behind the bar, stopping briefly for a word with a group of people gathered close to the back of the cafe, where a door led through to what Evelyn supposed were the private rooms of the building. The three people laughed good-naturedly and one responded, although Evelyn could not hear what was said. However, her attention was drawn to the speaker. She leaned closer to Lilian, as she settled back in her chair, and gestured towards the back of the room. "Who is Vernon talking to?"

Both Lilian and Dorothy peered in the direction Evelyn indicated. They seemed delighted that Evelyn was showing curiosity in the people in the room. "Which one?" Lilian asked.

"The one who looks ever so much like Vernon. That's why I'm asking."

"Aha! You mean Jos, darling," Dorothy told her.

"Of course. No wonder you'd notice her. She does look a lot like Vernon. They're twins."

"She's his sister?" Evelyn was a little surprised since, from this distance, the person in question had seemed more likely to be Vernon's brother. Her hair was short, not slicked back as her brother's but certainly cropped in a masculine style. She was in white shirtsleeves and a light tweed waistcoat, a loose blue cravat at her neck. Evelyn did not express her surprise.

"Yes. Jos Singleton, who is eleven minutes older than Vernon. She's an interesting one," Lilian said.

"How so?" Evelyn was already interested, but there was something more implied in Lilian's tone.

"Now, Lilian, be nice. Just because you're not her best friend, there's really nothing wrong with Jos." Dorothy smiled indulgently at Lilian, then turned her attention to Evelyn. "Jos is what you might call a free spirit. I rather admire her for it, honestly. She's like her brother but with a little more integrity."

"You really should give Vernon more credit," Lilian protested.

"I've known him longer than you, darling," Dorothy retorted.

"I don't know why you're always defending him, Lilian," James put in. "And his sister's just as bad, if you ask me. It's not really cricket, is it?"

"I don't think we did ask you," Lilian replied.

"Oh now, James, darling, are you worried she'll steal all the pretty girls away from you?" Dorothy teased.

Evelyn tried to follow their conversation but found herself growing ever more confused. She turned her gaze back to Jos and her two companions. One was a woman in a striking red dress, the fabric so sheer over her shoulders that the shadowy outlines of her collarbones and the valley between her breasts were visible. Although she was seated, Evelyn could see the glimmer of silver embroidery on the bodice of the dress. Her short chestnut hair was styled in immaculate waves and decorated with an ornate silver comb and red feathers. Her skin was strikingly pale, her lips coloured unnaturally red.

This striking woman was seated very close the person at her side. At first, Evelyn had assumed she was holding the arm of a man. The white tuxedo jacket, stiff-collared shirt, and black tie seemed to make it obvious. However, as she looked again, she realised she'd been mistaken. The shoulders were too narrow, the jawline too smooth. It was obvious when she looked directly at the woman's face, she was certainly no man. And yet her attire was masculine in the extreme, far more immaculate and sharply tailored than Jos Singleton, a few feet away. In addition, her dark blond hair was cut in a severe short style.

"Bet you're wondering about the others now too." Lilian had tired of laughing at her brother and had noticed where Evelyn's attention was drawn.

"Yes, I must admit, I was rather."

Dorothy smiled. "I can see the fascination. I'm not sure there's a man or woman in here who doesn't have a real crack on for one or the other, or both. Attagirl, Evie, you're fitting right in already."

"I don't know what you mean." Evelyn waited for an explanation from Dorothy. "Who are they?"

Lilian chose to enlighten her. "The one in the red dress is Courtney Craig. She's American, though she went to school here. Same school as Dorothy, in fact, though she was in the form above. Awfully rich, apparently her daddy is someone high up in banking in New York City. The one she can't let go of, with the Eton crop, is Clara Bridgford. Also at school with Dorothy. They were schoolgirl sweethearts and now they're as good as married."

Evelyn took a moment to process this information. "But they're both women," was her response, which did not, for a moment, convey the intrigue and confusion she felt.

"Oh yes, they most certainly are. Not the sort of thing that happened in West Coombe, I'll warrant!" Dorothy seemed to take delight in Evelyn's naiveté.

"I don't really think I understand," Evelyn admitted.

"And why should you?" James said. "Really, you two, this is Evelyn's first night here, must you really try to open her eyes to everything there is to know in just a few hours?"

"We were only trying to answer her questions." Lilian pouted.

James apparently decided to explain the matter himself, to draw an end to the conversation. "Evelyn, Clara, Courtney, and Jos are what's known as inverts. They feel the same towards other woman as normal women feel towards men. They form relationships with each other and act as though they're real couples. That's all there is to it, really."

"Oh…I see." Evelyn was taken aback by James's brusque and condemnatory tone.

"So there's nothing really to understand," James said. "And, yes, Courtney is certainly a beautiful woman but Dorothy is exaggerating how attractive they are."

"I am not! I could be charmed by Clara myself. Used to carry a bit of a torch for her at school." Dorothy winked at James.

"You're absurd, Dorothy."

"Oh, dry up, Mrs. Grundy. There's nothing wrong with it. Modern times, don't you know?" Dorothy was apparently unperturbed by James. "Evie, I'm sorry if we've overwhelmed you a little. This is just the world we live in."

"Oh no, don't apologise, I find it all fascinating." Evelyn smiled, still trying to process these new developments and trying to stop herself staring over at Clara and Courtney, still in conversation with Jos Singleton. Perhaps the gin was having an effect on her after all, since she thought she could understand why Clara was so attractive. Jos too, for that matter.

"Aha, the drinks. Just what we need." Lilian smiled up at Vernon as he approached with a tray of glasses.

"You know I employ waiters for this, Lily, darling." Vernon was only mildly exasperated.

"Of course. But I'm your star, aren't I?"

"Yes. You know you are. The earth moved for me tonight, every note was as if in a dream. I am eternally under your spell."

Dorothy laughed openly at Vernon's hyperbole. Even James smiled. Lilian frowned with mock melodrama. "Oh, how you tease me, Mr. Singleton."

"This is nothing, Miss Grainger, as you well know."

"Oh, please," James murmured as he took the first sip of his drink.

Vernon turned his attention to James. "Just because you're not my type, Grainger, you don't need to be so flat about it. Not stuck on me, are you?"

"I don't see why anyone would be, Singleton," James replied, without a hint of good humour.

"Playing hard to get. That's rare."

"Oh, Vernon, leave poor James alone. He's already suffering at our hands tonight." Dorothy gave him a stern stare.

"Anything you say, Dorothy, you know I can't resist your every command."

"Naturally. Won't you sit down for a drink with us? Or at least stay for a ciggie?"

"I'm a busy man, Dorothy. Besides, a chap named Sinclair has come in especially to see me this evening, and so far I've given him no more than a moment of my time. You'll just have to join me in the daylight hours, if you crave my company so badly. We can sip coffee in the sunlight."

"Coffee? Where's the fun in that?" Lilian interjected.

"Oh, I'm lots of fun, even when there's no gin, Lily. Anyway, how is our new friend?" He turned his enquiring gaze on Evelyn. "Are you enjoying your evening, darling?"

"Oh yes, very much, thank you." Evelyn could not help but feel nervous and wish he would look elsewhere, yet also flattered by his interest.

"Will we see you again?"

"I expect so."

"Then I will look forward to all the fun we'll have together. You do look like you'd be rather fun."

"Singleton, Evelyn's only arrived in London today—can you perhaps show her some common decency?" James glowered at Vernon, who looked mildly surprised. Evelyn did not appreciate the implication that she could not manage a conversation with Vernon by herself.

"Oh, I can be lots of fun, Mr. Singleton," she said, in as jaunty a tone as she could summon. "Only it entirely depends on the calibre of my playmates."

Evelyn did not miss the look of approval exchanged by Lilian and Dorothy. She did not look at James's expression but rather enjoyed the way Vernon narrowed his eyes and smiled, as if presented with a challenge where he had expected none. Distracted by this, she reached for her cocktail but misjudged the distance to the glass, managing to topple it over and into her lap. The ice-cold liquid soaked straight through her skirt and onto her thighs. Although she had righted the glass before the whole contents could spill, there was still a small puddle in her lap. She jumped up, embarrassed.

"Oh, darling! Your dress!" Lilian exclaimed.

"Where's the ladies'?" Evelyn asked urgently.

"Over at the back there, beyond the bar. Would you care for some help?" Vernon raised a cocky eyebrow.

"No, thank you." Evelyn hurried in the direction he'd indicated. Her route took her directly past Jos and her friends, but she did not look up for a moment as she went through the door with its frosted glass panels and into the beige-tiled washroom, where she reached for the white hand towel and held it to her skirt.

The sound of the music from the piano, which had been playing since Lilian had finished singing, filtered through the door but it seemed very quiet in the tiled space, with only the dripping of water from one of the copper-coloured taps making a sound in the room itself. There was a wooden bench along one side of the room. Evelyn perched on it and sighed, still dabbing at her skirt. Now she felt the effects of the gin she had consumed, and now she realised just how far away from home she really was. Alone in a bathroom with glazed beige tiles and a dripping tap, at the back of a cafe in London where jazz was played and friends argued and cocktails were ordered. Where women dressed like men and pretended to marry other women. Only this morning she had been in West Coombe. With Edward, and her parents. With familiar walls and rugs and mirrors. With tea and porridge for breakfast. Part of her ached for the familiarity and felt miserable that she had brought herself to this place, where she would never really belong. And yet it was so wondrous, so full of colour. Even to be miserable in this world was surely glorious. Was she living the life Edward had so badly wanted for both of them?

The door opened. Evelyn leaped to her feet, determined not to be discovered both dishevelled and staring into space in the ladies' washroom. She looked to the door and was surprised to see Jos Singleton appear.

"Hello there," Jos said, looking directly at Evelyn with eyes that were just as blue as her brother's. She ran a hand through her short hair, as if a little unsure of herself. "I'm dreadfully sorry to interrupt, but I couldn't help noticing, as you ran past, you dropped this." She held out a hand. In her fingers sparkled Evelyn's brooch, the diamond and ruby butterfly that meant so much to her. Evelyn stared at it, horrified she'd not even noticed it was missing.

"Oh gosh! Thank you so much. I had no idea I'd lost it, what with my spilling my drink and everything. And it means ever such a lot to me."

"You better take it back, then." Jos smiled and moved a little closer to Evelyn. Evelyn reached for the brooch and held it securely in her hand. "Perhaps the pin is broken?" Jos suggested.

Evelyn glanced down at the fastening of the brooch. "It looks fine. I probably didn't fasten it properly. I dressed in rather a hurry. Thank you again, Miss—" Evelyn stopped herself. She had been about to let on that she knew Jos's identity, which would reveal her former curiosity. Her cheeks grew warm.

Jos looked at her curiously. "It's Miss Singleton, but I much prefer people to call me Jos."

"Well, thank you, Jos, I'm so happy you brought me my brooch." Evelyn found herself quite captivated. Jos's nearly black hair was short cropped and sat close to her head, but with a natural curl which shone in the light. Her blue eyes were vivid beneath thick dark eyebrows and fringed with long lashes. Her complexion was almost Mediterranean, although there were a few freckles scattered over her nose. Now that Jos was standing right in front of her, Evelyn could see her whole outfit. She wore a light tweed double-breasted waistcoat fitted close to the curve of her body, at once masculine but showing her womanly curves more than any fashionable gown. Her trousers were wide Oxford bags in the same tweed as the waistcoat. The white shirt was a striking contrast with the rich colour of her skin, and the blue of her loosely tied cravat brought out that of her eyes. She wore her clothes easily, without affectation, and yet they seemed well-considered to show her form and colouring to their best. She looked a lot like her brother, Evelyn reflected, yet her expression was more open, with less of his assumed sneer.

"And might I ask your name?"

Jos's question made Evelyn realise she was staring and hadn't yet introduced herself. "Of course. Evelyn Hopkins." She held out a hand. Jos took it and squeezed her fingers gently. Her hand was warm, her fingers rougher and with drier skin than Evelyn expected. She found she wanted to hold on to the hand that was so quickly withdrawn. There was undeniably something compelling about Jos.

"I've not seen you before, have I? Not that I'm here often, but it seems like most people are regular patrons."

"No, I've not been here before. In fact, this is my first day in London. I'm from Devon."

"You've come a long way to visit the Yellow Orchid. Vernon must be doing something right." Jos smiled. "Sorry, Vernon, the proprietor, he's my brother. We're twins, actually."

"I've met Vernon. In fact, he's probably still at our table—that's where I left him."

Jos's smile faded briefly. "You're here with Lilian and James Grainger?"

"Yes. It's an awfully long story but I brought a letter to them, from their brother who died in the war. And they've been kind enough to allow me to stay with them while I'm in London."

"Oh, so you're not an old friend of theirs?"

Evelyn thought this an odd question and still sensed an edge of hostility in Jos's tone. "Not at all. I only met them today. It seems odd now, to be here with them and not to have known them this morning. And Lilian's friend, Dorothy, I only met this evening."

"Oh, Dorothy's swell, she'll be a good friend." Evelyn wondered why Jos had not said the same of Lilian, beginning to feel uneasy. "So will you be in London long?"

"I'm really not sure. Like I said, it's a long story and I don't have specific plans. I'm rather relying on Lilian and James's kindness, you see."

"I hope you'll be here long enough to tell me that story. It sounds like it could be interesting." Jos smiled now, the tension dissolving.

"I don't know about that. I'm not terribly interesting myself." Evelyn shrugged and laughed awkwardly.

"I think you seem interesting." Jos held Evelyn's eye contact for a long time and Evelyn found she could not look away. Then a thought seemed to distract Jos and she looked down at the floor, then at Evelyn's drying skirt. "It doesn't look like that will stain, anyway."

Evelyn looked down. "No, I hope not." The silence between them was not entirely comfortable. "I should probably go back out there, or they'll be coming in to find me."

"Of course." Jos turned to open the door for Evelyn, who hastily returned the towel to its rail. To leave the quiet of the washroom to enter the smoke- and sound-filled chaos of the cafe seemed jarring and yet enticing at the same time. She passed through the door Jos held open for her and looked back to take her leave properly.

"Thank you again for returning my brooch."

Jos smiled. "It was a pleasure to meet you, Miss Hopkins."

"Evie. I hope we'll meet again."

"Jos Singleton, you must introduce us!" A loud, accented voice came from close by.

Jos grinned at someone over Evelyn's shoulder. "I'm sorry, Evie, how impolite of me."

Evelyn turned to see the women she knew to be Clara and Courtney looking at her with no little intrigue in their expressions. Apparently, it had been the American, Courtney, who had demanded the introduction.

"Clara Bridgford and Courtney Craig, this is Evie Hopkins. I can't tell you much else about her, except that she's from Devon."

"Then you've shown a dreadful lack of curiosity, Jos." Clara held out a hand and Evelyn took it. "Good to meet you." Clara's voice was rich and deep. "What brings you to London?"

"I'm pleased to meet you too. It really is a long story though."

"Leave her be, Clara." Courtney placed a silencing finger on Clara's lips, then held her own hand out to Evelyn. "I'm also pleased to meet you. And might I say what a pretty brooch that is. I'm so glad we noticed it fall off and sent Jos in after you."

Evelyn could not help but wonder why Jos had returned her brooch, not Clara or Courtney. Perhaps they were simply unable to be apart from each other for a moment. Even now, they sat so closely their arms were touching. Evelyn shook Courtney's hand. "Thank you. The brooch is a family heirloom and I would've hated to have lost it, especially on my very first day in London."

"Isn't it quite a place?" Courtney clearly loved the city.

"Yes, it certainly is."

"I came all the way from New York City to be here."

"I thought that was to be with me?" Clara interjected.

"That too, obviously, darling." Courtney planted a small kiss on Clara's cheek, leaving a faint smear of lip colour.

"I only came from Devon, but it does feel like rather a long way, I have to admit." Evelyn was trying very hard not to be transfixed by Clara and Courtney. They were both strikingly beautiful and immaculately attired, but, above this, she could almost feel their dedication to each other. She began to wonder how James could be so disapproving. Their relationship was certainly unconventional, but something to frown on? She could not see it. What had he called them? *Inverts*, it was. She tried to make sense of it, but there didn't seem to be anything wrong with Clara and Courtney at all. What they had seemed actually quite appealing.

"Well, I very much hope we are able to hear what brought you to the corrupt streets of the capital one day soon," Clara said and sounded genuine.

"That would be nice," Evelyn said, surprised at such curiosity and unsure what the appropriate response would be. "I'm afraid I should return to my friends. Look, I can see them waving at me." Sure enough, Lilian was waving a hand in her direction. Vernon was no longer at the table with them, but Dorothy and James were both looking her way.

"Of course, we won't hold you up any longer," Clara said.

Evelyn smiled briefly at the three women and nodded her thanks once again to Jos, then returned to the chair next to James.

"We began to think you weren't coming back," Lilian said, her tone almost accusatory. "And what did Jos want? We saw her follow you."

"My brooch fell off as I passed by. She was just returning it to me." Somehow, Evelyn felt as though she needed to defend Jos from Lilian. "It was kind of her."

"Hmm, well, you should be careful being alone with her, you know."

Evelyn raised her eyebrows. "Why?"

"Smart question, darling! Yes, why, Lilian?" Dorothy chimed in.

"Well, you know her inclinations. And Evelyn's not all that worldly." Lilian clearly did not like being challenged.

"Jos is hardly likely to practice the art of seduction in the ladies' washroom."

Lilian was clearly annoyed at being ridiculed, her face florid. "You never know," she muttered.

"I liked her, from what I saw of her," Evelyn said. "She introduced me to Clara and Courtney too, they seem very nice. And very happy."

"Much happier than most couples I've come across," Dorothy said.

"That's not really the point, Dorothy." James spoke for the first time since Evelyn had returned. "Evelyn, you'll find most people are nice here. And most of them have drunk enough gin and smoked enough fags to be happy too. But you have to be careful."

"Please James, she's not a child." Dorothy seemed put out on Evelyn's behalf.

"I'm only saying she should be careful of people who are, well, unconventional."

"I appreciate the advice, thank you." Evelyn tried to sound sincere and took a large gulp of the remains of her cocktail.

"I think," Lilian interrupted, "it's probably high time we retreated to the house and to our beds. What say you all?"

"I think that's a top-hole idea. The night is young, of course, but I am rather tired." Dorothy seemed no less alert than she had at the beginning of the evening.

"Yes, agreed. Drink up, Evelyn," James urged.

Evelyn drained the remainder of her cocktail, undecided if she was pleased to be leaving the cafe or not. It had been an evening of discovery, and she hoped, before she had to leave London, there would be much more of that.

Chapter Seven

Jos Singleton spent a sleepless night, remarkable since she'd not even been drinking. Perhaps that was the problem, she reflected, as she sat in her winged armchair, contemplating the darkness. Maybe she'd become a little too reliant on scotch as a means to induce slumber.

Sleep had been difficult for her over the years. She supposed it was ever since her parents had been killed, peacefully asleep in their beds when the Zeppelin raid had demolished their house. Looking back on those last moments, cowering under the kitchen table, she still wondered if there was something she could have done. If only she'd not taken cover, if she'd gone upstairs and warned them. But she had assumed they were still out of the house, not already in their bed. The bomb hit their house directly, crashing through the roof. She'd been told it was a miracle she had survived herself.

She remembered regaining consciousness in a pile of rubble, hands pulling bricks and roof tiles and the remnants of the table from her wounded body. She remembered Vernon's face, the first thing she saw, peering at her full of anxiety and fear. She'd smiled to reassure him, before she had even begun to become aware of what had happened and the great loss they had both suffered. She'd always felt compelled to look after Vernon, even if they were the same age and even when their parents were still alive. He'd still been at his office when the bombs fell, or she might have lost everything that night. That Vernon was still alive seemed more important than the pain that racked her body.

Jos had not thought to ask about their parents right away. She was pulled from the rubble and carried on a stretcher to the nearest hospital. Her right leg was broken in two places, she had three fractured ribs, a broken left wrist and collarbone, and bruises to her head and face, but as she was told, she'd got away lightly considering the total destruction of their house. Only when she was properly settled in the hospital bed did they allow Vernon to visit her. And only then did she realise that their parents were not there to visit, nor had anyone mentioned them. She did not have to vocalise the question—she read the answer in Vernon's eyes. Their parents had died as she sheltered from the bombs.

Vernon said it wasn't her fault. That she would not have had time to go upstairs and wake her parents, even if she had known they were in their bed. If she had gone upstairs, she would be dead too and Vernon left all alone. The nurses told her it wasn't her fault when she couldn't sleep and told them of her anxiety by the light of the oil lamps they carried, halos of illumination in the darkened ward. Eventually, as she convalesced, she began to accept this.

But sleep was still difficult. She would dream of saving their parents, only for them all to die together. She would dream of their last moments in graphic detail. She would see the shadow of the Zeppelin looming and feel as though she was being crushed. Sleep became dangerous to her. Not only did the nightmares torture her, she could not help but linger on how her parents had died while they slept. Even when she did sleep, the cries and groans of the other patients in her ward would intrude into her consciousness. It was always worst at night, when there were no visitors to distract them from the pain and horror of it all. The nurses could not sit by her side all night, and she could not expect it. She made herself suffer in silence and darkness, telling herself she had to be strong. The world was full of death; it was not her place to be self-indulgent in her grief.

When Jos eventually returned home, she had been different. Vernon said the pain and loss had aged her, made her too serious. She did not fully agree with that assessment. It was rather that she saw life differently. She no longer wanted to fill it with the fantasy of acting, the illusion of pretending to be other characters. Although she'd stayed in the theatre, she'd chosen practical, realistic work. And she had decided that it was time to stop denying the desire for other women she'd been suppressing since her early teens. If death stalked so close, she would accept it and live her days just as she chose. No matter if she had to drink scotch to help her sleep. It turned out that most of her generation were doing just the same thing, with scotch, gin, or worse.

So now, in her armchair, she thought of all those long, sleepless nights she'd spent and realised this was different. She was not troubled by her past or by the sense of fear that sometimes gripped her. She was excited, in a way that felt hopeful and good. There was no point denying the source of the feeling. It was that brief encounter with Evelyn Hopkins.

Jos was no innocent. Her most recent dalliance with a beautiful woman was only weeks ago. Women looking to experiment, even if just for a night, with their sensual desires were everywhere these days. To sleep with a woman was decadent and daring, less risky than doing the same with a man, and Jos was interesting enough, it seemed, to get more than her fair share. The last entanglement, with a blond flapper named Daisy, had lasted a few weeks and she'd had fun. But neither of them had been serious in their commitment to each other. In fact, Jos found, she was rarely serious in her commitment. The women she encountered were probably even less concerned with the longevity of the arrangement than she was. Commitment to anything was rare these days. Apparently it was too old-fashioned to commit.

Jos did not really object to this. It made life much easier if she could satisfy her carnal desires and have a few light-hearted conversations, without having to bring her emotions into the picture. Too many women, once they got properly involved with her, wanted to know why she was the way she was. Wanted to save her from herself. If she ever got so attached to a woman that she told the story of her parents' death and her own narrow escape, she hated to see the pity in their eyes. She preferred her relationships brief, lacking in deep emotion, and more or less anonymous.

With this in mind, it was queer that she felt so drawn to Evelyn Hopkins. The girl was clearly out of her depth in London, with no real idea of the dangers she faced. And in the clutches of Lilian Grainger too! Jos sighed. She did not like Lilian. It was partly because her own brother seemed quite enamoured of her, of course, and she did not think any woman was good enough for Vernon, whilst he seemed quite determined to try the entire female population. Not that promiscuity concerned her, but it was rather the effect these women exerted on Vernon. Lilian, in particular, seemed to be a bad influence, and he'd been more moody since he'd been involved with her, more cynical than ever. However, her dislike of Lilian was also because Lilian seemed to sneer at her, only being polite when forced. For all of her fashion and claims of modernity, she suspected Lilian was rather conservative and struggled with the idea of Jos's love for her own sex. None of which would matter if it was not that Lilian would be exerting her irresistible influence over Evelyn. And somehow it already mattered to her that Evelyn did not disapprove.

She closed her eyes and tried to pin down exactly what it was about Evelyn that intrigued her so much. The obvious answer was that wide-eyed innocence. But innocence was not a quality that Jos was usually drawn to, since it spelled the way to outright rejection or too many questions. Evelyn was undeniably beautiful, with that luxuriant chestnut hair and lively eyes. But it was more that: her handshake had been firm and, despite clearly being far from her natural environment, Evelyn still exuded a certain confidence in herself. To be so far from home and yet still composed in this world was quite a feat. Evelyn was a strong woman, though Jos suspected she didn't consider herself as such. Strength was a powerful draw. As was independence of mind.

She'd only spent a few moments with Evelyn, but she already knew she wanted to know her more, to understand what had driven her to come to London, to follow the next chapter of the extraordinary story of a girl from the middle of nowhere suddenly in the heart of this turbulent, decadent world. Even, dared she hope, to be part of that story.

Evelyn dreamed of butterflies that night. Her brooch, so recently lost on the floor of the cafe, came to life and fluttered through a blue Devon sky. On a clifftop, above crashing waves, it settled on a yellow orchid. Another butterfly, this one not made of rubies and diamonds but a beautiful Common Blue, flittered into the scene and landed on a nearby cornflower, the same blue as its striking wings. Suddenly a shadow came over the scene and Evelyn felt fear and panic. Now she was the jewelled butterfly and something was bearing down on her. Her dream state did not show her if it was a boot or a net, but she was sure she would be crushed or trapped. And yet somehow her wings were too heavy, the jewels meant she could not fly. The Common Blue took off, flying free into the sky, where it disappeared, and she was still paralysed, could not move her wings. Still the shadow bore down and her panic only increased.

She awoke with a dry mouth, sweating into the sheets. The sheets did not have the familiar threadbare patches of home; the mattress springs were firmer. She opened her eyes wider, knowing she was somewhere away from home but not realising where for a few long seconds. She made herself focus on shapes of the shadows in the room to give her some sense of her bearings. London. This was London, she was in the Graingers' spare bedroom. They'd arrived home just before midnight and she had fallen asleep as soon as she'd climbed out of her clothes. Focusing on memories of the preceding evening helped, but she could not quite shake the terror of the dream, of that advancing shadow, that certain entrapment or death.

Evelyn sat up in bed, drawing a deep breath. The slight sensation of seasickness made her question just how much gin had been in her cocktails. She rubbed her eyes and reached for the electric lamp on the bedside table. Soft yellow light flooded the room. Her watch was on the bedside table. She took it up to check the time and found it to be just after five. It would soon be daylight. The idea of trying to sleep further was not appealing. Waking up at dawn was nothing unusual for Evelyn.

Her eye was drawn to the butterfly brooch, now lying on the dressing table across the room, along with the jewellery Lilian had lent her. Her dress was draped over the chair, evidence of just how tired she had been when she'd finally made it to her bedroom. She swung her legs out of bed and rose unsteadily to her feet. The dizziness was not quite as bad, now that she was fully awake. She picked up the butterfly and held it in her palm, contemplating the livid rubies and shimmering diamonds. Although she'd inherited it from her grandmother, on her mother's side, she had no idea what the history of the brooch was before that. Her grandmother had never told her, even when Evelyn had admired the brooch as a child. Certainly, such jewellery seemed far too expensive for her grandmother, a fisherman's daughter who married a fish merchant, to have been able to purchase for herself. Evelyn wondered what stories the brooch could tell.

For Evelyn, of course, the brooch reminded her only of the vision she had created with Edward that sunny day on a clifftop, when they'd known that one day they could fly. And yet, last night, she'd almost lost the brooch. It had fallen to the floor so easily. If it had not been for Jos, it could have been gone forever. Perhaps that was why she was dreaming about butterflies.

Thinking about Edward made her miss home. What business did she really have in this strange house, such a long way from her family. The letter had been delivered now. She'd had a glimpse of the life she'd suspected existed outside of her closed-off little world. She'd enjoyed it too. But perhaps it was time to go home. She could pack her bags now and be at Paddington in time for the first train.

Evelyn returned the brooch to its place on the dressing table and ran her fingers over the pearls borrowed from Lilian. They were beautiful. And it was very kind of Lilian. So far, everyone in London had welcomed her with more than open arms. Why would she leave that, when she could enjoy it for longer?

Still contemplating, Evelyn crossed to the window and pulled back the drapes. The street outside was deserted, still illuminated by the pale glow of the gas lamps. London seemed a city of ghosts. It was a place made of its past, of the stories of the people who inhabited it, of their own ghosts. In London, she did not feel peculiar, out of place. She was part of it. At rest as it was now, it had its own beauty. True, it was not soaring cliffs and sandy beaches, churning waves and dark woods. But it was a place full of human stories. There was so much more to discover, even so much more of herself to understand. It had to be here—she couldn't leave now. There really wasn't a question.

Her resolution in mind, Evelyn pulled out her suitcase, still not entirely unpacked, and removed the sheets of writing paper and pen she'd put into one of the inside pockets. She cleared a space on the dressing table, sat in the chair in front of it, and began to write.

Dearest Eddie,

I hope this letter finds you, and finds you well. And I hope there hasn't been too much of a fuss at home. I don't suppose anyone will think to blame you for all of this, but if they do, I hope you know it isn't your fault. I always wanted to get away. And now that I'm here in London, I know that we were right. I had to leave, to come here, to try to fly. Thank you—oh, thank you, Eddie, for helping me to find my way.

I found Lilian Grainger still living at the same address.

She's an extraordinary girl, quite different from me. Last night—on my very first evening here—I saw her sing at a jazz club. Can you imagine it, Eddie, me sipping cocktails and listening to jazz!

Lilian lives with her younger brother, James, and they were both very moved to receive the letter from Frank. They had some questions, of course, but thanked you for doing what you could to get the letter to them. It has given them some satisfaction to know something of how Frank died.

It is very early in the morning now. I am not sure what the day holds—I suppose getting to know my surroundings and discussing the terms of my accommodation with the Graingers. I am hoping I can stay for a while. They have been very kind so far.

I want you to know that I am thinking about you and missing you, in every moment. It's as though you are here with me, Eddie.

I will write again very soon. Do take care of yourself until then.

I love you, Eddie.

Your sister,

Evie

Evelyn smiled. Writing to Eddie was the easiest of all the letters. She knew he'd be happy for her, and pleased that he had been able to help her. To remind him how much she loved him was important, since she could not be there for him in person. The letter to her parents was much harder.

Dear Mother and Father,

You will by now have, of course, realised that I am not there. I hope Edward was able to pass my short letter to you, written in the hope that you would not worry. I am sorry for any anger or concern I have caused you. It was not my intention to hurt you at all, although I am perfectly aware that my actions will appear reckless and inconsiderate.

I will not attempt to explain myself because I am not sure I entirely understand it myself. When Edward managed to gather himself to show me the letter he had been keeping, for a friend of his captain, who lived in London, it seemed the most natural thing to offer to deliver it. I am aware that I could have arranged for it to be posted, or sought another solution, but it is apparent to me that I wanted to see London and it seemed of utmost urgency to set out at once.

There will be time for reproach when I return and I fully expect to bear the weight of your disappointment and anger. But I hope you will also understand that I have taken these actions in the pursuit of happiness.

The purpose of this letter is to let you know that I am perfectly safe. I am only a short train ride away from you. I have been accommodated by a brother and sister, Lilian and James Grainger, in Mayfair, so I am quite comfortable. I urge you not to worry for me. I will stay in touch.

With hopes of your eventual forgiveness,
Your loving daughter,
Evie

The idea of causing her parents pain or making them the subject of town gossip tore at her insides. She would have done neither intentionally and yet that was exactly what she had done, through making a choice that was entirely her responsibility. However, there was no going back now, so she could only hope they would be reconciled to her when the time came to return home.

She had two more letters to write. One to her sister and one to Michael. She began with a short note for Annie. She apologised, attempted the briefest of explanations, and entreated her sister to watch over Edward in her absence. Annie might not share the special relationship she had with Edward, but she did care.

Sealing the letter in its envelope, Evelyn stood up and walked over to the window. They sky was growing light; day had nearly arrived. She yawned and stretched her arms, ready to embrace a full day in London and see what it brought her. The prospect made her letter to Michael seem almost inconsequential. She'd already left him a note, and after all, the pain had already been caused. There was really nothing to say, so she simply assured him of her well-being and apologised for causing him pain. She added a hope that he would soon find a woman to love him as he deserved, to make sure there was no danger he would wait for her. Wherever the next weeks led, it would not be back to Michael. She signed off with affection and then it was done. She felt no regret, other than that she had hurt a good man, and thus knew her decision to be correct. He would move on and so would she, into a much brighter future.

Evelyn slid the final letter into its envelope and returned to the window. It was now quite light, with the haze of dawn. The buildings, though made of brick, still appeared grey and ghostly. There was movement in the street now. An old horse barrow made its way slowly along the street and a man in a smart suit walked briskly along the pavement. In the opposite direction, a couple in long coats walked past, arm in arm. There was sufficient light to make out the mottled damp on the flagstones of the pavement. London was coming alive. Despite the pain of writing her letters home, Evelyn felt a thrill at the thought of it.

❖

Breakfast in the Grainger household was an informal affair, eaten in the kitchen rather than the dining room. Grace had set out the breakfast things but she did not wait at the table. Her involvement stretched to nothing further than setting the kettle on the range to boil. She then left the room, ostensibly to clean the sitting room and set a fire in the hearth, but Evelyn was fairly sure she heard the servant make her way upstairs.

The kitchen, where she'd found James and Lilian when she ventured downstairs just before eight o'clock, was at the back of the house. A high-ceilinged room with white walls and a very large range at one end, it had tall windows to let in the daylight. The table was large and solid, a rectangle around which at least eight people could dine. There was no cloth, but lace-edged mats beneath each setting. It was a functional, comfortable room and Evelyn instantly felt at home there.

"I hope you don't mind, darling," Lilian said, after wishing Evelyn good morning. Lilian was once again in her colourful housecoat, her hair brushed but still a little dishevelled from sleep. "We don't like to be formal in the dining room—it feels so unnecessary for breakfast and it's so much extra work for Grace. Mater says we eat like servants, but I don't really see why there's a problem."

"Oh no, it's not a problem at all." Evelyn smiled, as James stood to pull out a chair from the table for her. He was already dressed in dark trousers and a crimson bow tie for work, though still in shirtsleeves. "Thank you." She settled herself in the chair. "Even this is awfully different to what I'm used to at home, you see. We always eat our breakfast around the kitchen table." Her mind flew to West Coombe, the family beginning a second day without her.

Lilian showed no sign of having noticed the shadow of sadness across Evelyn's face. "I realise we still haven't properly *talked*, Evie. I mean, about where you're from and what your life was like, and what you're going to do here in London." Lilian sounded full of curiosity. "And, as luck would have it, I don't have anywhere to go today at all. So, what say we cosy up in the sitting room with tea and biccies and have a good chinwag?"

Evelyn, who had been rather hoping to see a little of London, was at once flattered by Lilian's interest and disappointed. However, she could hardly deny Lilian, upon whose hospitality she was dependent. "Well, I don't exactly have other plans." She shrugged and looked at the breakfast on offer.

"Do help yourself to breakfast, you'll starve if you wait for Lilian to invite you." James gestured at the table. "We tend to keep it simple. There's porridge on the range and bread for toast, butter and marmalade. Oh, and the remnants of a jar of damson jam I brought from Cook when I last visited home. She makes the best jam, takes me back to my boyhood in an instant!" James grinned. Evelyn reflected how he seemed much more at ease and confident in his home, in this simple kitchen, than he had in the Yellow Orchid. She found this warmed her to him a little more.

"I'm happy with just bread and jam actually, thank you. If I might try the damson?"

"Of course. Here." James passed a small bowl of jam. She reached for a slice of bread from the board in the centre of the table. Lilian had just done the same herself, although she had opened the range and was holding the bread close to the flames on a toasting fork. Evelyn buttered her bread. "And another thing, Evelyn, don't let my dear sister bully you. If you want to go out and do some sightseeing today rather than satisfying her endless curiosity, then it's your choice. You don't have to do what we want, just because you're staying here."

"Oh, James, how dare you? I'm no bully! It's Evie's first day here. She needs time to settle before we start gallivanting, surely." Lilian looked at Evelyn with raised eyebrows.

"Well…I do want to see London, of course." Evelyn looked away from Lilian's expectant gaze. "But I want to get to know you too, and it's lovely that you're so interested in me."

"There, you see, James!" Lilian turned back to the table with her toast, triumphant.

"I see nothing, Lilian. The girl just said she'd like to see London."

"And spend time with me." Lilian buttered her toast with energy.

Evelyn looked from Lilian to James, unsure what to say. She was beginning to understand they would bicker about anything and it did not really matter how she responded. "I'm happy to go along with whatever plans either of you makes," she said in the end. "I do want to discuss the practicalities of my being here though. I have enough to pay you rent for the room."

"Nonsense! You're our guest, Evie." Lilian was dismissive.

James looked more thoughtful. "Lilian's right, of course," he said. "You are our guest and we don't need a contribution. I suppose it really depends on how long you'll be staying. We don't need anything from you, but if you plan to stay in London, you might want to think about lodgings of your own, or even renting part of this place."

Evelyn was grateful for James's pragmatism but bewildered when she attempted to see a way forward. All she knew was that she wanted to be in London; she wanted to see what this world would offer her. "I'm very grateful for your generosity in letting me stay. I honestly can't tell you my plans. Perhaps, Lilian, you can help me work them out today."

"Of course I can. By the time James is home from work, we'll have all kinds of things to tell him, I'm sure. And if you want to see London, we can always go out for a stroll, maybe catch a cab somewhere."

"That sounds excellent. I do have some letters to post too." It was important, whatever else there was to distract her, that the letters found their way home.

"Gosh, darling, you must've been up with the lark to write those."

"I think it was before the lark, actually." Evelyn smiled thinly. "I had a bad dream and couldn't sleep."

"Oh, you poor thing! You must tell me about it."

"You don't stop, do you, Lilian?" James shook his head. "I can take your letters with me and post them near my office, Evelyn. That way, you needn't worry."

"Thank you, that's very kind of you." Evelyn hoped she and Lilian would still be able to leave the house later. It would be rather frustrating to be in London and stay inside all day.

"No trouble at all. When you go out, you don't need to add a trip to the post office. Lilian, why don't you just go for a stroll across the park and show Evelyn the palace. That way, you don't need a cab and you can take tea at the Park Lane."

"What a smashing idea, James. That's what we'll do! You'll love the Park Lane, Evie—it's quite a new place and so very stylish."

Evelyn found she was not particularly interested in where they would take tea and far more interested in the sightseeing James proposed. "The palace?" she asked James.

"Yes. Buckingham Palace. It's only about ten minutes' walk through Green Park from here." James said.

"Oh, I've wanted to see it so much. A cousin of my mother's once sent a postcard from London with a photograph of the palace on it. I stared and stared at it and tried to make it come to life. I always knew I wanted to come to London one day, just to see the palace, if nothing else!" Evelyn said. She realised as she concluded that her disclosure had probably revealed something of her naiveté. Yet James and Lilian were both smiling and not apparently sitting in judgement.

"Then it looks like you're in for a wonderful day. I must go to work now, girls, so enjoy yourselves." James drained the last of his tea and left the kitchen. Evelyn sipped her own tea and helped herself to another slice of bread, even though she was suddenly so excited all hunger was gone.

Chapter Eight

In what was, apparently, an attempt to cement the intimacy of their growing friendship, Lilian suggested, after breakfast, that she and Evelyn could settle down and get to know each other better in Lilian's bedroom. Uncomfortable with the notion of sharing such a personal space with someone she barely knew, she was pleased to find that Lilian's bedroom, on the top floor of the house, was actually a very substantial part of the building. At one side was a large bed with a rumpled yellow bedspread and white pillows; along the wall opposite the doorway were several dark wardrobes, a chest of drawers, and a dressing table. Near the window and away from the bed, but under the sloping ceiling which revealed that the room was actually in the roof space of the house, was a small sitting area with two armchairs and a small coffee table.

When Evelyn followed Lilian into the room, she paused, surprised to find such a large room. She was also rather taken aback to find several shelves of books, for Lilian had not seemed remotely like a woman who would enjoy reading. Perhaps she had misjudged her. She began to think that a few hours getting to know Lilian might actually be quite an interesting experience.

"I think they intended this room as the nursery, you know," Lilian said. She picked up an indigo scarf from the seat of one of the armchairs and draped it over the chest of drawers. There were scarves and items of jewellery all over the room, so much so that every surface seemed to twinkle. Lilian did not seem to be untidy—she'd not left her dress on the floor or discarded her stockings over the coffee table—rather the sheer amount of decoration, jewellery, and ornament she owned was spilling out of every drawer and wardrobe and taking over the room. It added a mystical, oriental air to the room, Evelyn thought, only made more so by the presence of two large Venetian mirrors, both with modern geometric frames, which reflected the decorative chaos of Lilian's room and bounced the light from the window onto hidden jewels and strings of pearls.

"The nursery?" Evelyn refocused on what Lilian was saying.

"Yes, there's a small room next door which I'm fairly sure was for Nanny. Lord, when I think of our Nanny O'Neill, I wonder what she would think of me now. She was always so keen for me to grow up to be proper and act like a lady. I think I'd rather enjoy seeing her expression if she were to meet me now. What fun it is to be a glorious disappointment!"

Evelyn settled herself in one of the armchairs, from which she could see the rooftops outside the window. Lilian slouched in the other and looked thoughtfully at Evelyn. "You know, my parents don't approve of me in the slightest," she said. "They're happier with James, of course. But they don't really approve of anything modern. They only like James because he's such a dreadful stick-in-the-mud."

Evelyn listened to Lilian speak, unwilling to pass comment on Lilian's relationship with her parents or give an opinion of James. The potential for offence just seemed too great.

"They were fine until the war, of course. But then I was very young. And my wanting to help the war effort was patriotic, then. Funny how what a woman could do when we're at war is so different from what she is expected to do when the war ends, don't you think?"

"I suppose," said Evelyn. "I've read about the surplus women, of course. But I've never thought about it in quite that way."

"You've never really thought about your place as a woman?" Lilian looked incredulous.

"No." Evelyn felt compelled to adopt a defensive tone. "Why would I?" She thought of her flight from West Coombe and the weight of expectations and admitted to herself that in some small way she had thought about those things, even if she wasn't ready to say them out loud to Lilian.

"I don't know. Because you don't like being the property of a man? Because you don't like that even though women can vote now, it's only some women?"

"I've really never been interested in politics. It always seemed appropriate to me that, since it's men who make all the big decisions, it should be men who vote for them. I don't really know any women who are interested in politics." Evelyn surprised herself by being able to give a considered response, even if it made Lilian frown.

"That is far from the point, darling. The issue is that we should be equal. Women can be in parliament too, so all women should be able to cast their votes. Why shouldn't we be?"

"Well, when it was in the papers about the suffragettes, I remember my mother saying that they should be paying more attention to their homes and children, looking after their husbands better, and that if they did, they'd be happier."

Lilian was apparently stunned that any woman would express these thoughts. "But surely you don't think that too?"

"Well, no, not really. I don't think I'd go to prison for the right to vote though, like those women did."

"Fair enough. I saw some of the suffragette protests when I was very young. I even saw Emmeline Pankhurst once, as they dragged her away from the Buckingham Palace railings. We've always had family and friends in this part of London, you see. I thought it would be the finest thing ever to be a suffragette."

"But you never got the chance?" Evelyn's interest was drawn. Lilian clearly had more depth than had been revealed last night.

"Well, they stopped for war didn't they? Then, in '18, women were allowed to vote, so it all went quiet. I'm still involved in the campaign for women's rights though. I've helped them distribute pamphlets from time to time and listened to some speeches. If you want any books on the topic, I have several." Lilian gestured to the bookcase behind her.

"Thank you," Evelyn said. "I might like to read a little more about it."

"You really should. It's a battle that's far from over, you know."

"Of course." Evelyn really had little more to add on the subject. Instead she decided to move the conversation on. "You really do have a lot of books," she said.

"You're welcome to borrow any. I've gone through most of them. Have a look."

Evelyn rose from the low seat of the armchair and bent to examine the closest bookshelf to where they were sitting. There were a few copies of *Vogue* with garish cover plates showing the latest styles lying on the shelf. But next to them she found a group of novels and poetry collections, with many colours of binding, some with dustcovers and some with gold-embossed titles and author names. She read some of the titles: *The Rainbow*, *Sonnets to Orpheus*, *The Great Gatsby*. Evelyn had heard of none of them. A little further on she found *Mrs. Dalloway*, *The House of Mirth*, and a thick work called *Ulysses*. Not wanting to appear ignorant, she passed over these, seeking a title she recognised or something she could pass intelligent comment on. There were some books with French titles Evelyn could not read, and then she found a pamphlet, "The Morality of Birth Control," and *Ideal Marriage: Its Physiology and Technique*. At these, she frowned.

Lilian, watching her, noticed. "What's that you're looking at?" She leaned over Evelyn's shoulder to peer at the spines of the books. "Oh, I see! I'm not sure I can let you borrow *Ideal Marriage*, darling. It'd be awfully corrupt of me, you being innocent as you are."

Evelyn flushed. "I don't think I understand."

Lilian's smile turned into intrigue. "You don't understand?"

"What's the book about?" Evelyn wished Lilian would just answer her.

"Gosh, Evie, just how innocent are you? I thought everyone knew about that book. It's about sex, and how to do it well."

Evelyn stared at Lilian, unsure what to say. "Sex?" she finally said, weakly.

"Yes." Lilian's eyes narrowed. "You do know what sex is, don't you?"

Evelyn drew a deep breath. "I know what a man and woman do when they're married. I mean, as much as I can know, without being married myself."

"Without being married yourself? Don't you think it's good to know about how it all works before you get married? It's all very well understanding what goes in where, so to speak, but do you know how to enjoy it?"

Evelyn stared at Lilian, lost for words, wishing she'd never accepted the offer to look at Lilian's books. "I didn't know I was supposed to enjoy it," she ventured, in the end.

Her mind went back to the evening before her sister's wedding, the final night on which they'd shared a room together. Never especially close, Annie had still confided in Evelyn on occasions through the years. That night, Annie had been nervous about performing what she called her wifely duty. Evelyn had dearly wished she had more worldly experience with which to comfort and inform her sister. Their mother did not consider it a decent topic of conversation and there were really few other places to glean information. She'd felt dreadfully uninformed, and had done since. Now Lilian was looking at her incredulously, and Evelyn sensed she was on the verge of learning those secrets, whether she wanted to or not.

"Oh Lord! But there's so much to enjoy, darling." Lilian spoke with the tone of a woman who knew from experience.

Evelyn contemplated this. She did not want to reply in a way that sounded naive or judgemental, but Lilian was not married and Evelyn really did not understand. "You're not married, so how do you know?"

"Please don't tell me you're that wet behind the ears, darling? You know it's possible to do it even before you're married, don't you?"

"I thought only the worst kind of women did that." Evelyn repeated what her mother had always told her.

"Then perhaps I'm the worst kind of woman." Lilian did not look at all concerned. "But I'm not the only one, I can tell you. Why, nearly every woman I know must be on a one-way journey to hell."

Evelyn listened to Lilian and wondered just which man, or men, Lilian had done such things with. The waiter from the Yellow Orchid? Despite the disapproval she could not help, she was intrigued by what Lilian had said. The relations between a man and a woman could be something to enjoy. Something that did not depend on marriage. Apparently, it need not be as mysterious and frightening as it had always seemed. There was something of a relief in that, and it prompted her next question.

"I thought it was painful and just a wife's duty. Isn't it like that?"

"Oh no! Of course, I'm sure that's how some poor women experience it. But if you know what you're doing and so does your lover, well, then it's just another thing altogether. There's really nothing like it. Maybe I should lend you my book after all."

"I'm not sure I want to read it," Evelyn protested. Nevertheless, Lilian drew the book from the shelf and gave it to her. Evelyn took it dumbly.

"And I think you'll enjoy this one." Lilian handed *The Rainbow* to Evelyn.

"Thank you." Evelyn returned to her armchair, before any more of Lilian's books could create awkward conversations.

Lilian turned curious eyes on Evelyn again. "So there's really no one waiting for you at home? No one you're just dying to marry?"

Again, Evelyn thought of Michael. But he was not waiting for her and she certainly had no wish to marry him. She did not want to bring him into this new place, to give Lilian even more questions. "No, there's no one. I should really be married by now, of course."

"You're younger than me, and I'm not married."

"I'm different to you." She did not really need to explain why she was so different to Lilian.

"Why are you? You're a young woman, you're attractive, you're smart. What can I do that you can't do?"

Evelyn considered. "It's not about what I can or can't do. It's what I expect to happen in my life."

"Did you expect to be in London today?"

"No," Evelyn admitted.

"Then perhaps it's not really about what you expect to happen. Life's about what you want to happen, if you ask me."

Evelyn thought Lilian's approach was rather selfish and idealistic. But then Lilian seemed to have always been wealthy and popular, so it was not really a surprise that she did not approach life practically. And even Evelyn could admit the lure of going through life as Lilian did.

"I suppose I don't really know what I want to happen," she replied. "I don't even know how long I'll stay in London."

"Well, how long did you tell your family you'd be away?" Lilian asked.

Evelyn hesitated. The pause was long enough to raise another question from Lilian. "You did tell them you were coming away to London, didn't you, Evie?"

"Not exactly," Evelyn confessed. There was no point trying to live a lie while she was staying with Lilian. "I left letters for them. They'll know now."

"So you're a runaway." Lilian seemed delighted by the news. "How awfully cloak-and-dagger."

"Not really." She explained her early morning departure. "Hopefully they're not too worried."

"My parents wouldn't give a fig, but I expect yours are slightly different to that." Lilian reflected for a moment.

"I think they'll be very angry," Evelyn said thoughtfully. There weren't words to convey the level on which she suspected she had angered her parents.

"And they'll miss you?"

"I suppose so." She realised she'd barely considered the extent to which they cared about her. "I don't know. I never really felt like they liked me very much, if you know what I mean. They spent all of their money on Eddie, sent him to school when they made me leave when I was fourteen, that sort of thing. And then my younger sister, Annie, she was the one who led the life she was expected to. She's recently married and she'll be a perfect wife and mother. I could never settle, you see." It felt good to explain what she had always kept to herself, even if it was to someone like Lilian.

"And when Eddie offered you the chance to come to London, you took it, no matter the consequences." Lilian spoke softly, gently inquisitive now.

"Yes. I mean, I also wanted to make sure you got Frank's letter. That seemed ever so important too. But there were other ways of getting it to you without coming here on my own. I just wanted to see London so badly."

"And there's nothing at all wrong with that, Evie. I, for one, am very glad you did. And thank heavens it was my doorstep you landed on. It could have been anyone. Imagine if I was a stuffy old schoolteacher or something. Then you'd see a whole different side of London."

"Honestly, I didn't know what to expect. I knew London was big and exciting but I didn't really know much about life here. I still don't."

"Of course. And even a school ma'am could probably show you some thrilling museums and formal gardens. But if you really want to live, you came to the right place."

"I can see that." Evelyn smiled. "And I do want to thank you for taking me in. You needn't have done. And for being prepared to show me so much."

"Darling, so far you've only seen the Yellow Orchid. Now, it's a smashing place, no doubt, but there is more to London, even I can admit that."

"I'm looking forward to seeing much more. And to meeting more of your friends."

"I think we'll have to see about finding you some better clothes too." Lilian looked Evelyn up and down. Today she was in her smart grey skirt and cream blouse and this was seemingly unacceptable to Lilian, who frowned slightly. "I think I'll introduce you to my dressmaker. Though we could get something off the peg, of course."

"I don't have an awful lot of money," Evelyn said cautiously.

"Then we'll be careful. But you really can't keep dressing as if it's twenty years ago. It's so awfully liberating to wear what you want to."

Evelyn decided there was no point arguing that she was already wearing what she wanted to, and that she really had no desire to dress as elaborately as Lilian. She would fight that battle when it came to actually purchasing a dress. In an effort to change the subject, she decided to try to find out a little more about Lilian and her friends.

"It was nice to meet Dorothy last night," she said. "Are you old friends?"

"Reasonably, although we weren't at school together. I've known her since I came to London. It was Dorothy who told me about the Yellow Orchid. She's known Vernon for simply ages. She's almost like his sister."

Evelyn had not really paid much attention to the relationship between Vernon and Dorothy. However, the comment brought Vernon's real sister into her mind. "And have you known Jos long?"

"Not really. She's rather a standoffish sort. Of course, James is disapproving of her kind and that doesn't help us make friends." Lilian did not sound like she really wanted to make friends with Jos.

"But you're not disapproving?" Evelyn pressed. She was oddly fascinated by Jos and her friends.

Lilian looked awkward. "Not disapproving, exactly. I mean, I don't really think it's right, not the done thing so to speak. I mean, what can they really do with each other?" When Evelyn responded with a puzzled frown, Lilian looked mildly exasperated. "I mean sex, Evie. What can two women possibly do with each other?"

Evelyn flushed. "I'm sure I don't know. I can't begin to imagine…" Although, she found, as she said the words, she *could* begin to imagine. True, she was only contemplating what it would be to kiss a woman like Jos, in the way she and Michael had kissed, but the image was rather vivid.

"I will admit that Clara and Courtney have a good relationship. I don't really object to them. They've got each other and they're really quite eccentric, aren't they? Besides, Courtney's American, so it's not really any surprise. But still, one has to wonder if they wouldn't be happier if they found husbands. Or men to love them."

"It is rather extraordinary to think of two women courting each other," Evelyn said. "But somehow it doesn't shock me." It was just one in a list of extraordinary things that had happened in the last two days. "Does Jos live with Vernon?"

"No, but she spends a lot of time with him." Lilian seemed irritated by this. "She often calls in on the way home from her work at the theatre."

"She works in the theatre?" Jos seemed even more interesting now.

"Oh yes, did we not tell you that? She makes scenery. Doesn't just paint it, mind, she does all of the carpentry and things too. She might do more than too, I can't say I've paid that much attention. I think she's close by because she's working on a pantomime on Shaftesbury Avenue somewhere."

"She does the carpentry?" Evelyn remembered Jos's warm, rough fingers, the sensation of touching them as she looked into Jos's blue eyes.

"Oh yes. But then you can tell from looking at her that she's a tomboy—it's not really a surprise, is it?"

"No, I suppose not. Are there many women like her?" Evelyn realised how naive her question sounded as soon as she asked it.

"Well, that's a question, darling. Who can say? Obviously you met Clara and Courtney last night, they went to school with Dorothy. And I know a few others. One or two who bat for both teams too."

"Both teams?"

"They like men and women. For sex, at least."

Evelyn found herself, once more, lost for words. That anyone could like another person for the purposes of sex was entirely a revelation to her, let alone that a woman could like another female in this way.

"It's not just women either. There's plenty of men who like other men too. James is even more uptight about that one. Of course, the men tend to be relatively private about it because it's against the law for them."

"Is it? Why for them and not for women?" Evelyn could not work out why that would be the case.

"Oh yes. But that's because men can, well, do…something…a little more than women can. If you know what I mean." Evelyn did not know what Lilian meant but chose not to admit this and press the matter. "But they find ways of making themselves known to each other. Of course, the Yellow Orchid attracts all sorts of people. And one can't really complain. It's modern times, isn't it? What was it that Mr. Pound said about writing in modern times? *Make it new!* And really that's what's important isn't it?"

Evelyn reflected that if it was possible for women to love women and men to love men, it was likely not a new development or a modern affectation. Her one encounter with Clara and Courtney had showed her how genuine their love seemed to be. It certainly seemed far more sincere than much of what Lilian did and said in the name of being new and modern. She chose not to share these thoughts with Lilian. "How often do you go to the Yellow Orchid?" she asked instead.

"Oh, whenever we feel like it. At least twice a week in the evening and once during the day. I don't always sing, of course. Vernon hosts other singers and some top-notch bands. You'll keep coming with us, of course."

"Yes, I'd like that. It will be interesting to get to know Dorothy more. And Vernon too, of course."

At this, Lilian's face fell. Evelyn was intrigued. It seemed to be impossible to mention Vernon without Lilian reacting. Could it be that Vernon was the man she was involved with?

"Dorothy's one of my favourite people, of course," Lilian said. "But don't expect to get to know too much of Vernon. Oh yes, he's handsome and all, but he's a terrible man, really."

"I thought you were friends," Evelyn pressed, now even more curious.

"We are. But a woman would really have to be a perfect idiot to be tangled up with him. If you're looking for someone to discover the mysteries of sex with, I don't suggest you try Vernon." At Evelyn's astonished reaction, the tension dissolved from Lilian's face. "Not that you were, darling. I just know what he's like for latching onto any new face at the Orchid, especially the pretty ones. And you are pretty."

"Thank you." Evelyn smiled at the compliment, sure now that Lilian was somehow involved with Vernon. It seemed odd that for all of Lilian's openness she did not just admit it. Perhaps she was afraid of appearing foolish for falling for a man who was clearly neither faithful or particularly loving. Evelyn resolved to watch them more closely the next time she saw them together.

"In fact, by the time we get you a new dress and maybe a haircut, you'll have men flocking to your side." Lilian winked.

Evelyn was flattered but also aware that her desire to live her time in London well was rather different from Lilian's. It seemed remarkable that a woman who advocated rights for women as strongly as Lilian did seemed to think that the attention of men was a measure of success. "We'll see," was all she said in response.

"Oh, I know what I'm talking about, darling. I could show you how to have men eating out of the palm of your hand."

"I'm sure you could." Evelyn smiled and looked out of the window. Rows and rows of rooftops stretched across the view. So many houses, so many people, so many lives. She looked back to Lilian, reflecting that she could have done a lot worse than finding Lilian as her first friend in London. She would just have to be careful that Lilian didn't try to interfere too much in her decisions.

They were quiet for a moment. Evelyn was just beginning to wonder what Lilian was thinking when she broke the silence. "So, darling, shall we go our separate ways for an hour or so? Then dress and go to see the palace? And then I'll take you to tea at the Park Lane. It's a swanky place, you'll love it."

"I will do my best to dress appropriately," Evelyn said.

"Top hole, we'll be ready to leave at about two, how does that sound?"

"Perfect." Evelyn left Lilian in her bedroom. She took the books with her to her own room and set them on the bedside table. Her first thought was to go through her few clothes to work out what would best suit Lilian's swanky afternoon tea. When she'd done the best she could, she sat on the bed for a moment and contemplated the books. She had to admit she was intrigued at just what an ideal marriage was considered to be.

Chapter Nine

Side by side, Evelyn and Lilian walked along a wide, tree-lined path which led straight through the middle of Green Park. The winter trees had lost their leaves and the sky was a cold pale grey, but Evelyn still found the park beautiful. True, it was odd to see such a wide green space so surrounded by buildings, and every flower bed and row of trees was clearly there by human design rather than nature's hand, but she could understand why so many people sat on the benches either side of the path, appreciating the park.

It seemed that the park attracted all kinds of people. Some young men in the clothes of manual labourers were gathered around one bench, sharing a bottle of milk between them, joking loudly with each other. On the very next bench, a man in a bowler hat read *The Times*. A small boy in short trousers and a knitted jacket ran across their path, back towards where his uniformed nanny waited with a perambulator, attempting to soothe the crying infant within. Ahead of them, a young, smartly dressed couple strolled arm in arm and an elderly lady stopped to speak to a similarly aged acquaintance.

All of these people lived in London. The old and the young, the rich and the poor. And the majority did not know each other. On the other paths through the park, more people strolled, passing away a pleasant hour of leisure or using the park as a thoroughfare as part of a busy day. Strangers everywhere. In West Coombe that would have been impossible. Although she was not on conversational terms with everyone in town, she at least recognised them all. No one in West Coombe was truly a stranger. And the town had its old established rhythms, so you could usually guess what business a person was about at a particular time of day. In London, time seemed to be a different concept. There were no routines or rhythms and everyone was a stranger, caught up in his or her life. The anonymity appealed to Evelyn. Here she was, a young woman walking through a London park, feeling awfully self-conscious, and the only person who even noticed her was Lilian. It was oddly liberating not to be noticed, to know she wouldn't meet a family acquaintance around the next corner. Only now did Evelyn realise how much time she had spent hiding from observation and judgement. She liked her clifftop retreats precisely because she hardly ever saw anyone, let alone someone who would recognise her. In London, she did not have to retreat into isolation. She could be invisible and yet part of a crowd at the same time.

Of course, being invisible wasn't necessarily desirable. Perhaps, she contemplated, if a person was like Lilian and lived to be noticed and praised, it would be necessary to try to ensnare people's attention. No wonder Lilian spoke so loudly, was so gregarious, and dressed in such an extraordinary fashion. She wanted to stand out from the London crowds. Evelyn could hardly blame her, though it was further proof of how different they were.

Lilian had decided that Evelyn's skirt and blouse would do for tea at the Park Lane, but insisted on lending her a hat. It was a grey felt cloche and decorated with white and orange ostrich feathers, as well as a fancy silver and crystal ornament, where the feathers met the white ribbon which went around the crown. Evelyn wore Lilian's string of pearls again but had left her butterfly brooch on her dressing table, afraid of losing it again and made uncomfortable by her dream. Lilian also insisted in lending her a woollen wrap of grey wool, doing away with the need for her coat.

For her part, Lilian did not look quite so extraordinary as she had the previous evening. Her outfit was a single tone of midnight blue, skirt and coat matching the hat perfectly. A loose belt at her waist had a silver buckle which sparkled with crystals, and there was a similar ornament to the ribbon of her hat, but otherwise she was, for Lilian, dressed in quite a conservative manner. Evelyn noticed that the women of London wore a myriad of colours and styles. Some of the older women looked as though they had not fully escaped the last century, with floor-length skirts and corseted waists, many were stylish but dour, and others wore bright colours and short skirts more similar to Lilian.

It was these women to whom Evelyn's attention was most drawn, until a group of young women in what was clearly school uniform walked past, laughing together.

"Oh, how I miss my school days," Lilian exclaimed as they passed. "Don't you, darling?"

"Yes," Evelyn replied. "Although those girls are much older than I was when I left school."

"You mean you didn't stay on?" Lilian seemed to think this unusual.

"I left when I was fourteen. My parents needed my help and they could only really afford for Eddie to be at the High School."

"So you missed out on all the fun of being a senior then? Believe it or not, they made me prefect. Can't imagine it, can you?"

"No, I suppose not. I never really got to find out what that was like. Most girls from West Coombe didn't. Most of the boys left at fourteen too. If there was no need for us to carry on learning, we didn't."

"And, let me guess, it was common wisdom that girls only needed to be able to sew and cook and be good and obedient wives," Lilian scoffed.

"Yes. I did want to carry on learning, but I didn't really think to question it myself." Evelyn now wondered why she had just accepted this approach.

"And this is why women have still got such a long way to go, darling. You see. One day, it'll be realised that we're much more than just adornments, or wives, or slaves."

"I never really felt like a slave," Evelyn said, feeling compelled to defend her well-meaning parents, "or an adornment." In fact, the latter seemed a little hypocritical coming from the highly adorned Lilian.

"It's because so many women don't realise it that it still happens. Women who think it's all they can do to be the best wives and mothers they can be. And that's fine, but there's so much more. We're so much more. And some of us might not be wives or mothers."

"Of course." Evelyn nodded her agreement but was not quite sure what to say. Then her attention was distracted by the view through the bare branches of the winter trees ahead of them. "Is that it? Is that Buckingham Palace?"

Lilian smiled. "Yes, that's it."

At the edge of the park were tall, ornate metal gates between stone pillars. Through the bars of these gates could be seen the pale facade of one of the most famous buildings in London. Evelyn quickened her pace, full of excitement at finally setting eyes on a place she'd never thought she'd have a chance to see.

As they emerged from the park, they were on a broad road, the Mall, which swept up towards and went around a tall statue, situated a short distance from the black palace gates. The statue was surrounded by a pool of water and carved stones lions. Evelyn gazed in awe at what she knew to be the memorial to Queen Victoria. Although it had opened in 1911, Evelyn had read in the newspapers of its final completion only two or three years ago. She looked up to the gilded statue of Winged Victory at the very top, standing on a globe. It shone bright and proud, even in the winter light. Below that, the statues represented courage and constancy—she remembered that, although she could not quite remember the symbolism of every figure. The eagles certainly represented Empire, that she knew well enough, and she was fairly sure one of the marble carvings was the embodiment of justice.

Evelyn gazed at the gilded and pale marble figure, at the stony face of the Queen herself, and realised she was not feeling proud, or patriotic. When she looked at the modest war memorial in West Coombe churchyard, she felt a sort of horrified pride. The war had been so terrible, and Edward had been so damaged, and yet there was a certain nobility in the names of the young men who had died fighting for freedom. But this richly decorated statue did not take names and individuals into account. It raised a hymn of glory to the Empire, it suggested victory over the globe, and all in the name of justice and truth. Carved eternally in marble, it was the Britain of the last century, ruler of the waves, conqueror of the savage nations. And that Britain had carelessly sent her young men into battle on the myth of glory, as if they could conquer all over again. But the victory had been hollow in the end, merely a relief that it was over and no more would die. That patriotism, that misguided dream of greatness, was over. The statue, so recently finished, seemed like a memorial to more than Victoria. It was to a world that had been blown to pieces in the mud of France and Belgium. And yet, she thought, it was beautiful still in a ghastly and hyperbolic way.

Lilian was looking past the memorial statue to the palace itself, majestic behind its high, ornate gates. "I actually remember when they refaced this whole side. It looked quite different before. It was just before the war."

Evelyn tore her attention away from the memorial and looked properly at the palace. "It looks as though it's been here forever."

"Doesn't it? I suppose that's the idea. And look, seems like His Majesty is at home today." Lilian pointed to the flag flying from the pole in the centre of the roof. "That's the Royal Standard. They fly it when the King and Queen are in residence."

Evelyn watched the colourful flag flutter in the breeze, then looked down at the many windows in the pale, Portland-stone facade. The palace looked just as it had in the postcard she had gazed at years ago, only so much bigger than she'd imagined. And now she could almost see into the windows. She pictured the grand interior, wondered what King George and Queen Mary would be doing at this time of day. Did they look out of the window at the tourists clustering around their gates? How did that feel? To be the most important and famous people in this city full of people. Evelyn knew she would hate to be so conspicuous, for all the wealth and luxury that came with it. "It really is beautiful," she said to Lilian, who was clearly waiting for a reaction. "Very grand." In reality, the palace was almost too grand for Evelyn's taste. Although she was impressed, even captivated, part of her felt repulsed, excluded by the grandeur. It was a revelation to her, to realise that she was not awestruck by such a place. Lilian did not seem to be in awe either.

"Of course, I've seen plenty of the place, but I can see why visitors want to see it. It's so famous. You know, during the war, they moved all the important fixtures and fittings out, in case it was damaged. But nothing ever happened. Made the King lock his wine cellar too, to set a good example. Not that it made a difference!" Lilian laughed. "I know a few girls who came out in there, of course."

"Came out?" Evelyn asked.

"Yes, as debutantes. It's when a girl comes of age and is presented at court for the first time. You get to meet the King and curtsey and then there's a dance, with everyone in their best court dress. I used to be frightfully envious over it, of course. Now I think it's all rather silly, parading the marriageable aristocratic girls like that. Awfully stuffy too. Although I hear the King has had jazz at the palace, so times are changing."

Evelyn wondered now what it would be like to be one of those aristocratic girls. She was inclined, like Lilian, to think it was a rather silly notion. Still, she was aware of just how many different worlds there were, how many different ways life could be lived. The chance nature of where and when a person was born made such a difference to what they would experience. Only Evelyn had chosen to challenge that, by coming to London. She'd broken a pattern, done something thoroughly modern and independent. Of that she could be proud, even if she would never be a debutante.

They crossed the road to stand right up against the black painted gates. Evelyn peered through to see the red-coated guards in their black bearskin hats. Motionless, they looked like the toy soldiers Edward had played with as a child. It was odd that a soldier could still be a ceremonial, red-coated toy, when the reality was khaki and mud and death. There almost seemed a wilful ignorance of reality where soldiering was concerned, she thought. This was how storybook soldiers were still presented. The war was a dreadful nightmare, an abhorrence that would never be repeated. The witnesses to it were dead or damaged and the myth of red-coated glory could be restored. Very clearly, Evelyn saw what Dorothy had been trying to explain to her. This was a new world, a world their generation would make their own. They were not Victorians anymore, and they would break away from their love of Empire and glory and live as never before. This was the dream she had shared with Edward and now it seemed more than just a hope, but a duty.

"You look rather thoughtful, darling," Lilian said.

"I suppose I am. I can't say why, exactly. It's only, this place seems to be such a symbol of the past."

"Oh, it's the perfect symbol of the past." Lilian smiled. "Of course, when I see these gates I always think of the brave suffragettes chaining themselves to these very railings. But even that's a thing of the past now. It seems so ridiculously quaint, since the war, doesn't it?"

"It's something along those lines that I was thinking." Evelyn looked along the gates to the crowd of other sightseers who were peering through the railings. Was the fascination just that the palace was so famous? Or was it also the glimpse into the past, a yearning for days gone by, that drew them?

"Never ceases to amaze me how many people come to stand here," Lilian said, seeing where Evelyn was looking.

"I'm still surprised to see so many people anywhere," Evelyn said. "I think there's as many people here as there are in the whole of West Coombe. And certainly more interesting people."

"If you like to watch people, darling, you'll adore tea at the Park Lane. The rich, the famous, and the fashionable are the usual clientele. I adore the place."

"Are you the rich or the fashionable?" Evelyn asked.

"Aha, are you razzing me, darling?" Lilian grinned.

"Not really," Evelyn replied, hoping she'd understood correctly.

"Well, I might be fashionable, but I'm certainly not rich!"

Evelyn tried to hide her astonishment. "I suppose it's relative, really," she said.

"Oh, I don't mean to appear ungrateful for what I have. I know I'm not badly off at all. But compared to some of the folks who you'll see at tea? I have nothing."

"I can't imagine what it's like to have that sort of wealth," Evelyn admitted.

"I know plenty of them, of course. Turns out no one really feels wealthy, from what I hear. Perhaps we should all be more appreciative."

Lilian did not sound serious, while Evelyn found her flippant attitude to money rather distasteful. "We didn't feel wealthy at home either, of course. Especially not when we had to save for things like winter shoes."

Lilian was silent for a moment, clearly not missing the point of Evelyn's remark. "Of course, I give money to several charitable societies," she said in the end. "I do realise that there are people much worse off than me."

Evelyn nodded, not wishing to create any bad feeling with Lilian, who was, after all, her only real friend in London and her hostess. Lilian could not really be blamed for her background and upbringing, certainly no more than Evelyn could be blamed for her own. The gulf of difference was just rather apparent to Evelyn, as they stood at the palace gates. And yet she felt a thrill at the idea of tea in the Park Lane Hotel, surrounded by opulence and glamour, so she could not hold Lilian's lifestyle against her. There was a real allure to decadence and indulgence. She had first felt it at the Yellow Orchid and now she felt it again. Hypocritical though it made her, it was irresistible.

As though keen to change the subject, Lilian glanced at her enamelled wristwatch. "Well, what do you say we make our way back to the Park Lane now? If you like, we'll walk up Constitution Hill and you can see the Wellington Arch and Hyde Park Corner. It's only a little bit out of the way."

"That would be smashing, thank you." Evelyn was delighted at the idea of seeing more of the famous sights of London. She found it quite strange to imagine she was within walking distance of such places, even as she stood outside the gates of Buckingham Palace.

Lilian led the way as they walked to the right hand side of the Palace facade and along a wide avenue, lined with bare-branched trees. Several motor cars were travelling up the road. Evelyn had seen enough of them now not to find them remarkable, but to see so much traffic was still surprising. A double-decked motorbus advertising *Schweppes Orange Squash* on a large banner rumbled past.

"There's so much traffic these days," Lilian said, as the bus passed. "It didn't used to be like this. And I don't suppose you're used to it."

"Not at all," Evelyn replied. "I mean, it's not like I've never seen motor cars, or even charabancs—we got plenty of tourists in West Coombe with them. But nothing like as many as there are here."

"We'll have to take you on the Tube as well, of course. Filthy, stinking place that it is. But one simply must experience it, or you've not seen London."

"I hadn't even thought of that," Evelyn said, experiencing a new flush of anticipation. "I'll look forward to it."

"It's only a train in a tunnel."

"Still, it's not like we have a Tube in West Coombe."

"No, of course. Well, that's the Wellington Arch up ahead."

The memorial arch to the victor of Waterloo was as grand as Evelyn expected. A short distance across the grass, the colonnaded entrance to Hyde Park was just as elegant. Such architecture was at home in London, almost dwarfed by the buildings around it. In West Coombe it would have looked quite ridiculous, overly ostentatious. Evelyn wondered why she even made the comparison. West Coombe might as well be in a whole other world to London. London made her heart beat faster, it provoked her thoughts, it confounded and enthralled her. West Coombe had never done any of those things. With every new experience here, she knew her decision to be correct. She only wished she could tell Edward all about it. Perhaps the vivid details and colour would bring her brother back to her.

❖

The walk to the Park Lane was a short one, along a broad road. Hyde Park was to their right, to their left the graceful buildings of Mayfair. After only a few minutes, Lilian caught Evelyn's arm and they stopped in the street outside a tall, white-fronted building with grey granite columns either side of the revolving door entrance.

"Here we are, darling. Isn't it simply ritzy?"

"It's certainly very grand." Evelyn was not sure if she was excited or intimidated by the sheer scale of the building. It seemed a rather grandiose place to simply seek afternoon tea.

"Isn't it just?" Lilian smiled happily. Evelyn suspected that it was impossible for a place to be too ostentatious for Lilian's tastes. "And so very modern too."

"Of course." That was important to Lilian. Evelyn had not yet established in her own mind if that was a good thing.

"Come on then, let's stop dilly-dallying. You never know who we might find we're seated next to!" Lilian led the way through the revolving door.

The interior, to Evelyn's dismay, was just as grand as she had feared it would be. Of course, it was beautiful, there was no way to deny that. As they were led into the lounge area, there were high glass ceilings, as ornate as anything Evelyn had seen in a church. The black-and-white marble checkerboard floor was reflected in the same pattern spreading across the ceiling. The pale yellow walls were decorated with paintings of trees and birds. Fashionable patrons, most of them women, were seated at tables, sipping tea from china cups, large stands of sandwiches and cakes on the tables in front of them. There was a hum of chatter, the occasional peal of laughter. Waiters in cream jackets and black trousers circulated between the tables, carrying silver trays bearing more tea and delicate sandwiches. Somehow, the everyday business of food and drink seemed at odds with the surroundings. This place should be a museum or gallery, perhaps a room in the palace. To simply sit and take tea here felt uncomfortable.

As they were seated, Evelyn realised that this was the most out of place she'd felt since she'd been in London. Although the surroundings, the clientele, of the Park Lane Hotel teased her curiosity, her thirst for learning more of London, she had to admit she felt out of her depth. And she knew she had no desire to be comfortable here. She did not have to love everything that Lilian did. She did not have to be enthralled by all of London. And such a grandiose, formal place as this was not to her taste, beautiful though it was.

Lilian was looking around surreptitiously, clearly wondering if anyone of fame or fortune was present. Evelyn did not quite understand the fascination and was relieved when the waiter came to take their order. Again, she was struck by the notion of being on the wrong side of the transaction. Just as she could have found herself in the place of Grace, Lilian's servant, the waiter could, in different times, have been Edward or Peter. She could have been a domestic in the hotel, cleaning up after people like Lilian. The idea made her uncomfortable. She allowed Lilian to place their order, glad that she had not been asked for an opinion, hoping their tea would be brought to them quickly.

As she sat upright and uncomfortable, watching Lilian return to glancing around her furtively, in the hope of recognising a face, Evelyn thought back to the previous night. The Yellow Orchid was the height of modernity too, it seemed, and yet she was more comfortable there. In Vernon's little cafe, with the taste of gin in her mouth and jazz in her ears, she had felt at home. She had felt as though she was really living.

And of course, she'd also met some fascinating people there. Dorothy and Vernon, who seemed two sides of the same sardonic, modern, cynical coin, decadent through intention and loving every minute. Clara and Courtney, both beautiful and like no one Evelyn could have even have imagined to exist. Two women in love with each other. The idea intrigued her and she could not help her thoughts lingering on it. What would it be like to be in love with a woman? To kiss a woman? She tried to put herself in Courtney's place, to imagine Clara courting her, embracing her, kissing her. But of course, Clara was very much Courtney's, that was obvious to the world. But there was Jos Singleton too. Jos who had been so kind, so friendly. Jos with those blue eyes and warm fingers. What would it be like to be kissed by her pink lips? To look into those eyes and see love, shared secrets?

"Are you all right, Evie?" Lilian's voice startled Evelyn out of her pleasant reverie.

"Yes, why?" Evelyn asked, feeling defensive.

"No reason. Only you look a little flushed."

"I expect it's the excitement of being in a place like this. And of course, I'm a little tired."

"Yes. I'm sure a cup of tea will revive you. Plus, I'm fairly sure that the Sitwells are here, at the table right over by the wall. Isn't that exciting?"

"I'm not sure I know who they are." Evelyn only half listened to Lilian's enthusiastic explanation of who the Sitwell family were and why it was exciting to see them. Her thoughts had returned to Jos Singleton. To the way thinking about Jos made her feel, quite unexpectedly. Her head was light, her heart beating a little faster, and she was suddenly warm in a way that made her skin prickle. A queer sort of excitement rippled through her body. She had never thought of another person and felt this way. If this was how it felt to be attracted to someone, Evelyn suspected she was attracted to Jos. She should be alarmed by this, she realised. And yet it did not seem at all alarming. It seemed rather exciting and modern.

CHAPTER TEN

In her desire to return to the Yellow Orchid, Evelyn was frustrated for several days. She did not want to ask outright that they return, since she suspected Lilian would question her reasons. Explaining that she was fascinated to see Jos Singleton again was not something Evelyn expected to be well received by Lilian, who had not seemed particularly favourable towards Jos previously. So she remained silent on the subject and hoped to be taken to the cafe soon.

In those days, Lilian took Evelyn to see some of the sights of London. They visited the Victoria and Albert Museum and the Natural History Museum. On another occasion Evelyn was delighted to see Nelson on his column above Trafalgar Square and to walk the short distance to see the Houses of Parliament and Westminster Abbey. Lilian could not be prevailed on to enter the Abbey to view the illustrious tombs inside, but Evelyn was still excited to finally gaze at buildings she'd previously only read about or seen photographs of. Around every corner was a famous address or statue, a museum she'd never believed she would have a chance to explore. As the days passed, she still found it difficult to believe the reality of it. She was in London.

Her only source of growing consternation was the lack of news from home. Worlds apart from West Coombe though she was, part of her mind was always there, wondering what her family were doing. Edward was uppermost in her thoughts, but she could not help but think of her parents too, and of Michael and Annie. Were they thinking of her? Or was she so in disgrace, so beyond the pale, that she was not worth a thought? The notion made her feel cold. However much she craved this new life in London, it was painful to be disconnected from everything she had known, perhaps even rejected from that world now.

Of course, Edward would not be able to write to her. But she had expected that at least one of her letters would receive a reply, even if only an expression of anger and disappointment. Perhaps Michael expressing his heartbreak, her mother hoping she was safe but letting her know how angry her father was. At the very least she expected something from Annie. The total silence from home was all too easy to interpret as a lack of care or concern, and this gave her sadness a touch of resentment. Perhaps they barely noticed she was missing, or were even glad that she was gone.

In her quiet moments, Evelyn found these feelings were beginning to intrude more and more. In an effort to occupy her mind, she began to read the books Lilian had lent to her. To begin with, she picked *The Rainbow*, which, as a work of fiction, appealed to her the most. She was also fairly sure she'd heard of it, or at least of its author, Mr. Lawrence, at some point. Though the cover illustration suggested a light romance, she found the novel rather difficult to read. What seemed to be an account of several generations of the same family, their lives and loves, in the Nottinghamshire countryside, became far more intense and philosophical than the story warranted, and she grew rather frustrated. Perhaps she wasn't intelligent enough, or modern enough, to read such a book. She had only made it through about a quarter of the novel when she laid it aside and looked to the other volume Lilian had given her.

She took up the slim volume of *Ideal Marriage*. Just contemplating the subject matter made her nervous. Her mother would have surely told her she was evil for even considering opening the pages. And yet, frightened though she found herself over what she would learn, she was intrigued too, determined to banish the stupid innocence that so set her apart from women like Lilian. So she took a deep breath and began to read.

Once she began to read, she did not stop until the fading light in her room brought her attention back to the passage of time. The text, expressed as creatively as a work of fiction, showed her an aspect to the world she had barely considered. She read every word, learned every lesson. The text told her the anatomy of the sex act, the physiology of the body's response to arousal. The illustrated plates, rather artificially coloured in shades of orange, brown, and grey, revealed to her the secrets of her own body, showed her what a man's body looked like. What surprised her was that nothing she read was frightening. The author described a process by which married couples grew closer, by which they found mutual pleasure in each other. How could it be wrong to understand such a primal function of her own body? She was angry at her mother, at the other women who could have educated her, for not sharing their understanding with her. Or perhaps they did not truly understand either. *Ideal Marriage* suggested there were many, many marriages which were far from this ideal and could, in fact, be torturous for both parties. Was that what Annie experienced? Her own parents? If she had married Michael?

Relief flooded through her veins as she contemplated this. Chained to Michael, she might never have known that there was a realm of pleasure entirely hidden from her. Might have made him equally unhappy.

As she dwelt on the idea, she found she began to understand Lilian's point of view. If there was such pleasure to be attained, why did the ceremony of marriage actually matter? Of course, it was a sin to do something so indecent. And there was the fundamental fact that the act of sex was intended to produce a child for happily married parents. But Evelyn was not sure she would ever be married. And if that was the case, would she never experience the pleasure the book told her about? Or was it worth a risk? Lilian seemed to think so, Dorothy too. Neither seemed like bad women, or to be suffering any adverse consequences. The world was moving on, perhaps.

The author then implied that anything other than intercourse between opposite sexes was abnormal. Unavoidably, Evelyn's mind was drawn to Clara and Courtney, to Jos. Lilian and James certainly spoke of them and their desire for those of their own sex as abnormal. And yet, to converse with them, to watch them, they did not seem at all strange or wrong. Their desires seemed just as normal as any a woman might feel for a man. And now she understood the sex act, she found herself wondering about those women who loved each other. Surely they found ways of experiencing these mutual pleasures too? The book made it clear that sex was not purely about intercourse. If men and woman could tease each other's bodies for the purposes of fulfilling desire and arousal, women could certainly do the same for each other.

A woman's fingers could find the same places a man's could, her lips would be just as tender.

The image of Jos Singleton came back into her mind, uncalled for. And Evelyn felt a hot, forbidden curiosity that might just be, she thought, real desire.

❖

In the same afternoon as she finished reading *Ideal Marriage*, and with it taking up rather a lot of her consciousness, Evelyn realised for the first time that she needed to worry about James Grainger.

James was not a large part of her days in London. After a shared breakfast, he was away at his architectural practice until early evening. She admired how hard James worked. Lilian's idleness demonstrated that the family were wealthy enough not to require a salary to maintain them, yet James seemed to enjoy the process of earning his living. He certainly enjoyed architecture with a passion. Several of their dinner conversations were about architects he admired. He considered himself a modernist and very much disliked the heavy, backward-looking Gothic revival of the end of the last century. Evelyn thought James the least modern of her new acquaintances, so she was quite surprised to learn this. He relished straight lines, geometrical shapes and decoration, and was excited by the stylistic influences of Ancient Egypt, used in a modern way. His firm was currently involved in building a new factory for a large tobacco company, who wanted a building to increase their prestige and demonstrate just what an up-to-date firm they were. James was clearly proud of his work.

These conversations warmed Evelyn towards James. Although he remained rather awkward, it was a revelation to begin to understand the artistic streak that informed his technical work. James was every bit as engaged with the giddy, fast-paced London world as Lilian, only he looked on socialising and personal fashion as frivolities, preferring the permanence of bricks and stone and glass. As she saw more of his character, Evelyn found him easier to converse with and began to be glad when he returned home in the evenings, saving her from Lilian's talk of dresses and jazz and ceaseless gossip about people she'd never met.

On the evening that Evelyn finished reading *Ideal Marriage*, Lilian had gone out to visit an acquaintance who had the sheet music for a new song she wanted to sing at the Yellow Orchid. Evelyn was alone in the house when James arrived home. By the time he arrived, she had made her way to the sitting room, where Grace had brought her a pot of tea. She was glancing over Lilian's latest edition of *Vogue*, admiring some of the colour plates, when she heard the front door open. A glance at the clock told her it was James, though he was a little earlier than most days. She listened as he removed his coat and hat in the hallway. Then the door opened and she turned to smile at him.

"Good evening," she said.

"Good evening, Evelyn." James came fully into the room. Evelyn could smell the smoke of a winter evening in London clinging to his clothes and hair, felt a chill of outside follow him into the room. "No Lilian?"

"She went to visit someone, somewhere." Evelyn smiled wryly. "I have to admit I can't keep up with everyone she visits. I was invited but I stayed home to read instead."

"You have had a busy few days. With all the sightseeing."

"Yes, I've loved it though. I just wanted an easier day today."

"Naturally. Lilian's rather madcap I'm afraid—she's always been that way. I think in some ways, you and I"—he looked at her hesitantly—"are more similar to each other than you are to her."

Evelyn's guard went up in a way it would not have done without that awkward pause in James's statement. "Well, I think we both like a quieter life than Lilian," she said cautiously.

"Yes."

Evelyn wondered if there was going to be anything more. His face was pink, but she reasoned that he'd just been in the cold evening air.

"It is a shame that I am at work so often. I should like to show you the sights of London myself. I thought perhaps I could take some leave." He ended with a hopeful smile, making only brief eye contact before he looked away at something on the carpet.

Evelyn felt a knot of nerves in the pit of her stomach. She was all too aware of the implications of James's words, innocent though they seemed. He was not the sort of man to suggest sightseeing for the sake of it. He wanted to spend more time with her. And she was dependent on James's hospitality for her accommodation in London.

"That would be nice." She was not lying, she told herself. She liked James. Only now she cursed herself for letting on that she was interested in his work, for softening her manner with him. Clearly she had hinted at something she had not meant. "I wouldn't expect you to spend time with me instead of being at work though. Your work is important."

"Yes, it is. But we have a lull coming up, while they lay the foundations of the factory. Won't be much for me to do for a week or so."

"Oh, well, then surely you need a rest, some time to relax. I couldn't take that away from you." Evelyn was increasingly concerned. She couldn't reject James before he had even suggested more than a simple day's sightseeing. And yet somehow she felt she needed to turn him away from this path now, before he progressed any further along it.

"I would find it relaxing to spend time with you, Evelyn. I enjoy your company. I don't feel as though we've been able to get to know each other yet."

"That's true," she admitted reluctantly, struggling for anything to add.

"And I would like to get to know you further." This time he maintained the eye contact with her and Evelyn did not like what she saw. He seemed to be making an assumption at the same time as fearing rejection. Evelyn looked away, finding her gaze settling on the brown pinstripe pattern of his suit jacket. Her mind was racing for an appropriate response, struggling to avoid a feeling of repulsion. It was not that James himself was repulsive but the idea of any kind of intimacy with him was so uncomfortable it was almost repulsive.

"I would like that," she found herself saying, before she could help it. What else could she say? James had power over her, she was living in his house. Anger, at herself, burned inside her. Why was it so difficult to say no? She'd been unable to reject Michael face to face, and now James too. Why did they assume she would be interested and why could she not disabuse them of the notion as soon as it arose?

"Excellent." James was clearly pleased, probably misinterpreting her discomfort as coyness. "Shall we say one day next week then? Perhaps we can visit the British Museum and take lunch close by."

"Yes." Evelyn still avoided looking directly at James. She was relieved when she heard the front door open and the distinctive sound of Lilian's heeled shoes on the tiled hallway floor. Moments later, Lilian, still in her outdoor hat and coat, breezed into the sitting room.

"Oh, smashing, you're both here! I've got a new song to sing which is just the cat's pyjamas, I can't wait for you to both hear it. I want to go and see Vernon tomorrow and run the idea past him. Do you fancy coffee at the Yellow Orchid tomorrow afternoon, Evie? I'll ask Dorothy along too. Plus, we can find out what the New Year's plans are. It's always a top-hole evening at the Orchid."

"That would be lovely," Evelyn said with enthuasiasm. Suddenly the idea of visiting the Yellow Orchid was more appealing because she knew James disliked the place. "I've been wanting to go back there."

"Excellent! Now, is it dinner time? I'm famished." Lilian left the room to remove her coat and hat. Evelyn glanced briefly at James and then hurried after her, before he could speak again. Over dinner, she found her appetite much reduced, as a new tension clenched her insides. As if she did not have enough to make her anxious, with the beginnings of a new life in London, now she had to worry about James too.

Chapter Eleven

Lilian and Evelyn arrived at the Yellow Orchid just after half-past two in the afternoon. Considering Lilian had told Dorothy they would meet her at two, it was no wonder, Evelyn thought, that Dorothy looked a little less than friendly. However, that seemed to be Dorothy's default expression, so she tried not to be intimidated. She'd liked Dorothy when they'd first met, so there was no reason to be timid of her now.

The Yellow Orchid looked a little different by day, although the windows at the front were not large, so it was still largely illuminated by the electric lights around the walls. The yellow light was tempered by what daylight did creep in, making the room seem brighter but also a little colder. The clientele were less colourful and less exuberant, and there were far more empty tables. Lilian did not receive greetings from the daytime coffee drinkers, although she still walked across to Dorothy as though she were the queen of the establishment.

Dorothy did not bother to rise to her feet to welcome them. Instead she looked cooly up at Lilian. "Afternoon, Lilian. When will I learn to add at least a decent half hour onto any plans we make? Or simply to forget time entirely, since you seem to exist in your own world, free of such cares? Afternoon, Evie. Waiting for her to dress, were you?"

Evelyn could not help but smile. "Good afternoon. Something like that." Dorothy was exactly right. Lilian had been dressed and ready in one lilac dress before she'd decided it was making her skin appear sallow and disappeared to return in a navy and cream striped suit. Her skin had looked much the same to Evelyn, but Lilian had been much happier. For her part, Evelyn had borrowed one of Lilian's jackets to complement her grey skirt and added a dark jade velvet scarf which Lilian had given her, saying she never wore it herself so Evelyn might as well keep it. She was used to Lilian's disapproval of her appearance by now and was beginning to accept that one did not have to dress exactly as Lilian did to get by in the capital.

Lilian and Evelyn sat in the seats opposite Dorothy, who was smoking but did not seem to have ordered a drink yet. A waiter was with them in moments—not Clive, who had served them previously, but a rather younger man with pale blond hair, who seemed quite nervous of their party.

"Coffee, please, black," Dorothy said.

"Coffee for me too, but could you bring cream please. Evie?"

Evelyn had only previously consumed coffee on one or two occasions and had no preferred way of taking it. "Coffee with cream for me too, please." If it was what Lilian drank, she reasoned, it could not be too unpleasant.

As the waiter went away to fetch their coffee, Evelyn was aware of Dorothy looking at her from across the table. "So, my dear, it looks like London suits you. How are you finding it?"

"Oh, it's wonderful," Evelyn replied enthusiastically. "I've seen an awful lot of sights and Liliian's been very kind."

"I try my best, darling." Lilian smiled.

"It's quite out of character, I assure you," Dorothy retorted. "You're honoured."

"Well, I appreciate it very much." Evelyn glanced around her, wondering if Jos was in the cafe today. She had been telling herself it would be a good test of her true feelings, to see Jos and assess her reaction.

"Dorothy, you forget I'm such a top-hole educator. I've been teaching Evie the ways of the world! Which reminds me actually, did you read the book I lent you, Evie?"

"Which one?" Evelyn asked, trying not to blush.

"Yes, just what have you been inflicting on the poor girl?" Dorothy looked to Evelyn expectantly.

"Lilian was kind enough to lend me *The Rainbow* and *Ideal Marriage*."

"Well, that's quite a pair, my dear!" Dorothy raised her eyebrows. "Of course, I'm dying to ask what you thought of the last of that list."

Evelyn felt her face turning bright red. "It was quite... enlightening..."

"Well, just don't think it tells you everything there is to know," Dorothy said with a knowing smile. "That book is all well and good but it's awfully concerned with the holy act of marital coitus and not at all concerned with all of the other ways one can enjoy oneself."

Evelyn recalled the reference the book had made to "abnormal" acts and wondered what on earth Dorothy was referrring to. A very public cafe did not seem like the place to ask.

"Of course, the only way to find out is to try it for yourself." She winked at Evelyn, who sought a response and found none.

"Oh, Dorothy, you say I'm a corrupting influence, but you're far worse and you know it." Lilian looked indignant.

"And maybe both of us should just let Evie find the way herself." Dorothy was smiling at Evelyn again. "I'm certain she can find it."

"Thank you," Evelyn replied, hoping the conversation would now move on.

"I suppose the question is, have you set eyes on anyone who makes your heart beat faster yet, Evie?" Dorothy asked in a light-hearted manner. Evelyn was not sure if she was asking seriously or just to tease.

"Of course she hasn't," Lilian answered before Evelyn could draw breath. "Don't be absurd, Dorothy, she's barely met anyone yet." But Dorothy was not looking at Lilian; she was still maintaining eye contact with Evelyn. Evelyn was convinced Dorothy gleaned something of the truth in that moment, and found herself rather glad. She did not like it being a secret and she did not appreciate Lilian's assumptions about her. "And here's our coffee."

The waiter approached the table and set down a tray bearing a large coffee pot and three small cups and saucers, plus a jug of cream and a bowl of sugar crystals. The matching items of china were decorated with black triangles on a dark green background, the handles gilded. The rich aroma of the fresh coffee was enticing, and Evelyn breathed it deeply.

Lilian reached for the coffee pot and poured coffee into all three cups. Dorothy took hers and added a lump of sugar, while Lilian poured cream into the two remainining cups and offered one to Evelyn. She thanked Lilian and took a tentative sip. The coffee was hot and strong, but the cream softed both the taste and the heat. The bitterness was at first jarring but demanded a second taste. Evelyn swallowed it gratefully, enjoying the warmth.

"Oh, look, there's Vernon," Lilian suddenly exclaimed, setting her cup down clumsily. "I simply must tell him about my new song." She stood up and waved a hand until Vernon noticed her. When he finally did so, Vernon made for their table, coming to stand between Evelyn and Dorothy.

"Ladies, what a pleasure. And Lilian too." Vernon made a small, ironic bow. Today he was wearing a suit which was entirely mustard yellow, his cravat dark blue. Extraordinary though he looked, Evelyn could not help but smile. Her eyes were drawn to his face, where she saw the resemblance to Jos. Evelyn thought of Jos again, remembered the way her fingers had felt against her skin, and felt the heat rising inside her again.

"Vernon, you really are too much." Lilian pretended to pout but instead seemed quite pleased to be singled out.

"It's far better than being not quite enough, don't you think?" He flashed a brief smile. "How are you all? Dorothy?"

"I'm quite well, thank you, Vernon. Although I'm not sure your coffee is helping matters."

"Never satisfied, Dorothy, dear. That's why I love you so. It's a challenge to satisfy a woman like you."

"Not one you'll have the pleasure of taking on either." Dorothy's eyes twinkled.

Unlike Lilian, who seemed flattered and captivated by Vernon, Dorothy seemed to view herself as very much on a par with him and able to hold her own in any conversation. Evelyn much preferred her approach and envied the easy confidence, especially as Vernon turned his attention to her. Those blue eyes, so much like Jos's, sent a small thrill through her.

"And Evie? How is London treating you?"

"Very well, thank you." There really wasn't an appropriately witty response to such a simple question.

"You've not yet fallen under any terribly corrupting influences, then? Or felt the urge to flee back to your rural idyll?"

"Certainly not. I'm not so easily corruptible," Evelyn retorted.

"You'd be surprised who is easily corruptible," Vernon said darkly, "providing you're in the sway of the right person." As though he read something in her expression that connected him directly to her emotions, Vernon ran a finger over the back of Evelyn's neck, unseen to Lilian, though attracting Dorothy's keen-eyed gaze. Evelyn caught her breath; to be touched in so overtly sensual a manner sent an involuntary shiver of pleasure through her body.

Dorothy frowned her disapproval. "I don't think you'll find it's your job to corrupt every woman in London," she said, pointedly.

Vernon removed his hand from Evelyn's shoulder but appeared unabashed. "You're only envious, Dorothy, since I gave up upon realising you're an unassailable fortress. These days."

"What a flattering description."

Although she was listening to them, Evelyn was still silent, dumbstruck by the way Vernon's touch had made her feel. She had no interest in Vernon, yet to be caressed by him, to receive any kind of sensual attention in her current state of mind, was horribly compelling. She began to understand why, in this world, no one waited until they were married to experience such things. If you didn't have to love the person for the rest of your life, why not enjoy the sensual pleasure with them in the moment?

"Flattery is all part of my plan." Vernon turned his attention to Lilian. "You're quiet, my dear."

"Only waiting for you to notice me." There was an edge of the sullen child in her tone.

"How could I forget you? You wound me with the very notion."

"Well, now that you have noticed me, I can tell you about the new song I have for you. It's just fabulous."

"It sounds delightful. What say you come upstairs for a moment and we play it through on the piano. That's if Dorothy and Evie can excuse us, of course."

"Of course," Dorothy replied. Evelyn was not certain she liked the idea of being left alone with Dorothy, but she did not seem to have a choice. Lilian drained the last of her coffee and sprang to her feet, taking the bag containing the new sheet music.

"In that case, ladies, I might see you later. If not, it will be my loss." Vernon kissed his fingers and blew the kiss towards Dorothy, then repeated the action towards Evelyn. Evelyn copied Dorothy's response, which was not to respond, regarding him cooly. Vernon smiled and headed towards the back of the room. Lilian followed after him without a word.

Dorothy sighed. "Well, that's those two gone for an hour or so. Just watch out for the chandeliers rattling, if you know what I mean." She sipped her coffee.

Evelyn looked up at the ceiling, realising there were no chandeliers and entirely unsure what Dorothy was saying. "So Vernon has a piano upstairs as well as down here?"

"Oh yes, and he plays very well. But it's not all he plays very well, if you follow."

Evelyn thought she did but did not want to assume. "Vernon's very charming, isn't he."

Dorothy's expression hardened. "Oh yes, he is, Evie." She paused, appearing to consider her next words. "Too charming. Look, Evie, I don't really know you at all. But you're in London, you're looking for new experiences. It's only natural that Vernon would appeal. He simply doesn't have the moral compass not to flirt with every woman he meets. And he's an attractive man. But don't choose him."

"Don't choose him for what?" Evelyn was startled by this turn in the conversation and yet appreciated Dorothy's honesty.

"To be your first new experience. To see if you can experience that ideal marriage but without the marriage part. There are all kinds of reasons not to choose Vernon but the most important is that, ultimately, he doesn't care. I'm not saying that he's a bad man, I consider him a good friend. But he's really the depths of our generation's degeneration. He just doesn't care because he doesn't think caring is important. He believes in experience and pleasure and being the most incorrigible, but he will move on without a thought too. And you don't want that."

"How do you know?" Evelyn did not like the idea that Dorothy thought she knew what Evelyn wanted.

"Because I know, Evie. You're not from this world. Until this week I doubt you realised there were people in the world like Vernon. Like any of us, for that matter. And you can be part of this world, but don't let yourself drown in the cynicism of it. Don't think you can't do better than Vernon." There was a rare passion in Dorothy's tone.

"I appreciate you trying to help me," Evelyn replied. "But I am capable of managing my own life."

"I'm not patronising you, Evie. I'm only giving you the benefit of my wisdom. And I've seen the way you look at Vernon, and the way he looks at you."

"What do you mean, the way he looks at me?" Evelyn found this revelation fascinating.

"He looks at you as though you're the next tasty morsel in an endless banquet."

"Does he really?" Evelyn tried not to be pleased.

"Yes. But you don't want to be consumed, do you?"

"Of course not." Evelyn made an attempt to sound disapproving.

"If you're not sure, Evie, think about where Lilian is, right at this moment. What exactly do you think she and Vernon are doing?"

Realisation dawned on Evelyn. "Oh. You mean, Lilian and Vernon are—"

"Lilian and Vernon are not really anything, but at this moment they'll be enacting something you read about in that book, or something similar." Dorothy softened her words with a small smile. "You need to wake up to this world, Evie. Do you want to end up like Lilian? She's head over heels for him, though she tells herself she's not. And he does not care one little bit."

Evelyn pondered this and wondered why she'd not realised the way Lilian felt about Vernon previously. Then she felt unaccountably compelled to confide further in Dorothy. "I've been so innocent and naive, Dorothy. I want it gone, all traces of who I used to be. I want to be part of your world. I feel like I'm behind a window, separate from you all because of the things I haven't experienced. I don't want to be the innocent laughing stock or someone you need to look after and protect. I do have those feelings."

Dorothy's eyes registered understanding and sympathy. "Of course you do, darling. And you'll be very welcome in our world, as you call it. But Vernon isn't the gatekeeper, much though he'd like to think so."

"Why do you keep talking about Vernon?" Evelyn asked at last, realising she'd done nothing to dispell Dorothy's assumption. "I don't have any feelings about Vernon. I admit, he flatters me. No one has ever treated me in quite that way before and it has an effect on me. But, even before you told me about Lilian, I was only a little drawn to him."

"But when I asked if you'd seen anyone who makes your heart beat faster, I could read the answer all over your face, whatever Lilian has to say about it. Oh good Lord, it's not James, is it?"

"No, of course not." Evelyn was offended Dorothy would suggest it and tried to ignore the nagging anxiety of James's apparent feelings towards her.

"Well, that's a relief. I'd have credited you with very little taste if it'd been him, poor boy that he is. So who is it? Come on, spill the beans, darling. I won't tell."

"Really, it's no one…" Evelyn began.

Dorothy did not look convinced. "Oh, there's someone you've noticed, all right. And you've not met that many people yet. Let's see…" Her attention was drawn by someone who had just entered the cafe and was therefore behind Evelyn. "Jos!" Dorothy exclaimed.

Thinking her secret was discovered, Evelyn flushed, her eyes open wide at the notion of being discovered.

Dorothy's quick eyes noticed at once and realisation dawned on her a moment later. Surprise was followed by a broad smile. "Oh, Evie, attagirl," she said in a quick whisper. "You have impeccable taste. And you'll hate me for what I'm about to do." She raised her eyes back to Jos. "Come and join us, Jos. Lilian is demonstrating a new song for Vernon, and I don't expect they want disturbing for now."

"Afternoon, Dorothy. And Evie, lovely to see you in better circumstances." Jos slid into the seat next to Dorothy, not quite making eye contact with Evelyn. She shrugged her outdoor coat off and sat with an easy slouch. Today, she wore a long-sleeved knitted cardigan, the same shape as a formal man's jacket, with a white shirt and brown bow tie.

Evelyn tried not to stare, but once again, she found something extraordinarily compelling about Jos. "Good afternoon, Jos. It's lovely to see you again," she managed to say. Her mouth felt dry. She was at once terribly excited at this unexpected opportunity to spend time with Jos and entirely unprepared for the way it made her feel. Suddenly she felt as though she'd actually been drinking gin again, not coffee. Her head spun a little and her heart thudded faster. This was Jos, here, just a couple of feet away from her. A living, breathing woman, towards whom she had dared to admit her own sensual attraction. It was so ludicrous to be almost impossible and yet, as she faced Jos, she could not deny it.

"We were just discussing Evie's time in London so far," Dorothy told Jos, apparently trying to force a conversation from the awkward silence.

"And are you enjoying London?" Jos asked.

Evelyn had a impression of Jos as sure of herself but not entirely sure how she would be received. Evelyn wondered if Jos was sometimes greeted with hostility, which seemed awfully unfair. "Oh, very much. It's a wonderful place. So very different from anything I've ever known before."

"I can see why it would be. Mayfair especially. Vernon and I grew up in Greenwich. It's only across the river, of course, but I have to admit that Mayfair still makes me open my eyes a little wider." Jos looked briefly to Dorothy, as if for confirmation that she spoke the truth.

"I find it terribly exciting. I discover something new every day." Evelyn was relieved to talk to someone who seemed to understand how she was feeling, even if their experiences were really not the same. No one else she'd encountered so far had seemed to offer her any empathy at all.

"There's nothing like it, is there," Dorothy interjected. "Something to make the heart race at every turn."

Evelyn marvelled how, once again, Dorothy managed to describe her excitement with such a deadpan expression.

"Dorothy, my dear, you make it sound so very dry and quite the opposite." Evelyn smiled as Jos expressed just what she was thinking. "I know it's fashionable to be cynical, but really, you might smile occasionally."

This drew a smile from Dorothy. "It's not that I don't know how. It just doesn't always occur to me to deploy those particular muscles."

"You really are a marvel, Dorothy Bettany."

"I try my best. But let's not focus on me. How's the theatre?"

"Oh, just wonderful. It's pantomime season, of course. So everything is glistening and sparkling and merry."

"The theatre?" Evelyn enquired, intrigued.

"I work in the Royale, on Shaftesbury Aveune. I design the scenery and help with the props. I sometimes manage the stage too," Jos said.

"How wonderful!" Evelyn's image of the theatre was of a mysterious, glamourous world she did not fully understand. She'd been to several plays at the West Coombe town hall and once had been to see a pantomime at the bigger theatre in Plymouth. But the idea of a theatre here, in London, where everyone seemed to be performing in their day-to-day lives, was fascinating.

"It's not so exciting when you're there every day." Jos shrugged and looked down at the table briefly.

Evelyn found her modesty compelling. "I think it is," she said, pleased when Jos looked up and smiled. She held Jos's gaze for a long moment before losing her nerve and looking away, hoping her blush wasn't obvious. Jos seemed to see right into her thoughts and feelings. Could Jos possibly understand that something about her had kindled such emotions in Evelyn? Once again she felt herself growing warm, wanting to let Jos know that, if nothing else, she liked her and would like to spend more time with her. But how did one go about such things with a complete stranger, a woman, in this maddening London reality?

"Well, Evie, you have a lot of time on your hands at the moment and I imagine you're tiring a little of Lilian's company. Why don't you let Jos show you her theatre one day?" Dorothy winked at Evelyn, much to her consternation. She looked to Jos, who looked puzzled briefly but then smiled.

"I'd be very happy to show you behind the scenes. Any day you like really, although we have matinees on Saturday afternoons, so in the week would be best."

"I would like that very much." Evelyn found she did not feel shy about accepting the offer. "Would tomorrow suit you? I think Lilian is going out on her own in the afternoon and I'm a little tired of reading alone in my room now."

"That would be perfect. Do you know how to get to the theatre?"

"I think we might've gone along Shaftesbury Avenue one day. I'm not sure I can remember though."

Jos gave her directions. "Of course, it's a good mile, so you might want to take a cab."

"I used to walk much further than that at home." Evelyn was already starting to relish the prospect of an independent walk through London.

"Shall we say one o'clock then? Or I could meet you earlier on the route if it would help. I'd hate you to get lost on my account." Jos smiled, her words full of enthusiasm.

"No, thank you. One o'clock is fine. I won't get lost and if I do, I'll ask a policeman."

"You're such a tourist, Evie. We'll soon make you a Londoner." Dorothy seemed satisfied with how she had engineered the situation.

Evelyn was grateful to her since she was fairly sure that, left to her own devices, she'd have sat silently, wondering how on earth to further her contact with Jos. "I'm already starting to feel like I am a Londoner," she said.

"Not quite, sweetie. But nearly. It won't be long." Dorothy's words seemed to carry more meaning than was apparent on the surface. Evelyn smiled, rather thrilled to have Dorothy's approval. While Lilian was the shiny glamour of this new world Evelyn inhabited, she already felt like Dorothy was the essence of it. Dorothy's respect suddenly meant a lot to her, although not so much as the fact that she would spend time with Jos, alone, the following day.

"You'd almost think Dorothy had a checklist for becoming a Londoner, wouldn't you?" Jos joked gently.

"Yes. I'd like to know what's on it," Evelyn said, enjoying sharing the joke with Jos.

"I'll warrant it's not being born within the sound of Bow Bells. Maybe it's being born within the sound of the tills ringing at Harrods?"

Dorothy looked mildly offended. "Certainly not! I'm not so shallow and you know it, Joselyn Singleton." She smiled that vague, intriguing smile. "But I do have my opinions on what makes you part of this world. Number one would be a fascination for all that's new. A simply unhealthy passion for jazz. A desire to drink gin before midday, perhaps."

"This is still all awfully superficial, Dorothy, darling, don't you think, Evie?" Jos clearly enjoyed teasing Dorothy and relished sharing her humour with Evelyn.

"It is, I have to agree. I'd expect more from Dorothy." Evelyn drew confidence from Jos.

Dorothy's brow furrowed. "I'm not sure I'm happy you two are better aquainted if I'm going to be bullied so badly."

"Sorry, darling. You know I'm just pulling your chain. Do go on." Jos put a finger to her lips to indicate that she would remain silent.

"Well, you must also be thoroughly dissatisfied with everything and dream of something new and thrilling that you don't quite understand. You must think that the future is more exciting than the past but live in the moment and not concern yourself too much with what that future will be. You must have flirted with men and women and kissed plenty that you never intend to marry. You must feel the thrill and yet know it to be empty."

Evelyn and Jos stared at Dorothy as she concluded. With Dorothy it was difficult to know if she was sincere or in jest, yet her tone was intense, her eyes turned slightly glassy. Evelyn had the uncomfortable feeling of having witnessed the emotions at Dorothy's core, perhaps something she had not meant to reveal. She found Dorothy at once ridiculous and captivating. Jos's silence seemed to imply that she was equally unsure how to respond.

"Gosh, Dorothy, do you ever think that you dwell on it a little too much?" Jos said, eventually. "Surely, after all, the conclusion of your requirements is that one does not sit and talk about things but rather goes out and really lives."

"Oh, but where's the pleasure in life if one cannot postulate about it?"

"I think, perhaps, we have rather different pleasures, Dorothy. I don't want to talk about my feelings and their greater significance for the world. I want to feel them, to know what it is to be me, living my life. It's that which makes my flesh quicken. That and a good scotch, of course."

Dorothy allowed a flicker of a smile and turned her eyes to Evelyn. "What does Evie think about this? Where do your pleasures lie, I wonder?" The words were dripping with implications and yet Evelyn was drawn into the discussion without fear. It felt as though she was involved in something close to the edge, something dangerous and yet intoxicating. They were only sitting in a cafe, talking over coffee, and yet she felt as though she was breaking rules, drilling down to the root of what was important.

"I think I agree with Jos," she said giving Jos a long look to make sure her sincerity was not in doubt. "I could have sat at home in West Coombe and dreamed of a different life, philosophised about it. But I came to London to live it, to feel it."

"But those feelings count for nothing if they mean nothing," Dorothy said.

"But Dorothy, their lack of meaning is their ultimate purpose, if we are to be thrilled but empty." Jos looked back to Evelyn, apparently pleased they were in agreement.

"Can one feel, without thinking?" Dorothy asked.

"Yes. I think so," Evelyn said. "It's difficult to think without feeling though."

"The dilemma of my daily life." Dorothy drank the last of her coffee.

A giggle from the back of the cafe signified that Lilian and Vernon had returned. Jos looked towards where her brother emerged from the door to the private rooms above the cafe. Lilian was already heading back towards the table. Evelyn thought her hair looked ruffled, her lipstick freshly reapplied. Lilian's pupils were also rather wide and her cheeks pink. She could not help but wonder what Lilian had been doing just a few moments before.

"Did Vernon enjoy your new song?" Dorothy asked, wryly.

"Of course he did." Lilian took her seat and smiled, as though she really had just been performing the new song for Vernon. "Ah, Jos, good to see you. I'm sorry I was keeping Vernon occupied."

"Not a problem," Jos replied. Evelyn sensed a tension between them, which made her uncomfortable. "It gave me chance to get to know Evie a little better."

Lilian's smile faded slightly, Evelyn noticed. "Well, that's excellent. It's good you're making new friends, Evie."

"Jos is going to show me behind the scenes at her theatre tomorrow," Evelyn said, partly because she was excited by the prospect and partly because she was curious how Lilian would react.

"Really? That's very kind." Lilian was now not smiling at all. "Of course, if you want me to stay at home instead of going to see my dressmaker, I will do. I can take you to the theatre myself. We could actually see the play instead of getting our clothes filthy backstage."

Evelyn did not like the suggestion in Lilian's tone that her offer was far better than what Jos had suggested. "No, thank you. I know you've been looking forward to finally getting your dress for New Year's. I'm curious to see behind the scenes. We can go to the theatre at any time. If you don't mind." She added the last in the face of Lilian's downcast expression.

"No, I don't mind," Lilian said, her tone flat. Any further discussion was interupted by Vernon's arrival at the table.

"Sister darling, good to see you."

"I need to have a word, if you don't mind, brother dear." Jos got to her feet. "Dorothy, Lilian, it was good to see you. Evie, I'll see you tomorrow." She nodded at each of them then began to walk towards the back of the cafe.

"You mean I don't get to spend time with this delicious coterie?" Vernon had not directly followed Jos.

"No, not if you know what's good for you. I'm quite sure you'll see them again soon."

"In that case, ladies, it was brief but pleasurable." He lingered over the syllables of the word, sensually. Again, Evelyn found herself horribly curious to know what he and Lilian had been doing upstairs, her mind full of descriptions from Lilian's book.

"See you tomorrow, Vernon," Dorothy said. Lilian simply grinned.

"I'll look forward to tomorrow, Jos. Thank you again," Evelyn said, putting her other thoughts aside as rather uncomfortable to dwell on.

Vernon and Jos departed to the private door at the back of the cafe. Evelyn watched them go with some regret. However kind Lilian had been to her, she was beginning to find spending too much time with her was disagreeable. Even Dorothy was quieter when Lilian was part of the group.

As if to confirm Evelyn's misgivings, Lilian clearly decided it was time to turn the conversation to herself. "Have I told you about the dress I'm having made, Dorothy? Evie knows all about it, but I'm not sure I told you. It's a really nifty design."

Evelyn thought she saw Dorothy sigh slightly. "No, you haven't, darling. You simply must."

Evelyn sipped the last of her now-cold coffee as Lilian started to talk of crystal beads and ostrich feathers. But her thoughts were with Jos and what tomorrow would bring.

CHAPTER TWELVE

Evelyn awoke early the following morning and lay in bed staring at the white-painted ceiling in the grey early morning light. The house was quite cold and she did not feel inclined to leave the comfort and warmth of her blankets, but she knew she would not sleep any longer. She was already thinking about going to the theatre and meeting Jos.

Whenever she tried to think of the enormity of the fact that she felt drawn to Jos in the way she did, Evelyn diverted her thoughts to other concerns. There was no reason to dwell on that, she reasoned, since it was not something she could act upon alone. Would Jos feel the same way? How did these things work between women? So many questions arose which she could not begin to answer that she found contemplating her feelings for Jos made her nothing but anxious. Instead she lingered over the details. She had already decided to walk to Shaftesbury Avenue, taking enough money for a cab in case she did get lost. There was a peculiar thrill in the idea of being out in London by herself for the first time since she had arrived at Paddington.

She was also very excited at the prospect of seeing backstage at the theatre. It was an experience beyond those of the ordinary tourist and it seemed to mark a step towards her being part of this group of aquaintances, part of their London life. She smiled to herself, thinking that she would write a letter to Edward in the evening, after her theatre visit, and tell him all that had happened. Maybe she would even write to her parents, in the hope that she could dazzle them with the excitements of her new life.

Evelyn could hear Grace in the kitchen below, preparing the breakfast, and she decided to begin her day with a bath. She was still astonished by the luxury of the Graingers' bathroom, but growing quite accustomed to the convenience. She climbed out of bed, slipped a robe over her nightdress, and took her towels from the chest of drawers, already happily anticipating the warm water.

❖

The warm water was so pleasant, Evelyn even decided to wash her hair with the coconut oil shampoo Lilian had given her. At home, she had been used to washing her hair only once a week, usually on a Saturday evening. Now she found she liked the feeling of it being freshly washed and certainly much preferred Lilian's shampoo to the cake of coal-tar soap she used at home.

Her long hair was still wet when she left the bathroom, wrapped in only the thin robe, and she could feel the cool water soaking through to her skin. She was halfway along the landing between the bathroom and her bedroom when James's bedroom door opened and he appeared, dressed only in his trousers and shirt, the shirt open to reveal his chest and torso beneath. Evelyn glimpsed the hair on James's chest and the curve of his stomach before he clutched his arms to his body. Equally embarrassed, Evelyn held her towels tighter, aware that the robe showed the contours of her form in a most improper way.

"Oh, good morning, Evelyn. I thought I heard someone moving about but it's so early I thought it was Grace."

Evelyn wondered why it was more acceptable to appear half-undressed in front of Grace but did not say so. "Good morning, James. I'm sorry if I woke you. I wanted to have a bath."

"No. I mean, you didn't wake me at all." James had apparently now noticed Evelyn's state of undress and could not help a lingering look from her shoulders where her hair soaked the robe, down to her ankles and slippered feet. She wanted to tell him to stop looking at her, but that would have meant acknowledging that he was, and she did not relish the prospect.

"Good. I'm going to dress for breakfast now." Evelyn tried to move towards her own door.

"Of course. Oh, I meant to tell you"—James was still struggling to keep his eyes on Evelyn's and she grew increasingly uncomfortable—

"I managed to take two days of leave next week. So if you'd still like to go somewhere on one of those days, I'm available."

Evelyn felt dismayed and realised she'd forgotten James's intentions. However, she could not forget that it was his hospitality that gave her a roof over her head in London. "That's wonderful. Thank you. I couldn't possibly take up both days of your free time but maybe we could go to one of the galleries one afternoon."

"I could take you to the pictures," James said, hopefully. The pictures, Evelyn thought, was hardly a way to see more of London, but it was certainly a way for James to spend time with her alone.

"That would be nice too," she replied, with little enthusiasm. "Are they showing anything good?"

"They have *Wings* on at the Elite, with Clara Bow."

"Oh, the one about the war. Of course." Evelyn could not imagine a film she had less interest in.

"It's supposed to be very good. Very realistic."

"How wonderful. I'd be delighted." She forced a smile.

"Excellent." James looked genuinely pleased.

"Now, do you mind awfully if I make myself decent?" Evelyn did not hide her impatience.

Recalled to their states of undress, James suddenly seemed shy again. "Oh, of course. Apologies. Delighted you accepted though. See you at breakfast." Slightly pink in the face, he hurried off looking at the carpet. Evelyn let herself into her bedroom with some relief, though frustrated that her dependent situation and fear of causing offence made it impossible to refuse James, however much she wanted to.

Although she chided herself for cowardice, Evelyn decided not to join Lilian and James for breakfast. She knew James would leave for work within the half hour and she preferred not to see him again this morning. She did worry about what he was telling his sister. Had he confided in her that he planned to take Evelyn to the cinema, to court her perhaps? The notion made her desperately uncomfortable. Lilian, unusual and difficult though Evelyn found her to be, was still her first London contact, her first friend. She did not like the idea of Lilian forming incorrect ideas about her. And if she was to disappoint James, what impact would that have?

Of course, she reflected, she could be honest about her feelings towards Jos. But, unlike Dorothy, Lilian had expressed some distaste for Jos's way of living, and loving. Evelyn did not feel as though she could confide in her so easily, especially when nothing was by any means certain. After today's visit to the theatre, she might never see Jos again. She certainly did not need to share this with Lilian and realised that, in fact, it would make her feel vulnerable to do so.

Instead of eating her toast, she instead spent her time considering what to wear for her afternoon with Jos. While having no desire to be as superficial as Lilian, she found herself looking with dissatisfaction at the contents of her wardrobe. Jos was of the same world as Lilian and Dorothy, whose clothes were beautiful and well chosen. Yet there was some hope. Jos did not conform to Lilian's idea of fashionable, so perhaps she would not expect the same of others. In the end, she opted for her plain grey skirt and cream blouse, reflecting that she would be wearing her coat for most of the outing anyway. She would wear the red cloche and knitted scarf Lilian had given her a couple of days before.

Once she was dressed, Evelyn listened again to see if she could hear movement downstairs. She was fairly sure James would already have left for work, probably disappointed not to have seen her at breakfast. Eventually, she ventured downstairs, carrying the hat and scarf. As she reached the bottom of the stairs, Lilian entered the hallway from the kitchen. She was already dressed for the day in quite a conservative dress with a blue tartan pattern. Evelyn did not think it suited her at all but was not about to say so.

"Morning, Evie," Lilian said cheerfully. "There's still some breakfast left if you want some."

"I'm not that hungry this morning, but thank you," Evelyn said.

"Ah well, suit yourself. You're off to meet Jos this afternoon, aren't you?"

"Yes, I am. But I'm going for a walk first. I want to try being out and about by myself, without just following you around. Much though I appreciate all the time you've spent with me, of course." Evelyn felt nervous when Lilian spoke of Jos and wanted to move the conversation on.

"It's only natural that you want to be independent, Evie. I'm quite all right with not sheepdogging you everywhere. You be careful with Jos though, won't you? And those theatre people she spends her time with."

"You don't approve?" Evelyn raised a questioning eyebrow.

"I approve of the performing arts, obviously. And I'm all for a bohemian lifestyle, if one has the correct attitude for it. But they rather cross the line. I don't want you to be led astray, darling. I've already done enough of that." Lilian laughed, as if to lighten her clearly judgemental tone.

"Oh, I shall be on my guard." Evelyn wondered if Lilian noted the irony in her words.

"Excellent. Well, I shall be out for most of the day, and possibly into the evening too. So I'll see you in the morning, if not before."

"You won't be back this evening?"

"No. I'm going early to my dressmaker and I made an appointment to have my hair cut too. This evening I've been invited to drinks with an old friend from school, in Kensington, so I'm just not sure when I'll be home. Looks like it'll just be you and my darling brother." Lilian smiled and Evelyn was sure there was something implied by that smile that made her uncomfortable.

"I hope Grace isn't expecting me at a certain time," Evelyn said. "I'm not sure when I'll be home." The idea of an evening alone in the house with James was suddenly uncomfortable to her. If nothing else, it was possible she could claim to have eaten elsewhere and avoid sitting at the dining table with him.

"I think she's just planning to prepare some salad and cold cuts, so you needn't worry about the time. Although, really, how long can you possibly spend poking around in a theatre?" Lilian laughed but Evelyn did not join her.

"I don't know, but I expect it will be very interesting," she replied.

Lilian's smile faded. "Hmm, wouldn't be for me. But I suppose it's horses for courses, isn't it? I hope you have a lovely afternoon, darling." She gave Evelyn a quick pat on the arm and then made her way up the stairs.

"Thank you, you too," Evelyn called after her, before retreating into the sitting room where she sought the newspaper to help occupy the time until she needed to leave the house.

❖

Evelyn enjoyed the walk through the London streets. Already there were familiar landmarks, and already the sounds and smells of the sprawling city were nothing surprising. Walking a short distance along these streets did not feel at all adventurous now. Though she loved London, the pavements were a means to an end, taking her to meet Jos.

As she walked, Evelyn paid little attention to her surroundings. Although she had planned to absorb and remember every detail of her first independent day in London, the motor buses and shopfronts seemed to simply drift by in a blur. Beyond checking the street names to be sure she was still walking in the right direction, Evelyn barely noticed the shapes and colours around her. She thought of Jos, with some apprehension. Outside of the rareified world of the Yellow Orchid, how would it be to meet with Jos? What would they talk about? Would she still feel so compelled by her? And if she did, what did it mean? Was it possible for someone like her to act on such feelings? If Jos did not return them, how would she feel? The thoughts, not clearly articulated, occupied the whole of Evelyn's consciousness. She was at the theatre on Shaftesbury Avenue a full fifteen minutes early, scarce able to remember the route she'd taken to get there.

Uncomfortable at the idea of trying to get into the theatre and disturbing Jos before the appointed time, Evelyn contented herself with examining the facade of the red-brick building, probably built midway through the last century. A flight of broad steps led to the row of dark wood doors, with flawless glass panels and brass fixtures. Above each door was an ornate wrought-iron framework, supporting a stained glass canopy, which sent a rainbow of colour onto the top steps. Framed posters advertised *Dick Whittington* with a coloured picture of a woman in a long waistcoat and high boots, a cat at her side.

In the wide street, a motor car sounded its horn as a dray horse passed, heaving its cargo of beer barrels. Evelyn turned to watch the traffic. One of those fabulous open-topped buses sped along the other side of the road, a child waving from the top deck to anyone who might see. A baker's boy cycled past, clearly on his way home from a morning of deliveries, his basket now empty. Once again Evelyn marvelled at the bustle of London. Everyone was doing something, going somewhere important. She would admit that it was less friendly than West Coombe, less of a community, but it was far more fascinating. And people formed their own communities, even in this vast city. She had already found one, of sorts, with Lilian and her friends. Although Jos seemed a little outside of that community. Did Jos have friends of her own, away from the Yellow Orchid? Evelyn wondered if she would ever have the chance to meet them. She liked the idea of finding out more about Jos, of being considered part of Jos's world.

"Evie!" Jos's voice came from behind her. She turned to see Jos standing in one of the doorways into the theatre, propping it open with her foot. "Come inside, you'll catch your death out here."

Evelyn smiled and hurried towards Jos. "Hello! I was a little early and I wasn't sure if it was all right to come inside."

"Of course it would have been. But anyway, I'm here now."

"Yes, you are." Evelyn's eyes made contact with Jos's, and there it was again, that warmth, that sense of expectation of something, although she did not know quite what. Jos's expression seemed more open here, in her own territory, than it ever had when she'd encountered her before. Evelyn was glad Jos seemed relaxed.

"So, do you want the full tour?"

"That would be lovely, thank you. If you're sure you have time."

"Oh, I'm not really needed at this point, now the performances are under way. It's during those I have to be here. I'm only here today because they're making a few adjustments to some of the flats—that's the scenery, you know—and it's always best to supervise these things. Someone has to and, in truth, I just like being here."

Evelyn looked around the foyer of the theatre. The floor was light beige tiles, the ceiling a concoction of ornate plasterwork, and the walls were lined with decorated satin. The fixtures, including the large box-office counter, were all carved mahogany. Chandeliers hung from the moulded ceilings. It was not, perhaps, the most modern of interiors but it was certainly impressive. Evelyn rather liked the stately elegance that was not dependent on fashion. "It's a beautiful place to work," she said.

"That it is. Of course, it's not so refined behind the scenes, but it is more interesting."

"I'm sure it is. I really can't wait." Evelyn was genuinely excited, although whether by her forthcoming glimpse behind the scenes of the theatre or by spending the new few hours with Jos, she was not entirely certain. She ran her eyes quickly over Jos, from head to toe. Her hair was slightly touseled and she was in light tweed trousers and waistcoat, fitting the curves of her body. Her sleeves were rolled up to the elbow and showed smudges of dust. Her shirt was open at the neck, revealing her smooth skin and a trace of collarbone. Evelyn had never noticed the physicality of another person in the way she felt alert to every aspect of Jos's appearance.

"In that case, follow me. We'll go through the auditorium so you can get your bearings." Jos led the way towards a big double door with the words *Stalls Right* above it. She pushed the heavy pannelled door open and led them into a short passageway. "This is where the ushers take your tickets," Jos said as they walked, "and then you come through here to take your seat."

The passageway opened into the auditorium of the theatre. The red-upholstered seats of the stalls stretched across the space in curved rows. Above them, the ornate dress circle balcony looked too heavy with gold-painted plasterwork not to fall into the space below. Heavy velvet curtains framed the boxes close to the stage. Above the dress circle was the upper balcony. Although the space was not wide, it seemed to soar in height. In the centre of the ceiling was a very large crystal chandelier.

Evelyn had seen the interior of the theatre in Plymouth, palatial in its own way. But to see the inside of a London theatre, at a time when she and Jos were the only people present, was an entirely different experience. The space felt almost sacred, soaring high like a cathedral, shining with gilt decoration. She turned her gaze to the stage where the heavy safety curtain was in place, filling the whole of the white-painted proscenium arch. Even the safety curtain was decorated with a mural of flowers and cherubs.

Jos was smiling at Evelyn. "You seem impressed," she said.

"It's breathtaking," Evelyn said quietly. For some reason it seemed wrong to speak above a whisper.

"I suppose I'm used to it now, but I do think it's one of the nicer theatres I've worked in." Jos did not have the same reverential tone, but she did seem proud that her place of work had impressed Evelyn.

"It's so strange to be here with no one else. I've only ever seen a theatre when it's full of people."

"I know what you mean. It's not so much the emptiness that

surprises me, but the silence. Audiences are noisy, even when they're not talking, with all of their shuffling and coughing and rustling. Not to mention the actors and the orchestra. But when it's empty, it's so quiet. Even now, I sometimes pause and listen to the silence."

"I can see why you would." Evelyn thought it wonderful that Jos would notice such a detail, that she would stop to appreciate it too. After so many days with Lilian, who might notice the cut of a woman's dress from across the street but had probably never spent a moment in silence in her life, Jos was a wonderful antidote. She was more than that—she was fascinating to Evelyn, in a way she had never been fascinated by another person. Without even understanding what compelled her, Evelyn wanted to know Jos on every level, to see what more she could discover.

After a moment, Jos touched Evelyn lightly on the arm. "Don't expect such refined surroundings once we get behind that safety curtain. Come this way."

Evelyn followed happily, as Jos led them down the side of the stalls and then up the short flight of stairs to the stage. As they reached the stage, Evelyn glanced out at the auditorium, at the rows of seats facing her. "Gosh," she breathed.

Jos turned to see what had drawn the exclamation from Evelyn. "Oh, of course, I do always forget what it's like to stand on a stage for the first time." She grinned. "Why don't you take centre stage for a moment?"

"Can I?" Evelyn asked.

"Why not?" Jos took Evelyn's hand lightly in her own. Evelyn caught her breath and allowed Jos to lead her to the middle of the stage. She stood still, looking out to the invisible audience.

"It's hard to imagine, all those eyes, watching," she said. Jos had let go of her fingers and she rather missed the warmth.

"You barely see them when the footlights are burning and the spots are in your eyes. They're just shadows. Really, you perform for yourself and the people on the stage with you. And for applause that comes from beyond the light, of course."

"But to be the focus of so many people's attention…I can't imagine it."

"It's exhilarating." Jos sounded as though she spoke from experience, which aroused Evelyn's curiosity. "You can lose yourself in it. But then, as Shakespeare said, all the world's a stage, isn't it? We're all acting our parts, all the time."

"I don't know," Evelyn said. "Until recently I never really felt like I was playing a part. I just went on from day to day."

"Oh, but in London, you're part of one never-ending performance, Evie. The curtain never comes down. Only for some it's a farce and for others it's a tragedy."

Evelyn turned to Jos. "Which is it for you?"

A shadow passed over Jos's expression for a moment. "A farce, most definitely. Perhaps even a pantomime."

"I rather like the drama of it all," Evelyn said.

"Oh, so do I. But sometimes you need the interval, so you can retire and relax and stop playing the part, don't you think?"

"Yes, I do." With every thought and feeling Jos shared with her, Evelyn only wanted to understand her more.

"Well, Miss Hopkins, take your bow and we'll go and see what's behind the performance."

Evelyn laughed lightly and bowed, as she was told, to the audience of empty chairs.

Jos watched Evelyn, smiling, thinking it odd how happy she felt in Evelyn's company. Yes, Evelyn was unsophisticated and naive but she was also bright and thoughtful. Her natural beauty, unsullied by the usual artifice, seemed to glow. To Jos's mind, Evelyn was more worthy of being centre stage than any other woman she'd met. But she could not act on it, could she?

Evelyn was very different to the other women Jos had been involved with. There had been flirtations, passionate affairs, there had even been something masquerading as love, but the women had always known exactly what they were getting themselves into. Most of them had attempted to seduce Jos before she'd even decided she was attracted to them. Now she felt that the pressure was on her shoulders, if anything was to be possible between her and Evelyn Hopkins.

Jos was not yet sure of the extent of Evelyn's innocence but she was more than convinced that Evelyn's experience of the world did not extend to romantic relations between women. Yet having her here, away from the distractions of the Yellow Orchid, her brother's teasing, and Lilian's irritating influence, it did not seem like such a leap to imagine she could woo Evelyn, that there might be some hope for something between them. She had not missed Evelyn's sharp intake of breath when she had taken her hand a moment ago. The flush in her cheeks could only have one cause, really. And then there was Dorothy's rather obvious attempt at matchmaking in the Orchid. She'd known Dorothy for long enough to understand exactly what the confounded woman's intentions were. It wasn't just Dorothy either. Clara and Courtney were convinced she'd made a favourable impression on Evelyn in their brief first meeting. She just had to be sure not to scare Evelyn by moving too fast. Or make promises she was not sure she could keep. Because she did not want to commit herself to anything, however attractive a woman might be.

Evelyn straightened from her bow and looked at Jos. If nothing else, Jos could make sure Evelyn saw her at her best, and go from there. The theatre was her natural environment, where she was most comfortable. And Evelyn seemed geuinely keen to see the place, happy to be here with her.

"Come on, we'll go into the wings—I'll show you the flats and the tunnel that takes you to the other wing. Then we've got the dressing rooms, and if you're brave enough, we can go up there." Jos pointed upward. Evelyn's gaze followed her hand and into the area above the stage.

"I never knew there was anything up above a stage," she said.

"Oh, it's fascinating. But it is high and the stairs are steep."

"I'd love to see it."

Jos was pleased by Evelyn's enthusiasm. She liked a woman with curiosity and Evelyn seemed to have plenty of it. "Fabulous. Then let's go."

Jos led Evelyn from the stage into the wings. Jos loved the way the false, bright world of the stage suddenly became the practical, grubby working space of the wings. This was where the magic spell was cast, creating the illusion of the stage. Of course, she'd been part of the illusion in her early days, more interested in the chance to don a costume and act a role than in the practical tasks that allowed it to happen. But much had changed in her life since then. Now she actively sought a life away from false dreams with day-to-day realism, sceptical about the superficial. She'd not entirely lost her sense of magic, however. Perhaps the spell would work on Evelyn.

Jos showed Evelyn the flats which made the scenery at the sides of the stage. Cut from thin wooden boarding, and painted in garish colours to represent the fairy-tale version of old London town, where the story of Dick Whittington, three times mayor, would play out. The painted houses were in the Tudor style, dark wooden beams and pink plasterwork, but with painted ivy leaves to soften them, the creeping vine flowering with exotic fantasy blooms, their petals edged with glitter to catch the lights of the stage. Close up, with the brushstrokes visible, it was difficult to get the full effect. Yet Evelyn was looking at them with apparent fascination.

"I've never been so close to the scenery before," she said, running a finger over a place where the thick paint had real texture.

Jos watched that fingertip with an unexpected shiver of pleasure. "I painted this one myself," she said, with no small amount of pride.

"Did you really?" Evelyn looked at Jos with excitement in her expression, and real admiration. Jos could not deny that to be admired and respected by Evelyn for her artistic skills, was something that seemed to fulfil a craving from deep inside her.

"Yes. Like I said, I do a bit of everything, but I love to paint and we're lacking in painters. Some of the best were killed in the war, and it can take years to train anyone up to know what they're doing. So I help out where I can. I do enjoy the pantomime scenery. You're really creating the world of people's imaginations." She hesitated, astonished by how easy it was to talk to Evelyn, to begin to reveal something of herself. "Anyway, I'm happy you like it."

"It's beautiful. You're really talented." Evelyn sounded genuine, even when Jos tried to exercise caution. "Do you just paint scenery?"

"I experiment on canvases at home sometimes. But it's not the same. I'm not saying I'm terrible but my skill really lies in creating something on a big scale, that you should admire from far away. It's not art really."

"I think it is," Evelyn said. "And I'd like to see your canvases too."

Jos let her gaze linger on Evelyn's expression. From another more worldly woman she would have taken that as a suggestive comment. From Evelyn, it was difficult to tell. On the surface it was simply an expression of interest. And yet she sensed something below the surface. It might not be an attempt at seduction but, she concluded, Evelyn was trying to tell her that she wanted to know her better. That was a positive sign. All of Jos's senses seemed to spring to life, alert to any further signals she might receive from Evelyn.

After Evelyn had examined the flats and the way the painted boards created a sense of perspective in the way they were positioned towards the back of the stage, Jos led her through the dimly lit tunnel which allowed the actors to move from one wing to the other, to appear on the other side of the stage within a few seconds, to the astonishment of the audience. Evelyn smiled broadly at this secret revealed. Her smile was so genuine—so honest and so easy—nothing like the forced frivolity of most London women. Everything Evelyn did just seemed to make her more appealing, make Jos want her more. And there was no way she could deny that now. She did want her. But how would Evelyn receive her desire? The idea of being rejected in disgust, or out of fear of the unknown, was horrific.

Jos was still pondering this as she escorted Evelyn up the steep stairs at the side of the stage and into the galleries above. This was where ropes attached to pulleys to control the curtains and scenery, where the spotlights lurked in the darkness, their light projecting downward. Planks and platforms showed where stagehands risked everything to cross the void above the stage, or where they stood to guide the spotlight, all so the audience could be enthralled and delighted. So much technical effort, such a place of grubby industry, to create the myth of the magical world onstage.

The climb was several flights of very steep metal stairs, almost ladders. Jos had expected Evelyn to balk at the idea of climbing them, but she made her way up with remarkable ease. She was clearly physically stronger than her slender form suggested. Jos ascended the steps behind Evelyn, finding her eyes on a level with Evelyn's calves, watching the muscles flex as she climbed. Even though it was only her lower legs, it seemed a very intimate stolen view of a woman, and her body lurched with arousal she struggled to contain. She imagined running a hand over those legs, sliding it higher.

Drawing a deep breath, she looked down at her own booted feet, trying not to raise her eyes to Evelyn's form so close in front of her. However appealing it was to watch Evelyn, it was not the done thing to gawk at the woman when she had no way of knowing how Evelyn felt in return.

At the top of the stairs, Evelyn was slightly breathless, her cheeks pink through exertion now. Forced to stand close to her on the small platform that formed the initial landing, Jos caught the slight scent of sweat from her, such a human, earthly smell that it made it almost impossible to contain herself. Damn it, but she wanted to see Evelyn with sweat slick on her skin and the breath coming hard from between those rosy lips, lost in pleasure she was sure she could give her.

Jos bit her lip and concentrated on describing what the various pieces of equipment in the gallery above the stage did, hoping the raspy edge to her voice did not betray her.

Evelyn listened to Jos, fascinated to see the secrets of the stage revealed to her. She knew now that she agreed with her entirely and not at all with Lilian. She almost cared nothing for the illusion of the show that would be perfomed on the stage below; it was here, in the dust and the dim lights of backstage that the magic really took place. Or perhaps, ultimately, it wasn't about the theatre at all. Perhaps it was Jos. To be here, in this enclosed and secret space with her felt like nothing she'd ever experienced before. Every time Jos looked at her, she felt as though those blue eyes saw right into her. She'd felt Jos's eyes on her as they'd climbed the steep stairs. And now she stood so close she could feel the heat of Jos's body close to her, and all she wanted to do was reach out and touch her. To know what it was to kiss her.

How did she let Jos know? She was certain the tension between them meant something, that she was not alone in feeling it. She was sure that, if nothing else, Jos wanted to know her more. The look in Jos's eyes was almost hungry, and yet the way she bit her lip suggested she was trying to hide something, to suppress something. Did Jos feel the same way? And if she did, then what happened next?

Jos did not suggest they balance on any of the walkways above the stage, and Evelyn was glad. She could see the stage below and the drop was substantial. Evelyn did not feel as though she was concentrating well enough for balancing at such a dangerous height. She would rather be back on the ground and able to enjoy talking with Jos, doing what she could to tell Jos how she felt. She was pleased when Jos said they could climb back down and she would show her the dressing rooms and orchestra pit.

The climb down felt more precarious than the ascent had done, and Evelyn put her tumultuous feelings on hold while she made sure she reached the level of the stage safely. Jos went down the steps before her, and Evelyn felt safer knowing she was there. Once they were back in the wings, Jos led her away from the stage and into a rather institutional corridor, where the brick walls were painted cream and the heating pipes ran along the ceiling, with no attempt to hide them or make the area more pleasing. It was a marked contrast to the auditorium of the theatre but, in some ways, a more comforable place to be. They went down some stairs and turned to the left, where Jos opened a door into a dark space with a low ceiling.

"This is the orchestra pit," Jos said. She flicked a switch near the door and electic light filled the space. Evelyn saw a circle of chairs and music stands, empty and expectant. "We say pit but only the front part is actually a pit in front of the stage. We have this bigger area under the stage in case we need a bigger orchestra, you see. We don't fill it for the pantomime, but if we were staging an opera or suchlike, we'd need the full area."

"Of course. I never knew there was a space under the stage at all," Evelyn said.

"Not all theatres have one." Jos turned off the light. "Now, come and see the dressing rooms. None of the actors or actresses are here at the moment, so I can show you whichever ones I want. Shall we see the one we give to the leading lady?"

"Yes, that would be lovely." Evelyn realised she didn't really care any longer. Interesting though the theatre was to her, made more so by it being Jos's world, where she was comfortable, all Evelyn really wanted now was to spend time with Jos. To perhaps share a cup of tea with her and talk. Perhaps to risk a hint about her feelings.

A short way along the corridor, Jos turned into a doorway and twisted the handle. "This is Alexandra's dressing room. She's Dick Whittington himself."

Evelyn followed Jos through the door and into the room beyond. Where she had been expecting glamour, what she found was actually rather functional. The room was quite small with a ceiling that showed patches of damp in the plasterwork. The room did not benefit from any natural light at all, though the electric lights were quite bright, including the bulbs that surrounded the large mirror, clearly for the easier application of stage make-up. The dressing table in front of the mirror was a chaos of pots and bottles, tissues and sponges. Towards the back of the room was a metal clothing rail on which hung several stage costumes. Evelyn lingered on these for a moment, as the most tangible evidence of the colour and splendour of the stage itself. They were the typical costumes of the principal boy in any pantomime, long fitted waistcoats, tight breeches, frilly neckerchiefs. One outfit, clearly what Dick wore before he found his fortune, had brightly coloured patches sewn into it, clearly to suggest his poverty and need to mend his clothes. At one end of the rail was a much more ornate costume, in rich red and trimmed with gold thread. A matching tricorn hat hung over the end of the rail, plumes of ostrich feathers cascading from one corner. This was clearly Dick's costume for the finale, when he would marry the beautiful Alice Fitzwarren as a rich man, at the beginning of a happy ever after, and then take a final bow. Although she was sure the costume looked very rich and expensive in the stage lighting, here on the rail it hung limp and rather dull. The quality of the fabric was not high and the fastenings allowing the actress to make a quick change were all too apparent. Sometimes, Evelyn thought, it was better not to see behind the illusion.

"What do you think?" Jos said, watching Evelyn.

"It's really interesting to see all of this," Evelyn said. But she felt compelled to honesty with Jos. "I have to admit though, I almost don't like to see it. I love knowing the secrets of this place, but somehow, seeing the costume here, away from the lights, is almost sad."

"I think it's more like that in pantomime season. Everything on stage is so glorious, that everything behind the scenes seems so very drab," Jos said, looking around. "I prefer it here, away from the glare. But I do understand."

"I think it reminds me that it's all artifical, in a way," Evelyn said, relieved that she'd not disappointed Jos with her response to the dressing room. "More so than seeing all the scenery. You know the stage set isn't real, but I think I like to pretend the characters are, the fairy-tale world isn't just an illusion. Which is awfully silly when you think about it!"

Jos smiled. "I don't think so. There's enough artifice in the world, you have to suspend the cynicism and just believe in magic occasionally. Even when you know it's not really magic."

"Yes, that's it." Evelyn smiled. "There is rather a lot of artifice in the world, isn't there? I mean, I notice it more here than I did in West Coombe. No one really bothered so much there."

"Not everyone here bothers either, you know. Although there's nothing wrong with making your life a performance, if you're happy. I don't mind people worrying about their clothes or painting their faces or performing any role they like, as long as they're true to who they want to be. It's when the performance takes over the life, that's when it makes me uncomfortable."

Evelyn hesistated before she responded, happy that Jos was expanding more on her personal outlook on the world and reluctant to ruin their new level of intimacy. "I have to agree with you," she said, thoughtfully. "I don't know many people here, but, well, if I take Lilian as my example, she seems to be awfully focussed on living her life to the full, but then doesn't seem at all happy. When no one's looking, that is. She'd never let on, of course."

"You're a perceptive woman, Evelyn Hopkins," Jos said.

Evelyn warmed at the admiration in her tone. To be appreciated for her insights into the world was not something she was very used to. She enjoyed the way she felt comfortable talking with Jos, and even more, she enjoyed the idea that Jos understood her, valued her thoughts.

"I don't know if I am," Evelyn said. "I'm really just saying what I see."

"But not everyone would see it." Jos held her gaze.

Evelyn was aware of Jos's mind working behind the piercing eyes. What was she thinking? She ached to know more of Jos's thoughts.

"It's refreshing to talk to someone like you, Evie. And I don't mean that I see you as some sort of novelty. It's not just that you're not from London and you don't live the fashionable high life. Those are part of it, but it's also something about you that I can't quite put my finger on. You remind me that there are people in the world who see things the way I do." As soon as she finished, a tension came into Jos's expression, as though she was scared she had said too much.

Evelyn searched her mind for the appropriate words to both reassure her and let her know how touched she was by what Jos had said, how much she was beginning to feel the same connection between them.

Chapter Thirteen

As she walked by Evelyn's side along Shaftesbury Avenue, Jos felt a sense of pride to be seen with this bright, beautiful woman. It was not something she'd felt in any of her relationships, she realised. It was less a judgement of the women she'd been with and more a reflection on her own sense of being disconnected from them, even when walking arm in arm. Although she'd known Evelyn such a short time, she felt a sense of togetherness with her, a sense of being in the same place in the world. Of course, that was rather ludicrous, since she could not really have been much more different from Evelyn. But something like that wasn't really about where you came from or what was happening in your life. It was about understanding on a certain level, a feeling of connection and oneness of outlook. She felt this with Evelyn, and the sense only grew stronger with every conversation they had, every opinion that was shared.

Evelyn seemed relaxed as they headed for the restaurant she'd suggested for their evening meal. Jos wondered what was going through her mind. Was she relaxed, her naiveté preventing the suggestion of what could happen as the result of this evening? Or did she know full well what she was doing? Jos did not dare make assumptions. Whatever Evelyn's intentions and awareness, she had to be careful. Evelyn must not be rushed because that could end in tears, for both of them.

It had been on impulse that she'd invited Evelyn to Clara and Courtney's party. She would have been in attendance anyway, usually with the intention of locating and charming her next lover. Clara and Courtney's guests were almost exclusively the lesbians of fashionable London, their hangers-on, and those who were intrigued by them.

Women who loved women. The rest of the world might call them inverts and attest that they were mentally ill, but they knew otherwise and these gatherings were a celebration of that. Much though she was not a fan of being put into a neatly labelled group, it was pleasant to be in a place where she was not only accepted, but seen as one of the more interesting and desirable people in the room. It was also one of the only reliable ways to meet women who would not potentially be offended by her attentions.

Jos was nervous that Evelyn would be overwhelmed by such a Sapphic gathering. However, if she could cope with the decadence of the Yellow Orchid, a house party with a group of women was hardly something to fear. She was also very curious as to how Evelyn would respond. If she was right and there really was the spark of something like desire in Evelyn, how would being confronted with the reality of it make her feel? In some ways, Jos reflected, it was a kill or cure situation. Either Evelyn's eyes would be opened to the possibilities, or she would be horrified and overwhelmed and Jos's chance would be lost. She dared to hope that it would be the former. Evelyn was a strong woman with a real curiosity for the world so far beyond her experience. She had already met Clara and Courtney and would be under no illusions, surely, about the nature of the guests at the party. Besides, Evelyn had looked flattered and excited to be invited. Jos had really enjoyed the look of delight that had crossed her face.

As they walked, Evelyn looked lost in thought too. It was as though the walk from theatre to restaurant was the pause they needed, in company with each other but not talking, judging the other's responses. The quiet between them was companionable enough but spoke of their active minds. Jos wished she could read Evelyn's mind and know how welcome her advances would be. She knew she would have to take the initiative here, and that was not a role she was familiar with. The idea of rejection was actually quite terrifying to her.

She broke out of her reverie when, having turned onto the broad sweep of Regent Street, they arrived at the restaurant. "Here we are, this is the place I was thinking of. What do you think?" she asked Evelyn, before they went inside.

Evelyn took a step back on the pavement to look up at the sign above the door. The restaurant was named for its owner, Adalfieri de Pasqua, who had moved from Rome with his parents at the turn of the century. Jos considered him a friend and he could always find space for her in his restaurant. Jos watched as Evelyn read the name, in gold writing on a black background, and then glanced down at the windows, where there were fresh white lace curtains.

"It looks lovely," Evelyn said. Jos was pleased. She opened the door and ushered Evelyn through in front of her.

"Jos Singleton!" The exclamation went up as soon as she passed over the threshold. Adalfieri, a tall, wiry man with thinning hair but a certain handsome quality, was beaming at her from the centre of the room. He hurried towards her. "It's been too long, *mio caro*!"

"It's only been about a fortnight, Adalfi. But it's good to see you." Jos submitted to a warm embrace. Once he let her go, she was aware that his attention had fallen on Evelyn, who was looking rather awkward. "Mr. Adalfieri de Pasqua, allow me to introduce Miss Evelyn Hopkins. Evie, this is Adalfi, he's a very good friend and employs a very good chef."

"Only the best for Jos and her friends." Adalfieri looked at Evelyn with a knowing look in his eye. "It's good to meet you, Miss Hopkins."

"You too." Evelyn smiled, although she still looked slightly uncomfortable. Perhaps it had been a mistake to bring her here and subject her to Adalfi. Somewhere anonymous might have been easier. But she wanted to share things with Evelyn, including her favourite restaurant.

"I've not seen you before, I don't think." Trust Adalfi to be nosey, Jos thought, glaring at him.

"No, I've not been in London long," Evelyn replied, with the air of someone who was getting used to giving this explanation. "I'm from Devon, but I'm staying for a while. Jos has been showing me her theatre today."

"Has she now? I've not had that honour myself yet." Adalfieri raised an eyebrow in Jos's direction.

"You've never asked," Jos retorted. She loved him but wished she could tell him that today was not a good day for teasing. So he'd seen her bring other women here. This was different. "You know I'd show you around, if you wanted."

"Of course, of course, *mio caro*." Adalfieri narrowed his eyes, as if trying to discern more about the nature of Jos and Evelyn's relationship. Well, she would fill him in later, but this was not the time.

"We'd like a table for two, please, Adalfi. What are your specials this evening?"

"Your favourite table, by the window, is free. In fact, they're all free right now, you might notice—you're early." Adalfieri led them towards a small circular table with a pristine white cloth. There was a single evergreen sprig in the vase on the table, which was already set with silver cutlery. Each dark wood carved-back chair had a green cushion on the seat. Evelyn and Jos followed him, and sat as he pulled the chairs out for them, Evelyn followed by Jos. "Today's specials are the salmon or the beef. Would you like to see the menu?"

"I'm happy with the salmon," Jos said. "I recommend it, Evie, if you trust me?"

"Of course. I'll take the salmon too, please." Evelyn smiled and Jos could not help responding in kind, even though they were only choosing food in a restaurant. Even the most mundane activities took on a new colour and excitement when Evelyn was involved. Usually she felt as though she was fighting an uphill battle to impress a woman. With Evelyn it was easy to just be herself. She hoped that would last through the evening.

❖

Evelyn enjoyed the meal with Jos. The food was as delicious as promised and she found the comical, teasing intrusions of Adalfi, as she was told to call him, into their meal to be a fun diversion. Although she found it very easy to talk to Jos, she sensed they were both glad to be distracted from a focus on just each other. However interesting she found Jos, however intrigued and compelled she was by her own feelings, to spend an entire day with someone she did not know very well, and whose sentiments she was constantly trying to read, was rather intense. Aldafi's constant good humour and inability to stop himself interjecting in their conversation lightened the tone considerably. She had the opportunity to observe the fun side of Jos's personality. She could tease and be teased with equal good humour and wit. She laughed easily and did not back down. But her affection for Adalfi was very clear. Evelyn could tell then that Jos was nothing if not loyal, and compassionate towards those who returned those sentiments. She admired both traits.

Jos had a depth to her character she'd not been able to discover in anyone in London yet. Lilian was often nothing short of vacuous, James too reserved to reveal his true self. Dorothy liked to postulate and her intelligence seemed formidable, but it was very difficult to know what she really thought or felt. Vernon was a witty flirt but she knew nothing more of him. Jos had so much more to her. It was a depth that she longed to explore.

In some ways, Evelyn rather regretted the conclusion of the meal. A few more patrons had joined them in Adalfi's restaurant but the ambience was still peaceful and relaxing. She felt comfortable here with Jos and Adalfi, as though she had known them much longer than she had. She felt accepted by them. Adalfi had not cast a gaze of approbation over her outfit and decided she was not fashionable enough, or questioned her on her reasons for being in London. He clearly accepted Jos for who she was, and some of his jokes suggested that there wasn't much about her that he didn't know. He would not have been the sort of close friend Evelyn would have expected Jos to have, and yet he seemed to be a perfect counterbalance to her. When she was serious, he made her laugh; when that tension rose in her shoulders, he softened his tone and was gentle.

Adalfi was clearly a perceptive man, but he also undersood Jos, cared for her. This warmed Evelyn to him greatly. Apart from Vernon, Jos did not seem like someone who had a lot of people to care for her, or someone who sought out affection easily. But this didn't seem to stop Adalfi. Evelyn hoped very much that this would not be the last time she got to spend time with the restaurant owner.

Jos paid for the meal, despite Evelyn's insistance that she had enough money to contribute. As they were leaving, Adalfi asked what their plans were for the rest of the evening.

"We're off to Clifford Street. Courtney demanded a house party. It's been at least a month since her last one."

"And Clara wouldn't dream of denying her anything." Adalfi laughed good-naturedly. "Tell them I haven't seen them for a long time. I'm offended."

"I will do. I'm sure they'll be along before too long."

"Tell them if they're not, I will no longer guarantee them their favourite table."

"I'm sure such a dastardly threat will bring them to your door grovelling for forgiveness." Jos winked at Adalfi. "I'll bring them along myself one night soon. I miss you when I don't see you, you old goat."

"Perhaps I'll see all four of you," Adalfi replied, with a suggestive look at Evelyn, which made her shift awkwardly in her chair.

"Maybe you will," said Jos, a little more subdued now. Evelyn wondered what Jos had felt upon hearing Adalfi's suggestion. "Anyway, we haven't seen anything of Vito this evening, I notice."

"It's his day off. And that's quite enough questions, I think." Adalfi's eyes were twinkling and he had blushed slightly.

"I'll let you off this time, but next time I want the whole story," Jos said.

"If there is a story to tell, you will be the first to know," Adalfi promised. Evelyn was simply doing her best to understand the conversation. She thought she understood the gist of it and suddenly looked at Adalfi in a new light. Was he one of those men Lilian had mentioned, forced to break the law simply to fulfil their love for one another? If so, it seemed terribly unfair. Adalfi was a kind-natured man, certainly not someone who seemed likely to behave in a way that was obscene or abnormal, as it had been implied. Suddenly she felt dreadfully sorry for him, although he seemed happy enough.

"That's all I need to know for now then," Jos said. She rose to her feet. "Now Evie and I must be going, or else poor Courtney will be bursting with anxiety. She hates it when guests are late."

Evelyn rose and accepted Jos's help with her coat. Jos kissed Adalfi on the cheek in parting, and when he reached for her hand, Evelyn copied the gesture, keen to demonstrate her approval of Adalfi, who she had genuinely enjoyed meeting. "The food was delicious and it was really lovely to meet you," she said. "I'm sure it won't be the last time."

"I very much hope that's the case." Adalfi smiled as Evelyn turned to follow Jos from the restaurant.

The walk from the restaurant to Courtney and Clara's flat on Clifford Street was no more than ten minutes. When Evelyn saw the sign which told her they were on Savile Row, she could not help a flutter of excitement.

"Savile Row!" she exclaimed.

Jos looked at her curiously. "Yes, it is."

"It's famous. I read about Dr. Livingstone lying in state in the headquarters of the Royal Geographical Society here. And Sheridan lived here somewhere. And of course, there's all the tailors." Evelyn looked about her, gratified that the first shopfront she laid eyes on was a very upmarket gentleman's tailor.

Jos was smiling at her, her eyes dancing. "I forget how new and special this all is to you, Evie. It's wonderful. I don't know that I've ever really known anyone get excited walking along a street before."

Evelyn was a little embarassed, though Jos's tone did not suggest any notion of ridicule. "I'm sorry, it's not even that it's new, it's just there are places that seem almost mythical. You know, you read about them in books or newspapers but don't expect to see them. And it's not even the great buildings like Westminster Abbey or Buckingham Palace. You know they're real, they're the places the tourists go to see. But a street, a simple street, where so many important people have walked, going about the day-to-day business that makes up our history…they're the places you don't think to ask to see, the places no one takes you to when they say you're going sightseeing. But in some ways they're more special. Now I'm just one of those people who have walked along Savile Row too. It feels important." Evelyn looked to Jos for a response.

"I suppose when you grow up in London, you just accept those things. But I can understand why it would be exciting for you. And I think it's wonderful that you're excited about it."

"You don't think it makes me rather naive and silly?" It was the first time Evelyn had voiced a question that played on her mind time and time again since she had come to London.

Jos stopped in the street and turned to face Evelyn properly. She looked into her eyes earnestly. "Evie, you are one of the least silly women I've ever encountered. You are far from naive. You might be innocent in the ways of this corrupt urban world, but you're not naive. You're bright and observant and perceptive. And everything you experience here only makes you more complex and fascinating."

Jos caught her breath as the last word slipped from her lips. Evelyn noticed this, and the sudden tensioning of Jos's whole frame. She blinked and looked back at Jos, feeling more naive than ever as she found herself entirely unequippped to deal with Jos's compliment, clearly not one she had meant to voice there and then.

"You think I'm fascinating?" she said finally, in a quiet voice, barely daring to ask the question.

Jos took a deep breath. "Yes, Evie, I do. Now, I don't know how aware you are of, well, of me and of how I—"

Evelyn knew Jos was about to attempt to tell her of her sensual inclinations. She did not need to be told. She had to be brave, to help Jos and to make it possible for either of them to take any further steps. "It's all right. I know. I mean, I didn't know it was something that even existed before I came to London and I don't have the right words. But I know." She said the words hurriedly, almost scared to breathe in between them, in case she came to a complete stop. "And I think you're fascinating too."

Immediately she looked away, down at the stones of the pavement. She could not bear to look for Jos's reaction, even though Jos had confessed her feelings first.

Suddenly, Jos's warm, strong fingers were underneath her chin, lifting her face gently, until they were once again looking in each other's eyes. Jos held her gaze for a long time and Evelyn felt the allure of seeing deeper into Jos's soul. She opened herself to Jos, let her read her hopes and fears in her expression.

Eventually, Jos nodded softly. "Now that we've established that, what do you say we go to a party?"

She smiled and the tension between them dissolved. "I think that sounds like the cat's pyjamas." Evelyn grinned.

Jos rolled her eyes and offered her arm to Evelyn. Evelyn wrapped her hand around the crook of Jos's elbow and they walked towards Courtney and Clara's flat.

CHAPTER FOURTEEN

Clifford Street was a collection of grand red-brick Victorian villas. Many of them had shops or offices at street level and the upper levels were well-appointed flats. Clara and Courtney, who had no shortage of family money between them, lived in the upper two floors of a house about halfway along the street. Jos led Evelyn to the door, her heart and mind too full to know exactly how she was feeling in those moments. Simply to have Evelyn by her side, on her arm, and to know she had not misjudged the situation, that there was real potential between them, made her want to sing with joy. This feeling was so very different to her usual tired acknowledgement that a cynical society girl had a crush on her.

Evelyn had grown quiet since their mutual confession, but it was not an uncomfortable or awkward silence.

"This is a beautiful street," Evelyn said. "It's so funny, in London, even a street that's not famous can be more spectacular than the whole of West Coombe."

Jos smiled. It was only natural that Evelyn would compare every new streetscape to her home, although in some ways she thought it would be easier for Evelyn if she thought of home a little less. "One day, I'll take you to the East End, near the docks. It might make you think of West Coombe, since there's a lot of boats there. Or you might find that not all of London compares favourably to West Coombe. You've only really seen the West End."

"I'd like to see more of it. Maybe the places the tourists don't see." Evelyn was enthusiastic and, Jos sensed, glad that they were able to make easy conversation despite the new tension that existed between them.

"Oh, there's plenty of those. Of many different types. For example, you wouldn't get many tourists passing through this door." They stopped outside the blue-painted door of Clara and Courtney's residence and Jos rang the doorbell. Moments later, they were greeted by a young woman in the uniform of a maidservant. "Evening, Maggie, all right if we come in?" Jos greeted her.

"Miss Singleton! Of course. They're upstairs, in the salon. You're to help yourself to food and drinks, so I can have my evening off."

"Of course. Any plans?" Jos liked Maggie, however uncomfortable she was around servants generally, having not grown up with domestic help herself. She wished Maggie would be a little less deferential, but Maggie seemed to see it as part of doing her job well. Clara and Courtney treated her with respect and she seemed happy enough. Now Jos was conscious of Evelyn observing her interaction with the maid and also aware of Maggie glancing at Evelyn, curiosity in her expression.

"Nothing very special. I thought I might go to the cinema, but I'm rather tired so I might just make cocoa and read."

"You live a wild life, Maggie."

"Don't I know it?" Maggie was almost staring at Evelyn now. "Miss Courtney didn't say you were bringing anyone with you."

"No, well, she didn't know and she won't mind, I'm sure. This is Miss Evelyn Hopkins."

"Good to meet you, Miss Hopkins. Maggie Francis, I keep house for Miss Clara and Miss Courtney."

"Nice to meet you too," Evelyn replied. Jos could sense her slight unease. Evelyn would naturally have even less experience dealing with servants than she had herself.

"Well, now we've all met, let's head upstairs, shall we?" Jos said, before Maggie could ask any questions. She took Evelyn's arm and made for the flight of stairs that led to the flat above.

Clara and Courtney's apartment was rather upside down compared to the normal set-up of a house. The kitchen, bathroom, and bedrooms were all on the lower level, along with a very small sitting room and dining room, while the upstairs was given over to a large salon which made the most of the floor-to-ceiling windows with a view across the rooftops of Mayfair. The room was decorated immaculately in pale colours, which provided the perfect backdrop to Clara and Courtney's collection of fine art. On the chimney breast was a particularly large and striking Expressionist painting, which Clara was convinced was a fine investment, however much Courtney protested that it was ugly. Jos couldn't remember the artist Clara had named and had no wish to demonstrate her ignorance by asking for the information to be repeated. She made no attempt to explain the room to Evelyn as they reached the top of the stairs, merely led her through the archway and into the salon, from where gramophone jazz was emanating, combined with the hum of several voices talking at once.

A quick glance at Evelyn as they entered told Jos that she was paying little attention to the artwork on the walls and much more attention to the gathering of women in the room. Even though she was well known here, she found herself nervous on entering the room so conspicuously, so she couldn't help but wonder how Evelyn felt, despite the smile she had conjured. There were about a dozen women in the room and all of them turned to see who had joined them. Jos knew them all and was met with smiles, immediately followed by intrigued and knowing looks regarding Evelyn by her side.

"Jos!" came Courtney's New York accented voice from near the fireplace, where a table had been set up bearing various spirits and plenty of glasses. "Now you're here it's a real party! And you've brought Evelyn too, how simply jazzy."

"You can make mine a scotch, Courtney," Jos called back, grinning. Courtney's charm really was irresistable.

"But what about Evelyn?" This was Clara, who had risen to her feet and now came to stand next to Evelyn. "You don't strike me as a scotch drinker, my dear."

Jos was relieved to see Evelyn smile, genuinely. Just as she'd thought. A strong woman who was not easily intimidated. Still Evelyn's words drifted through her mind. *I know…and I find you fascinating too.* There was really no way to misintepret that. The only decision now was what she should do with that knowledge.

❖

It had only taken Evelyn a moment to realise there were no men present at this gathering and another moment to make the correct assumption that these were women who were like Jos, Clara, and Courtney. She did not like, even in her head, to think of using James's word, *inverts*, but she was not sure how else to describe them. Perhaps, she thought, she should be nervous in a room of such women. But she was not. She felt comfortable and welcomed. Besides, considering the feeling she had confessed to Jos, she was surely one of them, at least in intention if not in actuality. She liked the idea of finding women more like her. She was also excited to spend a whole evening with Jos, in a world where Jos seemed happy to be herself.

So now, when she smiled at Clara, it was a smile that held a certain confidence. Nervous though she was when greeting new people, and intimidating though it was to be looked at by a roomful of women she did not know, she did not feel out of place. Clara's and Courtney's welcome made it even easier to feel relaxed. They were pleased to see her, and they seemed to be pleased to see her with Jos too. She liked the idea of their approval.

"I'm not a scotch drinker," she replied to Clara. "So what do you recommend?"

Clara grinned. "Dangerous tactics, Evelyn."

"Now, Clara, I didn't bring Evelyn here to be corrupted by you," Jos said.

"Oh, how dreadfully disappointing," Clara replied, with a wink at Evelyn.

"I don't think Courtney would approve of you corrupting anyone except her," Jos pointed out, as Courtney crossed the room to join them.

"Are you talking about me? Should my ears be burning?"

"Talking about me, not you, sweetest." Clara wrapped an arm around Courtney's shoulders.

"We were discussing Clara's corrupting influence, actually," Jos said.

"Oh, well, then I'm the prime example. I was such an innocent before I met her."

"Don't believe a word of it," Clara said to Evelyn. "It was she who seduced me. Although, of course, I'm only in it for the money."

"If it's only the money, you're welcome to sleep on the settee tonight," Courtney said, pretending to look offended.

"Perhaps it's a little more than the money," Clara conceded. "She is rather a doll, don't you think?"

"Everyone loves me," Courtney said with a bright, insouciant smile. "And now that's established, here's your scotch, Jos. Evelyn, can I recommend the gin? With ice, of course, tonic if you want."

"That would be lovely, thank you," Evelyn replied. She'd enjoyed being part of another conversation with Clara and Courtney, who seemed to take nothing too seriously and yet to live a fascinating life.

She watched as Courtney went towards the drinks table again, admiring her black and gold dress, fringed all around the bottom. Courtney's clothes always seemed to fit her to perfection, but Evelyn did not feel any pressure to live up to her standards of fashion, not in the way she did when Lilian looked her up and down. She glanced at Clara, whose Eton-cropped hair was immaculate as ever and who was attired in a striped sports jacket. They were such a striking couple, it really was quite hard not to stare.

However, she was also increasingly aware of the other women in the room, still looking at her curiously.

Eventually, one of them called to Jos, "So, Jos, aren't you going to introduce us?"

The woman who had spoken was more plainly dressed, in a simple blue dress. Her hair was in a short bob and she wore no make-up. So not everyone in this world was fashionable or unconventional, Evelyn thought.

"Of course I am, Catherine. Give a woman a moment to enjoy her first scotch of the day, won't you?" Jos sipped her drink.

"No, I won't. You can't leave the poor thing just standing there, with us all looking at her."

"All right, settle down." Jos glanced briefly around the room. "Ladies, this is Miss Evelyn Hopkins, she's new in London, and we met at my brother's questionable establishment. I've been showing her backstage at the theatre today and I thought it would be nice for her to meet you all. So play nicely."

"We always do," Courtney said.

"Except when we don't," Clara added, nudging Evelyn with her elbow and winking. Evelyn giggled and waited for the second half of the introduction.

"Evie, you'll never remember their names, but here in the room we have Catherine Wakefield."

Evie nodded to the woman who had demanded the introduction.

Next to her on the settee sat a woman in a rather austere blouse, with short, straight dark blond hair.

"That's Stevie Robertson. Across from her are Gisela Blumstein and Abigail Blessing-Cooper." The two women, seated in separate chairs but close to each other, smiled at Evelyn. Gisela was a very slim dark-haired woman who wore a bright red dress and seemed the most likely of the gathering to compete with Courtney in terms of style. Abigail was a rather plump young woman, whose long platinum-blond hair was tied into a long plait which hung down over her shoulder. She wore a masculine black tuxedo, but it did not fit as well as Clara's and gave her a slightly ramshackle appearance.

Jos went on with her introductions. "The triumvirate on the chaise longue there are Lottie Green, Irene Jacobs, and Ronnie Mackenzie."

Evelyn smiled and realised she had no chance of remembering these women's names at all, just as Jos predicted. She barely had time to make brief eye contact with each of them. Lottie had bright ginger hair styled into ringlets and very pale skin. Irene had a very aquiline face and was wearing a vivid green dress. Ronnie was a little older, her dark brown hair beginning to grey. She wore loose trousers and sat with her right hand holding Irene's left.

Jos went on. "Helping herself to the best scotch is Suzanne Flint. Next to her is her sister Sarah. And last but not least, this is Caro Booth. I think that's all of them." Suzanne and Sarah were both tall and long limbed, with light brown hair, Suzanne's short and Sarah's worn pinned onto the top of her head. Caro wore an embroidered cap that covered most of her auburn curls, and her most memorable feature was a face liberally sprinkled with freckles.

Evelyn took a deep breath and looked around the room again. "It's good to meet all of you. Jos is right, I can't remember a single name, so do forgive me. Hopefully I'll remember by the end of the night."

"And if you don't, lass, we won't be offended." This was Ronnie, who spoke with a Scottish lilt in her voice. "There's no standing on ceremony here. Just a likeminded gathering and plenty to drink."

"Then might I suggest we start drinking?" This was Clara, who raised her glass to toast the room. "To new friends and a long night to enjoy them!"

"New friends!" was returned by most of the women in the room, who raised their various glasses. Evelyn was shown to an armchair. Jos, clearly reluctant to move too far away from her, perched on the arm. Evelyn was pleased that Jos wanted to stay close to her, despite being in a roomful of her friends.

For a short time, she sipped her cold gin slowly and simply observed the room. It seemed as though they had arrived in the middle of a conversation about a book that had recently been published, which the other women now resumed.

"Well, if she can get it published, that will be a fine thing indeed. A novel about us! Who'd have thought?"

"I suppose it's better than being a passing story about a girl and her teacher in *The Rainbow*. Do you know, I've never been sure whether I approve of Lawrence doing that or not. I told him so too, when I last saw him."

"At least he acknowledged we exist. That's half the battle sometimes."

"But a novel about us—do you think the reading public will cope?"

"I'm not sure if anyone will even publish it. And what price the chances of it being prosecuted if someone does?"

"I rather like the idea of my daily activities being too obscene to put into print." This was Clara, who came to stand at the side of Evelyn's armchair. "Don't you, Jos?"

Evelyn noticed Jos flush a little. She sensed that her presence placed a restricton on what Jos felt able to say, which made her slightly anxious. She did not want Jos to feel constrained by her in any sense. Part of what drew her so much to Jos was her apparent sense of liberty.

"Clara, you are incorrigible," Jos responded. "I don't think anyone would dare write a novel about you."

"Ha, perhaps not. Not one they'd want to publish, anyway. I shall always be an interesting background character, I fear. I add colour but no substance."

Jos smiled. "I don't think any of us would make the most thrilling of protagonists. Perhaps Evie would, with her big move to London."

Evelyn smiled at the thought. "I hardly think so. My life's been pretty dull apart from that."

"I'll bet it's more colourful now you're in the capital, eh? And certainly now you're spending time with Jos."

"Clara," Jos said with a warning in her tone. "We've not really spent much time together."

"It's quality, not quantity, darling." Clara ran a hand over her smooth hair, a knowing smile on her lips.

Evelyn was not sure whether to smile or feel concerned. What Clara implied was between her and Jos was real, their mutual acknowledgement in the street confirmed that. But to talk about it like this, to suggest it could actually happen—that it was happening—was something new and not entirely comfortable. Jos seemed equally on edge and Evelyn wondered if she was trying to make less of her feelings, in order not to make Evelyn feel pressured. She was not sure. It seemed safest, at this stage, to change the subject. "What book is it that everyone's talking about?" she asked.

"Oh, it's a friend of ours, John," Clara said, "I mean her name's Radclyffe Hall, you might have heard of her, but we know her as John. Anyway, she has written a draft of a novel about what it's like to be a woman who loves women. The thing is, Catherine's read some of it and she said it made us look awfully miserable. But then, even that seems to be better than not exisiting in books at all, don't you think?"

Evelyn hesitated for a moment. It was hardly something she'd had reason to think about before now. Even in this room, it seemed strange that such interesting and strong women could be written out of the world of literature because they loved each other instead of loving men. It wasn't as though they'd made a concious choice about it. Her own feelings for Jos had come from nowhere, unprompted, and felt as natural as any other feeling she'd ever experienced, even more natural and honest. To feel that way and yet find it led down a path of not exisiting seemed like a terrible position to be in. "I think it's definitely better to exist than not to," she said. "I have to admit I've not really stopped to think about it before now, but I'd say that even a book that shows the characters as unhappy would be better than no book at all. Perhaps if there's one where the characters are unhappy, people will think twice about things. And then someone will write a book where the characters are happy."

Jos was smiling. "I like the way you see things, Evie. It's simple."

Evelyn frowned, not sure if Jos was suggesting she didn't understand the complexity of the situation.

"Oh, Jos, you don't tell a lady she's simple," Clara said, seeing the frown.

"That's not what I meant, sorry, Evie." Jos hesistated. "It's more that you come to things with a fresh perspective. You've not spent so long thinking about it and discussing it that you're half-mad with it and entirely cynical. You see things as they are, which shouldn't be as complicated as people make it, really. That's what I mean by simple."

Evelyn smiled now, understanding the compliment. "I really just say what I think."

"As should we all," Clara said. "I make a policy of it myself. And what I think right now is that I need some of the very good food Maggie left for us." She raised her voice and addressed the whole room. "If any of you ladies can stop talking for long enough to eat, there's some tasty morsels over at this side of the room. And stop eyeing Courtney that way, Stevie, she's not one of them."

"Aww, and I thought I was tasty," Courtney said, pouting. "I mean, you like to eat—"

"Later, darling," Clara interupted smoothly, with a wink. "If you're good."

"Oh, I'm very good." Courtney approached Clara and gave her a brief kiss, directly on the lips. "You know that, my love."

"Don't I just." Clara ran a hand over Courtney's back and lower, caressing her bottom. Evelyn watched them, so openly showing their affection and attraction, astonished and yet captivated. The idea of something of what existed between them growing between herself and Jos was almost impossible to imagine and yet already tangible. She felt herself growing warm.

"You two need separating, if we're not all to feel sick by the end of the evening." This was Caro, interupting good-naturedly as she lit a cigarette in a long black holder.

"Yes, and you might remember that some of us are single with not a trace of romance on the horizon," Sarah Flint added.

"Hear, hear," came from Lottie Green. Evelyn smiled at the happy, if teasing, tone in the room. Clara and Courtney had gathered a group of interesting, intelligent women as their friends. And in this room, the idea that they all loved other women seemed a long way from remarkable. For them, it was normality. As such, Evelyn took confidence from them. If they felt that way, then it was entirely possible for her to do the same, surely.

As the night drew on, Evelyn talked mostly to Jos, although Clara and Courtney would join them from time to time. She learned a lot more about Courtney's life in New York and listened to a detailed comparison of the two cities from Clara. America was a place Evelyn had barely considered and certainly not a place she had dreamed of visiting. But Courtney's presence here in London, this woman who had grown up on the other side of the Atlantic, made anything seem possible.

Nor, she learned, was Courtney the only foreigner in the room. Gisela Blumstein was German, having fled her country in the immediate aftermath of the war, seeking a better life in England. She had travelled to England with a husband but had since been divorced, amicably, from him. Irene Jacobs was half-Belgian and had been living in Ypres when that town had found itself the centre of the battlefield. So she had sought the sanctuary of her mother's British family in South London. Suddenly, moving from West Coombe did not seem at all dramatic or unusual. Evelyn felt rather relieved to find this. Her Devon accent did not set her apart in a room of such diversity. To her surprise she realised she felt more comfortable with these women than she had at any time since she came to London. In addition, she wanted to know what they did, to know Jos like they knew other women. She wanted to share herself with Jos in the way that she saw Clara and Courtney share with each other, or connect with her in the way that Ronnie and Irene sat so comfortably hand in hand, even when conversing with different people.

The hours flew by. Evelyn barely gave a thought to the Grainger household, or to where she would say she had been if Lilian asked. It barely seemed important. She was happy and felt carefree. Besides, every word and look she exchanged with Jos drew her closer. She sipped her gin purposely slowly so that, although it relaxed her and made her more inclined to giggle, she did not lose the sharp edge of her perceptions or the sting of her desire for Jos, which only grew more and more. The women in the room seemed to already accept and understand that there was something between them and their acceptance made it seem more real, more possible. If only she knew exactly what was expected of her in such a situation. But all she could do was wait for Jos and try to demonstrate that Jos wouldn't panic her by taking another step along a path they both wanted to explore.

It was approaching midnight when Jos was cornered by Gisela and Abigail. Evelyn overheard the beginning of their conversation—it seemed Gisela had written a play about the current situation in Germany and they were seeking advice about how to put it into production. Evelyn liked the idea that Jos was considered an expert in such a creative field. She tried to listen to more of their conversation.

Suddenly, the place at her side was taken by Suzanne Flint. She smiled but looked at Evelyn rather intently. Clearly, Suzanne was a little more than tipsy, which made Evelyn cautious. "Hello," she said. "I'm doing terribly with names, but I think you're Suzanne. We've not had a chance to speak yet."

"Yes, that's me. Nice to meet you properly. Now, you must spill the beans, what's happening with you and Jos?"

Evelyn looked back in astonishment. "I don't know what you mean," she said. She had understood the question but she was not sure what she was supposed to say in response.

"Oh, poor thing. I suppose, being from the country, you're not used to our London ways. What I mean is, are you and she sleeping together?"

"No," Evelyn replied impulsively, before she had chance to consider it any further.

"Good. Because I wanted to warn you. It's not that I don't like Jos, I do. But I know more than one girl who's ended up in her bed and it's all ended very badly. Oh, I don't mean the night itself. From all accounts, she's very good at that. But she can't deal with being close to someone. It's since her parents died, I'm sure. But she'll love you by night and dismiss you by day, that one. I hear her brother's the same. Excellent at luring a girl in, terrible at showing any concern for her afterwards. So yes, flirt if you will, but prepare yourself. She won't commit to anything."

Evelyn was staring at Suzanne now. She didn't understand why she was being given this information and quite why Suzanne, who she'd not even spoken to until now, felt the need to provide this warning. At the same time, it was difficult to ignore the words. What if she did share everything with Jos, only to find it had been a mistake? How would she feel if Jos discarded her? The idea was horrendous. But would Jos do such a thing? It was even possible Suzanne was lying, although she had no apparent reason. Evelyn looked across at Jos, smiling as she explained something to Abigail, and found it hard to believe that she would mistreat anyone.

"Well, thank you for telling me but I'm not sure it's any of your business," she began.

"You needn't get on your high horse. I'm just being friendly. It'll take a phenomenal woman to get Jos Singleton to commit to anything, and I don't think you're it, sweetheart."

Evelyn was angry now, since Suzanne's words seemed critical of both her and Jos. "I'm sorry but I don't really know you at all," she said. "And, as I said, nothing has happened between us so it doesn't matter anyway, does it?"

Suzanne was about to respond when, much to Evelyn's relief, Clara appeared at her side. "Suzie, darling, are you sharing the benefit of your worldly wisdom with Evie?"

"Something like that," Suzanne replied.

"I suspect Evie's had more wisdom since she came to London than she can keep track of. What say we leave her to make her own way and her own mistakes? It's what makes us who we are, after all, isn't it?"

Suzanne smiled. "I suppose you're right. And things always turn out like they should in the end. Nice talking with you, Evie." With that she rose to her feet and went in pursuit of the drink her sister had poured for her.

"Don't listen to anything she says about Jos, Evie," Clara said. "She's got a terrible crack on for her, has done for years. Jos made the mistake of hinting that something could happen one night, when she was feeling a little low, and since then our dear Suzanne has believed that she is just the woman Jos needs to save her from herself."

"Does Jos need saving?" Evelyn asked. She found she trusted Clara's judgement.

"Not really. She's got some demons, but haven't we all? She needs accepting, not saving. Do you think you can do that?" Clara levelled her gaze at Evelyn.

Evelyn was briefly taken aback, but she knew the answer at once. "Of course I can. I wouldn't want to change her. I think she's wonderful just how she is."

"I won't lie, Evie. She's been with quite a lot of women and never settled for one. She's been known to leave a lady's bed before dawn, which isn't the done thing at all. But she's a good woman and I think I can say for sure that she won't do that to you."

Evelyn flushed at the idea of discussing sharing a bed with Jos. Clara seemed to notice, but went on regardless. "And you're going to have to make the first move. That's what I came over here to tell you.

She's terrified of pushing you too far or too fast. So if you want her, Evie, do something about it."

"How do I know for sure if I want her?" Evelyn asked, her heart in her mouth.

Clara smiled. "Oh, you want her, my dear. But in case you don't believe me…Does your heart beat faster when you think of her? Do your palms prickle with sweat and the urge to touch her? Could you look at her for hours and never get bored? Do you feel a deep urge at the meeting of your thighs when you imagine putting your lips on hers? Can you almost taste that kiss already?" Her words were spoken in a husky whisper and, watching her, Evelyn could see that Clara was looking at Courtney when she spoke, describing her own feelings. And yet indecent though it probably was to agree to it, she heard her own feelings described and could not help her response.

"Oh yes. That's it, I do. I want her." She heard the words and knew she would not take them back.

"You can have her tonight, Evie, and she won't leave you in the morning. I've known her long enough to be certain. But she won't risk doing anything else until she's sure. You need to make her sure."

"How?" Evelyn asked. "How do I convince her?"

"When the moment comes, you'll know," Clara said. Evelyn felt her hand squeeze her shoulder in reassurance.

"Thank you," she said.

"I'll get jealous if you two spend any longer talking to each other," interupted Courtney, coming to stand next to Clara.

"No you won't, my love, you'll just worry you're missing out on some gossip." Clara stroked Courtney's face affectionately. "And you're not."

"Hmm, well, even if I am, I always find out. You can't keep secrets."

"It's very true, I admit." Clara held her hands up. "Don't ever tell me anything you don't want Courtney to know, Evie. She tortures it out of me."

"I do nothing of the sort."

"It's cruel and unusual," Clara insisted, still directing her words to Evie.

"I'll show you cruel and unusual, dearest."

"Oh, promises, promises." Clara raised a seductive eyebrow, then grinned. "Shall I fetch us all another drink?"

As she went to do just that, Jos returned to Evelyn's side. "Sorry," she said, "I didn't mean to leave you alone."

"Evie's been fine, Clara and I have been looking after her," Courtney said.

"That's what concerns me," Jos replied. Evelyn smiled her reassurance.

"Really, I've been perfectly all right," she said, although Jos's concern for her was endearing. Clara's words were full in her thoughts now. As Jos smiled back at her, she knew she wanted her and she knew she would have to act. Now she only wondered when she would know it was the right time.

To Jos's mind, Evelyn looked more beautiful than ever, even though the signs of tiredness were beginning to show around her eyes. She was relaxed and comfortable, the effects of the gin bringing the colour to her cheeks. Although this was far from her home and far from the comfort of her family, she had a sense of seeing Evelyn as she truly was, of glimpsing something of her essence. In many ways it was remarkable how comfortable she was, here amongst strangers. Not just strangers—she could not deny it, Evelyn was oddly comfortable considering she was in a room full of lesbians and had just declared her own fascination for Jos. What Jos couldn't decide was if that was a good sign or not.

Was Evelyn so comfortable because she'd finally found a group of people she felt at one with, a gathering where she was able to be herself? Or was it that she felt so at ease because she did not feel the same tension, the same anticipation, as Jos did, was not feeling that her own situation was at all relevent to the other women in the room? How would she know?

There was something in Evelyn's expression that spoke of knowing rather than innocence, that told she was expecting something to happen. But Jos was frightened. She did not want to experience rejection but nor did she want to find herself in too deep. Her feelings for Evelyn were strong and she was uncertain where that could lead. That was not the case in most of her relationships. And Evelyn, who had surely expected her life to lead to marriage, would expect a reliable and trustworthy lover, someone to protect her. Jos was not sure she could fulfil that role if it was demanded of her. And yet, there was something so compelling about Evelyn, she thought she might be able to try.

The guests at the party began to leave after the clock on the mantel struck midnight. Evelyn and Jos drained the last of their drinks and continued in conversation with Clara and Courtney, until they were the only four left in the room. Evelyn was very content to listen to the stories other people wanted to tell her, Jos noticed, absorbing the information, clearly imagining worlds beyond her own. Now Clara and Courtney were telling her of their school days. Jos had already learnt the sadness Evelyn carried over the end of her own education. Now she was listening, intrigued, as Clara talked about the prefect system at their rather exclusive school.

Jos herself had left school at sixteen. She'd been passably academic but far too interested in learning about the world around her to stay into the upper forms. It always seemed a little odd to her to see young ladies of seventeen and eighteen still wearing a school uniform, running around playing hockey and calling their mistresses *ma'am*. But then Jos had always been told she was mature before her time. She'd never really considered it a failing. Yet seeing Evelyn's longing for the education she'd been forced to leave made her dwell on it for a moment.

The clock chimed half-past midnight. Jos was suddenly filled with a new anxiety. How did this night end? That moment was rapidly approaching.

"Good heavens! I know half-past twelve is hardly the latest we've all been awake, but I am beginning to consider my beauty sleep," Courtney announced.

"Actually, I'm a little sleepy too," Evelyn said. "And I still have to work out how to get back to the Graingers' house from here. Lucky I brought the spare key they gave me."

"I'm quite sure Jos will be the gentleman and make sure you get home safely," Clara prompted.

"Of course I will," Jos said, horrified that Evelyn might have thought otherwise. What Jos was really thinking was that she did not want to take Evelyn back to Lilian. She wanted to keep her by her side.

"Then perhaps it's time to call this little soiree to a close. Until next time. Are you doing anything for Christmas and New Year?"

"Gosh, it's Christmas soon isn't it?" Evelyn exclaimed. "I'd almost entirely forgotten."

Jos watched Evelyn's face and knew she was thinking of home. Christmas was a time of home and family after all. "It's next week," she said gently. "And no, Courtney, no special plans. Christmas will be quiet, I suppose, and I imagine I'll end up at the Orchid for New Year. It's always a good party there."

"I'll be there," Evelyn interjected. "Lilian is singing, so I said I would definitely be there. She has a new dress."

"I'm sure it'll be delightful," Clara said, with a small smirk. Jos saw Evelyn's discomforted reaction. She had to remember that Evelyn had been dependent on Lilian's kindness until now and that evinced a certain loyalty, even if she didn't have a lot of time for the woman herself. Clara continued, "I think we'll be there too. Especially if we're certain some of our friends will be there."

"I'll look forward to seeing you again," Jos said. She rose to her feet and placed her empty glass on the small table to the side. "So, we'll say goodnight for now." She leaned in to embrace Clara, followed by Courtney.

As Courtney's powdered face brushed past her ear, Courtney whispered, "Kiss her," just loud enough for Jos to hear but no one else.

When they parted, Jos looked at her dubiously, doubting she'd heard the words. But Courtney's expression was the giveaway. She had an imperative look about her that would take no arguments.

Evelyn had also embraced both Clara and Courtney, so they took their coats and hats from the hooks close to the door and descended the stairs, calling their goodbyes as they went. Moments later, from the immaculate, understated glamour and warmth of Clara and Courtney's flat they were in the cold of a late-December night. Under the lamplight, the street was full of long shadows and above them twinkled a host of stars in the strip of night sky they could see between the tall buildings. The clear skies promised frost in the morning.

Their breath came in plumes of vapour and Evelyn shivered slightly. Jos hesitated. Either they would begin to walk towards Hays Mews and the Graingers' house, or now was the time to do something. Evelyn was looking at her, expectantly. She felt full of confusion, of wanting to do the right thing by Evelyn, by her own feelings, of wondering whether to heed Courtney's advice or whether to show more patience.

In the end, her courage failed her. She looked into Evelyn's eyes for a long moment, then turned towards Hays Mews. "Come on then, it's this way to the Graingers' place. We'll be there in a few minutes. We shouldn't get too cold if we walk quickly enough."

She set off along the street, her heart crushed with disappointment but no one to blame but herself. Then she felt Evelyn's hand on her arm, pulling her back. She turned to find Evelyn looking intently into her eyes. Evelyn's hands were still clutching her sleeves and now her upper arms, pulling her closer, not letting her leave. She could see Evelyn's desire, her need. The cold disappointment burnt away in a flare of hot urgency and suddenly consequences were unimportant. She took Evelyn's face in her hands, noticing the cool smoothness of her skin, and pulled her closer. There was no fear in Evelyn's eyes. The desire was mutual. Jos pressed closer, feeling Evelyn's clothing rub against her own, Evelyn's breath on her face.

Their lips met, hot and dry against the cold of the night. Jos pulled back, the electric shock of the kiss almost too much. "Evelyn, I don't know…" She began to try to articulate in a whisper.

She was silenced by Evelyn pressing her lips back against her mouth. Jos wrapped her hand around the back of Evelyn's neck, let her fingers slide into her soft hair. Evelyn moved her hands from Jos's arms to her back as the kiss deepened, growing in passion. A small moan escaped Evelyn's throat, an expression of something raw and previously unexpressed, and it spurred Jos on with further confidence. She pulled Evelyn tighter into her body.

In the shadows of the street lights, sounds of the night-time city drifting past on the cold winter breeze, Jos felt as though something long dead had rekindled inside her as Evelyn kissed her with a passion that spoke of a real hunger.

Jos eventually pulled back. "Evie, don't go back to the Graingers' house tonight. Come to my apartment. It's not far from here."

She hoped Evelyn knew what she was asking. Somehow, she seemed to. Her nodded agreement was enthusiastic and wordless. Evelyn's eyes were shining, her breath coming quickly now, as Jos took her hand and led her through the city to her refuge.

CHAPTER FIFTEEN

Jos's first floor flat was on Dover Street, above a jewellery shop. They walked quickly and silently, the connection of their joined hands enough to maintain the heat between them. Evelyn dared not speak, lest the spell be broken.

She was full of nerves and worry about what was about to occur but could not force herself to change the course of the night. Her desire was too strong, as was her curiosity. This was what she wanted above all else in this moment. To be with Jos, in every way that she could be with her, even though some of those ways were a mystery to her. She wanted the mystery to unravel in Jos's hands.

The doorway at the side of the shop was narrow, as was the staircase leading to the flat above. Jos clearly did not spend as much money on her accommodation as Clara and Courtney or the Graingers. Insomuch as she could spare room in her mind to consider this, Evelyn decided it was something else in Jos's favour. Her home was comfortable and it suited her.

The stairs opened into a sitting room, with a settee, two armchairs, and a writing desk in the corner. Jos led Evelyn into the centre of the room, switching on a lamp on a small table by the settee. The room was bathed in yellow light, warm and soft. There was no fire in the hearth and the room was chilly, but compared to the outside it was comfortable. Evelyn took off her coat and Jos laid it aside in one of the chairs, adding her own jacket to it.

Evelyn, breathing hard and very aware of the pounding of her heart, stood in the centre of the room watching Jos. Jos was looking back at her, as if deciding what she should do. There was a certain tension in Jos's shoulders and Evelyn wondered what she was thinking. This would be much easier, she thought, if each knew what the other was thinking.

Jos approached her slowly, as if frightened she might attempt an escape. But Evelyn was going nowhere. She stood perfectly still as Jos came closer, then reached for Jos's warm hands, pulling her closer still. Encouraged, Jos leaned in and kissed her again. Evelyn felt the power of the kiss through the whole of her body. Even her fingers and toes seemed to tingle as Jos's lips moved against hers. Now she knew how a kiss was supposed to feel, everything felt clear, and she felt a flood of relief that she was here, now, with Jos.

Jos's hands were caressing her back, from her hips to her hairline. Evelyn revelled in the touch, moving with Jos, crushing herself closer to her. All she could feel was the deepest longing she'd ever experienced, the most painful hunger. Only Jos could satisfy it.

Jos stopped kissing her and took half a step back. Her eyes were glassy, her breath coming hard. "Evie, are you sure about this?"

"Don't I seem sure?" she replied, breathless herself.

"I would never do anything to hurt you. Tell me if this isn't what you want." Jos's plea was clearly from her heart.

"Jos, this is what I want. More than anything." She looked deeply into Jos's eyes and left her in no doubt. A low sound of desire came from Jos's throat as she pressed her mouth back against Evelyn's in a deep, passionate kiss.

This time Evelyn pulled back. "Are you sure this is what you want?" she asked, suddenly anxious.

"Oh God, Evie, yes." Jos tried to kiss her again. Evelyn did not doubt her desire.

"You have to know though"—Evelyn was quite embarrassed now—"I've never…I mean, I don't know what to do." She looked down, only to find Jos's fingers under her chin raising her face again.

"Evie, there's not a certain formula. I want to *be* with you. It doesn't matter what we do. You do what you feel." Jos paused, then grinned, a gesture that released the tension between them. "Although there are a few tricks I can demonstrate…"

Evelyn laughed with her, intrigued, almost unable to believe this was happening to her, that she could be so fortunate as to be here, with Jos.

"Can I take you to my bed now, Evie?" Jos asked. She was still holding Evelyn, who felt another surge of heat on hearing that question.

"Yes," she whispered. Jos took her hand and led her to a door on the far side of the sitting room. She opened it and turned on a lamp inside the door, to reveal a large bedstead with a brass frame, draped in a pale green bedspread. The room was fairly plain, with dark wood furniture and rugs covering the floorboards. Jos closed the bedroom door behind them and Evelyn felt perfectly safe in the small, intimate room with Jos.

Unsure what to do, Evelyn stood just inside the door. Jos came to stand behind her and reached up, massaging her shoulders gently. Evelyn relaxed at her touch. Then she felt Jos's lips on the soft skin at the back of her neck and her knees felt weak. Jos unfastened the button that secured the top of Evelyn's dress, at the back of the collar, and moved her kisses into the small triangle of exposed skin. Evelyn gasped at the intimacy of the touch, as Jos's hands came up to her hips, stroking the curve of her waist.

Evelyn turned to face Jos and leaned in for another kiss. Kissing Jos was such a pleasure, it was difficult to stop, until Jos took a step back. "Have a seat," she said, softly. Evelyn did as she was told and perched on the edge of the firm mattress.

Smiling, Jos began to unfasten the necktie she'd added to her outfit before they'd visited Clara and Courtney. She removed it quickly and then her fingers went to the buttons of her shirt. One by one, she opened them. Evelyn watched in awe, fascinated and compelled, as Jos revealed more of herself. Underneath the shirt, Jos wore a strip of fabric bound around her breasts, clearly with the intention of flattening them to her chest. Now, she loosened the pin at the side and unwound it carefully until her small rounded breasts were naked, pink nipples erect in the cool air.

Evelyn felt her chest tighten at such an intimate view of Jos's body. And now she did not want to be just a spectator. She was on her feet, helping Jos with the fastening of her trousers, her fingers fumbling but eager. Jos slid the trousers down her legs and removed them, taking socks and shoes with them and throwing the lot into a crumpled heap at the side of the room. Only her underwear remained. Evelyn stood back again, suddenly shy, allowing Jos to remove the last of her garments until she was entirely naked. Her skin was olive and smooth, with few imperfections except for a few faded scars on one of her legs. Her hips curved more than Evelyn expected. Evelyn's eyes were drawn to the triangle of dark hair at the top of her thighs. Jos seemed happy to let her look.

Without her clothes, Jos did not look vulnerable, just alluring. Her stance was one of confidence, of sensual energy and power. Evelyn wanted to touch her, to share that power. To see Jos like this, stripped of everything false, was moving in a way she had not expected.

Evelyn felt rather overdressed herself now. However shy she was, however dubious she could exude the same raw power as Jos, she wanted to join her in the intimacy. She began to fumble with the fastenings of her dress.

Jos came towards her. "Let me help."

It was Jos's hands that unfastened buttons and helped her from her dress, then her chemise and petticoat. In her girdle and stockings, nothing else, she felt exposed, crossing her arms over her chest, as the air on her skin made it clear just how naked she was. But Jos was understanding. She stood back and gazed at Evelyn, making no secret of her eyes exploring Evelyn's body.

"You're beautiful, Evie. A beautiful woman." She took Evelyn's hands gently and pulled them away from her body, dropping her eyes only briefly. "All of you." She leaned in to kiss Evelyn again.

Evelyn felt the press of her own skin against Jos's body, and the fire, briefly dampened by her shyness, rekindled. Now she wanted rid of the girdle and stockings, and pulled at them hurriedly, managing to put her finger through one of the stockings in the process. She did not care. In moments she was as naked as Jos and hungry for more kisses. This time, as they kissed, she could feel Jos's nakedness against the whole length of her body. Breasts crushed against breasts, hot skin caressed and pressed, and she felt the tickle of that thick hair against her thigh.

Still locked in an embrace, Jos urged her towards the bed again. Together they fell onto it. Jos's hand crept over Evelyn's body now, stroking her neck, the valley between her breasts, down over her stomach and thighs, and back to caress her breast softly. Evelyn gasped and arched her back, feelings more intense than any she'd ever known filling her every cell. She felt awash with emotions she could not explain, only wanted more of Jos's touch, felt a burning urge to be touched in places she'd never thought she'd want anyone to touch her.

Jos sat back, contemplating Evelyn lying on the bedspread. Under her gaze, Evelyn luxuriated on the soft bed, feeling beautiful in Jos's eyes, beginning to understand that she was just as alluring to Jos as Jos was to her.

Jos looked at Evelyn lying in her bed and her heart soared. True, she had urgent desires located rather a long way south of her heart, but Evelyn seemed to touch her soul as well as arousing her body. This was something different, special, and she would take her time to savour it.

She was enjoying seeing Evelyn's confidence growing. Where she'd expected shy awkwardness, she was finding Evelyn more relaxed and spontaneous. Now she stretched out on the bed like an artist's model, arms above her head, one knee bent. Jos could do nothing but gaze.

She began with a contemplation of Evelyn's face. She was smiling and relaxed, but not without an expression of wanting in her eyes, as she looked back at Jos. Jos smiled a reassurance. "I want to look at you, Evie." Evelyn's face showed the positive effect of this statement, as she resigned herself to Jos's attention.

Jos ran her eyes along Evelyn's long, slender arms to her graceful fingers and back over the pink skin to her delicately rounded breasts, their nipples darker pink than she anticipated. Her eye was drawn by the growth of chestnut hair beneath Evelyn's arms. Most of the women she'd been with in recent years had adopted the ridiclous trend of shaving that hair away, claiming it made them more feminine in their modern sleeveless dresses. Jos had very little time for fashion and certainly did not understand a trend that made women alter their natural state so dramatically. Hair in the underarm was a sign of a grown woman, and Jos loved the way a woman's natural scent caught in that hair and lingered tantalisingly. Lightly, she ran her fingers over the inside of Evelyn's arm, following the soft skin from the crook of her elbow all the way to those soft hairs, where her touch made Evelyn giggle slightly. Jos smiled and turned her touch into a full caress of Evelyn's breasts, making Evelyn breathe harder and arch her back again, as if craving more contact.

Now her gaze and hands slid lower, over Evelyn's flat stomach, around the curve of her hips and down towards her legs. Once more, she encountered downy hair where most modern women had unforgiving stubble from the razor. She caressed Evelyn's skin as far as her deliciately shaped toes, and then followed a path that went along the insides of Evelyn's thighs. Since Evelyn had naturally lain down with one leg bent, she was already partially exposed to Jos's hungry eyes. She let her fingers slide all the way to the top of Evelyn's thigh, until she could feel the damp heat so close to her skin.

Evelyn's breathing had changed now. Jos read a mixture of arousal and anxiety in her expression. She wanted Evelyn to feel safe with her. "Evie, can I see you? Can I touch you? I want it more than anything."

"What do I have to do?" Evelyn asked, her voice hoarse.

Jos cursed a world in which it was thought a good idea to keep a woman in ignorance of the pleasures her body could offer to her. Evelyn sounded so nervous. "You don't have to do anything, sweetheart. Just breathe, and feel, and let me show you…" She ran her hand over Evelyn's inner thigh again, this time applying just enough pressure to guide Evelyn's legs apart, to allow her gaze to fall entirely on her sex, with its curls of chestnut hair, already moist. Jos caught Evelyn's scent and it was like a drug to her. She slid her fingers slowly into that soft hair, seeking the silky wetness slowly, exploring Evelyn and letting Evelyn feel every sensation.

Jos knew women's bodies. She knew where to touch Evelyn to create the greatest pleasure. But for some time she held off, teasing and caressing. She did not want to deny the pleasure—she wanted to prolong it for both of them. Evelyn began to move her hips against every slight touch, letting Jos know she needed more, even without being fully aware of it herself. Jos moved her gentle touch to the spot she knew would send pleasure through the whole of Evelyn's body. All she wanted to do was pleasure her, show her the secrets of her body. She could feel her own body's response to Evelyn in the wetness on her thighs. But her need could wait, for now she wanted to focus on Evelyn and nothing more.

She could resist no longer, so she removed her massaging fingers and replaced them with lips and tongue. Evelyn's taste was perfection. Jos wanted to lose herself in her scent. Not all women tasted so good, but Evelyn she wanted to devour.

When Evelyn realised what was happened, she raised her head, clearly surprised to see Jos's head between her thighs, to feel the intensity of the new sensation. But she simply sighed in pleasure and relaxed. Evelyn's acceptance of the pleasure Jos wanted to give her encouraged Jos all the more.

Evelyn looked down the length of her body to where she could see the crown of Jos's head, her black hair blending with the chestnut hair of her own body. It was so awfully indecent to allow this to happen, she thought, with no inclination to act on the musing. Waves of sensation rippled through her, each more intense than the first, waves that did not quite break, rather building up a sense of anticipation, building, building. Jos's mouth and fingers teased and caressed and massaged. She could feel Jos's breath on her, Jos's shoulder against the inside of her thigh. She reached down and touched Jos's head, stroked her soft hair. This was Jos, who she had thought she could desire, a woman who loved woman, and her mouth was making Evelyn soar to places she'd never known she could reach.

The waves were more frequent now, changing to feel like ripples spreading out from where Jos's mouth moved against her. Now it was almost too intense and her legs started to tremble under Jos's attention. She tried to close them involuntarily, only managing to press them to Jos, who increased her pressure and urgency in response. Her hand twisted in Jos's hair, her other bunching up the bedspread, as the feelings grew so intense she did not think she could possibly survive this.

"Oh..." She moaned, her body tensing. Jos did not stop. Everything seemed focused on that one point of sensation between her legs. And then the wave broke, crashing over her with a release of the tension and a flood of pleasure. She cried out with the unfamiliarity, with the pleasure and the intensity, trying simultaneously to push Jos away and pull her closer, her hips jerking against Jos as she closed her eyes, her head tilting back against the pillow, and the wave broke again.

Eventually, Jos pulled away with a soft kiss. She sat at the end of the bed, looking at Evelyn with pleasure in her eyes. Evelyn, breathless and sweating, looked at her through a haze, speechless. What did one say at such a time? She could not begin to articulate what had just happened.

"Jos," she said at last, reaching out a hand and taking Jos's fingers in hers. "I don't know what to say. I've never—"

"Hush, Evie, you don't need to say anything." Jos leaned forward to stroke Evelyn's hair. "You know, it's been referred to as *la petite mort*, reaching one's climax."

"The little death?" Evelyn said, still breathless. "I can see why. I didn't know—" Evelyn could scarce believe it had been possible for her to feel this way all along and she'd never known it was possible. Might never have known.

Jos smiled. "I know. But now you do."

"I feel a little embarrassed." Evelyn wasn't sure if embarrassed was the correct word.

Jos slid up the bed to lie by her side, half covering her body with her own. "Don't be embarrassed, Evie. That was one of the most beautiful things I've ever bloody seen."

Evelyn heard real emotion in Jos's tone and barely noticed the profanity. She wrapped an arm around Jos and held her close. Now the burning desire was released, she felt just as strong a need to be close to Jos. They lay still and silent for some time, just together. Then something occurred to Evelyn. "Isn't it supposed to happen for both of us?"

Jos turned her face to look at Evelyn properly. "What?"

"The little death."

Now Jos grinned. "Well, there aren't any rules, like I said. Nothing's *supposed* to happen. But it can be nice if it happens for me too."

Evelyn suddenly felt her inexperience again. "But I don't know how—"

"I wouldn't expect you to, Evie. And I don't need you to. But if you touch me, and watch me, I can get myself there. If you would like?"

The idea of watching Jos do something so intimate was very compelling. Evelyn felt the heat stirring low in her body again. "Of course," she said. "Show me how."

Evelyn watched as Jos, her back propped against the white pillows, spread her legs very slowly. Her hand travelled up the inside of her thigh, her finger pressing into the dark curls of hair at the top. Jos looked nothing like those oddly coloured diagrams in *Ideal Marriage* and suddenly that book seemed ludicrous. This was something so very different to what it described and yet Evelyn could not feel as though there was anything wrong or perverse in this moment. It was glorious.

Jos used one hand to spread herself, while her other teased her pink flesh. Evelyn watched, captivated, aroused and yet uncertain. How could she help Jos feel the same pleasure she had just experienced? Jos's eyes were on Evelyn's face. Evelyn looked into her eyes then slid her gaze lower, over her firm breasts and back to where her hands worked. She was struck once more with how beautiful Jos was. Evelyn was fairly sure she could gaze at Jos's body forever, felt privileged to have the chance to do so. But she did not just want to watch. Her fingers tingled and twitched with the urge to reach out and touch her.

As if she knew, Jos gestured with her head that Evelyn should come closer. "Come near to me, Evie." Evelyn crawled up the bed to be close to Jos, their legs touching. "Do you want to touch me?" she said. Evelyn could hear the arousal in her voice, a tone deeper than usual.

"Yes, oh yes, I do," Evelyn breathed.

Jos reached out and took her hand. Gently, she pressed Evelyn's hand to her breast, as her other hand continued to move on her sex. Evelyn felt the soft give of Jos's breast, felt her nipple harden under the touch. She squeezed gently, enjoying the sensation. Jos moved her free hand to her other breast, gently pinching and stroking her nipple. Taking the hint, Evelyn did the same with her own fingers, drawing a groan of pleasure from Jos.

Now Jos took her hand and moved it lower. Evelyn breathed harder, felt Jos's smooth skin beneath her fingers as she trailed them over Jos's slightly curved stomach, to the curly mound below, and further still. She could feel the moving of Jos's fingers, feel a moist heat, and nearly stopped breathing as she felt Jos's silky flesh beneath her fingertips.

Jos felt a shudder of pleasure pass through her as Evelyn's fingers made contact. God, but she wanted Evelyn to touch her. She'd never slept with someone as inexperienced as Evelyn before, but it was oddly pleasurable to be patient, take things slowly, watch Evelyn discovering everything for the first time. Her own first time was so long ago, she barely remembered what it was like now. Yet somehow, with Evelyn, the sensations felt different, renewed and more exciting. She was getting close now, as she rubbed herself under Evelyn's gaze, holding back for Evelyn's sake, so that Evelyn could play more than a watching part in this. Now she forced herself to stop and direct Evelyn's fingers to where she needed the touch. "Here, Evie, just as I was doing…ah… yes, that's right."

Evelyn tentatively massaged Jos gently, then rubbed a little harder. Just looking at her, her face intent on the task in hand but cheeks burning with heat, eyes alight with pleasure, was enough to take her right to the edge.

"Evie...don't stop," she panted. Sweat was prickling all over her body now, the waves of pleasure mounting. Impulsively, she grabbed the back of Evelyn's neck and pulled her head down to her chest. "Your mouth, Evie, please," she asked, as Evelyn understood her desire and put her mouth on her hard nipple. Another few strokes of Evelyn's fingers and she could hold it no more. "Oh God, Evie..." she managed, before she had no more words and her climax overtook her. She shuddered, pressing her sex into Evelyn's hand.

As her body relaxed, she took Evelyn in her arms, holding her close. In this, she surprised herself. Sex was hardly ever an emotional experience for her. True enough, most women liked to hold her when they were done and Jos usually reciprocated the superfical, fleeting affection, even found it pleasant. But now she felt as though she wanted to crush Evelyn into her body, hold her so close there was nothing between them. Evelyn looked up at her, a soft smile on her face. "Are you all right, Evie?" Jos asked.

"Oh yes," Evelyn replied. "I'm more than all right. I don't think I have the words."

Jos returned the smile. "You don't have to find words. Just stay with me."

"I don't want to go anywhere," Evelyn said, settling her head against Jos's chest.

Jos closed her eyes and stroked Evelyn's hair. This was peace and it was something she rarely knew. There was no point questioning why she found it in the arms of a girl from the other side of the country. The question that remained was how long it would last. Because, in Jos's experience, it was never that long.

Chapter Sixteen

When Evelyn awoke in the morning, her head was still on Jos's shoulder and her arm draped across Jos's chest. As her vision cleared from slumber, she raised her head to look up at Jos. Jos, already awake, looked back at her. Her expression was questioning and Evelyn suspected Jos half expected her to wake full of regret. Instead, excitement stirred in her stomach and she smiled.

"Good morning," Jos said, relaxing noticeably at Evelyn's obvious happiness.

"Good morning," Evelyn replied. She pressed herself closer to Jos and luxuriated in the warmth of her body, the soft comfort of the sheets against her skin. She'd never slept naked on her own, let alone with someone else, and every sensation was new and wonderful. Briefly, she marvelled at how natural this felt, when it should have been more alien than anything that had happened since she'd been in London. But it was impossible to dwell on anything much, with Jos's eyes on her, Jos's hand stroking her skin softly.

Daylight was creeping around the edge of the curtains. Jos's bedroom felt very different to how it had in the lamplight of the night before. The gin, which gave the world soft edges, was entirely worn off. Yet the pale daylight and sober morning did not detract from the glory of being here with Jos.

"You've not run from my bed in horror," Jos said finally.

"No, why would I?" Evelyn replied, wondering if such a thing had happened to Jos in the past.

"I don't know. I suppose I was frightened that in the light of day you'd feel differently. Or that you'd suddenly realise what you'd done and decide it was a step too far."

Evelyn twisted and sat up so she could look at Jos properly. The sheets droped to reveal her naked shoulders and she had a moment of feeling vulnerable, until looking into Jos's face made her safe and confident. "I actually wish I could just stay here with you today. I don't want to go anywhere."

Jos looked relieved and then smiled a more lascivious smile. "Oh, you'd like a repeat of last night, would you?" She raised a questioning eyebrow.

"Of course I would." Evelyn paused to consider. "I never knew, I really never knew…"

"Why would you?"

"But it terrifies me to think that I could've gone through my whole life not knowing what it could be like. I could've never felt what I did last night, or what I do right now."

Jos's face grew more serious. "But now you do know, Evie. You don't have to be frightened of anything."

"Not with you here," Evelyn replied. As long as Jos was with her, she could achieve anything.

"No, Evie. Don't depend on me or anyone else. Just live your life."

"I am doing," Evelyn replied, unavoidably thinking of Edward's words all those years ago, of her promise. She smiled to herself, thinking that this last adventure was one she would not tell her brother about. "I'm flying."

"Like a bird?" Jos asked, apparently not quite following Evelyn's thoughts.

"No," Evelyn said. "Like a butterfly. Like my brooch, the one you returned to me that first night. I was wearing it because of something my brother and I talked about once. About being free to fly."

"And you are, Evie. To fly on beautiful wings."

Evelyn smiled. "They're fragile wings too." Her unpleasant dream came back to her. "I don't know that it's a good analogy sometimes. A butterfly is so delicate, its life so fleeting."

"Each butterfly lives a whole lifetime. A life of flying into the sky, drinking the nectar of myriads of flowers, drifting on the breeze. A rainbow of colour."

"I felt fragile on my own. But with you, it's different," Evelyn said. It was true. However much her confidence had grown during her time in London, she was still feeling a precarious loneliness, the lack of a real confidante. Now she had found Jos and surely she could now depend on her. It would be impossible to have shared what they had and not to continue that bond. Wouldn't it? Suzanne Flint's warning about Jos came back to her, countered by Clara's reassurance. A slight shadow had come over Jos's face, but their fingers were still entwined and warm together.

"I don't want you to feel like you're only strong because of what you're sharing with me," Jos said. There was a real insistence in her tone. "Your life is yours and you never know what might happen. You have your own wings and I don't think they're really so fragile."

Evelyn was quiet, unsure if Jos was trying to reassure her or hint that she could not rely on Jos, even if she wanted to. "I know that," she said in the end.

Jos must have sensed her slight confusion, since she reached out for Evelyn, drew her close, and dispelled all the doubts with a long kiss. Evelyn melted into the kiss, into Jos, as she felt Jos's hands slide over the curves of her body. In the end, the moment, this moment, was more important than any worry about the future.

As it turned nine o'clock, Jos walked Evelyn back to the Graingers' house. She did not want to but there was really no way to avoid it any longer. She had to be at the theatre by late morning and Evelyn really needed to return to what was, for now, her home. For Evelyn's sake, she was hoping Lilian hadn't missed her.

Walking around Berkeley Square, they passed a well-dressed young couple strolling hand in hand. Jos looked at them with some sadness. She wanted nothing more than to reach out for Evelyn's hand, walk with her as her lover should. Yes, walking arm in arm was acceptable and passable, but linking hands in a way that suggested romance was a little too much of a risk. She did not care for herself, of course. Her reputation was well-known. But she did not want to prompt any kind of speculation about Evelyn. She suspected Evelyn herself had not even begun to contemplate the consequences of her desire for her own sex. It would be a hard lesson and Jos almost regretted waking that urge in Evelyn. But it was impossible to really regret helping her be true to herself, whatever the cost. In Jos's book, honesty with yourself was more important than nearly anything else.

As they approached Hays Mews and Lilian and James's house, Jos came to a stop.

"It's just down here," Evelyn said, clearly not understanding why they'd stopped.

"I know where they live," Jos said. "Not that I make a habit of visiting Lilian and James but I have had cause to call on them on one or two occasions. I've stopped because I can't walk you to the door."

"Why ever not?" Evelyn asked, looking bewildered.

"I don't know if they'll have missed you or not, but it's not going to be very helpful to you if I walk you to the door. Since they know you were with me yesterday." Jos knew Evelyn would not easily understand her.

"But I have been with you. If they ask where I've been, I was going to tell them." Even as she said it, Evelyn's voice betrayed that she'd not really considered what she was going to say to Lilian until now.

Jos watched realisation dawn.

"I suppose I can't just do that though, can I?"

"You could. But I would prefer that you didn't, for my own sake." Jos did not want to find herself suddenly labelled as the corrupter of the innocent, not at this early stage. Nor did she feel like inciting Lilian's wrath and judgement while Lilian was still entangled with Vernon. "I wouldn't ask you to keep it a secret just for me though. It's for your own sake too. I know you're not used to this, Evie, but you do have to be careful who you tell about things like this. Lilian won't understand, and do you think James is any more likely to?"

Evelyn suddenly looked quite scared and Jos felt a deep concern for her, almost a regret that she'd brought such complexities into Evelyn's life.

"You're right," Evelyn said. "I can't tell them. Lilian would hate me. And I think James would probably tell me to leave his house."

"I'm sorry, Evie," Jos said, angry that any duplicity was needed.

"It's not your fault." Evelyn took Jos's arm. "And if you're worried, I don't regret what we've done just because I can't be honest with Lilian and James."

Jos breathed a sigh of relief that Evelyn had volunteered those words, without Jos having to ask. "Thank you, Evie. I'd hate for you to regret it. But what will you say if they've noticed you didn't come home last night?"

Evelyn thought for a moment. "Well, surely I can say that we took tea with some friends of yours and then I felt a little unwell, so they allowed me to stay for the night instead of having to travel home."

Jos considered this. It was an unlikely story and one Lilian would most likely not believe. However, she did not think that Lilian would suspect the truth either, so it was a good enough excuse. Perhaps it would do Evelyn good in Lilian's eyes to have a little mystery about her. "I think that will be good enough," she said. "If she asks which friends, tell her Sarah and Suzanne Flint. She knows of them, though they've only met very briefly. But because they're sisters, it won't seem like I've been taking you to gatherings where you might be corrupted. She wouldn't approve if you said it was Clara and Courtney."

"Very well," Evelyn said. "It seems silly to have to do this so we don't annoy Lilian though."

Jos understood that sentiment all too well. "It's not really about whether Lilian's annoyed. It's more about what she thinks of you—and me—especially since you're living here at the moment." There was something else too. She still did not trust that this would become any kind of long-term relationship. She was certainly not ready to commit to that herself. Telling anyone what had happened between them would tie her into something with Evelyn. Much as Evelyn delighted her, aroused her, made her heart leap with happiness, she did not dare trust that it would last, did not dare make that decision yet. Telling people would not help her remove herself from the situation should it not work out. She did not want to tell Evelyn this, of course. It was already plain that Evelyn expected more. Jos wanted more too but did not want to do anything that made it inevitable, just in case.

"I do understand," Evelyn said, looking worried as she watched Jos's expression. "Please don't think I mind. If it means we can be this way with each other, I'd lie to anyone I had to."

Jos smiled a bitter smile. "I know, Evie. I just wish you didn't have to. Now, you better get inside."

"When will we see each other again?" Evelyn asked.

"I don't know. What are you doing at Christmas?" She watched the shadow pass over Evelyn's face and knew the mention of Christmas had brought on a thought of home. She did not want Evelyn to be alone at Christmas, she realised.

"Well, Lilian and James are going to their family, out in the country somewhere. She invited me but I said I would feel a little strange intruding on it, and actually I'd rather be on my own, to write to my family."

Jos could hear a heartbreaking sadness in Evelyn's words and knew that, however brave Evelyn seemed, however well adapted to this life in London, thoughts of home and what she had left behind were still heavy on her shoulders. "Oh, well, if that's what you want to do—"

"It's not really," Evelyn interjected. "I mean, it is, I do want to write to my brother and my parents. But I don't want to be on my own all day. I just told Lilian that because I didn't want to have to go with them. I'd have hated it, I think." She looked expectantly at Jos, clearly awaiting an invitation but not liking to presume.

"In that case, would you like to come to my flat? I can't promise anything spectacular, but some friends will be coming around—no one you need to worry about—and possibly Vernon too."

"Vernon?" Evelyn looked dubious.

"He's all right, you know, Evie." Jos totally understood why Evelyn might have her doubts about her brother. "I know he's involved with Lilian but he doesn't really tell her anything, not if I know my brother. And he's a more honourable man than you'd expect."

"Of course," Evelyn said.

"And if he's been flirting with you, he'll soon stop when he sees you're with me," Jos concluded, knowingly.

Evelyn smiled an acknowledgement. "In that case, yes, I would love to spend some of Christmas with you."

Jos tried to stop a stupid grin spreading over her face. "I'll look forward to it very much," she said. "If you can find your way, come at whatever time you are ready." Then she leaned in and kissed Evelyn lightly on the cheek. "Perhaps you'll spend Christmas night with me too," she said softly.

Evelyn looked back at her with desire in her eyes. "Yes," she breathed.

"Until then, Evie." Jos took a step back, reluctantly. Evelyn nodded. Jos forced herself to turn and walk away, for once her mind more full of things to come than fears of what might happen.

❖

When Evelyn let herself into the Graingers' house, she found that both Lilian and James had already left. A hastily scrawled note on the table in the hallyway read: *Evie, I've gone to my dressmaker again. Last minute alterations. There's breakfast left if you want it. Didn't want to wake you. Lilian.*

There was little in the note to suggest whether Lilian had any questions about how Evelyn had spent the previous evening, but certainly her last words implied that the Graingers had not realised she had never returned home. That was a blessing at least, Evelyn thought. Though she understood the need, she had no desire to tell outright lies to Lilian and James.

She was glad to find she had the house to herself. She went into the sitting room and sat in the comfortable armchair, leaning her head back and gazing at the ceiling.

Her mind was so full of new memories, new ideas, of thoughts of the future, of lingering sensations and fears she'd never dreamed she would feel, that it was difficult to pick one thought from the maelstrom in her head. A memory would come of Jos's mouth on her body, of those intense pleasures she'd never imagined, and then it would be superceded by the gentle peace of waking with her body pressed close to Jos's. Tension would rise when she thought of having to lie, or when she remembered the warning she'd received about Jos, but then a happy anticipation would come when she imagined what Christmas with Jos would be like.

Her overwhelming feeling was one of excitement, of having overcome an obstacle she did not even know existed, perhaps even relief. One night with Jos seemed to have opened up a whole side of herself she had not previously understood. It was as though the part of her that was always dissatisfied, always searching for something more, finally had its answer. And that answer was Jos.

It barely occurred to her to find it strange that she should be experiencing these feelings, this fulfilment, from becoming romantically, sensually involved with a woman. Although back in West

Coombe, it would have been a strange and remarkable, perhaps even indecent, set of circumstances, here in London it did not seem any more extraordinary than the elaborate outfits, the stark haircuts, the frantic dancing, and the intoxicating jazz. In this world, was anything really extraordinary? She could not help the way she felt. And no man had ever inspired such feelings in her. Besides, had she not just spent an evening with a roomful of women who also felt this way about their own sex? They all seemed happy, intelligent, decent people. Who they chose to share their beds with, and their intimate moments, was surely unimportant. It was as clear as day that a woman could not only form an attachment to another woman, but could love another woman as deeply as husbands and wives loved each other, if not more so. Clara and Courtney demonstrated that. Of all the hopes and tensions she found were now roaming her thoughts and stirring in the pit of her stomach, that she had fallen for someone of her own sex was the least of them. Although she could not imagine what they would say at home in West Coombe.

The notion made her laugh out loud, despite the usual pang of sadness that came with thinking of home. Her existence here felt so separate, so different. She could hardly imagine Jos in West Coombe, let along being there with her, being presented as the person she was courting.

This gave her pause. Were they courting? After all, it was not as though courting, in this case, would lead to an engagement. She could not marry Jos. Besides, they had already been far more intimate than a courting couple was supposed to be. She already understood that amongst modern young people such intimacy was nothing to be surprised about, and she was sensible enough not to assume it meant there was anything deeper between them. It was not that they had shared a bed, it was more that they had shared real feelings, an emotional intimacy. She was drawn to Jos irrevocably and she was fairly sure that Jos felt the same. But it was difficult to fit such a connection into the known patterns of courting between men and women, as she had known them. Perhaps she would ask Jos, the next time she saw her, to define their relationship a little more clearly.

The next time she saw her. Happily, Evelyn put her concerns aside and dwelt again on the happy memories of the night before, teasing herself with the wonderful anticipation of the next time she would be with Jos.

❖

Evelyn spent a lazy day, revelling in her thoughts and memories, rather enjoying having a secret shared between her and Jos alone. She took a bath, remembering the touch of Jos's hands on every part of her naked body. Looking down at herself, she no longer saw a woman's body she barely understood. She felt at one with her body finally, fully aware of its potential for sensation and pleasure. Finally a grown woman who understood the mysteries she had been told she was not meant to understand for the sake of decency.

Late in the afternoon, when Lilian had still not returned and James was still at work, and tired after her late night, she retired to her room for a nap. As she drifted into sleep, she imagined she could feel Jos's arms around her once more. She dreamed of a butterfly, flying in a warm summer sky, and this time nothing came to crush that dream.

When she awoke, it was dark outside, and for a moment she was disorientated, thinking she'd slept into the night. However, a glance at her wristwatch told her it was in fact just before dinner time and the darkness was only that the days were so short this deep into December. James would still be at work, but she was fairly sure she'd been woken by footsteps outside her door.

Evelyn rubbed her eyes and slowly got out of bed. After a moment to steady herself and register that taking a nap had given her rather a headache, she went towards the door, listening. She was keen to find out if Lilian was home, and face any questions, if there were indeed any to come. The longer she avoided it, the longer she would be left wondering if she had been missed at all last night. At the same time, she rather hoped that the first person she saw would not be James. If she heard him arriving home from work, she was prepared to retreat back into her room until dinner time, when she would see them both together.

She heard no one on the landing outside, so she went out, blinking slightly in the electric light after the dark of her bedroom. Now she could more clearly hear that the sound of movement was reaching her from Lilian's attic rooms. "Lilian?" she called, but received no answer. Determined to get this first encounter over with, so she knew whether she would have to lie about her wherabouts or not, she crossed the landing and climbed the narrow flight of stairs that led to Lilian's part of the house.

Lilian was humming to herself, which possibly explained why she had not heard Evelyn's call. Evelyn came into the room to find Lilian seated at her dressing table, with her back to the door. The room was a little more disorderly today, with one or two dresses laid out as if they had been tried on. As before the room sparkled with gems and crystals and sequins, made even more lustrous by the yellow light of the lamps. Lilian was wearing a simple dark pink dress, which rather clashed with the red of her hair, Evelyn thought. She was bending to her left, though Evelyn could not see what she was doing.

"Lilian?" Evelyn said loudly, uncomfortable with watching Lilian while Lilian was unaware of her presence.

Lilian started and turned suddenly, her eyes wide with fear, which turned quickly to anger. A moment later her composure returned and a mask of ambivalence appeared. She hastily laid something down on the dressing table and got to her feet, standing rather obviously in front of whatever she had put down, as if to hide it.

"Yes?" she asked. "I mean, hello, Evie, sorry. I didn't hear you coming."

"I did call out. I didn't mean to interrupt you. I just wanted to say hello, since I've not seen you in the past day."

"Well, yes, hello. I did wonder if you were all right. You must've come in late last night. You weren't with Jos all that time, surely?"

"Oh no. Well, I mean, I was, but not alone. We visited some friends of hers, sisters. Suzanne and Sarah Flint."

"Oh yes, of course. Well, they seem like nice girls, if a little dull. I hope you had a nice time. I was late in myself." Lilian was still standing awkwardly but she had unconsciously shifted a little to her right, revealing more of the surface of her dressing table.

Evelyn could not help but look to see what it was she had been trying to hide, even while she answered. "Yes, I had a nice time. It's good to meet new people—I can't always rely on your friends, can I?" Evelyn smiled, hoping that sentiment wouldn't displease Lilian. Then her smile froze as she finally made out what Lilian had been hiding.

On the dressing table lay a small glass syringe, with metal fittings. She could not help but stare in horror.

Lilian saw her expression change and followed her eyeline. Evelyn looked from the syringe, to Lilian's slightly panicked expression, to the crook of Lilian's left arm. There, against her pale skin, was the tiniest trace of fresh blood. Lilian saw where she was looking and clasped her right hand to the place.

"Whatever's wrong with you?" she demanded of Evelyn, kindness gone from her voice. "Haven't you seen someone injecting medicine before? I got it from my doctor today."

Although it was not something she'd ever expected to encounter in real life, Evelyn was not so lacking in knowledge of the world that she did not know about drugs. There had been famous cases in the newspapers of actresses dying from taking too much, talk of the terrible influence of drugs on soldiers during the war. She was certain that opium and cocaine were now illegal because of their danger and ability to alter the mind. And because they had led to a dangerous black market trade. Suddenly, Evelyn saw Lilian in a new light. To imagine her as part of that dark, dangerous world was difficult but not impossible. A woman so selfish would surely do anything to fulfil her own needs. She stared at Lilian, finding herself beginning to pity her.

"I don't think it is medicine," she said carefully.

"And what would you know?" Lilian retorted. "You'd never even come across gin, let along cocaine."

"Is that what it is, cocaine?" Evelyn asked. "I have heard of that. I've heard that it can kill you."

"Oh, don't be daft. It only kills you if you take too much. You should try it. You've never felt anything like it." Lilian smiled now, but it was not a happy smile.

"I don't want to feel anything like it," Evelyn returned. "And I don't think you should too. Even if you think it's safe, isn't it illegal?"

Lilian laughed. "They only made it illegal because of the war. It's not like I'm a criminal. And plenty of people are doing it these days. It makes you feel so good. And God knows, we need that rush, don't we? You know it too, Evie. When you want to feel something more intense, fill that gap inside you. You don't know what it is, but then you find it... Well, this is how *I* find it. It helps me see how bright the world is, after all those dark, ghastly war years."

"But there are other ways to find that feeling," Evelyn replied, remembering how she felt in Jos's arms, wanting for nothing.

"Ha! The cocktails and gin are nothing on this. And ciggies I barely notice. What else do you suggest? Don't even think about sex! There's really nothing emptier than two people rubbing body parts against each other for a momentary thrill. Not that you'd know. I don't know why I'm explaining myself to you, anyway." Lilian's tone suddenly became dismissive. "Who made you the police?"

Evelyn's heart was heavy. She did not want to argue with Lilian, nor did she want to enter into a discussion about the best way to find fulfilment. All of a sudden, there was a darkness in this so very modern London world she had not stopped to look for. She felt her lack of experience again. Of course it could not all be bright colours and a life lived quickly, full of passion. Below the glittering surface was something altogether more sinister. Here was where the desperation lurked, the driving force that made them all—Evelyn included—try to burn brighter and longer, with more intensity. She suspected Dorothy might have had words for it, that longing, that need, but she did not have them herself. Only she understood it now. Lilian had lived through the pain of loss, seen her world destroyed by war, every bit as much as Evelyn had. Evelyn's escape had been to move to London, to seek a more complex and passionate life. Lilian had already had that life, but she numbed the pain with jazz and fashion and gin, she sang and drank and socialised. But eventually even that was not enough to escape the shadows, so she ran at a pace that was unsustainable without those drugs that now kept her so bright. Evelyn saw it clearly now, but wished she did not.

"I'm not the police," Evelyn said in the end. "And you must do as you like, of course. It's only that it seems awfully dangerous."

"I'll be careful, Evie, don't worry about me." Lilian smiled now, but Evelyn sensed a change in her, as if the warm friendship they had been acting out had begun to dissolve.

"All right," Evelyn said, keen to end this rather hostile encounter. Ultimately, she still liked Lilian and was still dependent on her hospitality. "You know more about it than me, I'm sure."

"Yes. You're still so awfully innocent, aren't you, darling?" Lilian's words sounded patronising now.

Evelyn decided it was best not to rise to her tone. "I am, really," she agreed.

"So it's probably best for me to remind you not to tell anyone about this too." Lilian narrowed her eyes and waited for Evelyn's response.

Evelyn wanted to ask why, if Lilian was so relaxed about taking cocaine, it mattered that it was kept a secret. Lilian's demand had given her away. Evelyn wondered if Vernon knew about her habit. She was more than certain that James did not. It was probably James, and therefore her parents and source of wealth, that Lilian was most concerned about. Evelyn chose not to ask any questions. "Of course, I won't say a word."

"Good, good." Lilian nodded. "Now, don't you have to get ready for dinner?"

Evelyn took the hint and went back down the stairs, leaving Lilian alone. She was not sure what to think of that encounter. True, she was inexperienced in the ways of the world, but Lilian's secrecy and barely concealed anger at having been discovered told her something was very wrong. How insecure in her happiness was Lilian, really? How easy would it be to push her over the edge?

As she returned to her room, Evelyn resolved to be careful of Lilian, though she very much wished that was not the case. She was pondering this when she heard feet on the stairs. Before she could dart into her bedroom door, there was James, the last person she wanted to have a conversation with in that moment.

"Good evening," he said. His tone was cheery and Evelyn felt a little guilty for the tension she experienced whenever she saw him. He was harmless enough and well intentioned. She just wished he did not seem so interested in her.

"Good evening, James. Good day at work?" She attempted a carefree smile. He did not seem to have noticed that she felt anything different.

"Yes, actually. We signed a new contract for the new Tube stations they're planning near Euston."

"That sounds exciting." Evelyn said.

"It is, very. I think the firm will let me lead on the design too."

"Well done. They must think very highly of you." Evelyn was in no doubt they did. She did not have to know James very well to glean that he would be a conscientious and reliable worker, and she knew he was more creative than he seemed on first appearances. James was essentially a good person, but it was a little as though he belonged twenty years earlier, before the war had changed everything, in a time when everything was still in its correct place.

"I like to think so," he said. "I think they respect my abilities."

"You're too modest, I'm sure," Evelyn said, her smile genuine this time. Perhaps she was overreacting regarding James. If Lilian was not her ally any longer, maybe James could be. "They are certainly trusting you with important projects."

"Yes, that's true." James seemed delighted by Evelyn's interest and encouragement. "Listen, Evie, I've been meaning to say sorry we've not gone to the pictures yet. I have every intention but time seems to have rather slipped on by, and now it's nearly Christmas."

"Please don't worry about it," Evelyn said. She was actually rather relieved that the outing had not materialised and was now dismayed that he had remembered. "I've been busy too."

"It's not really cricket though, Evie, to ask you and then not follow through. Now, you know we are away for Christmas, but perhaps immediately afterwards? Between Christmas and New Year, or just after?"

"Yes, of course," Evelyn replied without much enthusiasm. "Whenever you have the time."

"I will make time." He fixed her with that intense gaze again and all of her misgivings returned. There really were no two ways about it—James expected this to go somewhere. He was not just being friendly. In that moment she wished that Jos had not sworn her to secrecy. How she would have loved to tell James and watch his expression as he learned that she was not interested because she'd fallen for another woman, one he so disapproved of. Thinking of Jos, she would have rejected James in that moment, but for her new doubt in her friendship with Lilian. She did not want to find herself thrown onto the street by the Graingers. So she smiled back at James, trying to flatter without encouraging him.

"I'll look forward to it," she said.

"As will I," James replied. "Will you be joining us for dinner this evening? We missed you yesterday."

Evelyn knew he spoke for himself, not Lilian, who had been out the previous evening. "I will be joining you," she said, "but I'm sure my company is not that enjoyable."

"Then you're mistaken," James replied. Then, to her relief, he turned to go to his own room. "See you at dinner."

Evelyn smiled and retreated into her room. She leaned against the back of the closed door and stared across the room at the window. Suddenly everything had changed; her night with Jos, her discovery of Lilian's habit and the new tension between them, made everything different somehow. She no longer felt sure of her place in this new world. But part of that was Jos. And whatever else happened, she had Jos.

CHAPTER SEVENTEEN

The days until Christmas passed with excrutiating slowness. Christmas was when she would see Jos again and it was all she wanted to think about. She spent her days doing her best to avoid Lilian and James. Just seeing them at mealtimes was quite enough. Lilian had almost returned to her usual self; she was lending Evelyn accessories and recommending outfits, she was suggesting sightseeing tours and talking to Evelyn in her usual breezy fashion. Except Evelyn still felt a tension between them, as if Lilian was paying more attention than usual to her, waiting to be challenged or watching for the moment when Evelyn would betray her.

James had become more and more cloyingly attentive to her every need, passing her salt before she needed it, pouring tea when she did not want it. His face brightened when she entered the room. She might have hoped that he would be more awkward in his attentions to her and therefore less able to sustain them, but optimism seemed to have given him confidence and stamina. Her conscience told her she had to be honest with James, but she was unclear exactly how to do so without telling him about Jos.

There was no mention of visiting the Yellow Orchid again, which Evelyn found frustrating. At least it would have been a chance to glimpse Jos, perhaps to talk with her for a short while. Evelyn did not believe that Lilian would go so long without seeing Vernon or without drinking cocktails in her favourite cafe bar, so she suspected that it was rather the case that she was not invited. It was the only noticeable evidence of the new difficulty in her relationship with Lilian. She wondered if Dorothy had asked after her, and what Lilian had told her. And she was glad that, through Jos, she had friends outside of Lilian and her small circle.

About halfway through the week and finding herself with too much spare time, she decided she needed to see Jos. Although she tried to think of an excuse, she could not. In the end she resolved to simply tell Jos that she had missed her and wanted to see her. No one could object to being missed, surely? She was still unsure of the mechanics of a relationship like this one, but going to visit someone you had spent an intense night with did not seem like the wrong thing to do.

First, she tried Jos's flat. The walk from Hays Mews was a short one and she lost nothing by taking an afternoon stroll and ringing the bell. She was not surprised to find Jos away from home. She was presumably at work. However, the sun was shining and, despite the December chill, it was pleasant walking in the fresh air. Curious as to how she would be received alone, she turned her steps toward the Yellow Orchid. It was not Lilian's domain after all—it was a cafe open to the public. She did not need an invitation to go there, especially if her intention was to speak to the proprietor's sister. And going there alone was an act of defiance of Lilian's attempts to control what she did in London.

The pavements and landmarks of this part of Mayfair were becoming familiar to her now, if not entirely well-known. She found the streets of London fascinating, every building with its own majesty, its own sense of importance. Although she might not have taken the most direct route, it did not take her long to find the Yellow Orchid. Her heart beat a little faster as she pushed the door to cross the threshold. However, apart from one or two glances, her entrance attracted very little attention from the customers sipping their afternoon coffee, one or two already drinking cocktails. She paused inside the door, wondering whether to take a seat or ask for Jos at the bar. She did not recognise anyone in the room but she was certainly not the only woman on her own. The indecision was over when her eyes settled on Vernon, who had just entered from the back of the building.

Looking up, he saw her almost instantly and beckoned her over. She was pleased to see him. When she reached him, near the corner of the bar at the back of the cafe, he smiled broadly. Evie smiled back, remembering Jos's words about him and no longer feeling wary. Today he wore a cream and brown windowpane-check suit with a green bow tie. Every element of his outfit was in place. Whatever he'd been doing at the back of the cafe, it had not been manual work, that was for certain.

"Evie!" he said. "Delighted to see you. Can I flatter myself that you're here to suggest a private assignation with the dashing proprietor of the establishment?"

Evelyn could not help but laugh at him. Although she half suspected that, if she was willing, Vernon would proceed with such an assignation, it was now clear that he was nearly always in jest. There was a suggestion that he found everything to be verging on the ridiculous, including himself. His approach was almost modest in its own way and she found it endearing. "I'm afraid not," she replied. "Although I don't know how it can be that I'm resisting the temptation."

Now Vernon smiled a more genuine, open smile. Evelyn sensed a slipping of the facade that he presented to the world, that she was seeing the real man instead. "Perhaps because your heart lies elsewhere?" he said.

Evelyn looked into his eyes, the same blue as his sister's. Did he know? She knew Jos would tell Vernon eventually of course; Jos had said he would be there at Christmas. But did he know yet? She did not want to pre-empt Jos letting him know, nor give herself away unnecessarily. She decided to test the water first. "And where would my heart lie, if not with you?"

Vernon apparently saw the reason behind her question at once. "Evie, my dear, I know." He emphasised the last word to give it significance. "And I can't say I blame you. My sister is infinitely more handsome than I and considerably more trustworthy."

Evelyn found herself lost for words. Sharing what she had with Jos in the secrecy of Jos's flat was one thing. Suddenly being confronted with the reality in the words and eyes of someone else was rather more astonishing. She was not uncomfortable with the notion of Vernon knowing, only she was not sure how to react.

"Oh, don't worry, I won't tell anyone else," he said. "Jos's secrets are safe with me. Until you tell others about it, not a word will cross my lips."

"Thank you," Evelyn said. "I know it's important to Jos that it's a secret for now."

"And you're not sure you understand that, I assume," Vernon replied, with startling accuracy.

"Something like that," Evelyn said, curious what he would say.

Vernon took her arm and pulled her a few steps further toward the back of the room, where there was no way they would be overheard. "I wouldn't expect you to understand, Evie. But Jos is mostly protecting you. You see, people don't approve. Even in terribly modern establishments like this, people still stare at Jos and her friends from time to time. In the wicked world outside, you should hear what people say. I imagine Jos would hate for you to hear such things about yourself. Additionally, of course, Jos is always scared of what is waiting around the corner for her. She's been that way since our parents died. Never wants to commit to anything in case she loses it, in the way she lost our parents. Did she tell you about them—how it was a Zeppelin raid that took them?"

Evelyn nodded. Jos had told her, in the briefest of terms. Evelyn had not liked to press the matter further.

"Yes, she'll tell people that we lost them but not that she was at home at the time, that she's blamed herself ever since. That she's terrified she'll lose everything good that comes her way."

"But she won't lose me," Evelyn protested, moved by Vernon's words and wishing Jos was here herself, so she could reassure her.

"I'm glad to hear it," Vernon said. "But it's not really about what she thinks you will or won't do. It's that she thinks, if she commits to something—like telling people that you and she are a couple—she puts herself in danger of losing it."

"That's no way to live your life," Evelyn said, feeling sadness on Jos's behalf.

"No. But then which of us really can say we live an exemplary life?" Vernon returned with a shrug. "I certainly can't, as I'm sure you're aware."

Evelyn remembered his casual relationship with Lilian and who knew how many other women. She remembered Dorothy's warnings about Vernon. Perhaps he was affected by the same feelings as Jos; perhaps that was why he could articulate them so clearly.

"I suppose so," Evelyn replied. "I didn't mean to sound judgemental. I just meant that it must be very hard for Jos to be happy."

"We all find our ways, Evie. She's been particularly cheerful these last few days. I even caught her whistling a tune to herself."

"She has?" Evelyn felt a surge of optimism. If Vernon had noticed Jos seeming happy, then that was a good sign.

"Oh, most definitely. I can't think what's brought it on." Vernon's implication was very clearly that Evelyn was the cause of Jos's good cheer. "She's so happy it's almost sickening to her cynical reprobate brother."

"Well, I'm sorry about that," Evelyn said with a smile.

"I can cope. Anyway, we could make conversation all day but I understand we'll meet again at Christmas. How can I help you today? Not drinking on your own?"

"No," Evelyn replied. "I was actually looking for Jos. I just wanted to talk to her."

"She's at work until this evening. She did say she might pop by before she goes home. Would you like me to pass a message to her?"

Evelyn thought for a moment. "Do you have a pencil and paper I can borrow?"

"Of course. Step into my lair for a moment. I promise I won't bite." Vernon opened a back door and ushered her into a small office space. There was a desk with a chair behind it and several chests of drawers. She assumed it was where Vernon completed the necessary bueraucracy and accounting involved in running his establishment. He went behind the desk and found her a piece of cream writing paper and handed her his fountain pen.

"Thank you," Evelyn said, taking the pen. She thought for a moment, then wrote: *Jos, I came to see if you were at home or with Vernon, just to say hello because I was missing you. I will see you in a few days, at Christmas. I'm really looking forward to it. Evie.*

The note seemed rather cold and formal, but she thought it was better to leave a note than nothing at all. At least now Jos would have something in her own words. She like the notion that it would give Jos pause, a moment of thinking about her. She folded the paper and handed it to Vernon. "If you wouldn't mind giving that to her, I'd really appreciate it," she said.

"Of course, my dear. No trouble at all." Vernon stood aside so that Evelyn could leave his office.

She walked out into the cafe. "Thank you, Vernon," she said, hoping she conveyed her gratitude for his understanding regarding Jos, not just for the gift of his stationery.

"Not at all, Evie. I will reclaim the favour at a time of my choosing, naturally."

Evelyn smiled. It was impossible not to be amused by Vernon. "Of course," she replied. "See you soon." With that she turned and left the cafe, her thoughts full of the note she had left for Jos, the idea of Jos getting it and knowing Evelyn had come looking for her.

❖

Jos called in to see Vernon on her way home from the theatre that evening. She was tired after a day in which it had seemed like everyone involved in the performance had thought of a question to ask her. Despite this, she realised she was feeling happy. She knew all too well that the source of that happiness was Evelyn and the prospect of seeing her again in just a few days.

The days were passing slowly. She had considered going to visit Evelyn in the interim, but she did not want to pressurise her into anything. Evelyn had never been in any kind of relationship, let alone one so unexpected, and Jos had no way of knowing how she was feeling about this new development. She wanted to see Evelyn again, but it seemed the sensible course to give it time. Besides, she could hardly just call at the Graingers' and ask to see Evelyn, considering Lilian's and James's hostility towards her and Evelyn's current dependence on them.

When she arrived at the Yellow Orchid, she found that her brother had already retired for the evening, leaving his staff to run the cafe. It was a quiet evening, the pianist the only musical entertainment for the few patrons, so she did not blame him. Vernon had worked hard to make his business a success and it was only in the last year or so that he'd begun to take the occasional evening away from the cafe floor. She teased him that he was getting old and he reminded her that she was the older twin, by exactly eleven minutes. Usually, that rejoinder seemed all too appropriate; she did feel her age. But now, with thoughts of what might come with Evelyn filling her thoughts, she had a new energy.

Clive, who was standing at the bar when she arrived, directed her upstairs with a friendly greeting. She found Vernon relaxing in an armchair, his feet propped on a matching footstool. He was reading the newspaper, the room bathed in a gentle lamplight. He put the newspaper down when he heard her enter.

"Sister, dear!" he said. "Just when I was beginning to think you weren't coming to call after all."

"I said I would. I'm only late because everyone had something they needed me—and no one else—to do today." Jos sat down in another chair, facing Vernon. "How's your day been?"

"Oh, not so bad. Business is quiet but I don't mind that. I did have a visitor earlier, looking for you."

"Who?"

"Evie Hopkins. She left a note, here." Vernon picked up a folded piece of paper from the table at his side and leaned across to give it to her.

Jos took it quickly and read the few words inside. "Thank you. Did she say what she wanted?" The note was remarkably unhelpful, although it made her heart glad to know that Evelyn had wanted to see her.

"Not really. I think she was missing you and just wanted to say hello. It must be rather odd for her, after all, to spend one night with you, change her whole world, and then have to keep quiet about it and continue to make conversation with Lilian and James."

Jos read the note again and then levelled her gaze at Vernon. He played the fool, but he was capable of wisdom and insight. "Do you think I should go and see her?"

"No." Vernon's response was definite. "You're going to see her in a couple of days, after all. I think the note has served its purpose—she's let you know that she's thinking about you. That will sustain her until Christmas, I'm sure."

Jos raised an eyebrow. "How do you know for certain?" Her first instinct was to go and find Evelyn now, reassure her, tell her that she missed her too. Which was a first for her, she realised. She did not usually miss women when she was not with them.

"I don't"—Vernon shrugged—"but what are you going to do, knock on the door and explain yourself to James and Lilian Grainger?"

"It's unlikely," Jos acknowledged, "although I still don't understand why they disapprove quite so much of me when Lilian is clearly very approving of you."

Vernon laughed gently. "Lilian doesn't know what she approves or disapproves of. Just lately she's been even worse. I'm considering disentangling myself from her, I confess."

"That's most unlike you. Usually you wait until the ladies tire of you or see you with one of their friends and slap you."

"True enough. But Lilian is growing to be hard work. And I dislike her disapproval of you. She was fun for a while, and very energetic, but I've had to hear too many of her arduous views on the world now." Vernon sighed.

"She's one of your stars," Jos pointed out.

"London is full of women who can hold a tune and dance a Charleston. Besides, I'm all for amicable separations. She can still sing here, if she wants." Vernon did not sound concerned. Jos envied his ability to separate his emotions from his day-to-day life. She'd never managed it, despite many years of trying. "She was here today, just as Evie was leaving, and it was awfully tiresome. She's so endlessly bright and lively, but so prone to snapping if I make a wrong move. It's not like we feel anything for each other. The woman's using me every bit as much as I'm using her. One of us needs to draw a line under it."

"How very mature of you," Jos said, with gentle sarcasm.

"Not really. I'd marry her and be eternally unhappy if I wanted to grow up," Vernon said. "But we were talking about you, and your Devonshire beauty. I think she's rather wonderful, by the way. You have far better judgement than I do."

"Thank you. I don't think that was ever in question though." Jos looked down at the letter again. "She said she misses me."

"And?"

"It worries me. What does it mean?"

"That she misses you, I expect. Don't you miss her?" Apparently, it was simple in Vernon's mind.

"Actually, I do. And that's strange." Jos frowned.

"Only for you, Jos. I'm led to believe that most couples miss their other half at some stage."

Jos rolled her eyes. "Is that supposed to be advice?"

Vernon shrugged. "Not really. Just my thoughts. I think you have something good. Don't ruin it."

"Like I usually do, you mean?"

"Yes, that's exactly what I mean. You know it."

"But what if it only seems right because she's so innocent? I don't mean that as any insult to her, of course, but you must see it too. Everything's new to her—it will take her time to form an opinion, to understand the world around her. What if, given time, she decides this isn't for her?" Jos was relieved to have her brother to talk to, to have an outlet for her thoughts.

"It's a risk. But you have to take some of those in order to live, Jos. We've talked about this before. You can't always be safe."

"I do know that. But the other side of things worries me too. In Evie's world, men and women meet, court, and get married. I can't marry her and I don't even know if I would want to settle down in the way that Clara and Courtney or Gisela and Abigail have done. That's never been what I wanted."

"And can't what you want change?"

"It can. But I don't know if it has." Jos really didn't.

"All you can do, Jos, is spend time with her. Wait until Christmas now. You know she's still interested. See if you've changed, or not. If you haven't, be honest and be kind."

"You're right of course," Jos conceded. "It's not easy though. I find her irresistable, I have to admit. And I want to care for her." She did not add that she felt as though she could love Evelyn, that perhaps she already did. Vernon would probably infer that from her words anyway.

"And she seems to feel the same. Stop being frightened of what tomorrow holds, Jos. You can't read the future, so just live in the day you're in."

"I seem to think you've recommended that before."

"And yet you never listen."

"Well, that's what brothers are for, isn't it?"

"What, to give sage advice and be entirely ignored?"

Jos grinned. "Perhaps. But thank you."

Vernon smiled back. "Always welcome."

❖

The approach of Christmas turned Evelyn's thoughts to home. Christmas was, after all, a time to be with family. It was when you visited family members you'd not seen in months, put aside differences to share a mince pie. And here she was, miles from her family and with no idea how they thought of her. She was still worried by the lack of communication from home. A small part of her was tempted to take a train back to West Coombe. To visit them, to find out how she was received. That she did not was partly from cowardice, that she would find nothing but anger and hostility to welcome her home, and she was not sure she could face it. But it was also out of the sense that she would find herself trapped there. Once she was in West Coombe, London would be just a memory, and she was frightened she could not make her way back. Now, that would not only mean losing the excitement of a new life, it would mean losing Jos. She could not risk that.

However, she did feel compelled to write to her family again. She did not want them to think she had forgotten them, and perhaps, she would prompt a letter back. Ensconsed in her room, a fire in the grate and a shawl around her shoulders against the increasing winter cold, she wrote two letters, one to her parents and one to Edward:

Dear Mother and Father,

I hope this letter finds you well. I suspect it will at least find you warmer than me—London is much colder than West Coombe in winter!

I am, of course, writing to wish you a very happy Christmas. I hope that you have a jolly time. I am sorry that I cannot be there with you—it's an awfully long train journey and I am also not sure if you would welcome your wayward daughter. Please do write back, just a line or two, to let me know. I can arrange to visit in the New Year.

I will certainly think of you all on Christmas Day. I will be spending my day with some friends I have made. I have lots of friends now, here in London.

I am still relying on the generosity of some of those friends to allow me to stay here, but I am considering my options in terms of gainful employment. I will continue to let you know how that is progressing.

I will admit, I like London and am happy here. I am still very sorry for any heartache I have caused you. I hope that is beginning to subside. I do miss you all but I hope you will understand that I had to try to find a way to be happy and I could not find that in West Coombe. My biggest regret is causing you pain or shame. I hope earnestly that you forgive me.

I very much hope to hear from you soon.
With love at Christmas and always,
Your daughter,
Evelyn

Dearest Eddie,

I am writing to say Happy Christmas! I hope this letter makes it to your hands and you can read this for yourself. I hope you do have a happy festive season. I am very sorry not to be there myself. I would give anything to be able to see you, my darling brother.

I also want to let you know how happy I am here in London. Thank you for helping me find this life, Eddie. There is so much opportunity here, so many new friends. I have even found someone who I am developing something like love for. I never knew I could feel so strongly. Every day is a new adventure here—I am finally flying, just like we talked about, just as I promised. I only wish you were here with me to see it.

I miss you every day, Eddie, and I never forget that I am here because of you.

I will be spending Christmas with a group of very good friends. I am not sure if we will have dinner, like we would at home, but I know that I will have a good time with them. I would like to introduce you to some of them, and maybe one day I'll be able to.

I've asked Mother and Father about the idea of visiting. It will, of course, be difficult, but I can't imagine never coming to West Coombe again. I miss you all too much. I don't suppose you know why they have not written to me since I've been here, but I must admit that I find it worrying.

I know you can't write back to me, Eddie. I wish you could but please don't worry that you can't. It is enough that I know you think of me.

Have a very happy Christmas, Eddie. And know that I am happy too, because of you.

With the fondest love,
Your sister,
Evie

When she finished, Evelyn had tears in her eyes. She could not say whether they were tears of sadness, at separation from her family and the idea of a Christmas without them, or of joy and pride that she was finally living up to the dream she and Edward had shared.

Wiping the tears away, Evelyn hurriedly folded the letters into envelopes and set out into the chill outside for the post office. The letters would arrive on the day before Christmas, so at least her family would think of her on that day.

Chapter Eighteen

Evelyn awoke early on Christmas morning, more excited than she had been since she was a child anticipating gifts from Father Christmas. Lying in bed, feeling the warmth of the blankets and the chill of the room, she pondered briefly how maturity changes a person. As a child, simply knowing there might be a tangerine, some nuts, possibly a tablet of chocolate, and a new toy waiting for her was enough to cause an almost convlusive excitement. Now, a grown woman, it was the thrill of seeing the woman who caused shivers of pleasure to run through her body and nothing to do with Christmas at all. This would be a very different Christmas to any she had known before.

Climbing out from beneath the covers, Evelyn remembered, with a sense of relief, that she was alone in the Graingers' house. They had left for their family's country house the previous evening. Grace had been given both Christmas Eve and Christmas Day off work. For the first time in a long time, Evelyn was free to go through her morning routine and go down to breakfast without fear of an awkward encounter with James or Lilian. She considered this as she went to the bathroom to wash and tidy her hair. Living with the Graingers was becoming difficult. Even if no awkwardness had arisen between herself and Lilian, even if she did not have to contend with James's attentions, she was beginning to feel as though she had overstayed her welcome. There was only so long she could rely on their hospitality. What alternatives there were, she was not sure. She resolved to ask Jos's opinion as soon as there was the right opportunity to do so. Jos might have ideas about what work she could find, what sort of home she might be able to afford to rent. Knowing that she had Jos—and her friends—to ask such questions of made London seem much less daunting than it initially had. Ultimately, London was just a collection of smaller towns grown into each other. People worked and rented and formed communities. She could be part of that.

Having dressed and made herself tea and toast for breakfast, Evelyn sat for a while in the sitting room, leafing through the latest newspaper. She did not want to arrive at Jos's flat too early or appear too eager, even though she could not wait to see Jos. She thought again of the small gifts she had managed to purchase: enamelled cufflinks, with a modern sunburst pattern in black and white which she thought Jos would approve of, a fine cigar for Vernon, and a large tin of biscuits for any other guests to share. It had been enjoyable, shopping in London, even though it had seriously diminished the small amount of money Edward had given her. She was particularly pleased with the cufflinks, which she had told the assistant in the gentleman's shop were for her fiancée. She'd left the shop smiling at referring to Jos in such a way. No matter that the assistant had assumed she referred to a man. Jos was more of a fiancé to her than Michael had ever been, no matter her sex. Little did the young man in the shop know. She smiled again now, remembering. In some ways, the secret she shared with Jos was exciting simply because it was a secret, shared only between them and those who were close to Jos. To be part of that was rather thrilling.

❖

Shortly before midday, Evelyn arrived at Jos's front door and rang the bell. Moments later, Jos opened the door herself. Evelyn had found herself rather nervous at the thought of seeing Jos again. Any anxiety vanished as soon as she saw Jos's smile.

"Evie!" Jos's greeting was full of pleasure. "It's so good to see you." Jos took her hand and pulled her into the hallway. "I've missed you." These words were softer, spoken with more emotion.

"I've missed you too." Happiness flooded through Evelyn's body at being with Jos again. It was at once a new and exciting feeling and one that felt entirely natural, as though being next to Jos was something she had needed her whole life.

Jos pulled her closer. "I should have come to see you sooner. I wanted to after I got your note, but I wasn't sure what Lilian would think if I turned up at your door."

"I understand," Evelyn replied, still holding firmly on to Jos's hand. "I only left the note so you knew I was thinking about you."

"I know," Jos replied. "I've been thinking about you too, all the time."

Evelyn flushed with pleasure. Vernon had not been exaggerating then, when he had said Jos was happy. "Thank you," she said, unsure how else to respond.

"No, Evie, thank *you,*" Jos replied, her voice full of unexpected emotion. She leaned towards Evelyn, seeking her mouth in a kiss that was first romantic and then more passionate. Evelyn felt her whole body respond, as her hand found Jos's hip, felt the curve of her body, pulling her closer.

"So, who is it?" came a voice from the top of the stairs leading to Jos's flat. Evelyn started and pulled back from Jos, but Jos kept hold of her hand and laughed. Evelyn looked up the staircase to find Vernon standing at the top. "Aha, I see. Sorry to interupt the reunion," he said, turning to go back into the flat.

"It's all right, Vernon," Jos called after him. She turned to Evelyn. "There's only Vernon here so far, but I am expecting a few visitors throughout the day. Clara and Courtney said they'd pop in, and I think we might even see Dorothy. Not sure about any others so I can't promise a big party."

"I don't mind at all," Evelyn replied. "I'm happy to be here with you."

Jos smiled. "In that case, you're easily pleased. Come on, let's go and keep Vernon company. He gets awfully twitchy if he's on his own for too long."

Evelyn followed Jos up the stairs, marvelling at how relaxed and comfortable she felt but already decided that this was the best Christmas Day she had ever spent.

❖

Jos found seeing Evelyn again more exciting than she had been anticipating. Alone on Christmas Eve, she'd almost begun to regret inviting Evelyn to spend the day with her. She wanted to see Evelyn again but spending Christmas together seemed like a step forward into a relationship more committed than she was used to. Usually, even if she was involved, she told her girlfriends that Christmas was a time for family and she wanted to share it with Vernon. Those girlfriends were usually not overly concerned, having families of their own to see. To invite Evelyn into her day seemed rather intimate and she'd worried it would feel like too much.

Instead, seeing Evelyn at her door had been nothing but a pleasure. She'd forgotten just how beautiful she found Evelyn, just how intrigued she was to find out more about her. To kiss her again was unadulterated joy. She could have taken Evelyn to her bed and spent the day there quite happily, indulging both her lust and her craving for intimacy with her.

Now, as she watched Evelyn sipping a glass of sherry and conversing easily with Vernon, with whom she now appeared quite comfortable, she smiled to herself. Evelyn fitted well into her world, whilst changing it entirely. That was a combination she'd never managed to find before. There were women who were part of her world and women who wanted to reshape it. But no one who had slotted into her way of life and yet offered her the promise of so much more. True, there was still an uneasy tension in the pit of her stomach. This was unfamiliar territory for her and suggested a time of change in her life. She never handled change well. Yet surely she could overcome her insecurities, for Evelyn?

The afternoon was relaxed. Jos had not prepared a Christmas dinner but had rather arranged a hearty buffet meal on her dining table, with turkey sandwiches for the sake of tradition, along with a pile of mince pies, but plenty of more interesting options. She wondered if Evelyn pined for home, and her mother's cooking. She was nervous to ask, worried that she would cause Evelyn pain. And yet she knew she would have to talk through such things with Evelyn at some point. They could not go forward if she was scared to get closer and more emotionally involved with Evelyn.

For the first hour, Vernon dominated the conversation, as he was wont to do on most occasions. She was content to listen to Evelyn's responses, describing her home town to him, explaining her decision not to cut her hair as per Lilian's instructions. His questions were, typically, rather random, but Evelyn was open and comfortable responding to them. Jos mostly watched her, growing more and more familiar with all of her mannerisms. She had a habit of twirling a lock of hair around her finger when she was a little uncomfortable. Her smile came quickly and took a long time to fade from her eyes. When she was thoughtful, she bit her lip gently. Everything Evelyn did was somehow endearing to Jos. Was this what love did, when it was real? Made you notice the most ordinary of actions and consider them wonderful? She had to confess to herself that she was rather enjoying her experience of it.

Clara and Courtney joined them at about one o'clock. Jos was happy to see her friends and delighted that Evelyn seemed pleased to see them too.

"Evie! What a delightful surprise!" Clara said, on entering the room. She looked to Jos, raising an eyebrow. Jos had intentionally not told Clara and Courtney of what had occurred between her and Evelyn, partly to enjoy their happy surprise on discovering it. "Jos Singleton, you are a sly beast! Imagine not telling us."

"You're rather presumptious, Clara," Jos replied.

"Yes, Evie might be here with me, for all you know," Vernon added.

"Vernon, dear, she has far better taste and you know it," Courtney said, smiling indulgently at him.

"So I keep being reminded," Vernon said, with a mock pout.

"You poor dear." Courtney turned her attention back to Jos. "It is true though, isn't it darling? I told Clara it wouldn't take long. This is simply the best news for Christmas."

"Yes, it's true," Jos replied, looking at Evelyn, who had not managed to get a word into this exchange yet. Evelyn smiled, and Jos was glad. "You can consider Evie and me an item." She saw the pleasure in Evelyn's face.

Clara looked back to Evelyn. "Welcome to the club, Evie," she said. "Delighted to have you."

"Thank you," Evelyn replied. Jos thought she was, perhaps, a little overwhelmed by the attention. "I'm very happy."

"It's just the cat's whiskers, the cherry on the cake," Courtney said, happily.

"Darling, your metaphors are mixing again," Clara said with a smile.

"Oh, pipe down," Courtney responded. "I'm excited."

The doorbell rang again and Jos descended the stairs to admit Dorothy and her friend, Florence, whom Jos had only met on one or two occasions but was happy to welcome into her flat. Dorothy was an odd character, Jos found, and rather inconsistent in her friendships, but she enjoyed her company, recognising her intelligence and wit.

When she reached the top of the stairs, Dorothy's usual immovable demeanour was broken for a moment. "Evelyn Hopkins! I don't see you for what seems like weeks and then I find you here?" Thankfully, her exclamation ended in a smile.

Evelyn rose to her feet to welcome Dorothy. "Dorothy! I'm sorry I haven't seen you—"

"Oh, I know it's all Lilian's fault. She's stopped inviting you out with her, hasn't she? Very fickle woman, that she is."

Dorothy was nothing if not brutally honest. It was something about her Jos appreciated. She had once thought there was a possibility of a relationship between her and Dorothy, who professed that she could be seduced by men and women equally and sought no kind of commitment from either. However, when she discovered Dorothy leaving Vernon's bedroom one morning, all possibility of that was put out of her mind. She still liked Dorothy and was certainly the last one to judge her.

Evelyn, meanwhile, looked a little taken aback at Dorothy's understanding. "Has Lilian said anything to you?" she asked.

Clara rolled her eyes, "I still don't really understand why we all pay so much attention to Lilian. She's awfully foolish, don't you think?"

"She's been very kind to me," Evelyn responded. Jos admired the sense of honour that made Evelyn defend Lilian. "She's let me stay with her rent-free and she's been very helpful. Until recently."

"I don't say she's a bad person, not deep down," Clara replied. "Just quite a difficult one to spend time with. Wouldn't you say, Vernon?"

Courtney giggled at Vernon's brief discomfort and even Jos was amused. Her brother could handle the teasing. He shrugged. "Don't expect me to defend her. Of course, chivalry dictates that I should, being as the lady isn't here to defend herself. But our attachment is rather at an end, so I'm the last one to disagree with you all."

"I'm one of her better friends and I can't really defend her myself,"

Dorothy added. "Not that she's not entertaining company and she's an excellent source of gossip. But no, Evie, she's not really mentioned you. Which is what made me suspicious, if I'm honest. Lilian talks about everybody, all the time. I can't think what you've done to her. Unless it's your new friends she objects to, of course." Dorothy winked and looked at Jos.

"Lilian doesn't know about Evie and me," Jos said, understanding the implication.

"Oh, so there is an Evie and you, then?" Dorothy said.

"Yes, there is," Evelyn said. Jos heard a certain pride in her voice that made her heart glad. Evelyn seemed to like their relationship being known to their friends. That was an excellent sign.

"How wonderful! And I was the first to predict it." Dorothy's tone was entirely self-satisfied. "Of course, Lilian thinks it's Vernon you've got a crack on for, by the way, Evie."

Evelyn flushed and Vernon grinned. "Well, I wouldn't be surprised if she had, it would be entirely understandable," Vernon said. "You know I'm here, Evie, if that's where your heart really lies."

"Shut up, Vernon," Jos told him, in the way that only a sister could.

"Does she really think that?" Evelyn asked, looking concerned. Jos understood that she was still keen to keep Lilian's good opinion, despite the recent turn their friendship had taken.

"She did, a week or so ago, which is when we last spoke about you. Was awfully suspicious of you, especially since our dear Vernon hasn't been treating her so well just lately."

"I'm a terrible person," Vernon said.

"Yes, you are," Dorothy said, "but I don't think I blame you. Lilian's been very difficult in recent times."

"Hasn't she just?" he agreed.

"Why are we all talking about someone who isn't here, anyway?" Courtney said. "How about we put a record on the gramophone and drink some more sherry? It's Christmas!"

Jos was glad of her interuption. She could see the tension rising in Evelyn's expression and did not want her to dwell on Lilian, or what was being said about her. She went over to her gramophone and selected one that began with Jelly Roll Morton's "Black Bottom Stomp," guaranteed to lighten the mood and bring some festive spirit to the occasion. Then she went to stand by Evelyn, holding her fingers lightly, to reassure.

Evelyn squeezed her hand back and turned to look into her eyes. She saw nothing but happiness there, reflecting the feeling in her own heart.

❖

Evelyn felt Jos's hand grasping hers and her heart soared. Yes, she was a little frightened of what Lilian thought about her, of being the subject of gossip. But it was difficult to mind anything much with Jos by her side, with Jos so open about their relationship. To be in a room full of people who knew that there was something between them, and who were happy about it, was a rather wonderful feeling. She felt like a butterfly spreading its wings after emerging from the crysallis. The happiness in this room was sunshine; she needed to overcome any fears and to fly.

The afternoon was so delightful that she almost forgot to miss her family and her home. She ate far too much delicious food, drank too much sherry, and found she could hold her own in conversation, even with the likes of Clara and Vernon, who delighted in making sport of their words. She was pleased to see Dorothy relaxed and laughing and thought her new friend, Florence, though rather quiet, seemed very interesting. In the middle of the afternoon, they were briefly joined by Abigail and Gisela, the latter of whom insisted on sharing homemade Christmas stollen, her mother's own recipe, with them.

Despite the lively conversation and laughter of the afternoon, Evelyn felt the connection with Jos throughout. She was always conscious of where in the room Jos was, who she was talking to. Often, she looked in Jos's direction to find Jos looking back at her. On several occasions they found quiet moments, just to stand close, and there was more than one stolen kiss in the hallway. Every moment of contact, every exchanged glance felt special.

As darkness descended outside, Clara and Courtney took their leave first. Evelyn wondered what the rest of their Christmas would be like, once they reached their clearly happy home, alone. Dorothy, Florence, and Vernon all departed at the same time, since they would be walking to their homes in the same direction.

"Enjoy the rest of Christmas," Dorothy said, leaning in to plant a brief kiss on Evelyn's cheek. "I'm quite sure Jos will keep you entertained. I'm almost envious."

"Don't be ridiculous, Dorothy," Jos put in. "And enjoy the rest of the evening yourself." Evelyn saw the smile they exchanged and wondered what there had been in the past between the two women. There was still a lot she did not understand about the group of friends she found herself part of, but she looked forward to learning more of those mysteries, of counting these people as her community for a long time to come.

"Thank you, Dorothy. Hopefully I'll see you soon. Perhaps at the Orchid."

"Perhaps, I suppose it's rather dependent on Lilian."

"I should hope patronising my establishment is not entirely dependent on Lilian Grainger," Vernon said. "That would be terribly bad for business."

"Oh, don't worry, Vernon. We'll still come to see you." Dorothy patted him on the shoulder. "We'd miss you terribly if we didn't. Now, come along, you can escort two ladies home."

"How gentlemanly of me to offer," Vernon replied. "Thank you, Joselyn dear, for a lovely Christmas. I will see you soon. You too, Evie. Delightful to get to know you today."

Evelyn smiled, for once seeing Vernon without his contrived facade. "You too, Vernon. See you soon. Nice to meet you too, Florence."

"The feeling's mutual," Florence replied. "It's smashing of you all to be so welcoming. Dorothy said you were all nice people and I wasn't to be shy."

"Oh, we're not all nice, my dear," Vernon said. "Some of us are quite the opposite, if you ask nicely."

"Vernon, go home." Jos glared at him. "And Florence, just ignore him." Vernon pretended to look wounded.

"I intend to, don't worry," Florence replied.

Evelyn smiled at her. It was interesting to see this little group through her eyes for a moment. To Florence, the outsider, Evelyn was part of the group of friends—she already knew Vernon's sense of humour, she was in a relationship with Jos. Suddenly, she did not feel so new and awkward. She was already part of something.

Once Vernon, Dorothy, and Florence had left the flat, Jos returned up the stairs. Evelyn was still standing, waiting for her to return. Jos came straight to her and took her hands. For a long moment, they simply gazed at each other.

"It's been wonderful spending the day with you, Evie," Jos said softly, as if unsure how her words would be received.

"It's been one of the best days of my life," Evelyn said, without exaggeration. Jos looked moved. Simultaneously, they stepped closer into an embrace that became a long kiss. Evelyn had wanted to kiss Jos like this all day and now she did not want to stop.

The kiss broke but still they stood close together, foreheads touching. The gramophone was still playing the last record Jos had put on. A moderately paced jazz piece, led by a clarinet, filled the room. Evelyn had not heard it before, but she liked it. Jos appeared to notice the music in the same instant, suddenly moving to take Evelyn in a dance hold and beginning to sway with her. Evelyn laughed, enjoying the feeling of Jos's hips moving against her body, their hands twined, Jos's grip on her waist. Jos smiled widely, twirling Evelyn around, then pulling her closer. There could have been nothing better in that moment than dancing with Jos, laughing with Jos, being one with Jos.

As the strains of the music faded, they were still again. Jos's hand cradled Evelyn's cheek. This time her kiss had more intent and Evelyn's body caught fire in response.

The evening was filled with more kisses. It was filled with Evelyn exploring Jos's body, Jos's reactions to her touch, her own sensual power. And it was filled with Jos showing her just what her own body could do, how she could feel. Jos could be a tease, keeping her balancing on the edge for a long time before sending her into heights of ecstasy she'd never dreamed of. Inspired to confidence by Jos's response to her, Evelyn discovered the pleasure she could induce with her own fingers and mouth, by allowing Jos's gaze to fall upon her, by her own experience of their mutual arousal. Jos's body was beautiful and complex and she was hungry for every inch of it.

As midnight approached, they had moved from the settee and the floor of Jos's sitting room and into her bed. Sensual caresses had become an intimate embrace, passionate kisses become more affectionate and playful. Now Jos's hands explored her body again, and again Evelyn's senses woke to her touch, craved her contact.

Jos put her mouth close to Evelyn's ear, her breath an additional caress. "Evie, I want to be inside you, to feel your heat all around me. I want you to know how it feels…"

Evelyn understood immediately and found her body aching for what Jos described. In response she took Jos's hand and pushed it between her thighs. "I trust you," she breathed. Jos's fingers teased for a moment, then slid inside Evelyn's body. Evelyn felt the slight stretch of the unfamiliar sensation and then the flood of pleasure that followed as Jos filled her. Jos's thumb toyed with her where she needed the pressure, as their mouths were once more joined in a deep kiss. Evelyn lost herself in the sensations, of the feeling of belonging to Jos and of Jos belonging to her, in the mutual pleasure and ultimate intimacy they shared. She moved her hips against the pressure Jos gave her and moaned her arousal into Jos's mouth, and Jos took her over the edge into that little death once more.

As she fell through the layers of pleasure, she heard Jos's words. "Oh, Evie, I love you." She could not express it in the moment, but she knew without thought that she felt the same and her heart was full of joy.

Eventually, in the early hours, Evelyn lay in Jos's arms. Jos was asleep now, Evelyn listening to her regular breathing, feeling the rise and fall of her chest. She was sleepy herself, exhausted and satisfied, but before she fell into slumber herself she had time to reflect that she was at home for Christmas after all. This was her home now, wherever Jos was.

❖

When Evelyn awoke, Jos was already out of bed, doing something in the kitchen. Evelyn could hear her moving but could not work out what she was doing. After a few minutes, Jos's head appeared around the bedroom door. She smiled when she saw that Evelyn was awake.

"Good morning, beautiful," Jos said.

Evelyn smiled. "Good morning. What are you doing?"

"I thought I would make some breakfast. I hope you like scrambled eggs."

"I do. And thank you."

"You're welcome. My reward shall be a kiss," Jos replied. She came to Evelyn and bent to place a tender kiss on her lips. Evelyn reached for the back of her neck and held the kiss for longer.

"You should be careful, or it'll be you I'm having for breakfast and the eggs will burn," Jos said, as she pulled away gently.

"That wouldn't be so bad," Evelyn said.

"No, it wouldn't," Jos replied. She retreated in the direction of the kitchen, while Evelyn luxuriated in the warm bed. She was comfortable here, with Jos. It was a shame she had to return to the Graingers' today, even more of a shame that she had to keep this happiness a secret.

As they ate breakfast together on the settee, Evelyn in Jos's dark satin robe and Jos wearing just her trousers and an undershirt, Evelyn pondered this further. Although a huge part of the previous day's joy came solely from being with Jos, she could not deny that some of it also came from being around friends who knew how they felt about each other, of it not being a secret. However much of a thrill came from keeping something so exciting as a secret between them, she was much happier when people knew. Besides, being able to share her feelings for Jos with others was something she relished the chance to do. She wanted everyone to realise how wonderful Jos was.

"Jos?" she said eventually, as she finished her eggs and put the plate aside.

"Yes?" Jos replied. She had finished her own breakfast and was now nursing a cup of tea.

"I was just thinking. Do you really think it would be so bad if I told Lilian about us?" Evelyn saw a degree of tension creep into Jos's posture.

"Why do you want to?" Jos asked.

"I don't know really. It's just that, well, it's so wonderful to share it with people, like we did yesterday. And I don't like keeping it a secret."

Jos wished Evelyn had not spoken. The morning had been so perfect, after the perfect day before, and now Evelyn's words risked ruining it. It wasn't Evelyn's fault of course. She was right. But Jos was scared. Not of Lilian, but of herself. She did not really care what Lilian and James Grainger thought. But yesterday had been almost too perfect.

She cursed herself for feeling it, but she could not help it. Sharing her relationship with Evelyn with her brother and her closest friends had felt like the natural thing to do. She'd been pleased with how happy they seemed, how glad for her. But now that they knew, she felt a real pressure. What if something went wrong between them? It was by no means guaranteed, however strong their feelings, that things would work out. She knew from experience that good things usually went wrong for her. By telling people, she'd made a commitment. And she knew that Evelyn saw it that way too.

Telling close friends was, of course, one thing. But as soon as Lilian Grainger knew, everyone would know. She feared what the snide comments would do to Evelyn, knew she would have to be the one to protect her. She feared the warnings people like Lilian would feel compelled to give. What if Evelyn believed them, or if Jos could not protect her? In her mind she saw their relationship collapsing like a house of cards. She saw herself in the ashes of the relationship, clinging to her love for Evelyn, but ultimately betrayed by the world. Evelyn would not mean to do it, but it seemed so likely, this love seemed so precarious.

Her fear made her words more harsh than she had intended. "You can't tell Lilian. You need to understand that Dorothy and Clara and the others are not the same as Lilian."

She saw the confusion in Evelyn's face and hated herself for it. But then, Evelyn did need to understand. "I don't mean to sound angry, I'm sorry. But there are things you don't understand, Evie." She'd tried to sound kinder but now she realised that she was at risk of being patronising. So she stopped speaking and waited for a response.

Evelyn appeared to be trying to choose her words carefully. "It's not that I don't understand," she began, slightly defensive. "It's that I don't see why it matters if I tell Lilian."

"You live with Lilian," Jos returned, thinking that was the most obvious answer.

"I don't have to," Evelyn replied.

Evelyn's reply alarmed Jos. If Evelyn was considering moving out of Lilian's house, there was surely only one place she could be considering as another option. However strongly she felt for Evelyn, she was not ready for that level of commitment yet. She needed her own space. This was everything she had tried not to fear. Of course Evelyn would expect commitment. Relationships between men and women followed that pattern. They would meet, court, marry. Evelyn was looking for the equivalent of marriage, trying to fit their relationship into the world she was familiar with. Jos began to feel panic growing inside her, however much she was furious with herself for it. She struggled for something to say and, finding nothing helpful, stayed silent. Bitterly, she saw concern growing in Evelyn's eyes.

"I don't have to live with Lilian." Evelyn had clearly been waiting for a positive answer from Jos and, not getting one, was now trying to explain herself. "I have a small amount of money, I can pay rent. I wanted to ask you about finding a job in London anyway, so I don't have to live with Lilian. I want to spend time with you, I don't want us to be a secret."

The fear broke in Jos. Was this what happened when she told a woman she loved her? The very next morning that woman wanted to live with her, depend on her? It was why she tried so hard not to love. She was not fit to be depended upon. She would ruin it somehow. "Look, Evie, I can't marry you. I'm not a man. We can't do that. I can't fit in with what you expected to happen in your life. If that's what you want, I'm the wrong person for you to find it with."

Evelyn looked taken aback and Jos regretted the force with which she'd spoken the words. "I'm sorry, Evie. I'm just going to end up causing you pain. I should have seen it before now."

Evelyn looked lost and confused. She looked hurt and Jos saw tears rising in her eyes. More than anything she wanted to reach out and hold her, tell her everything would be all right and reassure her of her love. But she could not because she did not believe everything would be all right. She never had. She was destroying the best relationship she'd ever had before it had even started. How could she claim everything would be all right or reassure Evelyn of that?

"Last night you said you loved me," Evelyn said plaintively.

"I know," Jos said, forcing herself not to repeat that damaging sentiment.

"And I love you," Evelyn said, her tone more desperate now.

"I don't think you're sure of that," Jos said, regretting it immediately but not taking it back.

"But I am," Evelyn protested. Her tears were flowing now. Jos hated herself and wanted to wipe them away.

"Well, I'm not," Jos said. "It's not good for you to be with me, Evie, and you won't understand why. I think you should just go back to Lilian's and forget about me."

"I can't just forget about you." Evelyn sounded horrified. "I mean it, I love you, Jos. I want to be with you all the time."

"You must have heard my reputation, Evie. I don't have long relationships with women, I always ruin it. What makes you think you're any different?"

Evelyn stared at her in silence. She knew she'd struck the fatal blow. Slowly, Evelyn got to her feet and went into the bedroom. A short time later, she emerged fully dressed. She turned wide eyes on Jos, clearly hoping for something. Jos forced herself to look away.

"I don't understand," Evelyn said, her voice full of sadness.

Jos's heart broke. "No. That's the problem."

Without another word, Evelyn left the room. Jos listened to her descending the stairs, heard the door open and close. Evelyn was gone and Jos had done nothing to stop her because it was far better for Evelyn that she did not.

Alone, her own tears came because she knew alone was what she would always be.

CHAPTER NINETEEN

Evelyn was blind with grief as she made her way back to the Graingers' house. It was the only place she could think of to go, the only place where she could lock herself in a room and sob. The only place where she could dwell on her own stupidity and work out what she was supposed to do next. Her first, panicked thought was that all she could do was return to West Coombe, that London held nothing for her now.

She managed to restrain the obvious manifestation of her emotions long enough to make it to the sanctuary of her bedroom. Once there, she collapsed onto the bed and cried until the pillow was soaked with her tears and her throat ached. Still, she did not understand.

So few hours had passed since Jos had said she loved her, it was such a short time since she had known she loved her in return, since they had shared such happy intimacy. She could not believe anything that had led to that had changed. Yet, suddenly, Jos was angry with her, she was cold and apparently uncaring. Was this what Suzanne had warned her about? She'd been told to stay away from Jos. Perhaps those warnings were now coming true. Had Jos been leading her along, using her? The thought hurt more than anything she could imagine.

As the tears stopped and she lay still, exhausted, she remembered how she'd also been told Jos had demons, that women usually wanted to save her from herself, but that she was actually worth a chance, worth a risk. Surely Clara, who had told her that, knew Jos better than she did.

There was Vernon too, who had told her about Jos being terrified of losing everything good. Since their parents' death, Jos had blamed herself whenever things went wrong, was terrified of ruining her own happiness. Had Jos had seen her chance to be happy and done her best to ruin it before something went wrong? To prove herself right, even if it made her unhappy? Through her aching head, Evelyn tried to remain calm and consider this. Perhaps she had reacted in the wrong way. Maybe Jos needed to be reassured, to be helped to understand that she would not frighten Evelyn away.

She thought too about Jos's words about marriage. She did not expect Jos to be able to marry her. Although she did not see the exact route their relationship would take, she was happy to enjoy it, see how it unfolded. Jos seemed to be afraid that Evelyn wanted a level of commitment she did not. But, remembering Vernon's words again, she pondered this. Perhaps it was not that Jos did not want to commit to her; perhaps it was that she was frightened of what would happen if she did.

Slowly, as she lay on the bed, her tears drying, hope began to return. More than anything, she knew she could not walk away from Jos. It was time to prove that she was not just a naive girl from the countryside, but that she could handle this situation like the grown woman she was. She would fight for Jos because what she had experienced yesterday, and through the night, was the most complete happiness she had ever known. She had not come this far to let Jos's fears destroy that. She would talk to Jos that very day, make sure the situation was addressed before it got any worse. She would reassure her. Evelyn decided to give it a few hours. To return right now would only risk walking back into the same conversation. Let Jos regain her courage and her calm. And she'd allow herself to gather her strength and bring her emotions back under control, and she would win Jos back. Tonight, she thought, allowing herself a small smile, she would be in Jos's arms again.

❖

Despite her hopeful and determined resolution, it was still difficult to kill the time before she returned to Jos. She pottered around the house, forced herself to eat some bread and jam for her lunch, but still the time passed slowly. She decided to make herself wait until the clock had passed four o'clock. The time was arbitrary, but it seemed the right amount of time for both herself and Jos to recover and be ready to talk honestly with each other. She had to trust that Jos would be prepared to do so. She rehearsed what she wanted to say, imagining Jos's response. The conversation always ended in reconciliation. She could not allow herself to imagine anything else.

At about half past three, Evelyn was in the sitting room, considering that it was now time to find her coat and walk slowly to Jos's flat, hoping to find her at home, when she heard the front door of the house open. She went into the hallway just as Lilian and James entered, laden with bags and suitcases.

"Oh, hello, welcome home," she said, trying to sound enthusiastic. "Did you have a nice time?"

"Evelyn! Delighted you're home. It was a very pleasant visit home, thank you." This was James, who smiled broadly upon seeing her.

"Well, it was more pleasant for James than me, but I got plenty of presents, so that's something," Lilian added. She flashed a brief and insincere smile. Evelyn felt the same familiar tension that had characterised recent days with Lilian. In her emotional state, it bothered her more than it usually did, but there was really nothing she could do.

"How was your Christmas, Evelyn?" James asked.

"Oh, well, just quiet, you know. I didn't really do anything." She did not like to lie, but she could hardly tell the truth at this stage.

"Probably best, darling," Lilian said, without much care. She began to ascend the stairs, carrying a hatbox and small suitcase with her. "I'm off to take a bath, if no one objects."

"Of course, we don't," James told her. "Although it's remarkable how you make it seem as though you've just survived a terrible ordeal when all we did was visit home."

"It's not an ordeal for you, James, dearest, since Mater and Pater think you're the cat's pyjamas. However, for me, it's rather different. I'm not in favour."

"You know you only have yourself to blame."

"No, I entirely blame them. Frank was their favourite, and then they decided you were their favourite when they lost him. Maybe I look too much like him. Or they don't really like girls."

"You're absurd sometimes, Lilian."

"I know." With that, Lilian marched up the stairs.

James watched her go, frowning. "You know, Evelyn, Lilian's been much more absurd than usual just lately. Has she mentioned anything to you about what might be wrong?" James looked at Evelyn with an expression of earnest concern.

Evelyn thought about Lilian's deteriorating relationship with Vernon, about the illegal drugs. There were several reasons Lilian might be acting more strangely than her brother was used to, but none she could tell him about. "No, she's not really said anything to me at all," she said.

"Yes, I've noticed she's not as friendly towards you, either, if I'm honest," James said.

"Perhaps I've overstayed my welcome," Evelyn suggested. Moments later, she decided that was not the best tactic, since it prompted reassurances of quite the opposite from James.

"No, Evelyn, please don't think that. We're more than happy to have you here." His enthusiasm was rather intimidating, particularly when she felt so fragile and when she wanted nothing more than to go and speak to Jos.

"Well, thank you. I do appreciate it," she said, turning to walk away from James.

"Actually, Evelyn, I've been wanting to speak to you about that," James said, hurriedly.

Evelyn's heart sank. "You have?" she asked, turning to face him again.

"Yes. While we were away, well, it gave me a bit of time to think. And I realised that, with the new year coming, it's a time for making resolutions. I suppose I was inspired by seeing Frank's portrait at my parents' house too, to think what he would have done. He was an awful lot braver than me, you know."

James paused and Evelyn frowned. She knew she should feel for him, appreciate his lack of confidence, and be kind. But this was the wrong moment for that. "And what resolution do you want to make?"

James looked a little surprised at her direct questions, yet it also seemed to make it easier for him. "Evelyn, I think you're wonderful, you must know it. I've never met a girl like you in London. My resolution, if you will have me, is that I would like to marry you. Will you marry me, Evelyn?"

Evelyn stared. She had expected something along these lines from James, but not a proposal, not so suddenly and without any warning.

"But we've not even been for that walk you invited me on. Or to the pictures," she protested weakly, not sure what else she was supposed to say.

"We can do all of those things. It can be a long engagement, if that's what you would like, but I can't think of anyone else I would want to marry. I think I love you, Evelyn."

Evelyn raised her eyebrows. She almost wanted to laugh at James, though she was too aware of the gravity of the situation to do so. The idea of marrying James was ridiculous, particularly when he could only declare that he thought he loved her. He was watching her reaction.

"I know this is coming out all wrong," he said. "I didn't mean to ask you right away. I wanted to wait until this evening, perhaps, and work out what I would say. But the moment just seemed right. Maybe if you'll just consider it. I think you feel the same way."

His presumption sent Evelyn over the line from stunned ridicule to anger. Now he reached for her hand and tried to draw her closer. Still contemplating her response, she let him. But when, encouraged, he leaned towards her with his lips pursed for a kiss, she could not help herself. She pushed him back, rather more violently than she had planned.

"No, James!" she said, loudly, the emotions of the day affecting her tone. "I don't feel the same way at all."

James looked shocked but not prepared to accept her words. "I know you're not used to this sort of thing, Evelyn. I'm sorry if it's a bit sudden. But you must feel something, or else why would you have agreed to come out with me?"

Evelyn stared at him in horror, totally unsure what to say. "It is sudden, James, but that's not why I'm saying no. And I've not said so, but I was engaged once before, in Devon, so I am used to this. I didn't want to marry him and I don't want to marry you. I'm sorry."

James's disappointment turned to anger. "You were engaged before? So you ran away to London to get away from a marriage you didn't want to go through with?"

"No, that's not right at all," Evelyn said. "I came to London to look for a new life. My engagement was just one of the the things I left behind."

"You used our brother's letter to get here, to convince us to give you refuge, just so you could get away from a commitment you'd made?"

"You're not listening, James, which makes me even less likely to look favourably on you. I'm sorry you see it that way, but it's not true. After what happened to my brother in the war, I'd never do what you've just said."

"So why is it that you won't marry me, then? Give me a good reason." There was a challenge in James's eyes now, which frightened her a little.

"I don't love you, James."

"You could grow to."

"That's not how I believe a marriage should work." In desperation, she added, "Besides, there's someone else who I think I love."

"Who?" James demanded.

"It is none of your business." Anger flashed in Evelyn's heart, partly because she wanted very badly to tell him who she loved and yet she could not. She heard movement at the top of the stairs and suspected Lilian was listening. She did not care. "I don't have to tell you anything, especially not about who I love."

James responded to that anger with a pale-faced fury. "In that case you can get out of my house," he snapped.

Without another word, Evelyn took her coat from the hook in the hallway and did just as he asked. It was not until she had slammed the door behind her and was out in the street that she realised what she had done. All of her belongings and money were in that house. The house was her only place to stay in London. Lilian and James had been her first friends here. Without Jos, it was possible she had no friends here at all. For the first time since she had alighted the train at Paddington, London was huge and terrifying again, and she was alone.

There was only one course of action she could think of, and that was to do what she had planned to do anyway, to find Jos. There was even more at stake now. Surely Jos would put her fears aside to help Evelyn, even if she would not relent over their relationship. But if she could be persuaded that it was safe to love Evelyn, perhaps all was not lost after all. Jos was really all that mattered now.

She retraced her steps to Jos's flat, horribly aware of how much had changed since she had made this journey the previous day. Since then she'd been the happiest, angriest, and most desperate she'd ever been. Now, she could not wait to get to the door, to tell Jos what had happened, to bring about that the happy reunion she had been imagining.

She reached Jos's now familiar door and rang the bell. There was no answer. She rang the bell again, repeatedly. Eventually, she concluded that Jos was not home. She thought about where she might find Jos, or anyone she could still call a friend. Not entirely sure she could find her way back to Clara and Courtney's house and with no idea where Dorothy lived, the only place she could think of was the Yellow Orchid. Of course, Jos might be there herself. If she wasn't, she could probably rely on Vernon to help her.

As she entered the Orchid, she paid little heed to the fashionable patrons present, although she was aware that her hurried entrance and distressed expression attracted a few glances. She made straight for the office at the back of the room, knocking only briefly on the door before she went in.

To her relief, she found Vernon sitting behind the desk. He jumped to his feet when she appeared, his quick eyes taking in her emotional state before he uttered a greeting. "Evie! What's wrong?" he asked, crossing the room and taking her arm. "Is it Jos?"

Evelyn was so relieved to have found a friend, that she almost started crying. However, she needed to explain. "This morning it was Jos. She sent me away, told me she didn't love me," she told him.

"Oh she's an idiot, my sister. Evelyn, she doesn't mean it. You need to—"

"I know," Evelyn interupted. "At first I was devastated and then I was angry. I didn't understand. But then I remembered what you said about her, what Clara said, and I started to understand. I need to talk to her. I was hoping she was here, she's not at home."

"I'm sorry, I've not seen her all day."

"It's not just that though, not now," Evelyn said, feeling her chest tighten.

"What else?" Vernon was full of concern, his usual feigned insincerity entirely gone.

"James Grainger just asked me to marry him."

"Bloody hell, Evelyn! What did you say to him?"

Evelyn looked at Vernon. "What do you think I said?"

"Well, I don't think I hear the sound of wedding bells. I don't mean that. I mean, did you let him down gently?"

Evelyn sighed. "Not exactly. The last thing he said to me was *Get out of my house*."

"It's been quite a day for you, then." He smiled slightly.

She guessed he was trying to keep her calm. "Yes."

"Can I get you a drink? In fact, I insist on getting you a drink. Stay there." Vernon left the room to return moments later with a glass of brandy.

Evelyn sipped it, grateful for his kindness. "Do you know where Jos might be?" she asked, eventually.

"Afraid not. I have one or two ideas. There's places she takes herself off to when she's unhappy, places where she doesn't have to face anyone she knows. I imagine she's drunk far too much whisky and is currently feeling very sorry for herself. If she's pushed you away, she'll hate herself right now."

"I don't want that," Evelyn said. "I want to make her understand that I'm not pushing her into anything, I just want to be with her. And she won't ruin it."

"It'll take some convincing, Evie but, you know, I do think you might be the one to convince her, finally."

Vernon's vote of confidence made her feel slightly better. If only she could find Jos, there was hope. "I really hope so. I love her, Vernon."

"I know you do, Evie. She knows it too. She'll be back eventually, you can talk to her then. I honestly think you might have more to worry about with James." Vernon's serious tone was alarming. He was usually so quick to joke.

"What do you mean?"

"Well, haven't you been rather reliant on Lilian and James? Where are your clothes and belongings? Where are you staying tonight?"

"Remarkably practical considerations, for you," Evelyn said. "And I had already thought about them. The answer is that all of my things are still in their house and I don't know what I'm going to do tonight."

"Well, I don't object to you sleeping here if you have nowhere else. I don't think I'm a good choice to go to fetch your belongings though."

Relief filled Evelyn. If nothing else, she was no longer alone. "Thank you, I really do appreciate it."

"I do hope we can track my idiot sister down. She's the one who should be helping you. She might end up here, when she finally wants to talk about her misery."

"I hope so," Evelyn replied.

At that moment, the door of the office swung open, slamming against the wall. Both Vernon and Evelyn looked up, startled to see Lilian in the doorway, eyes blazing with anger.

"I might have known this is where you would be, you double-crossing little bitch!"

Evelyn, who had never been called any such thing in her life, was astounded and horrified. Vernon seemed equally speechless. It was not immediately apparent what was wrong with Lilian, merely that she was extremely angry. She had spoken so loudly that a hush had fallen in the cafe, the buzz of conversation gone.

"Lilian?" Vernon said eventually. "Is something wrong, darling?"

"Don't you call me darling! Not when you've been having your way with Evelyn, leading me on the whole time, you filthy excuse for a man."

It was now apparent what Lilian's problem was, but Evelyn was still not sure exactly how she should deal with it. "Lilian, you're wrong," was all she could manage. However, this seemed to make Lilian's anger intensify.

"Don't try to deny it. I take you into my home and share everything with you, and this is how you repay me? You rut in the same bed as me, taking my man from me, and you dare to refuse my brother when he offers you a decent marriage, better than anything else you'll ever be offered in your dead-end little town in Devon?"

"I was never your man, Lilian," Vernon put in, unhelpfully in Evelyn's opinion.

She glared at him. "You said you were, to get me between your sheets," Lilian retorted, loudly.

"I don't think I did, actually—it sounds most unlike me," Vernon replied.

"It doesn't matter what you said to each other," Evelyn interjected. "It's more important that we assure Lilian that there is nothing between us and there never has been."

"Then why are you here? My brother proposes, you tell him you love someone else, and when I come to confront Vernon, I find you here."

"Why were you coming to confront me because Evie doesn't want to marry James?" Vernon asked. "Hardly my fault."

Lilian's eyes were filled with venom. "Because I know about you two. You're the one Evie says she loves, aren't you? I've suspected it for ages and then I saw her leaving here the other day. She never told me she was here—why would she lie?"

"Are you spying on me?" Evelyn demanded.

"No, I came here to see Vernon. You got here before me."

"Am I not allowed to see Vernon without you assuming I'm sharing his bed? Or do you think we're all like you, Lilian?" Evelyn demanded, angry enough now to allow her contempt of Lilian to come to the fore.

"And what's that supposed to mean? Anyway, why would you come to see Vernon?"

"It's actually none of your business. But I wasn't here to share his bed."

"Surprising isn't it?" Venon said. "But it is true, Lilian. I can't say I didn't try, but Evie wasn't interested."

If Vernon thought his humour would help the situation, he was wrong.

"Well, she's a liar, anyway. Do you know she ran away from home because she was engaged? She let her fiancé down and used our brother's letter to find a way into our house so she didn't have to face the situation she'd created. What do you think to that?"

The pain of the accusation hit Evelyn hard, because Lilian was not entirely wrong. "While we're accusing people of things, don't forget the secrets I'm keeping for you."

Lilian's eyes narrowed, though her expression gave Evelyn the impression that she suspected Evelyn would not dare tell Vernon, or anyone else listening, about what she had witnessed. It only made Evelyn more defiant. Lilian had belittled her for too long. However much sympathy she had for Lilian's loss of her brother in the war, however grateful she was for her initial hospitality, the assumption that she had not only slept with Vernon but intentionally deceived Lilian about it was too much. "Vernon, would you believe I saw Lilian injecting herself with cocaine?" she declared.

Vernon stared open-mouthed at Lilian, who was looking at Evelyn with horror in her eyes. Evelyn realised then that to be humiliated in front of Vernon, within earshot of some her of audience at the cafe, was probably the worst thing that could happen to Lilian. That just showed how superficial she was.

After the brief moment of shocked silence, Lilian responded. She slapped Evelyn, hard, across the face, before Evelyn knew what was happening. The sharp sting of pain was nothing compared to the shock of the insult. Involuntarily, she took a step backward, falling through the doorway of the office and into the cafe proper. Instantly, she felt every pair of eyes in the room on her, as Lilian followed her out.

"Hello everybody, enjoying the show are you?" Lilian had her audience again and she knew how to make use of them. "Yes, some of you know me, you've seen me sing. Well, I want to introduce someone to you. This is Evelyn Hopkins. She came here from Devon, playing on my brother's memory to get herself somewhere to stay. Then she seduced my other brother, to the point where he proposed marriage to her. It was only then that she confessed that she'd run away from a broken engagement in Devon, without even telling her fiancé. On top of that, she's been busy between the sheets with the owner of this fine establishment, who was supposed to be committed to me. And I saw her taking drugs too—she injects cocaine. How do you like that?"

Evelyn heard Lilian's words through a haze of pain and humiliation. She could not argue in front of so many people. She was vaguely aware of Vernon coming to her defence, dragging a shrieking and swearing Lilian back into the office. But to hear her actions described in such a way, combined with such lies, on a day on which everything had already seemed to fall apart once was too much. She had not come to London for this. Tears blurring her vision, she ran from the cafe, not noticing if anyone tried to comfort or criticise her. She thought she heard Vernon call after her, but she was through the door and into the street, running far away from that place, from the false accustations and the ones that were dangerously close to the truth, from Lilian whom she had thought was a friend, from Vernon who could not help her find Jos, and from the memories of Jos herself. If Jos did not want to find her, perhaps Vernon was wrong. Perhaps he was too kind to his sister. Maybe Jos really did just want to abandon Evelyn now.

Out in the public streets, Evelyn made an effort to control the tears that had been flowing down her cheeks. She dabbed at her eyes with her pocket handkerchief and tried to look calm. She did not feel calm. She felt angry, then heartbroken. She felt homesick and then defiant. She longed for Jos and then wanted to leave London and never return. She hated James and Lilian, but pitied them in the same moment. She was stupid to have trusted anyone here, but then she was full of love for Jos and gratitude for the kindness of others. At once she felt crushed and resented Edward for sending her here, but still there was part of her that knew that this was all part of what needed to happen in her life. Even now she was still flying higher than she would have been doing in West Coombe.

She walked a long time, following one street after another without any real clue as to the direction she was walking. London was a city full of landmarks, almost impossible to be entirely lost in, but she did not know precisely where she was either. She would recognise a building or perhaps the name of one of the Underground stations she passed, then turn a corner and find herself somewhere entirely unfamiliar. Finally, she emerged into an open space she did recognise. It was Trafalgar Square. She recognised the fountains and Nelson on his tall column. She'd been a happy sightseer, still new in London, with Lilian by her side, the last time she'd been here. How much had changed. And yet the square had not at all. Nelson was still impassive. It was one of the things that fascinated about London, how it remained so unchanged by all of the stories that played out in its buildings and streets. So many people, so many stories, but always London with its familiar landmarks, its famous places. London was an entity larger and more timeless than its transitory population. Somehow this was a comfort. Whatever happened to her, Evelyn was only the smallest part of London, and London was just one city.

Emotionless now, more numb than angry, she trudged on. There was nowhere she could go. She could not return to the Graingers' house. She doubted she could ever go there again. She dared not return to the Yellow Orchid, much as she thought Vernon would help her. It was possible Lilian was still there, or that she had rallied her friends amongst the patrons. She could try Jos's flat again, but if Jos did not want to be found, even by her brother, what good would it do to turn up there now, especially with nowhere else to go? Such a need might only frighten Jos further. So she walked, waiting for an idea to strike.

Through Trafalgar Square she passed, on down Whitehall, where the business of government was conducted. She passed army buildings and government ministries; she passed the black gates of Downing Street and wondered briefly what Mr. Baldwin was doing at that moment. Then she saw, ahead of her in the middle of the wide road, something which drew her steps.

Rising from the grey road, carved in white Portland stone, stood the Cenotaph. The empty tomb memorial, unveiled in 1920 as the memorial to all the dead of the Great War. Ornate laurel wreaths decorated its angular flanks, the red, white, and blue of the Union Flag and various ensigns of the armed services hanging from their angled poles. In the diminishing winter light, it was bright and yet stately. Quiet, despite the bustle of the road all around it.

Evelyn waited for a car to pass, then crossed to the structure itself. Three shallow steps formed the base, on which were laid one or two poppy wreaths, as had become the custom of rememberance in recent years, blood red against the pale stone.

Reverence in her heart, Evelyn approached the memorial and laid a hand on the smooth, cold stone. It seemed as nothing at all compared to the many young, vibrant lives it represented. In fact, to memorialise those young men in hard, unforgiving stone felt almost tragic in itself. The Cenotaph, the empty tomb, was a thing of death. But those men had lived and would have continued living, had war not cruelly prevented it.

Caught in the emotion, Evelyn laid her cheek against the stone, closing her eyes. She thought of Edward, not dead but still lost to her. She thought of Frank Grainger, who had been so kind to her Eddie, wondered what impact his loss had really had on Lilian and James. She thought of the men they had known, the men who had died by their side, and those who had survived but carried the hell of the battlefield inside them. Her thoughts moved on to Jos and Vernon, their parents taken from them by explosions from the sky. To the men of West Coombe whose names were on a smaller memorial, near the harbour. She thought of the new friends she had found in London, wondered how the war had touched their lives. For it had touched all of their lives.

Perhaps, she thought, this memorial wasn't simply for the dead soldiers. Yes, they deserved it and the country mourned them formally every November. But she remembered the pressure there had been for this permanent memorial in Whitehall, carved in eternal stone. It seemed clear to her now that it was not just for the soldiers and sailors and pilots who were killed. Not just for the nurses and engineers, ordnance factory workers and civilians who died. The memorial was for all of them. For all who remembered a life before the war, who remembered those who had died when they were vibrant and vital. It was for a way of life which had slipped away. Carved here in stone was the world they inherited from their parents, it was the last testimony to the world under Victoria and Edward. That world had been swept away in bloodshed, and afterwards, nothing was quite the same. Everything was modern now. But the quiet dignity of the Cenotaph was a reminder of another time, the time before. It was the gravemarker of a time that had passed.

Evelyn was not of that time. She had been a child then. She was of the new world and it was that which had driven her to London. Edward's urging had simply shown her the path. The people of the time before, her parents, had accepted the world as it was, taken what they were given, assumed it was good and proper for a young man to fight and die for glory. They were different now, in a world where everything had died. They were left with dreams. The pursuit of those dreams was surely what made them modern, even if they did not really know what those dreams were. They pushed for something better, something more and went headlong into the world to find it.

Had she found it? In Jos's arms, she really thought she had. But that was gone now and she was not sure she would be able to win it back. So now her thoughts turned again to Edward, to her own loss, and how she wished he was there to help her in that instant. Tired of pursuing a life well lived, she rested against the cold stone, as the tears fell again. London swept by on the road, but she was still, calm and lying on a clifftop with Eddie, pondering the future.

CHAPTER TWENTY

Night fell. Such was the bustle and anonymity of London that no one came to question the young woman with her face pressed to the Cenotaph. Perhaps, Evelyn thought, this was not so unusual. Even though nearly a decade had passed, people had not stopped mourning their fathers, sons, brothers, husbands, lovers. They moved on, but the grief went with them. Evelyn wondered if people would always mourn here, when the war was forgotten and the soldiers long gone. Or would the memorial be torn down one day, when there was no one left to remember?

Her tears had stopped and yet there was an odd comfort in the solid block of stone. She did not want to leave it behind. But the darkness brought the cold of winter and she could hardly stand in Whitehall through the night. She had to try to return to someone familiar. Perhaps to Vernon, or even to Jos. Just for somewhere warm and something to eat. She would expect nothing but shelter and, perhaps, to be kept safe from Lilian's rage.

Sadly, she turned her aching feet towards the archway leading to Horseguards Parade. She knew if she could reach the Mall, and Buckingham Palace, she could find her way back into Mayfair. She would decide where to seek refuge when she got there. As she set off, it began to rain, a cold, icy rain that was nearly sleet. Hatless and with only her coat to protect her, Evelyn soon felt the chill creeping through her whole body, the freezing water tricking over her scalp, down her face, and seeping under her collar. She did not care. There was something cleansing about being drenched in this way. As her extremities went numb, her emotions felt the same.

Across the gravel of Horseguards and onto the Mall. Right on Marlborough Road to emerge near St. James's Palace and follow St. James's Street until she reached Piccadilly. She received a few curious glances from passersby, especially as she neared the well-to-do streets of Mayfair, but no one questioned why she was out in the winter rain with no hat or umbrella and no one offered her assistance. She was glad of it, convinced that kindness would feel like an intrusion to a grief that felt all consuming and yet impossible to explain. What would she tell anyone who enquired what was wrong? That the woman she loved had rejected her, and a friend she had only known for a short time had publicly accused her of seducing two men, playing on a dead soldier's memory, and taking illicit drugs? It sounded ludicrous. Evelyn could almost have laughed at just how outlandish her old self would have found such a tale. And yet here, in London, it did not seem so odd, somehow, in the city that swallowed stories and made them part of itself.

In the end, she turned her footsteps towards the Yellow Orchid. She considered it unlikely that Lilian would still be there and decided she was guaranteed a warm welcome from Vernon, whereas she could not be sure of the same from Jos.

She was approaching the cafe when a woman walking down the street towards her suddenly exclaimed, "Evelyn! What on earth are you doing? Oh, my dear, you gave us such a fright, disappearing like that."

Evelyn raised her eyes from the wet pavement to look at Dorothy. Warm relief flooded her cold body. Dorothy, of all people, would understand. "It's Jos," she said first. "And Lilian. Oh, Dorothy, I've made such a mess of everything!" She began to cry again.

"Nonsense," Dorothy replied. "Look, I know the story, as much as Vernon told me, anyway. You've not made a mess of anything. Come home with me—we'll get you dry and you can sleep in my spare bed."

"What about Lilian? You're her friend," Evelyn asked, trying to restrain the sobs.

"I don't give two hoots about what Lilian thinks. Besides, a woman would have to be heartless to leave you outside with nowhere to go. Come on. I'm not letting you back inside the Orchid, just in case. I'll nip back and stop Vernon worrying later." Dorothy took Evelyn's hand and led her along the street. Her house was only two streets over from the Orchid, a small terraced town house at the end of a rather quaint street. She opened the door and led Evelyn into the warm.

Dorothy's home was rather plain and matter of fact. She had everything she needed but nothing unnecessary. There was a smell of perfume and cigarette smoke, mixing with the scent of coal from the glowing hearth. Dorothy left Evelyn standing in the lamplit sitting room and went to fetch towels and blankets.

Once Evelyn was dried and dressed in one of Dorothy's nightdresses, a blanket around her shoulders, Dorothy sat to talk to her. "Now, I know what Vernon told me, but do you care to tell me what's happened yourself? He's awfully prone to exaggeration."

"It started this morning with Jos," Evelyn replied, realising she was grateful of the opportunity to relate what had happened. "I don't really know what I said, but she got very tense. I think I might have implied that I could live with her if Lilian decided I had to leave her house. And I questioned why we had to keep what's between us a secret. She got very angry, said I didn't understand and that she didn't love me after all. So I left. I really thought she would stop me when she saw I was actually planning on leaving, but she didn't."

"I sometimes think that woman is a lost cause," Dorothy muttered. "Sorry, go on."

"Well, I had nowhere to go but the Graingers'. They were away for Christmas, so I had the house to myself for a while. It gave me time to think and I remembered what everyone had told me about Jos, and what she must've been feeling. So I decided I would go back and talk to her, try to be more understanding."

"Which is really more than she deserves, if you ask me."

"Well, I'm afraid I love her."

"I can see that, darling. I could see it all day, yesterday. She's bloody lucky too." Dorothy smiled. "So what happened?"

"I didn't get to see Jos. I was about to go out when Lilian and James got home. I don't think Lilian had a very happy time with their family and she was in a strange mood. She stormed off upstairs and left me with James. I honestly don't know what came over him but he chose that moment to propose marriage to me."

"With no warning at all?" Dorothy looked honestly surprised.

"No. I had a hint that he liked me—he'd suggested we go to the pictures or for a walk in the park—but I didn't expect him to propose out of the blue." Evelyn was still confused by James's actions now. "Of course, I said no, but he wouldn't believe me. So eventually I told him that I'd been engaged before, in West Coombe, so it wasn't that I was scared of being engaged, and that there was actually someone else that I love. I didn't say who."

"I bet that went down very well."

"He was so furious, Dorothy." Evelyn felt a little frightened just seeing his face. "He told me to get out of his house. I have no doubt Lilian was listening from upstairs too and she did nothing."

"What's gone wrong between you and Lilian, darling? I know she's a perfect idiot, but for something like this to happen…"

Dorothy's interest seemed earnest rather than an attempt to gather gossip. Evelyn decided to tell her the whole truth. "I think it's more than one thing. Like you said, she thinks I'm involved with Vernon. She saw me at the cafe with him when I was actually looking for Jos. Of course, she wouldn't think I was with Jos—her mind is too narrow for that—so she guessed I had a thing with Vernon. When I told James that I loved someone else, I think her mind went straight to Vernon. It's not just that though. I happened to go into her room when she was injecting herself with cocaine. I know it was cocaine, I've read about it in the papers. She said it was medicine to begin with but then she didn't deny it, she just swore me to secrecy. I made my disapproval clear and she didn't like it. She's not really been the same since then."

"Oh, my Lord," Dorothy said. "I half thought she was on the stuff, she seemed so bright and full of energy all the time, even when her eyes were tired. But I didn't think she'd be brave enough to go out and get it. It explains a lot, really."

Evelyn told her the rest, about the slap and Lilian's lies.

Dorothy shook her head. "Vernon said he tried to talk sense into Lilian, but she informed him it was over between them and then stormed off. Somehow, I don't think he's devastated." Dorothy allowed a small smile. "But I'm so sorry, Evie. You didn't deserve to be treated that way. I'm not going to say you handled it all perfectly, but who would?"

"I'm not worried about Lilian, although I don't want her to think I used her brother's death to prey on her kindness. I'm more concerned that all of my belongings are in her house. It's Jos I'm really worried about." Evelyn hoped Dorothy would help her, somehow.

"I know, Evie. And I'm sorry she's so bloody stupid. She's been the same for years, never manages to hold on to something good. But I don't think she meant this to happen. She was different yesterday. She loves you, all right." Dorothy patted Evelyn's arm.

Evelyn tried to smile, despite the tears that threatened. "I don't know where she is."

"She'll be in a nameless public house where no one knows her, drinking as much whisky as she can afford. It's always how she deals with her own distresss. And no, there's no hope of finding her until morning, when she'll crawl home. I will help you, then. For now, you'd be best to sleep."

"What about all of my things, at Lilian and James's house?" Evelyn asked.

"I will go and fetch them in the morning, myself. Or summon the assistance of Clara and Courtney or someone else helpful who isn't at all afraid of Miss Idiot Grainger."

"Thank you, Dorothy," Evelyn said.

"No problem at all, sweetheart. You go through to bed now. I'm going to go back to the Orchid and let Vernon know all's well. He's uncharacteristically concerned."

"That's nice of him."

"Yes. Well, I'll put his mind at ease and then come back. So if you hear the door being unlocked, it's only me. Goodnight, try to rest."

Evelyn did as she was told, going through to the Dorothy's spare bedroom. The mattress was rather soft and badly sprung but Dorothy had put a warming bottle between the sheets and the warmth was soothing. Despite a racing mind and an aching heart, Evelyn fell asleep, exhausted.

❖

Jos slumped in her chair in the corner of The King's Arms in Shoreditch. The interior of the public house was a far cry from the modernity of the Yellow Orchid. Here, the dark wood fittings were of the last century, the paint on the walls stained with decades of tobacco smoke. Most of the patrons were working men, but they were so absorbed in their own conversations, pints of ale, and games of dominoes, that she was barely noticed in her dark corner. Those who glanced at her doubtless took her for a rather feminine young man. They'd have been more likely to notice that she was making rapid progress through a whole bottle of cheap scotch.

With every measure she poured, she hated herself more. There was no comfort in the heat of the alcohol burning down her throat. This was the life she'd tried so hard to leave behind. Meeting Evelyn was the pinnacle, the moment she had known that she had risen from the ashes. But she could not keep it. She'd let it slip through her fingers.

No, that wasn't fair. She took another drink. Evelyn hadn't slipped through her fingers. Jos had pushed her away. She knew it. When she thought back over the conversation of that morning she could not even follow her own logic. Why be so frightened at signs of commitment and love from Evelyn? In what way was that terrifying?

Now, she would give anything to go back. To be close to Evelyn in the warmth of her bed, to hold her close. Even to just eat breakfast at her side. Evelyn made the simplest of things seem pleasurable. She had thrown it away.

Jos was not prone to tears, but she found herself fighting them now. They were not so much of sadness but of fury with herself. How had she done this again? To the best woman she'd ever met?

She drank more whisky. It was far from a good scotch but it was starting to do its required job. There was a barrier between her and the world now. She felt removed from the lives of everyone around her, isolated in her misery but at least starting to be numb to the worst of the pain. There was nothing for her now, just a bleak, solitary future. Why not just accept it?

Jos usually took the coward's way out, running away rather than facing up to her troubles. As she sipped the scotch, she knew she was doing it again. If she shut herself in her flat for a few days, only going out to go to work, refused to answer the door, perhaps the mess she had made would just go away.

But what if Evelyn came to her door? Could she ignore the doorbell, knowing Evelyn was so close? And was it better for Evelyn that she did? What sort of life could she offer to Evelyn, anyway? She drained her glass and poured another. Perhaps Evelyn would be happier if Jos just left her alone. And yet, she had talked of love. How could Jos go against love?

She looked around the room and realised her vision had blurred slightly. It could have been the whisky or the tears, or both. Her hearing seemed to have lost its clarity too, and she heard the constant chatter of men's voices as if they were in a separate room, through a thin wall.

She would go to Evelyn. Not now perhaps, but in the morning. She would talk to her and she would see what response she got. She could not always be a coward. Evelyn might slap her face and send her away. If that happened, at least the decision was made for her. She would find Evelyn.

Her new determination in mind, she tried to stand up. But she had drunk more whisky than she realised and she fell back into the chair, her head spinning. Frustrated, she cursed under her breath. Then her eyes fell on the empty glass in front of her. There was some whisky left. Why not have another, for courage? In the morning, she would see Evelyn. But tonight she was drunk and anonymous and there was an old comfort in that.

❖

In the morning, Evelyn awoke to the sound of voices. It took her a moment to realise where she was, then all the grief of the previous day flooded back to her. She listened again to the voices in Dorothy's sitting room, daring to hope that one might be Jos, terrified that one would be Lilian. As it turned out, it was neither. She very distinctly heard Courtney's American accent and Clara's rather musical tone, in conversation with Dorothy.

Easing out of bed, finding her feet aching from the trudging of the day before, she wrapped a blanket around her shoulders and went through to the sitting room.

"Good morning, Evie," Dorothy said, with a gentle smile. "I hope we didn't wake you."

"I don't know if you did or not, but I'm glad to be awake. Do you know where Jos is yet?"

"Oh, Evie, she's treated you in the most rotten way," Courtney said. "I'd be furious."

"I just want to talk to her," Evelyn replied, realising she was not angry with Jos at all.

"She doesn't seem to be home yet," Clara said. "I was just saying to Dorothy that Courtney and I are going to try some of the pubs she's been known to frequent in the past. She tends to take herself towards the East End, where no one knows her and the whisky's cheap."

"You don't think anything's happened to her, do you?" Evelyn demanded, her blood running cold at the notion.

"No. She's done it before. Don't worry, Evie, she can look after herself. It's just that she doesn't want to be found sometimes. As soon as we find her, I will make her drink coffee and I will bring her to you."

"Thank you," Evelyn said. To have their support was comforting, to have their reassurances about Jos, even better.

"Now, before you woke up, Courtney and I went to see Lilian and we collected all of your things." Dorothy gestured to the suitcase resting near the door to the sitting room, and an additional leather bag by its side. She had not gained very much during her time in London. To see it all packed into a suitcase once again felt extremely sad, as though her time here had barely happened.

"Thank you for fetching it," she said.

"The thing is, darling, the postman had just called too. And there's some letters for you. I had a look at the postmark and it looks like they've come from Devon." In her hand, Dorothy held two envelopes. Evelyn took then from her, letting blanket drop to the ground. One, she thought, looked rather like Annie's handwriting. The other, the address written in an uneven scrawl, she knew was from Edward. That was the letter she chose to open first. It was badly written on a scrap of paper, the words difficult to make out. Yet there was still the trace of Edward's formerly graceful handwriting.

Dearest Evie,

Many thanks for your letters. I wish I was well enough to write more. Only know that you have made me happier than I have been since before the war, with your news from London. I wish I could visit and see you so happy and meet your new love. Thank you for thinking of me.

I miss you too, Evie. Always.

Now I must go but I had to write to let you know, I will always watch over you. Remember me as I was before. Continue to live the life I cannot.

I join my comrades. Remember me, as you do them.
Your loving brother, always,
Eddie.

Tears rose in Evelyn's eyes. It was impossible to misinterpret the letter. She cast it aside, moving on to the letter she was sure now was from Annie.

Dear Evelyn,

I do not know for sure that this letter will find you. I am not entirely sure if this is the correct address. I do not know if you still care about us here in West Coombe. If you have not become entirely selfish, maybe you do. I hope so.

I am writing to tell you that Eddie is missing. Today is Christmas Eve and we last saw him two days ago. As you know, he rarely leaves the house, so we cannot help but think something serious has happened to him.

I am writing for two reasons. The first is that I know he was closer to you than anyone, so you might know more than we do. Please do share any information you have. The second reason is to ask you to come home. Our family needs you at the moment and will, I believe, put your betrayal of us behind us, in order that we can be together.

I expect the earliest this letter will reach you now is the twenty-seventh. I will hope to see you then, or the day after. I am currently staying with Mother and Father, since neither is feeling strong enough to run the shop or even to make sure there are meals.

I very much hope you still care about us and can put aside your new fancy life in London to help.

With a reminder of your duty,
Your sister,
Annie

Evelyn could feel Annie's anger in every letter. Annie would never understand. Besides, that did not ultimately matter now.

Blindly, she handed the second letter to Dorothy. Better that she read it herself than Evelyn try to explain. "I have to go home," she said. "To West Coombe. Today. It's my brother, you see. Will you help me?"

Dorothy read through Annie's letter quickly. "Oh gosh, Evie. Darling, I'm so sorry. Do you really think—?"

"Do I think Eddie has killed himself?" The words hit Evelyn harder as she spoke them out loud. "Yes, of course I do. How could I think anything else?"

"I know, darling. It's just so horrible, I was hoping it might be something else." Dorothy had passed the letters to Clara, who was now reading them, Courtney leaning over her shoulder. Dorothy pressed an arm around Evelyn's shoulders.

"I need to get to Paddington and get a train," Evelyn said. She could think of nothing else and certainly could not allow herself to succumb to the grief, not while she needed to organise her journey.

"Do you need someone to come with you?" Dorothy asked.

"Yes, to the station. To make sure I get on the right train. But I will be fine to go home on my own." There was really no other way forward, much though she wished she could take one of them to hide behind, to defend her from her own family.

"Come along then, we'll go in a cab and make sure we find you a train." This was Clara, who smiled kindly, her eyes full of sympathy.

Just a few minutes later, Evelyn was in a cab with Clara and Courtney. Dorothy had stayed at home, vowing to find Jos and tell her what had happened. Evelyn barely had room in her thoughts to contemplate this. She certainly could not wait for news of Jos. Perhaps she would never see her again. It was decided now.

At Paddington, Courtney made enquiries at the ticket office. There was nothing like a direct train, but Evelyn could take a fast train to Bristol, the next express to Totnes, and then change there to the next local train she could find. It would be evening before she reached West Coombe, but there was really no alternative. Clara insisted on paying for the tickets and Evelyn did not have the strength to argue. She received kisses and good wishes from Clara and Courtney with little response before she boarded the waiting train. She welcomed their kindness, but her mind was entirely on Edward now.

Only as the train began to move out of the station did she realise what she was leaving behind and what she was going back to. She was not the same woman who alighted in this station all those weeks ago. She had been a child then, seeking an adventure. She had found a glorious, colourful Neverland but she was not really part of it. Now home called her back, inexorably, even against her will. She should have always known it would happen.

Factories and terraced houses became countryside and market towns as the train rattled forward. London was gone, like a dream. Like all dreams, it was difficult to make logical sense of it now it was gone. She stared, unseeing, at southern England drifting past the window. She'd not seen fields since she had arrived in London, but there was nothing soothing about being in the open again. She had rather liked being surrounded by the tall, ostentatious buildings of London. At least they were something, not nothing, like these empty fields.

The hours passed. She roused herself enough to buy a cup of tea from the buffet car and then returned to gazing out of the window. A wintery shower streaked her view with trickling raindrops, but still she stared. Her mind was too busy to register what she was seeing. She could not help the thought that came, at first just a nagging doubt and then a growing certainty the longer she focused on it. If she had stayed at home, in West Coombe, would Edward still be alive?

CHAPTER TWENTY-ONE

Darkness had fallen by the time Evelyn arrived on Main Street, West Coombe. The journey had been arduous, with a long wait at Bristol for the next Totnes-bound train. She was hungry and tired. Yet back in West Coombe, her senses came alive.

The familiarity was almost a relief. She might have been eager to leave the place but it had been her lifelong home. Every tree, hedgerow, and building was familiar. The sour salt smell of the sea was very different to the smoky air of London. Although she could barely admit it to herself, part of her belonged here, part of her missed this place.

She caught her first glimpse of the sea, black and smooth, reflecting the lights of the town. She'd barely even thought of the sea when she was in London, and yet here it was, the same as ever. Nothing had really changed.

To imagine that West Coombe had simply gone on without her was almost a surprise. Of course, she was not so selfish as to imagine that she was more important than anyone else in the town. It was just that it was strange to picture the town, here, the same as ever, while she was experiencing all she had in London. Just as, she realised, it was now very odd to think that London was there, going on. Clara and Courtney, Dorothy, Vernon, James and Lilian. Jos. They were all living their lives in places familiar to them just as they had before she had arrived. The buses were still travelling London's streets, jazz was still playing at the Orchid. She did not like to think of everything being the same, just without her there to witness it, be part of it.

Although it wasn't the same for Jos. She could be fairly certain of that. Now that she was off the train, her sense of her distance from Jos was very keen. Even if Jos wanted to find her, to hold her through the night, she could not. Jos was out of her reach now, and Evelyn had no way of knowing if Jos would care about that or not. Perhaps she was still out drinking whisky and seducing any easily led woman who came near her. Perhaps it was best that Evelyn believed that.

Evelyn approached her family home slowly. Now, all thoughts of London were overcome by the tension of being home. Despite everything, she prayed there had been a mistake, that she would walk through the door and find Edward there, in his usual chair. Whatever censure came from her family, she was sure she could cope with it if Edward was there.

At the door, Evelyn hesitated. She would never had knocked on it before but this was not her home now. Still, the idea of knocking on the door of her own family home seemed ridiculous and far too miserable to contemplate for long. Instead, she summoned her courage and went inside.

Evelyn found her family gathered around the large kitchen table. Her mother and father, Annie and Peter were all there. With them was Annie's husband. Edward was not there, just as she had known would be the case. At her entrance, they all looked up.

"Evelyn!" her mother exclaimed. For a moment, she sounded relieved and pleased to see her. Then her expression changed to one of cold anger. "You've decided to honour us with your presence, then?"

"Hello, Mother. And everyone." Evelyn paused. "Annie wrote to me and told me about Eddie." Was she supposed to fall on the floor and beg their forgiveness? Were they waiting for an apology? It was difficult to tell. "I'm sorry if I gave you all a scare, or if you thought it rather selfish of me to go off like that. I've come home to see if I can help with Eddie."

"Selfish is the word," her father said. "And I don't just mean that we needed the help in the shop. You disappointed a very good young man."

"But I didn't want to marry him, not really," Evelyn replied. It seemed like such a long time since she had accepted Michael's proposal. Clearly it was still far more important to her family than it was to her.

"You're a very silly child," her mother said. "Living in a fairy story. He's a good man and you were too selfish to see it. Too concerned with what you want to be a good wife."

Evelyn wondered if her mother could really hear the words coming out of her own mouth. "Mother, it would have been awfully selfish of Michael to marry me, knowing I didn't want to." Her mother seemed about to respond, so Evelyn continued. "Besides, it's in the past now. I wrote to him and apologised."

"He's found someone else, you know," Annie said, with a tone that suggested she wanted to hurt Evelyn.

How little her family really understood her. "I'm happy for him, in that case." Evelyn genuinely was. She hated the idea of Michael being unhappy because of her. He was a good man, just not one she wanted to marry. Annie looked dissatisfied with Evelyn's equinamity. "But I don't want to talk about that. Have you heard anything about Eddie?"

The common grief at Edward's loss seemed, momentarily, to unite them. Her mother gestured to the empty seat at the table and poured an extra cup of tea from the pot. Evelyn removed her coat and tried to feel at home, as she waited to hear what they knew about Edward.

"It was like I said in my letter," Annie said. "He was here, and then he was gone. He didn't say anything to anyone. You know, he doesn't walk about that much during the day. He's just always in his chair. Since you've been gone, he's been even less communicative actually. It's like none of us are good enough for him to make the effort." Annie said this with some resentment. Evelyn wondered why her brother's feelings were her fault.

"Anyway, Father was in the shop and it was wash day, so Mother was out the back. The next time anyone came to see if Eddie wanted a drink, or some food, he was missing. We've asked all around the village but no one has seen him. And you'd think they'd notice, wouldn't you?"

Evelyn felt the sadness creeping through her veins as she contemplated her brother's last hours. What would he do? What would he have thought and felt? The cold, heavy certainty of what had happened settled on her chest. "And there's been no sign of him?"

"No," her mother said. "We've had the whole village out searching. We've found nothing."

"Did he leave any clues?" Evelyn asked.

"No," Annie said. "But we did wonder if he might tell you something that he wouldn't tell us."

Evelyn thought for a moment. Should she reveal her brother's private communication to her? She looked at the pain in the eyes of their parents and knew Edward would forgive her. From her inside pocket, she drew the letter she had received that morning. "I think he wrote me this letter to say goodbye," she said, her fingers trembling. "I'd have thought so even if it hadn't arrived at the same time as Annie's letter. I think Eddie's was a little delayed because of how bad his handwriting is. So I got them both this morning." With some reluctance, she handed the letter to her mother, who passed it on to her father, and then Annie. She hated to share something that was private between herself and Edward. But her family were hurting and they needed to know. Edward would understand.

By the time they had all read the letter, Annie and her mother had tears in their eyes. Evelyn felt their pain, knew she had no right to claim this grief was hers alone. No matter that Edward had been closer to her than anyone else, he was Annie and Peter's brother, he was the eldest son of the family. It was a different loss to each of them but it was still a loss. It was also one they had been unprepared for. Eddie had survived the war. For it to finally have its full effect on him now, a decade later, made his survival seem so futile. They thought they were the generation who had surivived the war but they were still being killed by it.

"But what did he do?" Annie asked, voicing what they were all thinking.

"For there to be no sign of him…" their mother said, her voice hoarse with pain.

"It'll be the sea," her father said, gruffly. "No other way it's possible. Besides, it's easy. He was hardly in a state to plan anything."

They were all quiet, contemplating this. After a few minutes, it was as if her mother was suddenly reminded that her wayward daughter had returned to the fold. She turned sharp eyes on Evelyn. "You'll be staying, then, I take it?"

Evelyn was startled by the sudden question. "Yes. I mean, I don't have to, if you'd prefer me not to."

"Nonsense. You're part of the family, even if you turned your back on us. You'll stay here. What's more, we won't hear any more of your London talk. You'll stay here and you'll go back to your duties in the shop. With any luck, there's a man in the town who will still think of having you, before too long has passed." Evelyn's mother spoke the words as if there was no alternative.

Evelyn, who had not really stopped to contemplate if her return to West Coombe was permanent, was horrified. "I don't want to marry someone from West Coombe, Mother," she exclaimed.

"Then you'll be a spinster and help me take care of your father. Whatever you do, you'll stop daydreaming. It was Edward who made you daydream, and look what's happened to him. I won't lose you to it as well."

"Eddie wasn't daydreaming," Evelyn replied, angry now. "He was damaged by the war. It was shell shock, or whatever they're calling it these days."

"And yet he could manage to tell you to go to London, to take himself off and end it all? Funny kind of illness that's only bad when you want it to be."

"Mother, you can't mean it. You know Eddie wasn't choosing to be as he was."

"I don't really know what I know any longer, Evelyn. But I do know you're going to do the right thing by this family." Her mother sounded more tired than forceful. This made it even more difficult to argue with her.

"But I love someone in London," Evelyn protested, finally. The image of Jos sprang into her mind's eye. To feel such a connection with her, to imagine her so vividly, seemed very odd in her family's kitchen. Jos might as well have not existed. Yet she was so very real. Evelyn remembered how it felt to kiss her and almost smiled.

"Well, if he loved you in return I think we'd see him here at your side, wouldn't we? You're even more stupid than I thought if you trust a London man at his word." Her mother looked as though she was beginnign to pity Evelyn. Evelyn knew there was no point in continuing this exchange.

"I'm very tired, Mother. Do you think I might go to bed now? We can talk about it tomorrow."

"Go on then, go. Annie's in your room too." Evelyn's heart sank even further. Annie would fill the room with judgement and condemnation of Evelyn's actions, which did not seem conducive to a restful night. And she felt as though she needed to rest. She was almost too tired to grieve for Edward tonight. Tomorrow, she knew, the pain would overtake her.

❖

When the pain came, it did not subside. Although he had been a hollow shell of his former self for the last decade, Evelyn missed Edward horribly. He had been a constant presence in her life, even on his quietest and least communicative days. There had never been, she realised, a day in which she had been alive but Edward had not. Until now. Now he was gone.

There was still no sign of him. Every morning, men went out to search the coastline, particularly at the North Bay, where Edward could have been drawn by family memories of summer days. If he had thrown himself on the mercy of the waves there, it was almost impossible to judge where his body would have been carried. There were powerful currents in the water, as the estuary flowed around a sandbar and out into the open sea beween the rocky headlands. Perhaps he would be found one day, washed up miles away. Or maybe he would be lost forever.

On reflection, Evelyn preferred the latter. To vanish was more dignified somehow. It allowed Edward to join the ranks of his fallen comrades with their unknown and unmarked resting places. True, he would not have his name inscribed onto a memorial, but he was one of the war dead now. They did not need to find his earthly remains deposited on a beach.

Days passed, though Evelyn did not keep a real track of them. The New Year came and went without celebration. Evelyn gave a passing thought to Lilian, with her silly new dress. Had her New Year been the one she'd been anticipating so eagerly? Probably not, if Vernon had not relented towards her. Her sympathy for Lilian was only brief, until she remembered the last time she had seen her, the lies she had told the patrons in the Orchid. With hindsight, from this distance, it seemed astonishing that she could have prompted such a reaction. In light of what had happened to Edward, it seemed awfully trivial.

As days became weeks, Evelyn did not feel any more at home in West Coombe. Her family were polite, occasionaly almost seeming to care about her. But the sense of her betrayal was heavy in her home. They did not trust her. Not once did they ask her about London or her new friends. Not once did they suggest that she might want to go back. It was treated as an embarrasing incident not to be spoken about, to be forgotten, if not forgiven. Evelyn found it easier not to talk too much when she was with her family, adopting a sombre, taciturn diposition that could easily be taken for grief. She did grieve, but she also strove to protect herself from her family's disapproval. She regained a routine of helping in the shop, of helping her mother with housework and cooking and the occasional walk along the harbourside. She did not feel like her old jaunts onto the cliffs. She did not spend time daydreaming or reading. When she was not working, she was mostly trying not to think.

Her heart ached for Edward. But she knew that his was not the only loss she was mourning. The more time passed, the more she began to wonder about Jos. She believed she could trust Dorothy to tell Jos what had happened. But she had not left a forwarding address, so even if Jos did want to write to her, she could not. Besides, what would such a letter be? A goodbye? Evelyn was not sure she could stand the finality of that. Despite everything, she still loved Jos. If those two nights and few glorious hours with Jos were all she was to be allowed, then they would have to sustain her for the rest of her life. She was fairly sure she would never love anyone else in the way she loved Jos. She was certain she could never love one of West Coombe's men in anything like the same way. The thought repulsed her. There was only Jos now, and she was separated from her, perhaps forever.

Of course, it was entirely possible Jos would not want to write to her anyway. By now, she'd probably met a more interesting woman, or realised Evelyn was too naive and inexperienced for her. Or maybe she'd descended into the drinking again and didn't care about anyone. Evelyn hoped she was happy. And she went on, knowing she was unlikely to ever be truly happy again. If only she could have talked it through with Edward. Asked him how a butterfly was supposed to fly when its wings had been crushed. He'd flown away himself now, leaving her stranded. She almost wished she could follow him.

❖

The sea was dark, invisible in the night but for the white foam where it surged and crashed at the rocks on either side of the bay. The horizon was only perceptible because the sky was dark grey, not quite the deep black of the water. It was cold, the air full of spray. The sound of the waves and the wind in the trees on the cliffs above was all pervasive. Tonight, the North Bay was a place to lose yourself, not to think.

Evelyn wanted nothing more than to lose herself. Perched on the sea wall, built to keep back the power of the waves, her legs hanging above the sand, she did not care that she was cold. She felt it but enjoyed the numb, creeping sensation of it spreading from her extremities and towards her core. She felt reckless, drunk with grief and loss.

To end it entirely would be easy. To slide from the wall, cross the sand, let the waves wash around her ankles, then higher. She would have to walk out to sea to accomplish it. The beach was very shallow. But the tide was high and it would not take long to vanish. Just as he had done. As everything had done.

She knew this beach in the sunshine. She knew it as a place of family and bright days. Never again. Those things were permanently eclipsed and could never emerge from the shadows. Shadows she had cast herself.

Perhaps she was a coward. She was certainly more of a coward than he had been, for she knew she would not take that walk into the water. Living with the pain seemed a just punishment for her actions.

Yet did she repent? She asked herself again and again. Was she really in the wrong? Or had she simply been keeping a promise, more important than any other she'd made?

The rain started to fall, the edge of the approaching storm. The water soaked through her thin cardigan and the cotton dress beneath and cooled the last heat in her body. She felt the drops running over her scalp, her hair growing heavier with it, until the curls at the front were slick on her cheeks. Though instinct urged her to seek shelter, she would not. She would stay here. Perhaps she'd catch an awful fever, could take to her bed and pretend there was not a world outside. Just as the world seemed to have forgotten her. She let the rain soak her clothes, the wind lash her wet skin, and she shivered and remained where she was, hidden by the weather and the night.

At least half an hour had passed since the rain began. The tide had progressed towards her, the waves now beneath her feet, just touching the sea wall with each swell. She had stopped thinking, finally achieved the state of not caring about anything which she had so desired. A low rumbling sound blended with the wind and the waves. It was only when a flash of yellow light briefly came from behind her, casting her shadow against the approaching sea, that she took full notice of the accompanying sound, startled. Fear of being discovered was her first emotion and she turned, intending to stand and walk up the hill into the trees. Tonight she wanted only to be alone, numb.

As she rose to her feet, Evelyn gave an involuntary cry of pain. The cold had made her muscles stiff. She was forced to lean on the wall, pausing before she could flee. A motor car approaching along the coast road was not so unusual these days. But somehow, this car in the night-time felt like a threat. The illumination of its headlamps was too much to bear. She did not want to be seen.

Too late, she managed to walk a few paces towards the trees. The motor car, its rumbling engine now louder than the wind, rounded the corner and she was caught fully in the beams of light. Like a rabbit, she stopped, turning to stare, blinded as she looked fully into the two illuminated circles. The car itself was just a dark shadow behind them.

Abruptly, the car stopped. Evelyn, who had been expecting it to drive straight past her and leave her to her misery, felt her heart beat harder. Now she was afraid, of the stranger behind the wheel who had so obviously stopped because they had seen her at the side of the road.

She wanted to run, but stood transfixed instead, watching and waiting as the driver's door opened. A figure emerged, tall and broad shouldered, hatless.

A flicker of recognition warmed Evelyn for a moment, a flash of colour and light and joy, a world half remembered. But the cold edged it out. Not here, it was impossible. Too far away.

"Evelyn?" a familiar voice called.

Heat flooded back through Evelyn's veins, even as the incomprehension dizzied her. Relief made her breathless, as the driver of the car walked towards her and clasped her cold, weakened body in a strong embrace.

CHAPTER TWENTY-TWO

Jos held Evelyn, squeezing her close. Evelyn's clothes were sodden, her hair plastered to her head, and she was shivering. Hot tears rose in Jos's eyes and she cursed herself for not coming here sooner. It didn't matter how much whisky she drank, how many times she tried to tempt herself by gazing at other women, she only wanted Evelyn. To have left Evelyn to the disapproval of her family, without so much as a note, had been a horrendous misjudgement.

Of course, Vernon, Dorothy, Clara, and Courtney had tried to persuade her to write to Evelyn. She only knew the address because Evelyn had left the letter from her sister, Annie, behind at Dorothy's house. But she was still at odds with herself. If Evelyn had not left an address, perhaps she did not want to be contacted. Although she had good reason to return to West Coombe because of Edward's suicide, maybe Evelyn was actually glad that she was able to return. Vernon had told her what had happened between Evelyn and Lilian. Maybe that had been the last straw for Evelyn and she'd just wanted the simple life of home. Who was she, Jos, to bring havoc and confusion to that?

But now, holding Evelyn, feeling Evelyn's response to her, she finally admitted that she was wrong. Evelyn needed her, and she needed Evelyn. More than that, she loved her with her whole heart. If nothing else, their separation had taught her that. If it meant they would not be separated like this again, Jos was prepared to overcome her fear and commit to this woman. If it wasn't too late.

In the end, it had been Vernon who had forced her to come to Devon. He had borrowed the car himself, from a friend in Kensington. Jos was a better driver, but Vernon had accompanied her. She wondered if he'd joined her to ensure she made it to her destination and did not get cold feet along the way. She would not have done, but she did appreciate her brother's support. Several times along the journey she thought of Evelyn's loss, of how Edward Hopkins had galvanised Evelyn's life by starting her on her journey to London, and of how much grief Evelyn must now feel. Losing their parents had been bad enough but she could not imagine the pain of losing Vernon.

And so Vernon had occupied the passenger seat all through the long journey from London to south Devon. They'd begun with first light and only arrived now, after dark. The motor road swung down past one of the bays before entering the town. Jos's intention was to drive into the town and hope that Main Street would be as obvious as it sounded. However, as they passed the bay, she had seen the bedraggled figure in the headlights and recognised Evelyn at once. Relief and love fought for the uppermost place in her heart as she had called out to Evelyn and caught her in an embrace.

Now Evelyn pulled back a little to look into her eyes. "You've come. I didn't think you would."

"I'm so sorry, Evie," Jos said softly. "So very sorry. I was an idiot. I'm such a coward, you know. But I've learned my lesson. These past days and weeks without you, they've been the worst of my life. I want you in my life, Evie."

Evelyn's hand came up to stroke Jos's face with cold fingers. Jos leaned in to her caress. "I've missed you, Jos. I didn't write because I thought perhaps you'd be glad to be rid of me and move on." Her voice shook slightly, thought Jos was not sure if it was with the cold or with emotion.

"Please don't ever think that again," Jos replied. To hear such assumptions from Evelyn made her desperately ashamed of herself. "I will never want to be rid of you, I'm sure of it. I'm sorry it took me so long to come to my senses."

Evelyn smiled. "I love you, Jos. It's the one thing I've been certain of, through everything."

Jos's heart leapt with joy. "And I love you, Evie. With all of my heart." Jos closed her eyes and leaned her forehead against Evelyn's.

They stood that way for a long moment, heedless of the rain. Then the passenger door of the car opened.

"Might I remind you both that it's raining and we have a perfectly decent car with a perfectly waterproof roof?"

Evelyn looked to the car, surprised to see Vernon. Jos smiled. "Vernon persuaded me to come and find you," Jos told her. "It wasn't just Vernon, of course. Dorothy was furious with me. In the end she said she wouldn't speak to me until I saw you."

Evelyn smiled and turned to Vernon. "Thank you," she said.

Vernon nodded. "Good to see you, Evie. And you're welcome. Once again, I remind you of the rain."

Jos took Evelyn's hand and led her to the car, helping her climb into the rear seat, sliding in at her side. Vernon sat in the driver's seat. "So what do we do now?" he asked.

Evelyn looked thoughtful. She grasped Jos's hand tightly. "I think we have to go and see my family," she said.

"Very well," Vernon replied, starting the engine. "But you might need to direct me. And I hope to goodness you've thought of what you're going to say to them."

❖

The journey from the North Bay to her family's home took only a few minutes by car. Evelyn found it unusual to direct a vehicle through the dark streets of the town. Jos and Vernon were looking about them with curiosity. They seemed entirely out of place here, much as she had done in London. If she had not been nervous about taking them to see her family, she might almost have laughed at them. She sat close to Jos, wrapped in her arms, drawing heat from her body. Every part of her began to melt into Jos. It was almost surreal that Jos should be here, in the midst of her misery. She hoped desperately that she was not dreaming. If she was, it was the happiest dream of her life and she did not want to wake up.

By the time they made it to the house, a vague plan had formed for what they would say to Evelyn's parents. Evelyn, inspired to confidence by Jos's presence at her side, led them into the kitchen, where they found her mother and father, and Annie. Peter was out of the house somewhere. It was a shame, Evelyn thought, that she would not see her younger brother before she left. She already knew she would be leaving tonight. As she glanced around the familiar kitchen, her resolution did not falter.

Her family's faces showed various degrees of annoyance and surprise as their daughter and two well-dressed strangers entered the room.

"Mother, Father, Annie. May I introduce Mr. Vernon Singleton and his sister, Miss Joselyn Singleton. Friends from London."

Her family made no attempt to move to welcome the visitors. Evelyn pressed on, undaunted. "They've driven down to visit. Vernon, Jos, these are my mother and father and my sister, Annie."

"Delighted to meet you all," Vernon said. Even he seemed slightly off his stride in the face of such stalwart disapproval.

"Yes, it's lovely to meet Evelyn's family," Jos added. "She said so many nice things about you."

"Funny, we were under the impression she was so busy having a good time with the likes of you that she'd forgotten all about us," Annie said bitterly.

"Annie, that's not fair. I wrote letters so you'd know I was thinking about you." Evelyn was hurt by Annie's ongoing resentment. Part of her began to think Annie envied her newfound freedom, the experiences she'd had in London. Annie had never expressed an interest in any life other than West Coombe offered, but then she had never really considered the alternatives. And now she was married. Evelyn wondered how happy her sister's marriage really was.

"A letter's nothing though, not when you didn't even say you were leaving."

"I've said I'm sorry, Annie. I can't do much else."

"I assure you that Evelyn's mentioned you all on many occasions, always with loving sentiments," Jos said. Evelyn silently thanked her.

"So, who are you and how did Evelyn come to be your friend?" This was Evelyn's father, who was looking at Vernon with barely disguised suspicion.

"Well, I run a small…dining establishment, in Mayfair. Evelyn spent an evening as one of my patrons and I was introduced through a mutual friend." Evelyn was impressed at just how respectable and conservative Vernon contrived to make the occasion sound. "And naturally, after that, I was very drawn to her. Evelyn's a beautiful woman, Mrs. Hopkins. That's why I proposed marriage."

Evelyn drew a deep breath as her family's collective eyes widened. This had been the agreed plan, as it seemed to be what her family were most likely to accept. Introduce Vernon as the man she loved in London, claim they were engaged to be married, and then leave before too many questions could be asked.

"You're the man she loves?" Annie asked, staring at Vernon incredulously. Evelyn almost wanted to laugh at her astonishment.

"Yes. Why do you find that so unlikely?" Vernon asked. "With respect."

"I don't recall you asking for my permission, young man," Mr. Hopkins interrupted.

Vernon was caught off guard for a moment. "That's one of the reasons I'm here now," he said brightly, clearly pleased that he'd thought of an answer that sounded reasonable.

Evelyn listened to Vernon, realising just how ridiculous it was to pretend she was in love with him. He was giving a superb performance, but it was not the truth. The person she loved was standing to her other side. That love was pure and, whatever the consequences, her family would know about it.

"Vernon, it's all right, thank you," she said, pressing Vernon's arm. "I'm going to tell them the truth."

Vernon looked at her with a combination of surprise and approval and stepped back a pace. Evelyn took a deep breath. "You see, I'm not going to marry Vernon," she began.

"But you have to!" Annie asked. "We won't have a…a loose woman in the family."

"I've done nothing loose with Vernon, Annie," Evelyn replied, causing a stunned expression to overtake her sister's face. "Although, if I had, it'd be none of your business. I'm not going to marry Vernon because it's not Vernon that I love."

"I assume he knows this," her father said, still glaring at Vernon.

"Yes, Father. He was just trying to protect me. But it's time to be honest." Evelyn could not stop now, even if she wanted to. Every part of her was filled with the need to tell them the truth and damn the consequences. "I don't love Vernon. The person I love is someone I can't marry, even though I wish I could. I love Jos." To confirm they had not misheard her, she grasped Jos's hand in her own.

Her declaration was met with stunned silence. It was Annie who eventually broke it. "Are you implying that you love a woman in the same way as you could love a man?" she said. "Impossible! It's unnatural."

"Just look at the woman though," her father said. "Hardly looks natural, does she? Not right, a woman in man's trousers like that." He was looking Jos up and down now, as though he'd not really noticed her before.

"I won't stand for that, Father. Jos is the woman I love and there's nothing anyone can do about it. I know Eddie would have been proud of me. I always said I would fly away from here and be happy. Well, he can see me and he knows that what I'm about to do now, I'm doing for him because he can't. I love you all, as my family, but I will not stay here until I die of the misery of it all. Come on, Jos, Vernon. Take me back to London."

"Now, young lady—" Evelyn's father began.

But Evelyn was not listening. Her hand in Jos's, Vernon following them, she turned and walked from the house, without looking back.

❖

Evelyn lay on her side, looking at Jos, who was on her back in the bed at her side. She twined a naked leg between Jos's, just wanting to be closer, to feel Jos's skin on her own. She reached out a hand and placed it on Jos's chest, near her heart, and knew she'd found real happiness.

Jos smiled. She was clearly tired from the long drive, but apparently not ready to sleep. "Are you all right, Evie?"

"Oh yes," Evie replied. "I hope it doesn't make me seem heartless. I do miss my family. But I don't feel like I'm part of their world. You saw what they're like. Eddie was the only one who understood me, really. I do miss him."

Jos pulled her closer. "I know, Evie. And you can take all the time you need to grieve for him."

"I'm so pleased I didn't destroy everything," Evelyn said. "When I was in West Coombe, I was thinking of the mess I'd made in London. I feel awful, really."

"If you mean Lilian and James, I think they'll recover. You know, now she knows why Lilian's been so erratic, Dorothy's trying to help her. Of course, I think being away from Vernon will help too. He's not a healthy influence, really. As for James, well, he's young. He'll find other infatuations. I think you were just convenient for him—he didn't have to go looking for you."

"I'm sad to have lost their friendship. When I think of Eddie and Frank in the war, being good friends, I wish it had worked out differently." In some ways, Evelyn felt it was a disservice to her brother and his captain to have not worked harder on continuing a friendship with the Graingers.

"Perhaps you'll be friends with them again. Although I don't know how they'll cope with your choice of bedfellow."

Evelyn smiled. "I don't care how they cope with it, really."

Jos smiled in return. "I'm pleased. I was awfully frightened you wouldn't like being different, you know. Disapproved of by so many people."

"I think I've always been disapproved of," Evelyn replied. "At least now I get to be with you when it happens."

"You know, I don't think it matters that much that you're not friends with Lilian. Your Eddie and Frank, their friendship was sparked by the war. And that's over now," Jos said reflectively.

"It's funny though, isn't it?" Evelyn replied. "In some ways it seems like it's never over. It's still claiming people. It's still driving us all crazy with the desire to fill our lives before they're snatched away. In some ways, it's made us all dream of something more than we have."

"Well, I'm tired of being so awfully modern," Jos said, with a grin. "I don't need to dream about anything and pursue the next thrill. I have you, Evie."

Evelyn was filled with pure joy. Now, finally, she was flying high. "You think I'm thrilling?" she teased.

"Yes, I do," Jos said. "In oh-so-many ways. And I look forward to next thrill."

"Me too," said Evelyn, resting her head on Jos's shoulder, knowing there was so much more to come.

Author's Note

All the characters in this novel are from my imagination. However, the world in which they live draws very heavily on the reality of inter-war London. The places are fictionalised versions of real places—you should be able to follow Evie's route around London on a street map. I won't claim I've represented a minutely accurate picture of London in the Roaring Twenties, but I've tried to be as faithful to the details as possible. The Park Lane Hotel existed—and still does—as, of course, do the attractions of London and the streets of Mayfair, much the same then, outwardly, as they are today.

The publications referred to are all real. These include *The Well of Loneliness* by Radclyffe Hall, discussed at Clara and Courtney's party, which was indeed published in 1928 and then prosecuted for obscenity for daring to portray a lesbian relationship. *Ideal Marriage: Its Physiology and Technique* is a real self-help sex manual by Theodoor Hendrik van de Velde published in 1926, with revised editions in 1965 and 2000.

My story refers to the real events of the First World War—the Great War, as it was known—such as the battle at Valenciennes, which really took place in November 1918. In the four years between 1914 and 1918, there were approximately 888,000 British and Commonwealth military deaths and 124,000 British and Commonwealth civilian deaths. Over one and a half million soldiers returned wounded, a large number of them suffering, as Edward did, from shell shock. Today this ill-defined condition is usually acknowledged to be a form of post-traumatic stress disorder, but at the time was generally seen as a form of insanity or symptom of underlying weakness or cowardice.

The huge impact of the Great War on all levels of British society was undoubtedly a significant turning point and a cataclysm which was still causing tremors at the end of the next decade. A generation of young men had been lost, their families and lovers left grieving. Soldiers were still dying of the after-effects of the conflict, or living with the disabilities it caused, throughout the 1920s. Although the British experience of the 1920s took many of its cues from the American jazz age, the liberated, decadent pursuit of happiness is also the flip side of a country that thought it knew itself attempting to recover and questioning itself for the first time in generations. The old certainties of the class system and Empire were fading with memories of the Victorian age, separated from the new generation by the horror of the war.

About the Author

Born in Nottingham, England, Rebecca S. Buck now lives just outside the city with her partner, slowly renovating their Victorian house. Her day job is in the museums and heritage sector, where she specializes in education and engagement. Her first novel, *Truths*, was published in 2010. Her second, *Ghosts of Winter*, was shortlisted for a Lambda Literary Award. History is her passion, but she's also a big fan of travel, where every new place visited presents a new setting for a story.

Find her on Twitter: @rsbuck

Books Available From Bold Strokes Books

Dyre: By Moon's Light by Rachel E. Bailey. A young werewolf, Des, guards the aging leader of all the Packs: the Dyre. Stable employment—nice work, if you can get it...at least until silver bullets start to fly. (978-1-62639-662-3)

Fragile Wings by Rebecca S. Buck. In Roaring Twenties London, can Evelyn Hopkins find love with Jos Singleton or will the scars of the Great War crush her dreams? (978-1-62639-546-6)

Live and Love Again by Jan Gayle. Jessica Whitney could be Sarah Jarret's second chance at love, but their differences and Sarah's grief continue to come between their budding relationship. (978-1-62639-517-6)

Starstruck by Lesley Davis. Actress Cassidy Hayes and writer Aiden Darrow find out the hard way not all life-threatening drama is confined to the TV screen or the pages of a manuscript. (978-1-62639-523-7)

Stealing Sunshine by Tina Michele. Under the Central Florida sun, two women struggle between fear and love as a dangerous plot of deception and revenge threatens to steal priceless art and lives. (978-1-62639-445-2)

The Fifth Gospel by Michelle Grubb. Hiding a Vatican secret is dangerous—sharing the secret suicidal—can Felicity survive a perilous book tour, and will her PR specialist, Anna, be there when it's all over? (978-1-62639-447-6)

Cold to the Touch by Cari Hunter. A drug addict's murder is the start of a dangerous investigation for Detective Sanne Jensen and Dr. Meg Fielding, as they try to stop a killer with no conscience. (978-1-62639-526-8)

Forsaken by Laydin Michaels. The hunt for a killer teaches one woman that she must overcome her fear in order to love, and another that success is meaningless without happiness. (978-1-62639-481-0)

Infiltration by Jackie D. When a CIA breach is imminent, a Marine instructor must stop the attack while protecting her heart from being disarmed by a recruit. (978-1-62639-521-3)

Midnight at the Orpheus by Alyssa Linn Palmer. Two women desperate to make their way in the world, a man hell-bent on revenge, and a cop risking his career: all in a day's work in Capone's Chicago. (978-1-62639-607-4)

Spirit of the Dance by Mardi Alexander. Major Sorla Reardon's return to her family farm to heal threatens Riley Johnson's safe life when small-town secrets are revealed, and love may not conquer all. (978-1-62639-583-1)

Sweet Hearts by Melissa Brayden, Rachel Spangler, and Karis Walsh. Do you ever wonder *Whatever happened to*...? Find out when you reconnect with your favorite characters from Melissa Brayden's *Heart Block*, Rachel Spangler's *LoveLife*, and Karis Walsh's *Worth the Risk.* (978-1-62639-475-9)

Totally Worth It by Maggie Cummings. Who knew there's an all-lesbian condo community in the NYC suburbs? Join twentysomething BFFs Meg and Lexi at Bay West as they navigate friendships, love, and everything in between. (978-1-62639-512-1)

Illicit Artifacts by Stevie Mikayne. Her foster mother's death cracked open a secret world Jil never wanted to see...and now she has to pick up the stolen pieces. (978-1-62639-472-8)

Pathfinder by Gun Brooke. Heading for their new homeworld, Exodus's chief engineer Adina Vantressa and nurse Briar Lindemay carry game-changing secrets that may well cause them to lose everything when disaster strikes. (978-1-62639-444-5)

Prescription for Love by Radclyffe. Dr. Flannery Rivers finds herself attracted to the new ER chief, city girl Abigail Remy, and the incendiary mix of city and country, fire and ice, tradition and change is combustible. (978-1-62639-570-1)

Ready or Not by Melissa Brayden. Uptight Mallory Spencer finds relinquishing control to bartender Hope Sanders too tall an order in fast-paced New York City. (978-1-62639-443-8)

Summer Passion by MJ Williamz. Women loving women is forbidden in 1946 Hollywood, yet Jean and Maggie strive to keep their love alive and away from prying eyes. (978-1-62639-540-4)

The Princess and the Prix by Nell Stark. "Ugly duckling" Princess Alix of Monaco was resigned to loneliness until she met racecar driver Thalia d'Angelis. (978-1-62639-474-2)

Winter's Harbor by Aurora Rey. Lia Brooks isn't looking for love in Provincetown, but when she discovers chocolate croissants and pastry chef Alex McKinnon, her winter retreat quickly starts heating up. (978-1-62639-498-8)

The Time Before Now by Missouri Vaun. Vivian flees a disastrous affair, embarking on an epic, transformative journey to escape her past, until destiny introduces her to Ida, who helps her rediscover trust, love, and hope. (978-1-62639-446-9)

Twisted Whispers by Sheri Lewis Wohl. Betrayal, lies, and secrets—whispers of a friend lost to darkness. Can a reluctant psychic set things right or will an evil soul destroy those she loves? (978-1-62639-439-1)

The Courage to Try by C.A. Popovich. Finding love is worth getting past the fear of trying. (978-1-62639-528-2)

Break Point by Yolanda Wallace. In a world readying for war, can love find a way? (978-1-62639-568-8)

Countdown by Julie Cannon. Can two strong-willed, powerful women overcome their differences to save the lives of seven others and begin a life they never imagined together? (978-1-62639-471-1)

Keep Hold by Michelle Grubb. Claire knew some things should be left alone and some rules should never be broken, but the most forbidden, well, they are the most tempting. (978-1-62639-502-2)

Deadly Medicine by Jaime Maddox. Dr. Ward Thrasher's life is in turmoil. Her partner Jess left her, and her job puts her in the path of a murderous physician who has Jess in his sights. (978-1-62639-424-7)

New Beginnings by KC Richardson. Can the connection and attraction between Jordan Roberts and Kirsten Murphy be enough for Jordan to trust Kirsten with her heart? (978-1-62639-450-6)

Officer Down by Erin Dutton. Can two women who've made careers out of being there for others in crisis find the strength to need each other? (978-1-62639-423-0)

Reasonable Doubt by Carsen Taite. Just when Sarah and Ellery think they've left dangerous careers behind, a new case sets them—and their hearts—on a collision course. (978-1-62639-442-1)

Tarnished Gold by Ann Aptaker. Cantor Gold must outsmart the Law, outrun New York's dockside gangsters, outplay a shady art dealer, his lover, and a beautiful curator, and stay out of a killer's gun sights. (978-1-62639-426-1)

White Horse in Winter by Franci McMahon. Love between two women collides with the inner poison of a closeted horse trainer in the green hills of Vermont. (978-1-62639-429-2)

Autumn Spring by Shelley Thrasher. Can Bree and Linda, two women in the autumn of their lives, put their hearts first and find the love they've never dared seize? (978-1-62639-365-3)

The Renegade by Amy Dunne. Post-apocalyptic survivors Alex and Evelyn secretly find love while held captive by a deranged cult, but when their relationship is discovered, they must fight for their freedom—or die trying. (978-1-62639-427-8)

Thrall by Barbara Ann Wright. Four women in a warrior society must work together to lift an insidious curse while caught between their own desires, the will of their peoples, and an ancient evil. (978-1-62639-437-7)

The Chameleon's Tale by Andrea Bramhall. Two old friends must work through a web of lies and deceit to find themselves again, but in the search they discover far more than they ever went looking for. (978-1-62639-363-9)

Side Effects by VK Powell. Detective Jordan Bishop and Dr. Neela Sahjani must decide if it's easier to trust someone with your heart or your life as they face threatening protestors, corrupt politicians, and their increasing attraction. (978-1-62639-364-6)

Warm November by Kathleen Knowles. What do you do if the one woman you want is the only one you can't have? (978-1-62639-366-0)

In Every Cloud by Tina Michele. When Bree finally leaves her shattered life behind, is she strong enough to salvage the remaining pieces of her heart and find the place where it truly fits? (978-1-62639-413-1)

Rise of the Gorgon by Tanai Walker. When independent Internet journalist Elle Pharell goes to Kuwait to investigate a veteran's mysterious suicide, she hires Cassandra Hunt, an interpreter with a covert agenda. (978-1-62639-367-7)

Crossed by Meredith Doench. Agent Luce Hansen returns home to catch a killer and risks everything to revisit the unsolved murder of her first girlfriend and confront the demons of her youth. (978-1-62639-361-5)

Making a Comeback by Julie Blair. Music and love take center stage when jazz pianist Liz Randall tries to make a comeback with the help of her reclusive, blind neighbor, Jac Winters. (978-1-62639-357-8)

Soul Unique by Gun Brooke. Self-proclaimed cynic Greer Landon falls for Hayden Rowe's paintings and the young woman shortly after, but will Hayden, who lives with Asperger syndrome, trust her and reciprocate her feelings? (978-1-62639-358-5)